WATERCROSSING

PHANTOM ISLAND

3

WaterCrossing

KRISSI DALLAS

Cover design by Kristen Verser
Interior design by Sarah Kirchen
Dorian Island Map designed by Sonia Pennington

Published in the United States of America

ISBN: 978-0-99973-112-3
Juvenile Fiction / Fantasy & Magic
12.03.15

For my mom, Bonnie
The most important Hydro in my life
There is true healing power in a mother's love.

Dorian Island

THREE WEEKS AGO

He slowly rolled his head in a circular motion, stretching the taut muscles in his neck. He was careful to keep any grimace of pain from showing on his bloody face—not that any form of expression felt possible through the swelling. His dark eyes flicked unceasingly around the sparkling cavern, observing their faces, their body language, and any possible weakness that might provide a route of escape.

With his wrists locked into the armbands, he had no access to his life force, and he was outnumbered by about seven to one. However, he knew the armbands and the beating had been a formality. After all, one does not defy the Guardian—not even if one is the future ruler and present son of the Guardian. In his culture—and in his family—orders were made to be followed. He had apparently stepped into a situation he did not know nearly enough about, and perhaps that was why he made the choice to protect her instead. His mother and father had acted as if he had just brought about the destruction of the Island itself and, truthfully, he had gained some satisfaction in knowing he had thrown a kink into their carefully laid plans.

Not more than an hour ago, he had watched *her* disappear—a shimmering, hazy image moving out of his arms and into a foreign, otherworldly portrait. And it had been his seemingly brilliant idea to make her cross over…only now he could not erase the image of her golden hair whipping around, her face contorted with confusion and panic, the horrifying sound of her screaming his name before she disappeared…

He closed his eyes and allowed himself to feel the torture of the moment again before consciously pushing away the emotion that threatened his calm and cautious exterior. That was the problem with *her*…she made him feel what he had been trained to ignore. And like the weakness of his Pyradorian nature, the emotion was almost uncontainable at this point.

He glanced again at his mother across the room and studied her cool manner as she was deep in conversation with his father. She was very adept at staying calm and in-control, no matter what the situation. Though Abrianna had been openly furious with him for what he had done, she was the one who had quickly put an end to Eli's beating. He knew his father was probably the only person on the Island who could overpower him physically—and that had definitely been proven true with the current state he was in. But as he observed his parents, he could see no love or tenderness between them—only a shared desire for power and importance, a desire that bordered on greed.

His mother turned sharply away from Eli then and made a quick motion with her hand to a servant across the room. She had a delicate, graceful way about her…but that delicacy was an act he knew well. She carried the weight of authority and the cunning of intelligence in that one small flick of her hand. The servant jumped into action and met her halfway as she swept toward her son.

"You did not hold to the plan, Gabriel," she said coldly. He met her gaze without flinching.

"I was never aware of a plan to torture our Pilgrim and her friends," he replied haughtily, because even though he had collected his thoughts, his emotions were still very close to the surface.

"Torture? Is that what she told you?"

"She did not need to—I saw the armband marks. I know you threatened her. I just do not know why yet."

Abrianna stared at him in silence for a moment.

"I had no choice but to place her in armbands—"

"Do not try to justify your actions!" he snapped, ignoring the presence of the blue-eyed servant standing behind her. "I told you those could kill her!"

"I would not have allowed that, Gabriel, but you should understand better than anyone how powerful she is. I could not risk her using a life force against me," Abrianna tried reasoning with him.

"In the Dome?" he scoffed. "Impossible."

"The realm of possibility extends further for people like her."

"*People?* You mean there are others like her?" Gabriel narrowed his puffy eyes at her. Abrianna paused and watched him carefully, wondering just how much he had discovered since the Travelers had arrived.

"It is possible."

"You mean her father." He stated it boldly to force a reaction from her. She flinched—it was almost imperceptible, but it was there. And he knew then he had struck on some kind of buried emotion. It was in her eyes, even if it was not on her face.

"What did she tell you about him?"

"It hardly matters what she told me, *Mother*. She knows nothing of what happened to him, though I suspect you do know…in fact, I believe he is here on the Island somewhere as a prisoner. As *your* prisoner."

"As a matter of fact, he is on the Island…and has been for six years," Abrianna admitted offhandedly. He was surprised at her candidness.

"Well, that is an important detail you failed to share with me!" he growled. "Where exactly are you keeping him? And why? It is time you tell me the truth, or I will—"

"You will what, Gabriel? You already destroyed Whitnee's hope of retrieving her father…not to mention the fact that you sent away one of the most gifted people to arrive on this Island."

"She was in danger here—"

"Oh, please…do not act as if you were being noble." She waved him off with that delicate hand. "You allowed your Pyra emotions to control you. You were thinking with the affections of a lustful boy instead of with the rational mind of a ruler. It is disgusting, and you will have to correct this problem immediately."

He hid his emotions well at her words. If she only knew how small she could make him feel…He gazed up at her with ferocity in his eyes. "I want the truth about her father."

Her eyes slid sideways toward the silent Hydro servant behind her. "That is a conversation for a more private setting. For now, Michael will clean you up. In light of present circumstances, your duties with the rebels have been reassigned." And she gave a slight nod to Michael who pulled a bright blue bottle of sparkling Water from his guard pouch. He knelt in front of Gabriel, but Gabriel pulled his face away.

"What is my new assignment?"

Abrianna gave a short look over her shoulder at Eli, who continued shooting dark glances their way. Then she lowered her voice, "I am sending you to the Mainland to bring her back. Eli does not wish for you to go. Needless to say, his trust in you has been broken. But I believe she will listen to *you*. I do not care how you get her here—use whatever force or *persuasion* you choose, but bring her only. We do not need her friends interfering this time." She gave him a piercing stare before adding, "Failure is not an option, Gabriel. She wants her father back, and I agreed to help her with that."

"And what did she agree to help *you* with?" Gabriel asked knowingly, trying to ignore the way his heart had quickened at his mother's words, the pathetic way hope flared in his chest at the thought of seeing *her* again.

"It does not matter. We need her. She is the key to everything. Do not fail me," she commanded, but it almost came across as pleading. She glanced back at Eli one more time and then turned to the servant. "Michael, fix his face and any other injuries he might have. I do not want one scratch or mark on his body."

"What if I am tired of blindly following your orders? What if I choose not to do this?" Gabriel asked defiantly.

She raised her voice in authority. "There is no choice here. Your loyalty is to this Island first—not to some girl who bats her eyes at you and makes you feel good about yourself. She does not truly *know* you, nor does she respect the position you hold." Her words were like knives cutting into his chest. She gave him a condescending look. "Did you even tell her about your...*commitments*? Or was that just one more thing you lied to her about?"

He gave her a grim look.

"I will take that as a no, then." Abrianna shook her head in pity. "What a shame...and she actually trusts you. The reality is, Gabriel, that we cannot afford to get close. The burdens we bear to our people are too much for others to understand. You cannot let yourself feel anything toward her, especially if she is the Pilgrim. That is not the Pilgrim's purpose, and you need to start treating this situation with a bit more reverence. You had your fun and your little romance, but you know that is as far as it can ever go. Quit torturing yourself by thinking there is more."

He bristled visibly at her words, amazed as always at how she was able to manipulate him. "When do I go?"

"Soon. There are some adjustments I must make to the portal. It will take some time. But soon..." She gave him a last piercing look. Then she walked purposefully away so Michael could erase the evidence of her husband's abuse...something Michael had done for them on several occasions. She was moving toward Eli when the slight, familiar ringing sounded in her head...a sound only she could hear, a sound she dreaded at that moment.

And then the voice she knew so well entered her mind, almost whispering...*I felt something.*

She sighed and paused in her stride across the cavern. *Yes, that was the portal*, she answered, but not aloud.

Is she gone then?

Yes, just as you asked.

She chose not to disclose that it hadn't happened *exactly* as he had asked. In fact, it had been quite the opposite. Her own plan had failed, thanks to Gabriel's intervention.

Then why are your guards moving me again? What is going on?

She tried to hide the weariness in her response. *I cannot discuss this right now. I will come visit you soon and explain.*

Explain now. *What have you done? If she is really gone—*

Then you would still sense her here...do you?

There was a pause.

No, I guess not, he replied slowly. *Please, Bri, stop these experiments. I have done all I can for you. Maybe it is time things change. Maybe I can go home—*

Stop calling it that. This *is your home!* Without guilt, she admitted, *Besides, you are the only reason that she will come back.*

There was panic in his voice. *You can't bring her back...You promised me you'd send her home!*

I never promised to let her stay there. You know we need her here.

No, we do not! I left everything behind in order to keep her away from here. She tried to steel herself against his words, but then he said, *Bri, you have no right to do this. You are out of control! If you don't stop—*

She shut off the communication. His pleas faded into silence and the ringing sound vanished. His desperate concern for a distant place and a family that was not hers was too much for her to handle.

That was when she realized she had been standing frozen in the middle of the cavern alone. Eli was staring at her again, his face a mask of frustration and jealousy. He knew. She stared back unapologetically before spinning back around and moving toward her son again. Michael had his Water-soaked hands pressed to Gabriel's face and a faint blue glimmer showed his healing progress.

"Gabriel," she said sharply, and his eyes slid upward to meet hers. "Do not get any ideas. I know how you think, and you will not be able to find her father before you go. Do not even consider trying. Your only option in fixing your mistake and helping Whitnee is to hold to the plan this time, son. It would be unwise of you to forget your place again." It was a warning, and she used every bit of intimidation she possessed in her voice and demeanor. He had to follow orders this time.

Gabriel remained silent, and though he showed no emotion, his hopeful heart sank.

RESEARCH

A BEAUTIFUL MIND

Tap, tap, tap, tap, tap. My fingers drummed the steering wheel at about the same chaotic rate as my heartbeat. I peered obsessively at the rusty, paint-stripped bathroom door that Morgan had disappeared behind nearly ten minutes ago. We were at a rest stop out in the middle of nowhere, trying to get to Boerne, Texas, to meet a psychologically disturbed person we'd only ever heard about in stories. So, was I more nervous about the fact that we were about to do something which could be classified as really stupid or that Morgan's bladder was once again going to delay us?

As my tapping grew more violent, a familiar hand shot out from the passenger's seat and firmly pressed on my fingers.

"You have *got* to stop that," Caleb warned. "She'll be out as soon as she can."

"How long does it take?" I grumbled. "We haven't even stopped for Starbucks yet."

"She does this all the time," he remarked.

As if she had been waiting for that cue, Morgan came stumbling out of the bathroom, and Caleb released my imprisoned hands. She was apologizing as she opened the back car door.

"I'm so sorry, y'all. I feel a little sick to my stomach…" She slid in and shut the door quickly. I was backing out before she had even buckled her seat belt.

"Probably the camp food," I suggested flippantly. "Thank goodness we get real food for a weekend. I can already smell Papi's Fourth of July fajitas!"

"Or it's nerves. I can't believe we're going to do this. We can still back out…" Morgan stated in a fearful voice.

"Morgie." I groaned. "I have to do this. This guy could have information about my dad. He's the only other person we know of who has been to the Island." I veered back onto the highway, checking my GPS for the next exit.

"True, but he could also be a psychotic serial killer," she pointed out.

"Not all emotionally disturbed people turn into serial killers, Morgan," Caleb jumped in and then grinned sarcastically. "I mean, take Whitnee, for example…"

"If I were, I know who my first victim would be." I widened my eyes in his direction, earning a playful wink that almost made me blush. "Besides," I continued, my eyes back on the road, "his mom sounded very nice on the phone when I told her we wanted to come visit."

Morgan snorted. "He's like, what? Forty years old and still living with his mother? Come on! The guy can't be a normal, functioning adult!" I could hear the distress in her voice. Ever since Morgan lost her best friend in a bicycle accident in the sixth grade, she had a perpetual worrisome side to her. Why she selected me, a perpetual risk-taker, as her best friend, I'll never understand. Only Morgan's steadfast loyalty and need to look out for me kept her involved in all my adventures.

"Listen, I did my research as well as I could with the stupid dial-up Internet at camp. He has no criminal history that I could find, works at the local grocery store, and has lived with his mother his whole life."

"Except for one brief summer when he was twelve in which he wandered off from Camp Fusion and was found in *California*," Morgan cut in, and I gave a sigh.

"But we know the truth about that," Caleb reminded us.

"Right. He accidentally transported to the White Island, until my dad, who was working at camp, rescued him and sailed back to California where they were found," I finished. It all sounded so ridiculously impossible. "I'm dying to know what really happened while they were there."

"I still don't see how this will help us at all with your father," Morgan insisted. "I mean, didn't Ben say they both lost their memory of the Island when they sailed back instead of transporting back through the portal?"

"Yes, but Ben also said that Dad's memory eventually returned."

"Wow," Caleb breathed. "Even if this guy's memory came back, who would believe that he found an island no one has ever heard of or ever traced on the face of the planet? I did my research too and found nothing about the White Island or Dorian Island anywhere. Just a few mentions about phantom islands or lost lands. It's as if we imagined the whole thing."

I bristled at his words. "We did *not* imagine it. Don't forget that my dad was born on the Island, and I am ninety-nine percent sure that he's still alive there somewhere—"

"I know, I know, Whit. I wasn't saying that it wasn't a real place, only that there is no scientific reason why anyone should believe our story," Caleb soothed.

The three of us fell into a thoughtful silence.

He was right, of course. I could imagine returning to school for my senior year only to get the expected question about how my summer went. An honest answer would go like this: "Well, I went back to work at Camp Fusion as a mentor, but then I started seeing my dead dad across the river. Yes, I know that sounds crazy, but seriously…when I went to explore, I accidentally transported to the White Island where I healed myself and created a tornado to fight off a giant bug, who later ended up talking to me in my thoughts! What do you mean you don't believe me? I learned to control Wind, Water, Earth, and Fire, and the people on the Island believed that I was the answer to one of their ancient prophecies about a blonde Pilgrim who would come to rescue them from their current problems. Oh, but just as I was about to find my dad with the help of the evil Guardian on the Island, I got shoved back through a portal by a gorgeous Island guy with some mad Fire skills—"

But then I would have to stop…because I couldn't even go that far within my fictional conversations.

Caleb, Morgan, and I had been away from our homes in San Antonio for five straight weeks—well, almost six weeks if you counted the five days we time-traveled with two of our campers to the Dorian Island (informally called the White Island by its natives). But since nobody ever knew we were missing, it created an illogical and unsolvable time problem.

"I hope Amelia's okay this weekend," I commented aloud, thinking of my favorite little camper.

"Is she with her mom for the weekend?" Morgan asked.

"Yeah…and she hasn't seen her in over six months. Not since her parents divorced." I bit on my lower lip. Amelia had been a brat at the beginning of the summer, but after having been a key part in our unexpected tropical excursion, she had made a total one-eighty turn in her behavior. I loved that kid like she was my own sister, and I worried that being around her dysfunctional parents would cause her bad attitude to relapse.

I glanced over at Caleb. His green eyes were focused on me, and he smiled encouragingly. "You've done a great job mentoring her, Whit. She'll be okay."

"I hope so…" I sighed. "What about Kevin? Did he make it off okay with his grandparents?"

Caleb nodded. Kevin was the other mischievous camper who had found himself on the Island with us. His parents had been killed in a boating accident, and he now lived with his grandparents. You would never know the kid had been through so much tragedy; he still showed an incredible amount of passion for life and adventure. Unlike Amelia, he did not act out his hurt in self-destructive ways.

I focused back on the road before saying to Caleb in a mocking voice, "And will Claire survive without you this weekend?" I never should have said it...I knew that. Especially when Morgan groaned from the back seat.

"Why do you have to go there, Whitnee?" Caleb snapped.

"Just making sure *you're* not still going there," I snapped back.

We had just met Claire this summer at camp, and Caleb had kind of hooked up with her right before we found the Island—and unfortunately right around the time Caleb had confessed his more-than-just-friends feelings for *me*. You would think that would complicate my tight-knit friendship with him. And it did for a while...even more so after I met...well, someone else. But Caleb and I were working through those issues and, truthfully, I didn't want anything else to complicate the progress we had made.

"Claire and I put the brakes on the whole relationship... for *obvious* reasons," Caleb admitted, staring away from me out the window.

"Are you sure? Because to hear her talk about it..." I couldn't help the pathetic way I needed to argue with him over this issue, even though I knew he had broken up with Claire in an effort to be honest with her. After all, Caleb was still convinced I was the one for him, and leading Claire on was not okay. I pictured Claire and her humongous brown eyes and the way they seemed to fill with hope every time she talked about Caleb or saw him around camp.

"Who cares what she says? Shouldn't you believe *me*?" he challenged.

"You never talk about it! I have no clue what's going on in Caleb-and-Claire land." *Aww, their names even alliterate. How cute,* I thought bitterly.

"Whitnee, I told you he officially ended the whole thing a couple of weeks ago," Morgan piped up. "Give him a break."

21

"Yeah, and speaking of that…why did you tell Morgan that and not me? Since when do we keep secrets from each other?"

"Trust me, I wouldn't dream of telling either of you anything that I didn't expect the other one to hear about," he muttered and ran his hands through his dark hair, which had gotten longer since we'd been away. I tried not to notice the attractive way it started to curl out on the edges, and the way the sun reflected the natural bronze highlights that had shown up from his time outside as the sports activity camp instructor. He was starting to look…well, like a cute guy I *might* be attracted to and not just my loyal best guy friend.

Grr.

He suddenly turned on me with intensity. "You really wonder why I wouldn't talk to *you* about Claire?" His voice had an edge to it now…an edge I didn't particularly care for.

"What? Why? You think I'm jealous? Because I'm not!" I totally was, though. Even I could admit my own stupidity at this point—but only to myself.

He shook his head in frustration. "Whit, sometimes you drive me nuts," he mumbled, and then gave his attention to the rolling hill country outside.

I shot a frustrated look at Morgan in the mirror.

She lifted her eyebrows at me in warning and mouthed, *Drop it.*

"Exit in one mile," the GPS lady instructed in her monotone voice.

I gripped the steering wheel tightly, feeling my heartbeat pick up again. We were almost there. All my careful investigation and research about the camper who had crossed the river at Camp Fusion years ago was about to come to fruition. If I was going to find a way back to the Island and rescue my father, I needed to know everything I possibly could about his previous life there and his strange disappearance. This guy just had to remember something important…something that would help us.

William Allen Kinder suffered from a severe case of schizophrenia, diagnosed when he was a teenager. Because he had exhibited extreme emotional trauma at the age of ten after his father died, the boy's mother sent him to a camp where children went to deal with tragedies. Nobody realized then that little William had more than just emotional trauma to deal with. He suffered from delusions and episodes of paranoia. The summer that he was at Camp Fusion, William kept telling his mentor that he saw a "pretty lady with black hair" across the Frio River. He said that she stared at him every time he went to swim and he thought she was sad. This was an apparent delusion since nobody else ever saw her, and everybody knew there was nothing over there for miles.

One day when his camp mentor was not looking, William climbed the rope ladder that hung down the cliff on the other side of the river. Once he set foot over there, he was not seen again until he appeared in California weeks later with Nathan Terradora, my father.

This was the man I had finally located. This was the man whose modest residence we were now staring at hesitantly from inside the car.

"I think this is a bad idea," Morgan fretted.

"Do you want to stay in the car, Morgan?" I offered.

"Absolutely not!" she exclaimed, and then held up something in her hand. "I'm taking the pepper spray in though, just in case."

"Oh, *geez*, Morgan," Caleb grunted, spinning around to see the little can in her fist.

"What? You can't be too careful these days…I mean, we live in the time of Internet and cell phones. You don't just go over to strangers' houses anymore without being announced," she told us matter-of-factly.

"I told his mother we were coming," I reminded them. "Remember, she thinks we're doing research for the camp about former campers. Kind of like a where-are-they-now deal."

"Seriously? She bought that story?" Caleb raised one eyebrow—the one with a childhood scar slashed across it.

"Yeah, so just let me do the talking," I told them, moving my hand to the door handle.

"Holy beep, we are *so* gonna die," Morgan muttered.

"Uh-oh. She's starting to beep out her cuss words again," Caleb whispered in my direction. I shook my head in amusement. Ever since Morgan had taught our Island friend, Thomas, that cuss words sometimes get "beeped" out on our TVs, she had started using "beep" as her own cuss word—probably because Thomas had found the idea so entertaining. Though she didn't talk much about Thomas, I had a suspicion she missed him more than she let on.

Morgan chanted under her breath as we left the safety of the car. "Our names will be put out on the Amber Alert everywhere, and our faces will end up on those mass e-mails. You know the ones that get forwarded to everyone and their dog and you have to keep scrolling down just to see what it's even about? And nobody will ever know that we disappeared somewhere in Boerne, because we *didn't tell anyone* we were—"

"Morgan!" Caleb and I interrupted her at the same time, exchanging exasperated looks.

Her frightful blue eyes were wide as she closed her mouth, choosing instead to chomp down viciously on her gum.

"Just don't get all trigger-happy on us, okay?" I said, eyeing the way she was clutching the pepper spray. "Put that in your purse or something." Still, her gruesome speculations had only served to make me second-guess this little escapade.

I swallowed with difficulty before speaking again. "We'll be in and out quickly. My mom is expecting me home for dinner, so I have no intention of dying tonight."

Even though I appeared calm, I was still clinging to my cell phone, ready to dial 911 if the situation called for it. As we slowly approached the porch, Caleb by my side and Morgan bringing up the rear rather closely, I couldn't help thinking now that this was probably one of the dumbest things I'd ever had the mind to do. Morgan was right—people didn't just stop by people's houses anymore. And just because I researched this guy didn't mean he wasn't holding his own mother hostage and hiding dead bodies beneath the floorboards of his house. The Internet was not the end-all, be-all source of true information. What if he totally went all *Tell-Tale Heart* on us?

"If you notice a funny smell," I whispered, "we're leaving immediately."

I barely had time to notice the odd looks Caleb and Morgan gave me before the front door suddenly swung open. The three of us sort of jumped and grabbed onto each other reflexively before a very sweet, grandmotherly woman appeared, her face etched with all kinds of wrinkles.

"Well, hello!" She spoke with a Southern drawl. "You must be the children from Camp Fusion…Come on in now. Will and I have been expecting you." She was perhaps the least intimidating person I had ever seen. And somehow I found my breath again and smiled carefully at her.

"Hello, I'm Whitnee," I replied, stepping toward her with forced confidence and holding out my hand.

She took it into her two wrinkled hands and gave it a squeeze. Caleb and Morgan introduced themselves, and I noticed Morgan relaxed a little too.

The interior of the house was small but well lit with the summer evening sun streaming through all the windows and exposing floating dust bunnies. I took a deep breath and was relieved to smell cookies instead of rotting dead bodies. So far, so good. She invited us to sit on the couch while she went and got Will, all the while mumbling about how pleased she was for him to have visitors.

When we were alone, Morgan whispered, "What does it mean if the house smells like cookies?"

Caleb smirked. "Evil Keebler elves have invaded?"

"She's a witch luring us in with goodies so she can eat us?" I offered.

Morgan rolled her eyes. "Y'all are both sick."

I don't know what exactly I expected Will to look or act like, but when he came through the door, the first thing I noticed was that his hands fidgeted obsessively. He kept closing them into fists and then flicking his fingers out as if flashing the sign for the number five over and over again. Fist and flick. Fist and flick. The second thing I noticed was how he never completely looked at us. He would glance and look away, making me wonder if he really *saw* us.

"Will, honey, this is Whitnee and Morgan and Caleb. They came all the way from Camp Fusion to visit you. You remember Camp Fusion, don't you?" The old lady spoke kindly as she directed Will to the loveseat opposite of us.

Will nodded and said hello. I had never been around a schizophrenic person. I wasn't sure how to act or what to say now that I was there.

"Hi, Mr. Kinder—" I started.

"You can call me Will," he interrupted me. "Named after my father. Do you know anyone in the Air Force?"

"Um…" I glanced over at Morgan and Caleb, who looked equally perturbed by his bizarre behavior.

"Will's father was in the Air Force," his mother explained. "He sometimes thinks out loud from one subject to the next. Will, I think they want to ask you some questions." His mother looked at me expectantly.

"Right…" I paused. I had prepared in advance for what I was going to ask, but now everything I had planned had escaped my mind. I stared helplessly at the strange man for a moment. His hair was a graying dirty blond, and his thick glasses and wandering eyes kept me from seeing his true eye color. A sense of pity overcame me.

"So, *Will*, what do you remember about Camp Fusion?" Caleb jumped in once he saw me go blank. So much for me doing all the talking. I released the breath I must have been holding and listened.

"Swimming...lots of swimming and running," he answered, one hand still flicking in and out slowly.

I found my voice. "Did you get to swim in the Frio River? It's very cold, isn't it?"

"Very cold. I went to Colorado too. It was cold there, but different. I saw a mountain and went inside of it," Will said.

"Actually, Will, we just drove through Colorado, remember? You didn't go inside the mountain," Ms. Kinder gently corrected. "But we did see a lot of mountains along the way. Gorgeous mountains...like nothing you see in Texas." She smiled and then stood up. "I need to check my cookies. I'll be right back. Just be patient with him." She shuffled slowly out of the room. The three of us continued to stare at Will and his fidgets.

His voice dropped conspiratorially when she was gone. "Not in Texas. I went inside the mountain where it sparkled everywhere like stars. Can you find the Big Dipper?" He glanced at me again in his strange way.

I nodded. "Yes, I have seen the Big Dipper. It's pretty amazing. Do you like looking at the stars, Will?" I replied, wondering if he was going to say anything that made sense to me. How could I get around to asking about my dad when he kept changing the subject away from Camp Fusion?

"I like the stars. The Big Dipper follows you wherever you go." He looked up at the ceiling as if he could see the Big Dipper right then.

"Uh-huh." I nodded. "Well, besides swimming and running... and looking at the stars at Camp Fusion...is there anything else you remember from that summer?" I prodded him as gently as possible.

He shook his head as he answered, "I traveled far that summer."
Now we were getting somewhere.

"What do you mean you traveled far? Where did you go?" I
leaned closer.

"I went swimming, and there was a fire. I have to be careful
because I can set things on fire, and it won't burn me, but it can
hurt other things. I made fire at Camp Fusion, lots of it. But I
don't do that anymore. It's too dangerous."

I sucked in a breath. Was he talking about being a Pyra? The
Pyradorian tribe was gifted with the Fire life force, and they had
hazel eyes that lit up gold. Maybe while he was on the Island
somebody gifted him with the life force of Fire! I moved to the
floor right in front of him and knelt. *Dangit*, I couldn't get him to
look at me close enough to see what color his eyes were.

"Will? Do you remember a man named Nathan? Nathan
Terradora?" I asked breathlessly.

His hands immediately stopped their fidgeting, and his whole
body went still. I waited for him to move.

"Will? Are you okay?"

He stared off into the space away from me and didn't say anything, as if he had slipped into a coma.

"What's wrong with him?" Morgan whispered.

"Will? You knew a man named Nathan. He helped you get
back from all your traveling, didn't he?" I spoke softly but couldn't
help staring intensely at him. "Please tell me what you remember,
Will. Nathan was my dad, and he's been missing for a very long
time. If you can remember anything about that summer, I would
really like to know."

And then as suddenly as Will became catatonic, his head
snapped back toward me, and his eyes met mine for the first
time. He *looked* at me, really looked at me. And his eyes were a
dull hazel….

I continued in a whisper, "You remember him, don't you? Will,
you went to an Island that summer, didn't you?"

"Were you there?" he asked, never taking his eyes off me. His hands started fidgeting again...fist and flick.

"No, I was not even born yet. But you know Nathan, right? We look alike," I explained, trying to be patient with his thought processes.

He squinted at me. "Do you live on the Island? Your eyes are gray, like the sky when it rains."

"Yes, I am an Aerodorian...a person of the Wind tribe. But I live here in Texas," I told him, wondering how much he understood about the Island.

"Yes...yes. You know Nathan...he was Aerodorian too. He helped me. He found the cave, the one that the pretty lady made. She wanted us to stay, but Nathan said no. I swam a lot that summer. It chased me if I got too close." He was getting increasingly excited as he spoke.

"What would chase you? What cave? Do you mean the portal?"

"No portal. No way to escape. We found the cave, and then there was a fight. But we ran and we left." He flicked his hands out quickly, but then his face fell. "Nobody believes me. I made Fire, and I saw the stars, and nobody believes me. Do you believe me?" He looked at me sadly, and I wondered how many times he had tried to tell people what he found that summer, only to be told it was just the start of many delusional episodes. He stared down at me so earnestly; it was almost child-like.

"Yes," I whispered, "I believe you. I've been there...to the Island. All three of us have been there." I heard Morgan suck in a breath at my candidness. I pointed at her. "Morgan is a Hydrodorian... from the Water tribe. And Caleb is a Geodorian, like the Earth tribe. Did somebody gift you with a life force when you were there?" Did he understand the tribal words? It felt strange to say them here so far away from the Island.

He stared at me a moment longer before he shot up out of his chair and almost tripped over me.

"Come see the Island! I will show you...I go there all the time," he practically shouted before grabbing my arm and roughly yanking me to my feet. I was stunned at his strength as he started to pull me down the hallway. I did not miss how quickly Caleb was on his feet, lunging for me, and the way Morgan's hand moved to her pepper spray in her purse. I should have been scared at the man's sudden forceful intensity. For all I knew, he could be dragging me off to the basement to hack me to pieces. But I couldn't bring myself to fear him—there was too much honesty in his voice. Disturbing as his behavior was, I knew he wasn't lying about the Island. And if he had been under some sort of delusion when he found the Island, then I needed to be checked for schizophrenia too.

"Whit!" Caleb cried as Will pulled on me sharply.

"It's okay. Come on," I told him and reached for him with my free arm.

I felt his strong hand connect with mine and hold on tight. Morgan was right behind him, and we all cautiously followed the excited man down the hallway, the smell of freshly baked cookies wafting behind us. Will paused at a closed door and flicked his hand at it a few times before opening it.

What we saw before us was breathtaking and almost frightening at the same time. He was indeed showing us the Island...or his version of it anyway.

"Whoa," I breathed, taking in everything I could in one quick sweep.

The room was lined nearly floor-to-ceiling with pictures and drawings. There was a simple desk with pencils and papers and watercolors scattered across its surface. The musty scent of dried paint and aging paper had settled heavily in the room. A large bookshelf held various books and objects, all with an oceanic or tropical theme. I took a step inside, my hand still firmly tucked into Caleb's, even though I could feel the reluctance in his grip.

I slowly moved around the room, inspecting the pictures up close. "Did you draw these?"

"Yes, it is my Island. I live here, but I don't play with Fire, because it might burn up all the paper. Fire is dangerous, so I don't do that anymore." Will looked at us expectantly, as if we should praise his caution.

One whole wall featured deserted beach scenery. Some of the pictures were framed and looked store-bought. The rest of them were simply hand-drawn with pencil and an occasional splash of color. The pencil drawings were actually very good. One picture caught my eye because it looked like a dilapidated stone building nestled in a jungle.

"Look at this." I motioned to Morgan and Caleb.

"It's the Watch Tower ruins on the Southern Beach..." Caleb mumbled incredulously.

"Stay away from the tank," Will warned us.

"What is the tank?" I asked him, staring at the near-perfect resemblance of the Watch Tower ruins. I had never heard of anything called "the tank" when I was there.

"It is dark and cold there. Scary. Have you ever been to a haunted house before? I hate them, hate the dark, hate the sounds," he whispered.

We left the Watch Tower ruins picture and moved along the next wall. Some pictures featured various symbols, some of which included each tribe's specific birthmark. He had definitely been to our Island.

"What are these pictures of?" Caleb asked. There were a few generic depictions of what could have been tunnels or chamber rooms. The rocky walls were flecked and looked gritty. One had an odd symbol I had never seen before—like four swirls that moved around each other and met in the center.

"The cave. It is where they fought. I liked it there, though. It was warm, and it sparkled like the stars...Have you seen the Big Dipper?" he asked me again, and I nodded distractedly.

What cave was he talking about? It had to be the one where Abrianna, the Guardian of the Island, kept the portal, the key to the Mainland. I was puzzling over this when my eye found a picture in the middle of the next wall. It only grabbed my attention because the penciling was darker than the others, as if Will had pushed down too hard on the paper. As I studied it, I found a few tiny tears in the paper. It was the most disturbing image on any of the walls, because it was of a creature with sharp fangs poised to strike the onlooker. And it had large, sightless eyes…and scaly skin and—*gulp*—gills.

"What is *that*?" I pointed with a horrified grimace.

Will came up behind me, and his voice dropped to a low volume, as if he didn't want anyone outside the room to hear us. "The water beast guards the tank. Do you believe me? Nathan believed me, and he is my friend. But we forgot. We forgot everything, and I wish I could forget again. I don't play with Fire anymore. I am very careful," he promised me, his big hazel eyes glaring seriously at the picture. "You need to be careful. Do not go back. Stay at Camp Fusion and watch the Big Dipper."

INDEPENDENCE DAY

"So why do you think his family plays along with his Island fascination if they just believe it's one of his hallucinations?" Caleb mused.

With still shaky hands, I reached through my driver's side window and dumped some change in the Starbucks tip jar while I waited for our drinks. My mouth was so dry...I just needed a drink.

"None of that made any sense to me," I muttered. "And Ms. Kinder wasn't exactly happy when she found us in the *island room.*"

"Can you imagine that guy having a Pyra's ability? Wonder what kind of damage he caused? You know he did. He kept bringing it up," Caleb said.

"I bet they regretted gifting *him* with a life force. And what was all that going-inside-the-mountain talk?" Morgan pondered from the back seat.

"And the Big Dipper?" Caleb added.

"And the tank and the water beast thing? *Ugh.*" I shuddered at the picture that had already burned its way into my fragile brain... I mean, I was already the world's biggest wimp when it came to being around fish. Just simple fish! Not like sharks or piranhas or whatever...I'm talking anything from your average pet goldfish to a grilled salmon entrée. I hated them all. No fish for me as a diet or as a companion. The idea that something like that gruesome creature in the picture could exist on the beautiful, exotic Dorian Island, much less in Will's imagination, was just disturbing to me.

"I don't think I'll ever forget that visit as long as I live." Caleb spoke quietly. "I've never been around somebody like that. I mean, how much of that was real and how much of what he said was just made up?"

"Grande vanilla bean frap?" the barista interrupted.

I took the drink and passed it to Caleb.

"Those pictures he drew were definitely of the White Island," Morgan said. "He even had one of the Blue River where the Hydrodorians live."

Of course she would have noticed that. As a peaceable and fun-loving group, the Hydrodorians had accepted blue-eyed Morgan as one of their own. And we had discovered there that she was naturally adept at using the Water life force without much training.

"Grande caramel macchiato?"

I passed the drink back to Morgan. "I feel so sorry for him. Can you imagine what that would be like to never know the difference between reality and your own imagination?"

"Pretty sure my compassion for him disappeared when he grabbed you and started pulling you farther into the house..." Caleb trailed off with a serious look on his face.

"I really didn't believe he would hurt me." I shrugged and then accepted my unsweetened passion fruit tea.

"*Ugh*," Caleb commented on my choice. "I don't know how you drink that."

"It's like sipping a liquid sweet tart," I said, defending my favorite fuchsia-colored tea. "I don't know how y'all drink coffee. Now *that's* gross." I thanked the barista and guzzled down half of my drink before the window finished rolling up.

"And you call yourself an American..." Caleb shook his head in mock pity.

I grinned. "Well, I am half-Dorian, you know."

An hour and one more potty stop later, I had dropped Morgan and Caleb off at their homes with promises to see each other for fireworks the next night. We had come to a consensus that much of what Mr. Kinder had said was useless to us, and we were no closer to finding my dad than when we began. Despite that depressing fact, we had still found the overall experience interesting. Just knowing that somebody else—even though he was quite a disturbed individual—had actually been to our Island made the place feel real all over again.

When I finally pulled up to my house, Mom was already charging out the door to greet me. "*Mija!*" she cried, pulling me into her warm and familiar arms before I had even gotten both feet out of the car door. There were tears in those dark brown eyes as she hugged me.

"Hey, Mom." I sighed, realizing how much I had missed her. I loved everything about my mother—the faint Spanish accent that always colored her English, the way her smile lit up her heart-shaped face, the rich dark hair that I was slightly upset I hadn't inherited. And, of course, I loved the fact that she *understood* me.

When she pulled back, she searched my face. "You look different," she remarked, her eyebrows scrunching.

"Really?" I laughed, reaching back into the car for my bag. "Well, my hair is longer—it's been six weeks, you know."

"Five weeks," she corrected.

Oops.

"Right." I smiled, straightening up.

"No, something is different," she insisted. We exchanged puzzled glances.

"Don't know, Mom…" I shrugged.

She gave me that Mom Look she used when trying to decipher if I was being truthful—the one where her head tilted back, her lips pursed, and her eyes squinted at me. I tried to act normally. I could never share my Island experiences with her—at least not until I had confirmation that Dad really was alive. I dreamed about the day I would be able to share that with my mom—to see the look on her face when we could all be a family again. Just thinking about that had me diving into my pocket where I kept Dad's wedding ring—the wedding ring that Abrianna, the Guardian of the Island, had produced in an effort to prove to me that he was on the Island. But as I twisted the ring around my finger inside my pocket, I couldn't help thinking that Abrianna's story still didn't make complete sense.

"So you're kind of late. I've been trying to keep dinner warm," she chastised lightly as I followed her into the house.

"Yeah, sorry about that…" I dropped my bag in the living room and couldn't resist my excitement as the smell of dinner pervaded the atmosphere. "Oh, Mom…that smells wonderful! I'm *so* hungry."

"I made your favorite. Brown-sugared ham, mashed potatoes—with lumps, of course—and broccoli soaked in butter," she announced as she began fixing us plates. "It's one fabulous calorie fest, and you look like you could stand to put on some weight. I remember the food at Camp Fusion…not much to write home about. Fix our drinks while I get this ready."

I sighed happily as I poured us each a glass of iced tea. Glancing around my home at the little personal touches my mom had added everywhere made me so thankful for my life. It had been rough not having Dad around the last six years, but Mom had still made our house into a loving and comfortable home. This was our refuge, our little spot where the two of us could just be girls. This house was so symbolic of the new life we had created as a family of two. It was feminine and held new kinds of memories. The traces of Mom's perpetual quest for new hobbies were everywhere. We had certainly been through many different adventures together… Cooking experiments that went horribly wrong. Tae Kwon Do lessons until Mom sprained her ankle. Painting my bedroom a deep pink and stenciling little zebras on each wall until our hands were blistered and we wanted to give up. (After my bedroom in Aerodora, I was already planning on repainting with lavender and dragonflies.) One time we decided to take up scrapbooking, but that hobby soon ended when each scrapbooking session turned into a crying fest over our family pictures. That was when the late night chick flicks and therapeutic ice cream binges helped. Yes, Mom and I had definitely created a good life together.

A life I had no idea was about to be threatened until Mom dropped the bomb on me.

Dinner started with me filling Mom in on everything at camp (most of which she already knew from our frequent phone conversations). I even confessed a little bit about Caleb and the confusing feelings I was having. She watched me knowingly, a hidden smile at the corners of her mouth.

"Quit grinning like that!" I warned her. "I'm not saying I want to date him. I mean, what if there was someone else out there...?" I paused, my thoughts instinctively returning to the Island and the person I left behind there, but then I shook my head. "Caleb is such a good friend. I don't want to lose that."

"Sometimes friendship makes the best foundation for romance, Whit. I mean, you two already love and trust each other...I have no doubt that Caleb would treat you with respect and place your needs above his own."

"I don't doubt that, either," I replied. It was hard to explain my hesitance, especially since she didn't know anything about the Island. "I guess I like the idea of being swept off my feet..."

"Being swept is fun too. But it doesn't always last. Once the reality sets in and the butterflies in the stomach are gone, you need something of substance to stand on. And falling in love with a friend is more like a slow-building flame that can burn for a long time."

"You're biased because that's what happened with you and Dad," I reminded her with a raise of my eyebrows.

"Maybe," she admitted with a distant smile. "But I had the sweeping romance too—before your dad. And maybe having already had that experience showed me that your dad was the real thing." She trailed off then and started meticulously folding her napkin into triangles.

"You still miss him." I spoke quietly. It wasn't a question, but it wasn't exactly a statement either.

"Every day," she said and then abandoned her napkin to fold her hands on the table in front of her. "Whit, I want to tell you something."

Something about the way she said it set my heart to pounding.

"What?"

"It's not easy to say…and I want you to have an open mind, okay?"

"O-*kay*," I replied slowly. This was definitely weird. Mom had never been nervous to tell me anything before.

And then she just said it, almost like a confession. "I've started seeing someone."

Silence.

I stared at her.

"What do you mean?" I asked stupidly. Of course I knew what she meant, but that couldn't possibly be what she *meant*.

"I've been dating someone this summer…since you've been at Camp Fusion. He was a friend of Suzanne's from work, a widower, and she introduced us…We have a lot in common, and he has been so kind to me, Whitnee. In fact, I invited him to Papi's tomorrow for the party. I thought maybe you'd want to meet him…Oh, Whit, stop making that face. You're killing me here." She paused, and I took a second to compose my expression.

"Wait, *Suzanne* introduced you…Caleb's mom?"

She nodded.

"Well, why doesn't *she* date him?" I sputtered. "I mean, she's single too. Why did she have to step in and play matchmaker here? That's kind of irresponsible of her—"

"*Whit.*"

"*Mom.* You can't date someone!"

"*Mija*, I know this is weird for you…To be honest, it's a new concept to me too. But I was really hoping you would be okay with it—"

"Why in the world would I be okay with it?" My voice sounded loud. Why was it coming out so sharp and *loud*? Even my heartbeat was too loud in my own ears. Mom was becoming defensive—I could see it in her face and hear it in her voice.

"Because you are a rational and mature seventeen-year-old, Whitnee. I thought you would understand. This isn't about replacing your dad or anything like that—"

"*Replacing* him? Sounds more like *forgetting* him!" This was not happening. This *couldn't* be happening. Not when there was a chance that Dad was alive…a chance that I could bring him home.

"You never get over losing someone you love, but it's been six years, *mija*. And you're going away to college next year. Is it wrong of me to not want to be alone the rest of my life?" She looked at me with those honest eyes the color of milk chocolate, and yet I could feel the anger starting to burn through me.

"Oh, please! Six years is all it takes to move on from the supposed love of your life? And you're the one trying to give me advice for my own love life! What if Dad were to come back?"

"Your father is not coming back, Whitnee."

She said it so softly, but it seemed to echo around the room. It was the first time she had ever said it out loud. And it hurt both of us to hear it.

And then I opened my big, fat mouth. As I yelled at her, I could not control the tears that began spilling out of my eyes. "What if he was alive, Mom? What if I told you I knew where he was and I could bring him back home? Would you still date another man? Would you be in another relationship when Dad came back? If the situation were reversed, Dad would never give up on *you*! He would never date another woman, because he loves *you*!"

"Enough!" she shouted at me and stood to her feet. "I don't want to hear any more. You are obviously upset and not thinking clearly…This was a mistake." She shook her head, and I could see her hands trembling with anger as she started to clear the table.

"Oh, it was definitely a mistake, all right! My mistake for believing all these years that you loved Dad! That you would never give up on him!" I couldn't control the hurtful things coming out of my mouth, even though I knew I would regret them later.

"I'm not listening to this," Mom said. "We'll talk about it when you're calm."

"Ugh! I can't believe this!" I screamed and took off toward my bedroom, grabbing my bag on the way. "Do what you want!" And then I slammed my door shut and threw myself across my bed. I dug my face into my pillow and cried, trying to muffle the moans that ripped from deep in my chest. It was an angry cry as much as it was a mournful cry. And when I was finished, I pulled back and took in deep, raspy breaths. That was when I saw through my puffy eyes the little note on my bed that said, "Welcome home, Whitnee. Love, Mom." I threw it on the floor and squeezed my eyes shut.

Welcome home, indeed.

I avoided Mom the rest of the night, ruining what she had planned as a chick flick movie night for both of us. She came into my room once to try to make things better, but I was a little numb. This whole freaking summer had been a stressful, life-altering experience, and Mom just didn't understand that. How could she when I had not told her everything? But was it asking too much to want some sense of normalcy when I came home?

Once I calmed down, I replayed my conversation with her over and over again. I'm pretty sure that I only came across as a spoiled, selfish brat. And maybe I was…but, seriously, how could she pick *now*, this summer of all summers, to start dating? I mean, I was starting to seriously believe Dad was alive out there; I'd had real conversations with him in my dreams. Granted, none of that had happened since I'd left the Island, but when I was there, he had felt so close…so real…so *alive*. I spun his wedding ring around my finger again, wondering if I should have just showed it to her. What would she have done if I'd just said, "Look! It's Dad's ring! He's alive!"

Would she have flipped out on me? Sent me to a mental hospital? No, even she couldn't ignore the personalized inscription inside. So what then? Would she believe me if I told her everything about the Island? Then again, I was still so mad at her for cheating on Dad. Okay, technically it wasn't cheating, but seriously…She was trying to move on with her future while I was just on the verge of digging up the whole entire past.

What a mess. The more I had time to stew on it, the more I knew I had to find my dad. It was time for him to come back before every part of us that had clung to him over the years was gone. I had to find a way back to the Island. Failure was just not an option.

I should have had the best sleep of my summer being back in my own bed. But, no—the guilt of my conversation with Mom, the fear of losing Dad forever, and the worry over finding the Island again kept me tossing and turning and sweating all night.

The next morning it felt like this huge distance between Mom and me had settled in.

"Whitnee! You better…running late…getting in the car… *now!*" Mom's voice came out in short, clipped phrases over the loud, energetic music pumping through my bedroom.

I sagged against the bathroom counter, wishing I could just stay home in bed for the day. Dropping my brush into my toiletry bag, I shuffled out of the bathroom and turned my iPod speaker off. I had barely slipped into my flip-flops before she was calling my name again.

I resisted the urge to yell back and instead flew out of the room and headed straight for the car without a word. Arguments between Mom and me were rare, and when they did happen, we usually didn't stay mad for long. After all, we only had each other.

Once we were buckled in and on our way, Mom spoke quietly. "Robert is still planning to come to the party." As if I needed to be reminded that I would have to spend the whole day with *Robert*—the loser who was breaking apart my happy family. "Are you going to be nice to him? Or should I tell him not to come?"

In order to appear somewhat aloof, I started digging in my toiletry bag for my lip gloss. A tiny part of me felt like I had already pushed things too far with Mom and I needed to give a little in her direction. "Of course I'll be *nice*. I don't really care anymore." I shrugged and pulled the visor down for the mirror. Being nice would be easy…as long as I just avoided him (and Mom) as much as possible.

Mom wasn't buying my nonchalance. "You not caring about something…there's an idea." I think she smirked. "Whit, it's okay for you to care. It's a big change. I know that."

"Can we not talk about Robert?" I found my tube of lip gloss and was desperately trying to act like acquiring the right amount of gloss on the applicator was the most important thing at the moment.

"Well, what *do* you want to talk about? Camp Fusion? Your dad? The fact that last night, for the first time in five years, you acted like he was alive somewhere? You've *never*—"

"Mom." My stomach lurched and it wasn't from her bumpy driving. "I was just trying to make a point, okay? Please drop it."

She sighed heavily. "I just wish I knew what was going on with you this summer. You feel so far away from me right now, Whitnee." Her words almost broke my heart. I knew what she meant. She was less than a foot away from me, but there was far more separating us than a center console.

For a moment, the truth almost popped out of my mouth. But I swallowed it down by scrupulously applying gloss to my lips and focusing on my reflection in the mirror. I sure was glad Caleb would be at Papi and Mimi's house today. I needed a friend. Morgan's parents had their own family activity planned for the afternoon, but Caleb's single mother, Suzanne, had become my mother's best friend over the last five years. Since Caleb's father had died in a car accident and Caleb's three older sisters had already moved out on their own, he and his mom were often invited to our family functions.

After a few painful moments of silence, I reached over and flipped on the radio. Mom didn't protest, but I don't think she was happy about my lack of response. I honestly just didn't trust myself or my ability to say the right thing.

"Papi and Mimi can't wait to see you," Mom finally changed the subject. "You know Papi will bring his guitar out at some point and want you to sing."

I used the pad of my ring finger to smooth my lips and gave a half-smile at her words. "I figured." Any time my full-blooded Spanish grandfather threw a fiesta, it was known to feature delicious home-cooked Mexican food and a free concert by Papi and me. "I just wish he wouldn't make me sing in Spanish. Clearly I did not inherit that bilingual gene from you. I can't even roll my Rs..." Mom cracked a smile as I attempted to speak Spanish in a really bad American accent.

"Poor little white girl," Mom teased. "You are your father's daughter, for sure."

I lost touch with my smile then and just replied, "Yeah. Guess so."

With a sigh, I leaned closer for one last glance in the visor mirror. My skin was tanner, and my golden hair had indeed grown longer and lighter since I had last seen myself in this mirror. Sometimes I wondered if using the four different life forces on the Island hadn't changed me physically in some ways. I used to think my gray eyes were a boring and forgettable color...until they would glow silver on the Island, marking me as a member of the Aerodora tribe—the tribe that could harness the power of Wind.

It actually physically hurt for a moment as I allowed myself to think about the Island and what I had left behind. As foreign as that beautiful place was, as strange and different from my world as it was, I felt a connection to it. Maybe because it was the only place where I felt a real connection to my dad.

And that was when, sitting there staring at my reflection in the mirror, I thought I saw my eyes flicker with a bright silvery glow. They flickered about three times, like an old attic light bulb trying to find its power source before clicking on. I gasped and leaned in closer to stare at my eyes, daring it to happen again. And when it didn't, I let out the breath I must have been holding. I could've sworn...

I slammed the visor closed and leaned back into the headrest, my heart pounding. Mom gave me a sideways glance, but I stared straight ahead at the road.

Man, the power of missing something that badly must really have an effect on someone's imagination...because it had to be imagination. I mean, it was impossible to access a life force from the Mainland. There was no way my eyes really could have just lit up this far from the Island.

"How could she even *think* about dating someone? Why *now*?" I screeched, pacing around Papi and Mimi's expansive kitchen.

Caleb was perched casually on the kitchen island, slowly swinging his feet. His head nearly grazed the silver pots and pans hanging above him. His watchful eyes followed my every move, but other than that he did not appear surprised at my reaction.

"It is weird timing..." he agreed gently.

"*Weird* timing? It's the *worst* timing *ever*!" I threw up my hands in dramatic frustration. "My dad is still alive out there...I just know it! And I'm closer than ever to finding him and bringing him home—"

"Whit." Caleb sighed with a shake of his head.

"Caleb...*don't*." I stopped my pacing to give him a warning look. I was not up to his skepticism at the moment.

"There has been no sign of the portal opening back up—" he began.

"It's just a matter of time."

"How can you be so sure?"

"I don't know...I just can't believe that *somebody* wouldn't open it back up for me as soon as possible." I didn't meet Caleb's eyes then as I picked up my pacing at a slower rate.

"You mean Gabriel." It wasn't a question, but it hung in the air between us, creating a thick cloud of awkwardness.

I turned away from Caleb to play absentmindedly with the pack of new kitchen sponges on the counter. "He told me before I left that I would find a way back to the Island," I said softly, pushing away my memories of the handsome Pyra boy who had turned my love life upside down several weeks ago. Though some of my experiences on the mysterious White Island had already faded in vividness, the moments shared with Gabriel had not. I still painfully remembered every look, every conversation, every kiss, and...*ugh*. I couldn't do this. Was Caleb trying to torture me by bringing up his name? That relationship was going nowhere.

"Well, he told *me* before we left to take care of *you*," Caleb responded quietly.

Bristling a bit from that part of the whole strange journey, I squeezed my eyes shut and hissed, "And if both of you hadn't decided to take control of my decisions, I would have my dad here, and I wouldn't be dealing with my mom dating another man!"

"We've been through all of this, Whit. I'm sorry things happened the way they did, but we can't change that now. If I'd known we could find your dad, I never would have pulled you through the portal."

"I know, I know." I sighed and turned back around, squeezing the pack of sponges in one fist. "I'm not upset about that any-more...or I shouldn't be. I guess the idea of my mom dating would be upsetting even if I didn't know there was a possibility of finding Dad," I admitted.

Caleb shrugged and gave me a mischievous smile. "How long did you think your mom would stay single? I mean, not to weird you out or anything, but your mom's still pretty hot for her age—"

"Caleb!" My eyes widened, and I threw the sponges at him. "That *does* weird me out! Don't talk about her that way!"

He batted the package away easily with his hand. "All I'm saying is that it makes sense."

"Stop it! You're supposed to be on my side," I reminded him with a roll of my eyes.

"I am on your side. I just don't think you should be freaking out yet. They've been on a few dates…It doesn't seem like it's anything serious," he pointed out, absentmindedly tracing his finger along his temple near his hairline—a recent habit I was starting to notice.

I narrowed my eyes. "Is your scar bothering you?"

"Huh?"

I pointed to his head where he had suffered a pretty serious injury on the Island.

With a shake of his head, he said, "The new scar was the first thing Mom noticed when I walked in the door. It's like she keeps record of every mark on my body."

"What did you tell her?"

"Well, I *didn't* tell her that I got hit by a coconut and you healed my injury with magical Water powers." He grinned.

"I told you to let the HydroHealer get rid of the scar."

"And I told you I wanted to keep it. I will always know how I got it—and who really healed me." His eyes were illuminated with affection for me.

I tried to ignore his implications, but the emotions within me were getting too near the surface. I dropped my face into my hands. "We have to get back to that Island, Caleb! I *have* to get Dad back!"

"We'll get back if it's meant to be, but there's nothing you can do to speed the process along. You need to calm down."

"I am calm!" I snapped. His logical nature was starting to irk me. "I mean, how would you feel if it were your mom dating another man?" I pointed out.

"Actually, I think I might like for my mom to get remarried someday. I worry about her being by herself when I move away." He shrugged. "As long as he was a good man and treated her well, I think I'd be okay with it."

I stared at him. "Well, geez. Thanks for making me feel like a jerk!"

"*But*...unlike you, I know there's no way to bring my dad back. So I suppose it's a little easier to move on with my life. And if your mom really believes your dad is gone, she probably feels the same way. Remember, you're the one who hasn't told her the truth. I think someday you're going to have to let her in on things, Whit."

"She'll think I'm crazy."

"Maybe at first."

"Well, I'm not doing it until I know something for sure. Until then..." I leaned against the counter and faced Caleb straight on with a frown. "I feel terrible, you know. I said a lot of mean things to her. And I want to apologize, but..." I squeezed my hands in frustration. "Watching her out there with another man is just too much! I don't like seeing him look at her. I don't like her caring about what he thinks of me or if we are getting along okay...This just can't be my life! If I could, I would just, I don't know...create another whirlwind and blast him away from here!"

And I don't know what happened or why it happened, but my emotional intensity was so high that when I threw my hands out to demonstrate how I would use the Wind life force, a huge gust of air came right out of my palms and hit Caleb full-force. The pots and pans above his head clanged together, some even flying off their hooks and crashing on the kitchen floor. Caleb himself was almost thrown backwards, his hair flying around his shocked face. And then it was over.

THE YUM VORTEX

We gaped at each other as the last pot finally stopped rattling on the floor and settled into silence.

"What did you just—?" Caleb started at the same time I cried, "Did I just—?"

But our mutual shock was interrupted by the sound of my mom's voice calling my name from another room in the house. I was so stunned I could only stare wide-eyed at him when he whispered loudly, "Your eyes are glowing! You can't let anyone see you like that!" He jumped off the kitchen island.

"Where…what…?" I stuttered, panicking. No, I wasn't ready to explain this to my mom. Without a rational thought, I grabbed Caleb and pulled him into the pantry. There was just enough space for the two of us to stand inside…rather closely. Like body to body. The pantry had one of those lights that clicked on when the door opened and turned off when it was closed. As soon as I shut the door behind us, we were plunged into darkness.

On one side of me was the door; on the other side were shelves of canned goods and food. Something was jamming into my back, and the front of me was pressed in close to Caleb—since when had he gotten so tall? And, dang, he smelled good. Something distinctly male and yummy that permeated my senses beyond the boxed foods and spices surrounding us. His face was barely illuminated by the glow of my eyes.

"You're looking at me," he whispered with a small laugh. "I forgot how weird it was to see people's eyes glow in the dark."

"I can't believe this is happening…We'll just stay in here until they stop glowing. Won't be long," I told him, keenly aware of his nearness now and worried that I liked it too much. I heard Mom calling my name again, closer. I wished she would go away for a second so I could figure out what the heck was going on. I wanted to know if I could use the Wind again.

Now that I had a moment to allow my heartbeat to settle down, I discovered that it only pumped faster with Caleb taking up so much of my personal space. In fact, I found myself leaning in closer to him…and not just because of whatever was knifing me in the back, but because he just smelled so good. And I *wanted* to be close to him.

"You smell different," I couldn't help whispering. "Is that a new cologne?"

"Yeah," he answered in that quiet voice, and I swear he leaned down a little toward me. "You like it?"

"It's nice. I mean, I definitely *like* it…"

Oh my *gosh*. It was, like, making me feel all fuzzy and confused. And it wasn't just the smell. It was the way he was just *there* and so much taller than I think I had remembered. And the way we were all entangled in this little pantry…*Oh heaven, help me.*

"Whit?" He said my name so softly.

"Hmm?"

"Do you know how easy it would be to kiss you right now?"

Dangit. He was feeling it too. Could he tell how easy it would be for me to *let* him kiss me? I was definitely in trouble here.

My stomach came to life with energetic little butterflies, and I let out a small laugh that didn't sound very natural. I couldn't seem to find anything especially witty to say, because all I could wonder was, what *would* it be like to kiss Caleb?

"You're not answering me," he breathed, and I felt his fingers graze my shoulder and push my hair aside.

When his hand gently rested on the nape of my neck, I shivered and my stomach nearly dropped to the floor. I was very aware of the easy access this position gave him to pull my face closer to his.

"You better say something to stop me, Whit, because I've been wanting to do this a long time…and we're trapped here in a pantry. And you smell pretty good yourself…"

His face was definitely moving closer, and instead of turning mine away, I was certainly keeping it slanted upward toward him. Was this really what I wanted? Once I kissed him, there was no going back…

"Say the word, Whit, and I won't…"

I sighed. "Caleb, I—"

And that was when the pantry door swung open and bright light blinded us. My heart felt like it went into cardiac arrest as I jumped painfully backward into the thing punching me in the back. Caleb pulled away so fast, he knocked over a couple of canned vegetables, and we both grunted in pain.

"Oh! Um, hello," Mom stumbled. "I was just, uh—Papi needed…didn't expect you to be in…" She reached right in between Caleb and me and grabbed a jar off the shelf. We stood there in mortified silence. "I'll let you two…okay. Bye!" And before she shut the door on us again, I didn't miss the knowing grin that was spreading across her face.

And then we were back in the dark. It was a few seconds of stunned silence before I heard Caleb's laughter start.

"What is so funny about this?" I asked. "My mom thinks we were making out…in the pantry!"

"I'm sorry…it's just…I don't know. You freaking destroyed the kitchen with Wind, I almost kissed you, and then your mom interrupts us…Talk about a crazy five minutes!"

"I wouldn't have let you kiss me," I retorted, suddenly realizing how dangerously close I had come to that. *What was I thinking?!*

"Oh, right. You think I can't tell when a girl wants me?"

"Shut up." I opened the pantry door with a pout and stepped back into the sun-lit kitchen. How dare he bring up other girls in this moment? Like I wanted to know that... "You read it all wrong. It was dark."

This made him laugh harder as he followed me. "You're so cute and annoying when you pretend like something didn't happen..."

"Nothing did happen."

He grabbed me by the waist and spun me around, gathering me very closely to his body again. Then in a high-pitched voice, he mimicked dramatically, "Oh, Caleb, you smell so nice! I want you to kiss me now!"

I whacked him on the arm. "I did not say that. And get control of yourself before somebody else sees us!" And I wiggled out of his embrace, though I did find him entirely too attractive in that moment. That was when I looked around at the kitchen...the pots and pans that had fallen haphazardly on the floor and the island. "Do you think she thinks we...did this?"

"Yeah, baby." Caleb grinned wickedly and let out another hoot of laughter. There was no way...my mom was smarter than that.

"Will you stop being a guy and snap out of it? Holy crap, Caleb, I just used a life force on the Mainland!" I faced him with my palms out. "Let's see if I can do it again."

"Whoa! Point those things somewhere else," he warned, pushing my hands away from him.

We got quiet while I concentrated on the sensation of breathing, the cool movement of air flowing throughout my body. But no...I couldn't make contact with the actual life force. I definitely sensed it, but the right connection wasn't in place.

"It won't work," I stated, dropping my hands.

"Are you sure?"

"Yeah, I can tell. But I definitely feel something different...Oh my gosh! You know what this means!"

"I have no clue."

"It means we're closer! It means something is trying to reconnect—maybe they're opening up the portal back at camp! Wouldn't that be great?" I was so excited I could barely keep myself from launching back into his arms. It was euphoric to realize we might be closer to the Island than we thought. But I didn't miss Caleb's hesitance in joining my celebration. Slightly deflated, I mumbled, "What's wrong?"

"Nothing. It's great, Whit. I'm sure it's just a matter of time before we go back." He gave me a weak smile.

I knew then what he was thinking. Going back to the Island also meant seeing Gabriel again, and that was not exactly a pleasant concept in Caleb's mind—for obvious reasons. Though I had never told Caleb the depth of my relationship with Gabriel (like the stolen kisses), he knew. He had an uncanny way of reading me, and he could see it in my face even when we were still on the Island.

I sighed and looked deep into his green eyes, wanting to take away the hurt I knew he felt. "Things will be different this time, Caleb. I was an idiot before. I'm over…the whole thing."

"Sure you are…" He nodded and gave a little laugh that probably came out more bitter than intended. He moved to start picking up fallen pots and pans. I watched him silently for a moment, wondering if there was something more I should say on the subject or if I should just let it go. Lord knows I still had those feelings for Gabriel, but I really thought that it was mind over matter at this point. And I was working pretty darn hard to believe that what happened on that magical Island between him and me was nothing but a distraction.

So I opted to drop the subject.

"We've got to call Morgan…and Ben!" I exclaimed, wondering if anything was happening across the river at camp.

"First, we've got to clean up this mess and rejoin the party before rumors about us start." Caleb grinned boyishly. And then his face dropped. "Shoot! What if your mom told my mom—"

"Oh, no!" I gasped. We did *not* need our mothers conspiring about us. "Let's go!"

"I told you it was just a matter of time, Whit! We're going back soon—I just know it!" Morgan exclaimed after I filled her in on what happened in the kitchen—well, the first part of it anyway.

"I hope you're right." I sighed, pressing the phone to my ear and peering out the window at Caleb talking to the adults by the pool. He looked so relaxed around my family. My aunt was scolding one of her three energetic boys for shoving his little brother headfirst into the shallow end of the pool. I could tell Aunt Letty was speaking half in Spanish and half in English, like my family had a habit of doing when upset.

I was pretty sure I came from a family of spicy Spanish Pyras—if there was such a thing. (I had started making a habit of secretly classifying everybody I knew into a particular tribe.) Aunt Letty could go off on someone with that fiery Latina attitude of hers that reminded me way too much of the emotional Pyras on the Island. It didn't help that my cousins were all under the age of eight and definitely upped the volume of a room anytime they were around. They were so cute with that tan Spanish skin and rich dark hair. We didn't look blood-related, even though we totally were. I loved them dearly and was slightly jealous that they were already way more bilingual as children than I was at seventeen.

Turning my attention back to Morgan on the phone, I confessed quietly, "Okay, so after that happened in the kitchen, Caleb and I hid in the pantry—"

"Why?"

"Because my eyes were glowing, and Mom was looking for us. So while we were in there…I don't know, Morgie. Something weird happened. Between Caleb and me."

"Do explain, because I've seen that pantry, and it's not that huge…" I could hear the smile in her voice.

"Well…I think I got caught up in the yum vortex!" I confessed in a loud whisper.

She started laughing. "Caleb has a yum vortex? Wow, you really do have it bad."

"I don't have anything bad…He had on a new cologne, and you know how weak I get when a guy smells good and I just get that whiff and it's like *mmm…*"

"It's the vortex of yumminess. Sucks you in and makes you forget all sense of reason," she finished for me.

"Morgie, what's wrong with me?"

"You like him, Whitnee. Just admit it. I know you do, and you know you do. Why is it so hard for you to just say? Is it because of the Gabriel thing or what?"

"Well, I mean, is it possible to like two guys at the same time? But differently?"

"Maybe…especially since you've never dated much before. You've always been so picky. Maybe you're just trying to figure out who you're most compatible with…"

"They're both so different, though."

"It's true," she agreed. "I've always thought that you and Caleb are great together…when you're not fighting, that is. The problem is you've never been physically attracted to him."

"Until now…" I sighed and heard Morgan chuckle.

"I've been wondering when you would figure it out…We need to face the facts here, Whit. Our very own Caleb has turned into quite the hottie over the last couple of years. If it weren't for his feelings for you, we might have already lost him to some annoying girlfriend."

I cocked my head to the side and glanced again out the window. "Really? I mean…yeah." I stared inconspicuously at Caleb through the window and wondered if I would have checked him out in public had I not known him…*Hmm*. Yeah, I just might. I was certainly checking him out now. I gave a little growl of frustration.

"So how are things with your mom?" Morgan changed the subject, causing me to switch my gaze to Mom by the pool with Suzanne and Robert. Mom spotted me through the window and frowned. I turned away.

"Weird…just avoiding the whole thing right now. I can't wait for you to get here and meet this guy. Caleb's being all logical about everything. I need someone to be a Robert-hater with me."

"Actually, Whit, I don't think I can come later."

"Morgie, fireworks together on July Fourth is tradition!"

"I know, and I'm sorry. But I really don't feel good. Maybe it's a virus or something, I don't know. But my parents aren't going to let me go back to camp tomorrow night if I don't kick it. So I think I'm going to have to sit the fireworks show out this year."

"That sucks—"

Mom came into the house at that moment and gave me a stern look. I held up my index finger at her.

"Hey, Morgan, I have to go. I'm sad you can't come! But I'll see you at church in the morning, right?"

"Hopefully. Depends on how I feel. Promise me you and Caleb will behave tonight?" She laughed again.

"Whatever. I promise!" I shook my head and stifled a laugh. And then we hung up. My smile died when I turned my attention back on my mother.

"You need to come outside and be social, Whitnee. I know you're avoiding getting to know Robert, but you're being rude to the family."

Maybe she was right. "Okay, I'm coming now," I said with a sigh. She turned to go back out the door, and I stopped her. "Hey, Mom?" She spun back around. "Um, I…" There was so much I should say to her, needed to say to her. But I started with the simplest. "What happened earlier with Caleb and me in the pantry… it wasn't what it looked like. I promise."

"I know." She actually gave me a small smile and took a few cautious steps toward me.

"How do you know?" I was surprised.

"Your lip gloss was still on."

Okay, so now I could feel my face flaming. "Well, we were just talking about something in a quiet place…and I know it looked bad. But you know I have high values when it comes to dating and physical relationships."

"Yes, I know, and I'm proud of you for that. But, Whit, if you want to keep those high values, you are going to have to be careful what situations you allow yourself to get into with a guy…Once you're there, the temptation is hard to fight. I just want you to be smart about how you handle yourself."

I nodded and stared at the floor, contemplating just how great that temptation to kiss Caleb had been. I could sense her moving closer to me.

"Whit, don't get mad at me for prying here, but…the way you look at Caleb…it is definitely different now."

I met her eyes then.

"What do you mean?"

"I mean that something is changing between you two, and I can't quite figure out why you're so hesitant to just enjoy it."

I took a deep breath, warring within myself over what to say to her. Now was certainly not the time to tell her the real story. "I guess I'm just scared of hurting him," I finally muttered. At least it was the truth.

She nodded. "As much as I'd love for you to date someone like Caleb, I have to agree that you should take this one slow. You seem torn for whatever reason, and Caleb deserves all of your emotions when the time is right—not just part of you."

Geez, she was hitting everything just right.

"Mom? Since you're being so honest with me, can I be honest with you?"

"Of course. That would actually be nice since I feel like there are things you're not telling me lately."

I ignored her intuitions and just came out with it. "Robert is *boring*! Oh my gosh, look at him!" And I gestured out the window to the man in a button up short-sleeved shirt who sat by the pool with his legs crossed. "He is so not your type! You're like, this adventurous person and he's like, the sit-at-a-computer-all-day kind of guy. He's nothing like Dad…I mean, he's just kind of *there*. Nice guy, but come on!" I finished dramatically, throwing up my hands.

I was shocked when she started laughing. In fact, she laughed pretty hard, and I just stared at her, not really sure what to do. Finally as she wiped an escaped tear away, she looked at me.

"Oh, *mija*…you're right. He is completely boring!" Her laugh was sort of high-pitched, like she couldn't believe she had just admitted that.

"Then *what* are you doing, Mom?" I asked incredulously.

She sobered up and paused as if trying to find the right words.

"Whitnee, I have had a lot of fun in my life…and you're right. Your dad and I always got a thrill out of new experiences. I hope we did a good job raising you to seek out your own adventures, but…" She sighed heavily. "I'm tired, Whit. I'm getting older. I don't want to find another man like your dad. Maybe I'm ready to finally settle down and just be boring, you know?"

"No, I don't get that."

"Well, I don't expect you to completely understand. Just know that I like Robert because he's different than Dad. Can we just leave it at that for now?" She wasn't smiling anymore. In fact, she looked now like she might cry.

I nodded slowly. "Okay," I agreed. I didn't understand her reasoning for the same reasons she didn't understand mine over Caleb. There were deep emotions there that we just couldn't put into words. But it did give me some hope that maybe Mom wasn't quite head over heels for the guy. Things would change if—or when—I brought Dad back. Before we opened the door to rejoin the party, I told her confidently, "I don't think you're through with your adventures, though, Mom."

The rest of the afternoon progressed less dramatically. Caleb and I eventually got in the pool with my cousins, where we let the boys chicken fight on our shoulders. I even played some Marco Polo with them, until I discovered Caleb cheating. He was way too good at immediately swimming in my direction. Secretly, I think it was just an excuse for him to grab onto me and dunk me underwater. I will admit that Caleb's lean athlete's body didn't look bad at all in a swimsuit. Add *that* to the list of things I had forgotten to notice about him.

Morgan was right. When did Caleb become the poster boy for All-American, boy-next-door, homegrown hottie? I don't know what it was, but flirting with Caleb had taken on a new angle. And I'd be lying if I said his attention and excuses to be physically close to me weren't welcome. Eventually, though, our antics in the pool only served to increase our appetites. So while drying off in my large, snuggly towel, I had no qualms about scarfing down some fajitas with the boys.

"Eddie, you're about to lose your chicken!" I warned my six-year-old cousin as his fajita slowly fell apart. He was the middle child and kind of my favorite of the three. He seemed more attached to me than the other two. Eddie was the scrawny, intellectual kid in the family. He asked the kinds of questions nobody thought about, and he often seemed lost in his own imagination. Probably an Aero. Even his two energetic brothers didn't seem to bother him. He had positioned himself right in between Caleb and me and was taking his time eating, kicking his little feet that didn't reach the ground from his chair.

After helping him rewrap his fajita, I sat back in my chair, slightly regretting how much I had eaten. That was when Papi came back out on the porch—with his guitar in hand. I groaned inwardly, knowing what was coming.

"Come sit with me, Whitnee! It is time to sing!" Papi exclaimed in his dramatic way.

I had always thought I inherited my musical ability and my flair for dramatics from my Papi, Mom's dad. But after meeting Ezekiel, my dad's real father on the Island, and learning about his theatrical personality and aptitude for music, I wasn't sure I ever had a chance to inherit a quiet and meek personality between my two grandfathers.

I lazily pulled myself up off my chair and moved to the porch swing with Papi. I wrapped my towel a little tighter around me, suddenly a little shy knowing Caleb's eyes were glued to me. I mean, it wasn't like he hadn't ever been a part of this scene, hadn't ever witnessed Papi making me sing in front of family and friends…but it was the way he was watching me that felt different. It was like he had a right to watch me, to appreciate me in ways that nobody else could. And it was a sweet feeling that I could sit there in my swimsuit and towel with wet hair and no makeup and know that Caleb still cared about *me*. Because even though he didn't say how he felt, I could feel it. I could see it in his tender green eyes that were now observing my hesitance. He gave me a quick wink, and I averted my gaze to watch Papi tune the guitar before Caleb could see the effect that wink had on me.

Everyone angled their chairs toward us—including Mom, Robert, Suzanne, Mimi, Aunt Letty, Uncle Paul, and a few of Papi and Mimi's neighbors who had been invited to the party. My cousins continued working on their meals at the porch table with Caleb.

"My only granddaughter, Whitnee, *canta precioso!*" Papi announced, and I shook my head at his boasting. "Which song should we do, *niña?*" he asked, picking a few chords on the old guitar. But before I could answer, he started one we had been singing at holidays since childhood. So I harmonized with him. Eddie joined in with his mouth full of food.

Everyone clapped when we finished, and then Papi started another song, one he had made me sing alone since I could learn the words—"El Pino"—a holiday favorite in our family. The bad thing was that all the lyrics were in Spanish.

"Oh, Dad…quit torturing her. You know Spanish is not her strength," Mom jumped to my defense.

"Shh, shh, Serena. She can do it. I know those Spanish roots are somewhere deep down inside her." I gave her a grateful look for at least trying to rescue me.

The backyard was alive with the outdoor sounds of a late summer day and the lilting strumming of Papi's guitar. Papi looked to me and nodded when it was my cue to begin, and my voice filled the air, weaving into the chords of the instrument. I sang the words I knew so well in the language I barely understood. As I sang, I mostly kept my eyes on Papi and his fingers moving deftly over the strings of the guitar. Just once during the song did I allow myself to look at Caleb. He had that look of intensity on his face that seemed reserved for me lately, and I wondered what he was thinking about. I was so distracted by it that I messed up one of the lyrics—only to have Eddie call out the right word for me. I gave him a smile when Aunt Letty shushed him.

When the song was over, they clapped again and Caleb whistled. I really hoped that was it, but no, Papi wanted to do one more song and make everyone sing along. So we did…and had fun clapping and singing to each other. Even Caleb sang a little, and I knew singing wasn't his thing. After that, it was time to change so we could load up the cars and drive out to the golf course where we went every year for fireworks. It was a fun tradition to bring our blankets and chairs out on the green where we were almost directly under the explosions.

I went back to the guest bedroom so I could change into my clothes and throw my chlorine-riddled hair up into a messy bun. I had just dropped my towel to the floor when there was a knock at the door. Still in my bikini, I went and opened it. Caleb was standing in the hallway—in just his swim trunks with his towel hooked over one shoulder. His hair had dried haphazardly and was a wavy mess on his head, but he was cute. He was way too cute.

"Your mom told me you needed this." He handed me the toiletry bag I had packed for the day.

"Oh, yeah. Thanks." I smiled up at him and took it out of his hands. He turned to walk away, but then he came back, his mouth open as if he was going to say something. I just stood there, gazing up at him expectantly. Then he pressed his lips together and shook his head slightly. "What?" I prompted.

"You, uh…" he stumbled and then grinned boyishly. "You need to get dressed."

Okay.

"Well, I was about to before you interrupted me."

"Good." He backed away, still facing me with a silly grin.

I narrowed my eyes at him and leaned against the doorjamb. "What is that smile about, Caleb Austin?"

"Nothing." He shrugged. "I just, uh, hope we don't ever meet in a dark pantry when you're wearing *that*. Not if you expect me to have some self-control…"

My mouth dropped open, which made him laugh out loud before he disappeared around the corner, calling over his shoulder, "See you in the car!"

I shut the door and leaned against it for a moment, smiling like an idiot.

Truthfully, we really did miss Morgan at the golf course. It was the first year since I'd lived in San Antonio that she didn't come with us, and we had our phones out texting her so she would still feel a part of the event. Caleb and I had laid a blanket out on the ground next to the three boys, and the adults sat in lawn chairs behind us. The remaining streaks of daylight across the sky were illuminated pink and purple, a beautiful backdrop to the freshly manicured green of the golf course. Caleb was tossing a ball around with Luis and Eddie. Marcus, the four-year-old, was already preparing to hide under a blanket in Aunt Letty's lap. He was afraid of the boom when the fireworks exploded. Maybe Marcus wasn't a Pyra either.

I sat there, listening in on Mom's boring conversation with Robert about the economy while I casually observed Caleb playing with my cousins. He was a natural with kids. He was in the middle of chasing the ball that Eddie had thrown way off-target when he must have received a text. He reached into his back pocket and pulled out his phone, read the text with no expression, and then started texting back. Once he finished, he jogged toward me and tossed the phone on the blanket beside me along with his wallet and keys.

"Watch those for me. I can't chase this ball with everything in my pockets."

"Who's texting you?"

"Oh, just Dillon and the guys," he replied nonchalantly. Dillon was his best friend and fellow teammate during football season.

"It's practically dark, you know," I called after him as he went to finish his game of catch. I lay on my back and peered up at the darkening sky. I could faintly see the Big Dipper. My thoughts immediately returned to yesterday and poor Will Kinder. I wondered if he was looking at the same stars right now. Did it have a special meaning for him to look up and see such a pattern in the sky? Did its consistency and faithfulness to appear every night give him comfort when his mind was so jumbled up?

And speaking of consistency…what exactly did it mean that I had been able to use Wind on the Mainland—in my grandparents' house? On the Island they had made it clear that it was the land itself that held the connection to the life forces. When Dorians moved too far away from the Island, they lost their abilities. How did I connect to it from so far away? Secretly, I had been trying to reconnect with the feeling all afternoon—with no luck. When I had called Ben earlier, he hadn't answered his phone. I was desperate to get back to camp tomorrow and find out if anything was happening across the river. When I hadn't been distracted by Mom and Robert and the changes happening between Caleb and me all day, my mind was already turning over the preparations I would need to make before going back to the Island.

I was reliving the bizarre experience in the kitchen earlier when Caleb's cell phone vibrated and lit up on the blanket next to me. I picked it up to see the message coming in and immediately wished I hadn't. It was a message from Dillon.

> Dude, ur wasting ur time w Whit! Hot girls here, Laura & her friends—come over ltr!

Caleb was wasting his time with me? What did that mean? And Dillon wanted Caleb to come over because Laura was there...? *Ugh.* Laura was the head cheerleader at our school, and Caleb had kind of liked her last year. It hadn't really bothered me then, but it certainly bothered me now. Stupid Dillon. I thought he and I were friends! What was he thinking telling Caleb I was a waste of—

"What are you looking at?"

Caleb and the boys had quit their game because the show was about to start. Eddie and Luis collapsed onto their blanket next to us, and Caleb dropped beside me. I still had his phone in my hand, and I quickly gave it back to him.

"Nothing. You got a text." I shrugged, focusing my attention back on the night sky. Where was that Big Dipper again?

Caleb was silent as he took the phone and read the text. I pretended not to notice.

"Did you read this?" he asked carefully.

"Huh? The text?" I played dumb, but Caleb knew me too well, and I was not so good at playing the nonchalant girl. He gave me a look, and I mumbled, "I didn't mean to read it...I thought it might be Morgan."

"No, it's okay that you did. I just...wouldn't have wanted you to see that." He lay down beside me and rested his head in the crook of one arm.

"Well, yeah, it kind of stinks to know Dillon thinks I'm a waste of time—"

"That's not what he means. You know Dillon likes you."

"Well, what the heck is he talking about?" I sputtered, losing my cool. "And why is he trying to get you to come hang out with Laura and those girls? Just because they're pretty and popular? I guess I had forgotten about your crush on Laura, but if you'd rather be there with her instead of here, then—"

"Whitnee, you sound jealous," he interrupted me, and I couldn't bear to look at him.

"Well, so what if I am? I mean, first Laura, then Claire, and now we're back to Laura? You sure know how to make a girl's head spin, Caleb."

"It's not like that," he insisted.

"Then what is it like?" I hissed. "Because according to your friends and, I don't know, maybe to you too, I'm just a waste of time."

"Would I still be here if you were a waste of my time?"

"I don't know. Would you?" And then I turned my head to meet his gaze. *Dang*, it hurt to even consider the idea that Caleb would give up on me like that…that after everything we'd been through together he'd just run off to some random girls from school. It had nearly killed me when he kissed Claire right after he shared his feelings with me. And that was before we'd found the Island. Now that we shared such a huge secret, I couldn't imagine losing that closeness with him again.

He heaved a sigh as he stared back at me. "The guys just think that you're never going to like me back. They think I'm wasting my time spending it with you when there are other girls out there. They just don't get it, Whit, that's all."

"Well, maybe I don't get it, either," I said bitterly. "I mean, what's in it for you to be my friend, to work with me all summer, and even hang out with me on your one weekend break? Because, let's be honest…you know my life is completely turned upside down right now. You know I'm not ready to get involved in a dating relationship with you. And who knows when that will change? So really, what are you doing hanging out with stupid, boring, ugly me?"

"Stop it," he said forcefully, obviously noting my headfirst fall into self-deprecation. Then he propped himself up on his elbow so that he could look directly down into my face. "First of all, you are not boring. Far from it, actually…You could be the Pilgrim, the savior for an entire race of magical people. If you think I'm bored with that—"

"Oh, great. So you stick around because I'm a sick fascination for you—"

"Will you let me finish? *Geez*, Whit, stop talking for a sec! Don't forget that I've been pretty loyal to you for the five years prior to your discovery of the White Island, so don't even try to act like this is a new thing. Second of all, I'm not that into Laura. I told the guys that last year to get them off my case about *you*, and as for Claire…you and I both know she was just a distraction, a reflex reaction, after you rejected me."

I opened my mouth to cut in on that, but he held up a warning hand. "*Third*, you're gorgeous, so I really don't want to hear you call yourself ugly again. And, finally…" He paused before saying gently, "You once said that when I found the right girl, I would wait for her and work hard everyday just so she would feel cherished…and you were right. I firmly believe that there are some things in this world that are worth waiting for, worth fighting for, even if it takes a long time. And you are that girl."

I sucked in my breath. "Well, when I said that before, I didn't mean…um, maybe you shouldn't say that yet."

Was that seriously the most brilliant thing I could think of to say?

"Just know that I am right where I want to be," he finished.

"I don't deserve that, you know," I admitted. "But I don't want you to give up, either." I'm not sure if it was the right thing to admit or not, because saying that to a guy was like giving him hope. And I certainly had no idea what my future held. I just knew that right then I wanted Caleb in it somehow.

"Well, *that* is a new expression I've never seen before…" he mumbled, his eyes watching me curiously. I wasn't sure what emotion was playing on my face, but he seemed fascinated by it. After all, Caleb prided himself on knowing and understanding all of my constantly changing facial expressions.

And that was when the first boom of the fireworks show happened, nearly scaring me to death. He laughed and lay down on his back again, and we watched the glorious display of color and light exploding in the sky above us. We *oohed* and *ahhed* and took pictures on our phones to send to Morgan. Eddie cuddled up to the other side of me. Eventually, I felt Caleb's hand reach for mine in the space between our bodies, and I gladly held on to him.

THIS ISN'T THE BLUE LAGOON

Sunday was weird. Morgan didn't come to church, and when I called her afterward to see if she could go shopping, she was really sluggish and sleepy. We only had three weeks left at camp, and one of our closing activities was the lip sync contest among the mentors and campers. This event fell under my responsibility as the music and drama activity camp instructor. With a "Travel Through the Decades" theme, Morgan and I picked the eighties for our group's entry. And what better song was there for us to perform with our campers than "Girls Just Wanna Have Fun"? I had limited time to do some costume shopping and was a little disappointed when Morgan acted as if she'd forgotten all about it.

Fortunately, Mom went with me and helped pick outfits for Morgan and me. After all, she knew the eighties better than me. ("Oh, *mija*, you have to scrunch your hair and tease it really high. Here, grab some extra hair spray!") It was a pleasant enough time, but I think that was mostly because Mom and I avoided the heavy topics. I don't think either of us wanted to ruin our last afternoon together before I left. Eventually Morgan had called back with the news that she had to take her own car back to camp. Caleb and I agreed to just ride with her this time, even though it was weird...I was usually the driver among the three of us. Before I knew it, she was picking me up and stopping in long enough to say hi to Mom and apologize again for missing the fireworks fun. She looked pretty pale and wasn't acting quite like herself. Even Mom noticed. As soon as I hugged my teary-eyed mom good-bye and got in the car, I turned to Morgan.

"Are you okay? You look terrible."

"Thanks, Whit." She grinned weakly and sagged a little once it was just the two of us. "Actually, I feel pretty crappy. After we pick up Caleb, do you mind driving? I just don't think I'll make it."

"Is it still your stomach?"

"Yeah, I had to fake like I was totally fine or my parents wouldn't have let me come back—you know how they are." She rolled her eyes.

Morgan's mom was the worrier type...with some major over-protective tendencies. (A Geo, maybe?) Morgan was the middle child between her overachieving brother and uptight sister. If there really was such a thing as middle child syndrome, Morgan had it. She was the only laid-back person in her immediate family.

"What do you think it is?" I questioned.

"Nothing. Weeks of bad camp food," she answered with a shrug. "You know I always have 'bathroom issues.' Nothing new."

Definitely nothing new...If I had a dollar for every time Morgan had rushed off to the restroom in my presence over the years, I'd be rich.

"So why did we need to take your car?"

"Oh, I just have to make a day trip back for some appointments before camp is over. Just the classic back-to-school stuff. Dentist, physical...no big deal." She sounded casual...almost too casual. Was that my imagination or was Morgan acting funny beyond just being sick?

"Really? Why couldn't you have scheduled all of that once camp was over?"

"You know my mom. Her OCD can't wait. She already called Steve about giving me permission too." She sighed. "I was kind of ready to go back to camp. I couldn't handle all of her hovering, you know?"

And Morgan's mom did hover. I had seen it firsthand.

"Well, you know I never mind driving…especially your nice, new car!" I wiggled my eyebrows at her.

"Be careful," she warned. "Now I want to hear about everything I missed last night before Caleb gets in the car."

And my stomach gave a little jump at the anticipation of seeing him again after yesterday. I couldn't help the strange, new twinge of excitement just thinking about him…and Morgan caught my expression before I could mask it.

"Oh, girl, you better start talking!"

Our trip back to Camp Fusion was quicker and easier once I took over driving. Caleb took the front seat so Morgan could lie down in the back. She actually fell asleep, so Caleb and I played music and enjoyed the trip together without much talking…and with no potty stops.

When we finally arrived back in the deep hill country of the Frio River, it was nearing sunset. The sky had turned pink and cast a lazy glow over the tall trees and Texan brush along the dirt road. I drove purposefully to Ben's cabin downriver.

"Morgan, wake up. We're here," Caleb called softly to her in the back seat. She didn't stir. "Morgan." He reached back with one arm and jostled her a little. Slowly, she came out of it. "Hey, you okay?"

"Mmm-hmm," she muttered and sat up, looking rather dazed.

I exchanged a worried glance with Caleb, who seemed just as perturbed by her behavior. Before we had even parked the car, Ben's tall and regal figure appeared in the doorway of his cabin. His long graying hair was pulled back into a characteristic ponytail at the base of his neck, and he had on big work boots, worn jeans, and a Camp Maintenance t-shirt. His gray eyes sized up our vehicle moving too quickly on the dirt road, but he grinned when he saw us through Morgan's windshield.

"Ben! What's happening with the portal? I tried calling you!" I called in an excited rush of words as soon as I emerged from the car.

Ben's face immediately registered confusion, an emotion Caleb apparently read before I did because he interrupted me. "Slow down, Whit. Say hi to the man first."

I had reached the porch by then and gave Ben a quick hug. It was still a strange thing to know that he was my great uncle—a blood relation from the White Island on my father's side.

"Glad you three made it back safely. You are earlier than I was expecting…" His gray Aerodorian eyes glittered with a smile at us.

"Morgan slept, so we didn't have to make any bathroom stops this time," I explained jokingly with a smile aimed at Morgan, which she didn't return.

"Morgan?" Ben's expression was concerned. "Why don't you come sit down? Can I get you something to drink?"

Morgan nodded. "Sure."

She looked so pale and strangely lost. Her clothes even bagged around her, as if they were weighing her down. With her skin taking on a translucent quality, she resembled one of those beautifully tragic, blue-eyed ghosts in scary movies. And then I shivered for even thinking something so morbid. Maybe she should have stayed home another day. What if she was contagious?

"Morgie, do you need to go back to the cabin first?" I asked.

"I'm fine," she answered softly, settling into a porch chair and slumping over her stomach a little bit.

She definitely wasn't fine, but I let it go since her face grew more serene as she took in the view of the sparkly clear Frio River. I followed her gaze to the riverbank flanked by large trees with twisting and gnarly roots dipping into the water. I shuddered inwardly, knowing those dark roots in the water were where the fish hung out. *Ick.* My eyes drifted upriver to the section where campers played in the water on the hot summer days. From here I could see the cliff in the distance that we had climbed in our exploration of the forbidden side of the river—when we immediately transported to the White Island. There was nothing over there—no weird lights or orange wisps of mist creeping around, which had definitely happened when the portal opened for us.

"Now, what's this about the portal?" Ben questioned as soon as he came back with cold drinks for us.

"Did you feel anything happen over here? Did it open up?" I asked.

"No…I haven't seen or felt a thing. What would make you think it had?"

"Ben, you won't believe this, but I used Wind on the Mainland… yesterday!" I exclaimed.

His eyes widened, and he leaned forward in his chair. "Are you sure?"

"Oh, yes…" Caleb jumped in at the incredulous look on Ben's face. "She practically threw me across her grandparents' kitchen. Plus, the pots and pans hanging above my head didn't just go flying off their hooks by themselves." Then he gave me a little wink, as I'm sure we both remembered the pantry escapade. I *really* needed to tell him to stop winking at me—the effect it had on me was getting harder to hide.

I turned my attention back to Ben. "How would something like that be possible?"

"Well, it's not…The life forces come from a direct connection with the Island itself. This is something we absolutely know is true. Nobody can access them without being in direct contact with the land," he assured me, a perturbed look on his face. "Describe to me exactly what happened."

So Caleb and I recounted the story in as much detail as possible, which meant I had to tell Ben a little more about our conversation, including the part about Mom now dating someone. He raised his eyebrows at that but did not comment.

"Well, it would make sense that because you are a Dorian, you would be more sensitive to feeling the Island and the life forces wherever you are. But I am a Dorian too, and I felt nothing different..." He trailed off, clearly confused. "So, then, we must assume that you have a special connection to the Island, because never in all my years on the Mainland have I ever been able to use a life force here. I can sense them sometimes, particularly when there is portal activity going on. But I've never actually used one."

"Could it have to do with her being the Pilgrim?" Morgan piped up quietly. Morgan had admitted on the Island, and still believed, that I was the one the Island prophesied would come to deliver the people out of dark times.

"It's possible." Ben nodded. "If you are the Pilgrim, your powers could be great enough to bridge land and ocean."

"But my dad fits the Pilgrim prophecy too," I added, glancing meaningfully at Morgan. "How did the prophecy go again?" Caleb asked.

"This is the gift you shall receive," Ben and I started reciting at the same time until he let me finish. After all, I had memorized this thing and played it over and over in my head since Abrianna first presented it to me.

"A Pilgrim resembling a native, yet of a pale color and missing birthmark, will appear in the midst of dark times. From this all-gifted Pilgrim, the tribes will learn the way to true peace, and the White Island will prosper."

They were silent for a moment before I said, "Seems to me that Dad is the real Pilgrim—the whole resembling a native thing? He was *born* there, even though he looks nothing like the natives."

"But the all-gifted part..." Caleb pointed out. "That is you, Whit. You can use all four life forces. Ben, are you sure Whitnee's dad only used Wind?"

Ben sighed heavily. "On the Island, children do not receive life force until they are about five or six years old. Nathan received life force much earlier than others...He was special. I remember him being able to do strange things when he was just a toddler. However, I never saw him use anything other than Wind. Unless..." And he stopped.

"Unless what, Ben?"

"Whitnee, there is so much I don't know. I left when Nathan was only sixteen years old. And when he found me here, he was almost twenty years old and very private about what had happened on the Island since I had been gone. He gave me general descriptions of how Abrianna was running things. But honestly, I always felt like he was hiding something important...There were things that had happened there that he did not want to share with me. And when he left to retrieve that one camper—"

"You mean Will Kinder," I jumped in.

"Yes, poor Will. What an unfortunate situation...He was never supposed to transport. Abrianna had opened the portal, waiting for Nathan to cross over. Technically, Will could not have transported by himself. The portal only connects to that life force sensitivity within a true Dorian."

"Then how did it happen?"

"Honestly, I believe it was something about Nathan that caused Will to transport...We were the only two out there. Nathan was in the river, and I was cleaning up the shed when it happened. I know it wasn't me, because I felt nothing." He paused and looked incredibly sad as he avoided making eye contact with me. "I should have been the one to go after Will, but I just couldn't...I wasn't ready to face life on the Island again, much less see Abrianna. So Nathan followed him, and I stayed."

The depth of Abrianna's deception really struck me then. Ben had loved Abrianna like a real daughter. They had developed the portal together, only for her to push him through so she could gain her own power and glory. It was so underhanded and horrible that I could understand how the whole situation must have broken Ben's heart.

"I'm sorry, Ben," I whispered.

"After so long I have come to terms with it. But I still have no desire to return there. My time on the Island is over," he said and then continued with his memories. "I was actually shocked when your dad didn't return quickly with Will. I started telling people how he was involved in search and rescue to explain his absence. But nothing prepared me for when I got a call from him, saying he was in California with no memory as to where he had been, nor why he was there with Will. I discovered later he hadn't just forgotten what had happened on that trip to the Island, he had forgotten its entire existence."

"And you decided not to tell him the truth about his background so he could move on with a new life here…just like you had," I finished, wondering at how people make such choices. I still wasn't sure that Ben had done the right thing. And if I wasn't mistaken, Ben wasn't sure either. "So, what do you think Dad was hiding about the Island?"

"I don't know, Whit. Sometimes I wondered if he had developed abilities in all the life forces and was afraid to admit it…I mean, he spent a lot of time out on the Island by himself—I told you that it was like he had this special relationship with the land. He seemed to understand each tribe uniquely, as if he belonged to all of them. It wasn't until Nathan's memory began to return that I suspected more about his abilities. His memory would come back in little pieces. He'd remember one thing here or there about life on the Island, but he couldn't decide if he was remembering reality or just a dream. I tried to put the pieces together, but there was still a lot that didn't make sense. I even started to suspect…well, I'm not sure you want to hear this." He paused and looked at me.

"No secrets anymore, Ben, remember?" I reminded him. There had been too many secrets for too long.

"I know, Whit, but there are still things you might not want to understand yet."

"Ben." I gave him a stern look. After everything else he had revealed to me, there was very little I couldn't handle hearing at this point.

"Okay. There were times when I suspected…that is, it seemed like *maybe* Nathan's relationship with Abrianna became…*complicated* after I left the Island," Ben said carefully.

"What!" I blurted.

I saw Caleb's eyebrows shoot up, and Morgan turned her foggy gaze directly on Ben's face.

"They were raised as brother and sister, Ben! That is so…I just can't believe it. What in the world would give you that idea?" Okay, so maybe I couldn't handle just *anything*. Gross. Oh my gosh, *gross*. I hated Abrianna.

"Whitnee, I only speculated. And, yes, they were raised together, but they are not related at all. And, truthfully, they were best friends as children. The woman you met on the Island was not necessarily the same girl your father knew growing up. She became that way by feeding her own selfishness. But if anybody brought out the best in Abrianna, it was Nathan. He knew how to calm her down, how to make her smile, how to protect her—usually from herself. And I know your father loved her—certainly not the way he loved Serena—but the way you love family. However, I did get the impression—again, it is just my intuition, Whit, okay?—that Abrianna was the one who complicated things. Even her marriage to Eli…that sounds like something she did out of spite. She did not love Eli like that."

I was reeling inside a total *Blue Lagoon* moment. Raised as brother and sister, living on a beautiful exotic island only to… *Arghhh!* I couldn't even complete the thought.

"How do you know Nathan chose to come back? That she didn't just send him back by boat hoping that he would forget everything?" Caleb came to my rescue by slightly changing the subject.

"Well, either something didn't work right with the portal, or he couldn't get to a portal and had to leave by sea. The fact that Abrianna eventually began contacting Nathan through dreams—the same way Nathan contacted Whitnee this summer—was clear evidence that she had been trying to find him again. She wanted him to come back. She had even opened up a portal in Hawaii, remember? In Kauai, where he disappeared six years ago."

"Geez, Ben, I wish you would have told me all of this six years ago…" Sometimes my eyes crossed just trying to think through all of these details.

"It has taken me years to figure out the truth. And even now I am discovering more through your experiences. I did not feel like I could share the truth with your mom and you immediately—I was so sure Nathan would show up again. The fact that he remained gone for six years…well, I never saw that coming. Even I started to believe he really had died until you found the Island. It doesn't make sense. We know the portal works because you used it this summer. We know sailing back has got to be an option. So where is he, and why is he still there? That I just don't know."

"He said he was trying to protect me," I mumbled, remembering the dream I had of him on the boat in Hydrodora…when he told me about the portal and how to leave.

"And I can see why…" Ben said quietly. "You are worth protecting. Look at all you can do. People will be after that kind of power on the Island. Especially Abrianna. And if she's found a way to take your abilities, then you should definitely be careful."

"Yes, but she said she can't just *take* them. I have to *give* them to her…willingly. And if I did, she would send Dad home with me."

Ben's face grew dark then, and he looked as if he was deep in thought. Then, very seriously, he leaned toward me and spoke gravely. "Whatever you do, Whitnee, don't give them to her. Trust me on this—it doesn't matter what she promises you. Do you understand?"

I nodded slowly. "Of course," I answered, even though we all remembered how close I had come to releasing my life force abilities to her just to see my dad again. Funny how I could see more clearly now that I was out of that situation.

"So am I understanding that we still don't know why Whit was able to use Wind on the Mainland?" Morgan asked. We looked to Ben again.

"All we know," Ben said darkly, "is that something—perhaps the Island itself—has formed a very strong connection with Whitnee. A connection that I fear only one other person can understand or explain to her…"

"Her dad," Caleb murmured, watching me closely.

"Exactly," Ben agreed. "He has the answers we need."

"Well, then we go back and we get him this time, right?" I said fiercely. "We don't take no for an answer, and we don't give in to Abrianna's manipulations. After all, I have something she wants. She won't hurt me."

"Don't be so sure," Ben warned. "Abrianna has gone to quite some lengths to get what she wants. And if Nathan has been there on the Island all these years, then she's definitely holding something over his head. My guess is that it's you, Whitnee."

"That won't work this time, Ben. I know too much—she can't manipulate me again. She probably doesn't even know you're still around to give me all this background information." Ben opened his mouth as if to say something, then closed it. "What? You think she does know you're here?"

"I have a feeling she knows more than we think. I think she has watched things on this side for a long time."

"Okay, whatever. It doesn't matter what she knows." I waved my hand and then looked straight at Ben. "The fact is that I know the truth. And when that portal opens again, I'll be ready."

THE LOST ART OF THE D.T.R.

After that enlightening conversation with Ben, I drove back to the cabin, and Caleb helped us unload our belongings. All of our girls, except Amelia, had already arrived back to camp and were so excited to see us. I gave each of them a round of hugs and then excused myself briefly to go drive Caleb to his cabin. When we pulled up in front of the cabin porch, I got out of the car and met him around the back at the trunk.

"You think Morgan will be okay?" he asked casually, pulling his suitcase out of the trunk.

"I hope so. She looks awful, doesn't she?"

"Yeah. Not acting like herself at all. Maybe she just needs another day or two to recover."

I nodded and slammed the trunk once his stuff was out. That was when he grew serious.

"Listen, Whit," he began, and I knew immediately I was in for a lecture. "I know you're all fired up about going back to the Island…and I hope we do get to go back and find your dad. But we can't make the same mistakes as last time, you know?"

"I know," I replied quietly, not meeting his eyes. I remembered too well the mistakes I made and could have made if I hadn't been stopped. I remembered the mistake of letting my attraction for a certain Island boy dictate my motivations…

"I mean that we have to stick together. We have to think smart, and we can't keep secrets from each other. Hey—will you look at me?"

I turned my eyes up to meet his concerned gaze, and he half-smiled.

"There you are. Look, I don't want anything to happen to you. If it were up to me, I would lock you in a tower somewhere where nobody could hurt you—"

"Caleb—" I started, annoyed that he would prefer me locked in a prison.

"Calm down. Your free spirit is one of the things I love about you. And you'd find a way to escape anyway…you always do." He leaned casually against the car and crossed his arms, a grin on his face. "That's why I've settled for the stress of following you on all your adventures, risking heart attacks and restless nights, all in the name of Whitnee Skye Terradora."

"Okay, you and Morgan need to stop acting like I'm the only one who attracts trouble. You two have caused your own messes too." I pointed a finger at his chest.

He grabbed my pointing hand and pressed it flat against his chest in one swift movement, his face turning solemn again. "Seriously, you have got to be careful, okay? The stuff we're dealing with on that Island is real and dangerous."

I took a step closer to him as he leaned against the car. "Of course I'm going to be careful. I already told you I'm going to do things differently this time." I fixed my gaze at his hand covering my own, right above his heart.

"I want to believe that." He sighed and looked up at the sky. Then he finally addressed the topic we'd been avoiding the last two weeks. "I just worry that you're only acting this way with me because I'm here…and *he's* not."

I slowly pulled my hand away at his words, and his face tilted back down to see my expression. I just stared at him in the twilight.

"What am I supposed to say to that, Caleb?"

"I don't know. Say it's not true. Say you don't care for him as much as I think you do and that you want a real chance with me. Say there's more here between us than just friendship. Just say… something."

"There's more here between us than just friendship," I repeated without hesitation. It was the first time I had actually admitted it out loud…to Caleb. I guess now was as good a time as any to have a D.T.R. (the define-the-relationship conversation that two people had to have in order to figure out where they were heading). And it usually started with the confession of feelings. The cat was out of its stupid bag now.

He watched me quietly until I spoke again. "What's wrong? Isn't that what you wanted to hear?"

"I guess I'm waiting for the *but* to come in…"

"You know the *but*."

"Oh yeah, I know all the *buts* pretty well now," he said. "I like you, Caleb, *but* I don't want to ruin our friendship. Yes, Caleb, I feel more-than-just-friends feelings for you, *but* I'm not ready for a serious relationship. I would date you, Caleb, except for the fact that I still have major complicated feelings for a guy I don't know very well who lives on an Island across the universe!" he finished.

"Conversation over," I replied tartly and spun around to walk away. Just when I finally found the courage to admit my feelings for him, he had to go *there*. He ran ahead of me and planted himself in my path.

"Whit, don't run away from me—"

"I'm not running away. I'm just not discussing this with you." I was really keeping a tight rein on my anger at the moment. You'd think he would appreciate that. I went around him and reached for the car door. His hand came down on mine, not allowing me to open it.

"You know what scares me the most about all of this?" His voice was intense.

I didn't answer, just took a step back and folded my arms across my chest, listening.

"It's the fact that you *don't* talk about him. It would be normal if you said his name or did the girly giggling thing, but you don't. You keep everything about him and what happened on that Island locked inside your own mind. Even this rule of yours that we're not allowed to say his name…It's like you're trying to convince *yourself* you don't feel anything for him. And that scares me. Because you wouldn't work so hard at it if it wasn't that big of a deal to you."

Dang. It sucked how close to the truth he was.

"Caleb, it's the same reason you don't like to talk to me about Claire or Laura…because I'm the girl you like! Why would I discuss Gabriel with *you*, of all people?"

"But you don't discuss it with anybody, Whit. Not even Morgan."

"Because I'm trying to let it go, okay!" I ignored the fact that he and Morgan had obviously been discussing my issues. This D.T.R. had gone horribly wrong. "Geez, Caleb! You're so hung up on proving my feelings for Gabriel that you've totally ignored the fact that I just admitted that I like *you*."

He paused for a moment and stared at me. "Okay."

"Seriously. I *do* like you as more than a friend, and that scares *me* more than anything else I've experienced lately—including shooting cyclones *out of my hand*!" I blurted, throwing my hands up in the air. "But what am I supposed to do with those feelings? I don't know! And, yes, things with Gabriel are…complicated… but I can't do anything about that now. If things went wrong with him, well, I'm not losing much! But with you…I mean, I stand to lose a *lot* if I screw it up. And that's a much bigger deal to me than you realize. I'm just trying to take things one step at a time. So quit trying to figure me out—that's my job!" I was breathing hard now from my emotional outburst. Caleb just stood there, a thoughtful expression on his face.

"Well, at least you finally admitted it…I was starting to think it was all in my head," he finally said.

"It's not in your head," I assured him. Then I reached for his hand. "Please be patient with me. I'm scared to commit anything to you right now, Caleb."

"I already told you I would wait." He squeezed my hand. "But I can't help the bad feeling I have that once we get back on that Island and you're around him again...I don't know, Whit. Only you can decide how you're going to handle that. I just hope I don't come out on the losing end again."

I heaved a deep sigh, wanting this conversation to be over.

"I should get back and check on Morgan. Plus, the girls are waiting on me."

"Come here." He pulled me into a comfortable hug. "I'm sorry I upset you. I don't want us to fight any more. Fighting with you is just not fun for me like it used to be."

I nodded with my head pressed tight to his chest. "I know what you mean." At that moment light from the cabin door spilled out, exposing our sentimental moment.

"Caleb? Whitnee!" It was Kevin at the door. He came running out, oblivious to interrupting anything private.

"Hi, Kev," I greeted the twelve-year-old as I pulled self-consciously away from Caleb's embrace.

"Hey, dude! How was your weekend?" Caleb slapped Kevin on the back.

"It was okay. It would have been better if we'd gone to the Island again—"

"Kevin, shh…" I warned, looking around to make sure no one else was nearby.

Caleb laughed. "You can tell me all about it inside. Whit's gotta get back to her cabin. Here, take my pillow." Kevin grabbed the pillow and started toward the cabin door again.

"Goodnight, Whitnee!" Kevin called out.

"Night, Kev!" I replied and waved, then opened the car door. Caleb hesitated, as if he wanted to say a more proper good-bye. So I made it easy for him by escaping into the car. "See you in the morning, okay?"

"Okay." He shut the door for me and then waved as he walked up the steps.

I started the engine of Morgan's car and watched him disappear into the cabin. I had finally done it—finally admitted I liked Caleb. And where did it leave me? Wasn't sure yet. I wasn't even sure if our D.T.R. had ended up defining anything after all.

I began my short drive back to the girls' cabin, trying to ignore the fact that most of what Caleb had said scared me too. If it was just a matter of time now before the portal opened up for me, then I was destined to come face-to-face with Gabriel again. And I had *no idea* how that was going to go down. The only thing I knew was that the anticipation of it made my heart race a little. Clearly I had more mental and emotional preparation to do…

Monday morning Morgan woke up looking and feeling a little better. At least her color had returned, and she seemed more like herself. Amelia, however, had been in a sour mood since she came back later than everyone else the night before. She only communicated in grunts and looks and definitely hadn't uttered a word to any of us about what happened over the weekend. I had learned not to push her when she was in this state, but I couldn't help worrying about her. We had made so much progress this summer—I didn't want any relapses with her. I knew one of two things would happen: (a) her emotions would die down soon, enabling her to express her frustrations in a healthy way; or (b) she would continue acting this way until she exploded in a mess of tears and screaming, leaving the rest of us to deal with the aftermath of her meltdown.

My other sweet campers, Bailey, Madison, and Emily, just seemed more tired than usual that morning. Truthfully, we were all kind of dragging after our weekend away. I started out the morning playing some peppy music to help the girls wake up.

My four girls had group session with a therapist after breakfast, and mentors were encouraged to attend those sessions with their campers. Sometimes the girls shared deep thoughts with each other, and some days they were just quiet and didn't have much to say. That was when they were encouraged to journal and engage in some thought-provoking activities, like setting positive goals for the week. I had a feeling today would be a quieter session.

At breakfast we sat with Morgan and her girls. We were soon joined by Caleb's sleepy boys, and I watched as Kevin sat next to Amelia and tried asking her about her weekend.

"Did you have fun with your mom?" he questioned.

"Sure, yeah. It was fun," Amelia answered with the level of excitement someone would show at a funeral.

"So it was pretty bad, huh?"

"I said it was fine."

"No, you said it was fun, and you're lying," he accused. "Do you want to talk about it?"

"No! I don't!" She raised her voice in frustration at him. "Why is *talking* all anybody ever wants to do around here? I'm sick of talking. It fixes *nothing!*"

Kevin's eyes were wide at her outburst. "Sheesh. I was just trying to be nice. You're such a Pyra—"

"*Kevin,*" I jumped in. Sometimes he and Amelia forgot other people didn't know about our Island.

"Well, she's acting like one," Kevin defended himself.

"Well, if you were a real Hydro, then you would know when to shut your mouth!" She stood up and took her tray with her. "I'll meet y'all outside when you're done."

So maybe she was going to choose option B this time—full-out explosion. I just let her go, sensing she wanted to sulk on her own for a bit. Besides, I wanted her to calm down before the group session. I had seen her snap at the other girls this summer, and it was pleasant for nobody.

As we watched her shove her way out the door, Emily asked, "Isn't a pyro somebody who's, like, addicted to playing with fire or something?"

"Something like that..." I mumbled, kicking Kevin under the table as a warning.

"What? Why'd you kick me?" He gasped.

Ah, middle schoolers. So smooth about everything.

"What did she call you? A hydro?" Bailey chimed in. "Is that like a new thing I don't know about?"

"No, they just have nicknames for each other," Madison explained, then turned toward Kevin. "I've heard y'all talk about the weirdest stuff...If you and Amelia are forming a secret club or something, can I join too?"

"We don't have a club," he told her, then turned to me again. "What happened this weekend? Is she okay?"

"Don't know yet," I told him with a sigh.

"Should I go apologize to her right now?"

I smiled at him. He really was a sweetie. "Maybe later. I think she needs some alone time right now. But you should be more *careful* about what you say." I raised my eyebrows at him. He nodded and rolled his eyes. "So where's Caleb?" I asked him.

"I dunno. Steve stopped him for something on the way over here."

Steve was the director at Camp Fusion, and he had a particular trust and respect for Caleb. If Steve needed a job done right, he called on Caleb. I knew that had a lot to do with what we now referred to as Caleb's Geo traits. He was dependable, loyal, and approached everything through logic. He was somebody you could count on to follow through with a task and do it well.

"Hey, Whit," Morgan called from down the table. "Will you walk my girls to group? I have to go back to the cabin really fast."

"Sure." I nodded, glad to see that she had eaten a little from her tray. About the moment that Morgan was leaving, Caleb entered the cafeteria—with Claire by his side. They looked like they were deep in conversation, oblivious to all the noise in the cafeteria.

Now I know it was probably just innocent, but my mind flashed back to that horrifying moment on the rock cliff when I stumbled upon them kissing. And seeing that in my head, combined with the intimate way they were conversing, I just couldn't help feeling a little uncomfortable with it.

And therein was the problem with Caleb and me. He liked me. I liked him. But there was no commitment there beyond friendship. Which *technically* meant that neither of us had a right to get jealous of the other one because, well, we were *technically* free agents at this point.

I suddenly wanted to get out of there before I had any more of an opportunity to become a stupid, jealous, territorial friend. I didn't want to be that kind of girl. After all, Caleb had been pretty serious about his feelings for me...Except he had said the same things the night before I caught him making out with Claire, soooo...

Yeah, not helping. *Must get out.*

"You girls ready to jet?" I looked around and found that they all seemed finished with their breakfasts. I rushed them to the spot where we dumped our trays, trying to edge out of there without saying a word to Caleb. Not that he was noticing anything but Claire and her big eyes with thick eyelashes like a mascara model—

"Where are you going in such a hurry, Whit?"

Dangit.

Just two more feet to the door and I would have made it. Turning slowly around, I plastered an innocent smile on my face. Caleb was coming toward me, having left his place in line with Claire. She was watching closely from behind him—but in the way that girls watch something without trying to be obvious that they're watching.

"Just getting the girls to their session!" I replied brightly. He looked good today...all fresh and clean in his blue shirt and khaki cargos.

"Do I not get a *good morning* or at least a *hey* before you leave?"

"Hey...good morning," I mimicked him.

He sauntered right up to me…like, really close, so that I caught a whiff of that awesome cologne. Oh, dear…not again. Not in the camp cafeteria.

"Is it just me, or am I detecting a little bit of attitude with you this morning?" he questioned lightly, with a grin on his face that was a little too confident.

But I didn't back down—just matched his gaze with my own casual expression. "Nope. No attitude here. Just got things to do… and we had already eaten…and you were apparently busy…talking to different *people*—"

"Man, I love it when you're jealous." He laughed.

My mouth dropped open at his dead-on observation. "I'm not—!"

"Don't ruin it with your denials. It's a good sign." He smiled and then leaned down toward my ear to whisper, "Don't worry. It was you that kept me up thinking all night."

Stupid, stupid yum vortex…

"Like in a good way…or bad?" I asked.

"Mostly good…I can still picture that bikini—"

"Caleb!" I slapped him on the arm. As I backed away to follow my campers out the door, I gave him a flirtatious smile. "See you later."

"I look forward to it…" he called after me. I barely caught the look on Claire's face behind him before I was gone. And I couldn't decide if it was disappointment or anger.

MANIC MONDAY

Morning group session was definitely quiet. None of the girls particularly wanted to talk about their weekend. Amelia was especially defiant about being called on to share, and I think that really ruined any kind of warm, fuzzy feelings the rest of them might have had about opening up.

So the session ended early with the girls given the assignment to go somewhere quiet on camp property and journal their thoughts about the weekend. Once the girls dutifully left, the therapist pulled me aside and asked me to find some one-on-one time with Amelia that day—just to see if she would open up to me about whatever was wrong. I promised I would try.

My heart really did hurt for Amelia. I used to have a huge problem understanding her and even relating to her bad attitude. But I had learned that deep down Amelia was exactly what the therapist said—a child who needed some love and attention. Yes, she was a spoiled brat, but that was because her parents had always thrown material things at her to replace time spent getting to know her. It was sad, but I hadn't figured out yet how to correct years of bad parenting in just a five-week period. And from what I could see, no therapist could do that either.

The day progressed in the same manner it started—pretty routine. I conducted my music activities with the younger kids before lunch, met up with my own campers for the afternoon, and then spent free time down by the river.

I confess two things here: one, I was definitely checking Caleb out again as he swam with the kids and launched himself into the water via the rope swing. And, two, when I wasn't checking Caleb out (about every thirty seconds), I was checking out the other side of the river, looking for signs of…anything. How would I know when the portal opened up? Last time there was no visible sign of it happening until we set foot on the ground. Of course, someone had tried to lure me to that side by flashing holographic images of my dad over there (a unique ability that only Pyras have). Surely if *someone* (okay, I meant Gabriel) had opened the portal back up this weekend, wouldn't he give me a sign?

As I sunbathed on my favorite flat rock ledge watching my campers, Caleb, and the forbidden side of the river through my oversized sunglasses, I did start to feel more impatient about getting back to the Island. After all, our eight-week program at Camp Fusion only had three weeks left in it. That meant something had to happen by then, or I was out of ideas. By the end of July, it was time to start thinking about my senior year of high school. Caleb would start having athletic training in preparation for football season. Morgan would probably pick up shifts at her old lifeguard job in her neighborhood—anything to keep her out of the house and in the water. I still had summer reading and projects to do for my advanced classes, as well as the traditional back-to-school activities student council had to prepare and implement the first week of school.

Time was passing quickly…and starting to run out.

"How are my girls doing?" Morgan's voice interrupted my thoughts as she joined me on the rock ledge.

"Did you get off lifeguard duty early?" I questioned. I hadn't been expecting her for another fifteen minutes or so.

"Yeah."

"Well, everyone's fine here—having fun. How do you feel?" I surveyed her carefully. She didn't look *that* much better up close. At least her green complexion had vanished in the sun.

"Better," she replied. "Still a little weak." She lowered herself beside me, and I noticed how thin her legs looked in her swimsuit…and Morgan was already a skinny person.

"Are you eating enough, Morgie?" I couldn't help asking.

"Yeah. Why?"

"You look like you've lost weight."

"Great. Just what every girl wants to hear!" She smiled, but it didn't seem genuine—even behind her sunglasses.

"No, I mean, you're too skinny. We need to fatten you up a little bit."

"Okay…*not* what every girl likes to hear. I don't want to be fat!"

"You're so not fat. I just think that—"

"I know what you mean, okay? Can we just drop it? I promise I'm eating."

I stopped, because her tone almost seemed a little sharp. That was totally not like her. But she had just been pretty sick…and I'm sure she hadn't held down much food the last few days. Maybe I was being overprotective and she was being oversensitive.

"Okay, good. I'm glad you're feeling better," I replied, kindly dropping the subject.

"Speaking of feeling better…how is Amelia?"

"Unresponsive. She's snorkeling with the girls out there, but you know…being underwater is safe because she doesn't have to talk or get along with anyone there." I pointed out Amelia in her black tank top (covering a very inappropriate swimsuit) kicking along. Her face dipped into the water as she moved.

"What do you think happened?"

"Maybe she had such high hopes of how things would be with her mom after so long…and maybe things just didn't go the way she expected. Her therapist told me to spend some one-on-one time with her today, but it's like Amelia knows that and is avoiding me completely. I don't know what to do. I can't force her to talk."

"She'll come to you when she's ready," Morgan assured me.

But by the end of the day, Amelia still hadn't lightened up. So I went to the Snack Shack and bought her favorite flavor of ice pop, hoping to entice her to come chat with me before it was time to settle in for the night.

"Look what I got you…" I sang as I entered the cabin and danced over to her bunk.

She was sitting there, plastering on more mascara, which was ridiculous when she would soon be going to bed. The amount of makeup Amelia wore was always a good indication of her emotional state. Less makeup meant she was happier with herself and others. Heavy makeup was a red flag to get out of her way.

"I'm not really hungry," she replied, pausing long enough to see what I had for her.

"Good thing, because this is mostly water and flavored syrup. Won't do much for the appetite, but it sure is delightful on a hot, summer day." I waved it in front of her face. "Come on…You know you want it…"

She looked as if she was fighting the temptation to smile. "Fine. But you better not be trying to trick me into talking."

I gave a look of mock innocence. "Who, me? I would never use ice-cold treats to lure campers into a false sense of security that would ultimately allow them to open up about their deep, dark feelings to their favorite mentor!" I batted my eyes at her. "Now, follow me, my pretty, out onto the porch…" I held the ice-pop out invitingly as I backed away.

She rolled her eyes. "You're such a dork."

"I know. But you love me anyway," I called over my shoulder. She was already following me.

Once we were settled outside on the porch rocking chairs, I handed over her treat.

"Sooooo," I began, opening up my own ice pop.

"We're not talking about my weekend."

"Okay, that's fine. What *do* you want to talk about?"

"What's up with you and Caleb? Y'all are acting different."

"Oh, I get it. You want me to open up and tell you all my secrets, but I don't get to know yours?" I raised my eyebrows at her.

"So you admit there are secrets between the two of you."

"No, nothing is necessarily different with Caleb," I began, but then thought maybe if I was a little transparent with her, she would become that way too. "Well, okay, maybe I might have admitted I liked him, but it's not going anywhere right now. We just had a really good weekend together."

"Did you kiss him?"

"No!" Geez, she was blunt. "None of your business anyway."

"It's not like I haven't seen you kiss a guy…" She wiggled her eyebrows, making me blush despite myself. "And speaking of that, what would *Mr. Hot Tamale* think of you and Caleb?"

"Amelia, *ew*. I told you to stop calling him that."

"Well, you won't let us say his real name, so that's my code name for him."

"Having a code name defeats the purpose of *not* talking about him in the first place. It's not his name that bothers me."

"You mean you just want to act like he doesn't exist?"

"Pretty much."

"My therapist calls that *avoidance*, Whitnee," she pointed out.

"You know, maybe you should consider a career in psychiatry… with all your questions and terminology…" I rolled my eyes at her.

"Which brings us back to my question. What would *Gabriel* think of the way you're acting with Caleb?"

I couldn't help the way I glanced self-consciously around us to make sure nobody was listening. "Amelia, it doesn't matter what he thinks of Caleb. He's not here. And neither one of them is my boyfriend, anyway."

"But they both want to be your boyfriend."

"You don't know that," I objected, then added, "Okay, yeah, Caleb makes no secret of it, but we really don't know a whole lot about Gabriel's real feelings."

"I thought he was pretty obvious when we were on the Isl—"

"But we're not there now, are we? So who knows? He could have already found another girl to…" I didn't know how to finish that sentence, and I especially didn't like the twinge I felt in my stomach at the thought. "Never mind. I don't want to talk about this either."

"So you know how I feel then."

I shrugged. "Fine."

As she gazed out at the campgrounds before us, I examined her carefully. Amelia was a pretty girl who had unfortunately grown up too fast. Her hair, which was normally dyed black and cut short, had been fading, revealing gorgeous golden-brown roots that highlighted all the different colors in her hazel eyes.

"I think you should let your hair go natural," I commented.

"Maybe. I was thinking of going blonder once Camp Fusion is over…"

"That would be pretty too," I agreed.

We sat in silence for a few minutes, eating our ice pops and just being comfortable with each other.

Finally, she spoke. "I know I'm being rude." I didn't say anything, just listened, like the therapist suggested. "But I don't want to talk about it, because I don't even know what I think."

"I understand that feeling," I said, because I really did.

"And it really annoys the heck out of me the way everyone wants to know how things were with my mom. It's not any of their business!"

"Ever considered the fact that people ask because they care about you?" I asked gently.

"Yeah, well, it's annoying! I mean, what if the weekend totally sucked? If I tell people that, then they start feeling sorry for me, and I don't want that. I've got everything I could want. I don't need people feeling sorry for me!" Her voice had risen to a higher pitch. "Everybody here has some kind of sad story…Maybe life just sucks, Whitnee. I don't know how you always stay so happy and normal even when all these crazy things happen to you…like your dad and the Island. I would go nuts and cry and scream at someone if I were you."

"I did a little of that this weekend too…especially when I found out my mom is now dating another man."

That caused her to stop short. "Are you serious?"

"Yep. Never saw it coming…and I had a total meltdown at first. Said some not-nice things."

"You did? Really?" She stopped rocking in her chair to stare at me curiously. "But aren't you pretty close to your mom? Can't you just tell her that your dad is—"

"Not yet…I don't know. Look, I only shared that with you because, yeah, you're right. Sometimes life has sucky moments. But it's our choice to either sulk about it or move ahead and try to change the future. I'm not a sulker. I'm a changer."

"I want to be a changer…but every time I try to change, it doesn't fix anything. I'm so sick of trying and then getting let down by *people* who are supposed to love me." She sighed, and I could see her eyes filling up with tears, which, of course, made my own eyes prickle.

"Well…*I* love you, Amelia, and I think you've made some pretty awesome changes already this summer." It was the only thing I could think of to say. If I could officially adopt her as my little sister and bring her home to live with me, I would. But just moving into another family would never fix the rejection she felt from her own family.

She wiped her eyes with the back of her hand. "Thanks for the ice pop. But I think I'm going to go to bed early tonight. I just don't feel good." She wouldn't look at me as she stood to her feet.

I grabbed her arm gently as she passed me. "Hey," I said softly, "Anytime you want to tell me the real story, you know I'm here, okay?" She nodded and then walked back into the cabin.

It wasn't the breakthrough I wanted, but at the same time I couldn't help pondering how much territory Amelia and I had crossed this summer. It wasn't just the nature of our relationship that had changed—even though that had changed drastically since visiting the Island together—but the maturity we both just demonstrated was different. Old Amelia would have yelled at me for prying and made some bitingly sarcastic remarks. Old Whitnee would have had zero tolerance and total impatience with her. And yet I only felt compassion, because I knew the heart behind what she was saying.

Huh. It felt good to know I was already avoiding old mistakes.

"Hey, what's that?" Morgan questioned Amelia as all of us girls scrubbed our faces and brushed our teeth at the sinks. Amelia had random dots of a white, gooey substance globbed all over her face.

"Toothpaste," she replied as if we should have known that. She was already dressed in her pink pajamas with the zebra print lining.

"What's it doing all over your face?" I clarified, drying my own face with my towel.

"Zit control."

"Huh?" Morgan looked skeptical.

"I read about it in my magazine this weekend. If you put toothpaste on your zits, it gets rid of them faster. I just started sleeping with it on my face…I wake up in the morning and…gone!"

"Doesn't it get all over your pillow?" Emily asked.

"No, it dries really quickly. See?" And she touched it delicately with her finger. "Wanna try? This toothpaste is really strong."

I shrugged. "Why not? I have a couple of zits I wouldn't mind being rid of…" I walked toward her as she extended her arm out with the tube. "Whoa, girl, you smell like the dentist."

I dabbed the toothpaste everywhere I had a zit or the potential for a zit. The result made me look like a cartoon character with the chicken pox. I might have gone a little overboard, but the tingling sensation was kind of nice, and the scent was definitely refreshing.

"Emily, go get my camera!" Madison laughed at us.

"No!" Amelia and I chimed in at the same time. "No pictures allowed! I'm serious," I told Madison, who was still giggling.

"Oh, I guess I'll try it too..." Morgan conceded, reaching for her own glob. Her skin was pretty close to perfect, so I wasn't sure where she would use it.

By the time we had returned to the room, hit the lights, and started our sleepy playlist of calming nighttime music, my toothpaste face had indeed dried. And I fell immediately into a deep sleep.

Maybe it was the scent of the toothpaste, I don't know, but at some point I started dreaming of the fields of Geodora. I was walking along the dirt road toward the breathtaking flower field where the Geos grew and displayed all their exotic arrangements and unique blossoms. The flowers seemed to be glowing in their gorgeous array of color beneath an abnormally large orange moon. I was completely alone, but I didn't mind. It just felt so good to be back there. The night was still and peaceful. There was one single golden flower in the center of the field that caught my attention. It almost seemed spotlighted by the moon, and I was drawn to its beauty and its unique smell—like vanilla and peppermint. It stood out from the rest of the flowers. As I moved closer to inspect it, the flower started speaking to me in the deep resonances that I had recognized on the Island as the Earth life force. But it wasn't translating right. I couldn't understand the message, so I kept drawing closer and closer, straining to hear.

If I could just touch it, maybe I could figure out what it was saying. So I reached out...and the moment my hand grazed one golden petal, the flower turned into Elon. Sweet and fragile Elon...the younger sister of Eden, clad in the white dress that tied around her neck. Her hair hung loosely over her small shoulders. She had been my favorite...the one who had promised to create a flower the color of my hair...her special Whitnee flower.

"Elon? Is that you?" I stared at her in amazement. She looked around us as if in a daze. "Elon, it's me—Whitnee. Don't you remember—?"

And then she scared the crap out of me by grabbing my arms and gasping, her face a mask of terror.

How did someone so small and dainty have such strength?

"Whitnee, watch out! They are coming!" she whispered, her voice tight and stretched, almost like she wasn't breathing.

"Who? Who's coming?" I glanced wildly around me.

Suddenly all the flowers grew sinister, dripping with liquid colors that started to blur around me. Even the moon began to turn from an orange glow to a murky red. Dark shadows of people I could not quite bring into focus started advancing from every side.

"Whitnee! They have come for you! Go! *Go!*" she cried desperately beside me.

I threw my arms around her, wanting to protect her from the menacing shadows around us. Who were they? They were close enough to touch, so I did the only thing I knew to do.

I thrust my hands out in panic, and a perfect arc of green surrounded the two of us crouching in that meadow. The protection of the Earth Shield would save us. They couldn't get us under here...

And then I woke up, sweating as if I were still exerting that much energy. I was back in my bottom bunk with my pillow beneath me and my blankets in a heap at my feet...and a glowing, fluorescent-green shield encompassing my entire bed.

MELTDOWN

I sucked in my breath and released the life force, my hands quickly relaxing in front of me. The green shield disappeared, and I scrambled out of bed very quickly, my chest heaving. I stared at my bed like it had suddenly grown fangs and tried to attack me.

Was I still dreaming? I turned circles in the dark, making sure nobody was coming after me. Elon was gone, but there were eight campers and Morgan fast asleep in bunk beds around me. No sounds could be heard except Madison's light snoring.

Had I really just done it again, or was that just part of my dream transferring to my waking reality? I stepped out into the middle of the room, bunk beds flanking the four walls around me. Very quietly, I threw my hand out and projected the fluorescent shield in front of me, hearing the slight hum it made when it was working.

I gasped and dropped it again. I was definitely awake now. I reached in the darkness for the flashlight that hung on my bedpost. Quickly I turned it on and slipped into the bathroom. My heart stopped—a pair of glowing eyes watched me as I approached. I froze mid-step in fear, turning the beam of the flashlight on the person, afraid of whom I might find there. I was, in turn, blinded by my own flashlight.

It was my eyes. Reflecting in the mirror above the sinks.

I clicked the flashlight off so I could stare at my irises, lit up like a nuclear substance under a black light.

"Ohmigosh, ohmigosh…" I chanted, trying to keep the hysteria at bay.

I jumped back into action. Clicking the flashlight on again and slipping slightly on the tile floor of the bathroom, I hastened back into the bedroom and practically launched myself up to Morgan's bed. I landed hard on top of her legs. She jolted but didn't come out of it very quickly.

"Morgan, wake up," I whispered loudly near her face. "Wake-up-wake-up-wake-up—"

"Huhh…?" She twisted uncomfortably, and I shook her by the shoulders, making the flashlight beam jump all over the room.

"Get up! We have to go! We have to go *now*." I tried to sound as urgent as I could while being quiet at the same time.

That was when her eyes fluttered open. She took one look at me, and I saw her eyes go wide and her mouth open to scream…I covered her face with my hand before she woke everybody up.

Talking quickly, I told her, "I just used a life force! See my eyes? I need you to calm down and listen to me!"

Only, why she would listen to me when I was acting crazy myself, I don't know. She stopped squirming and gazed at me in terror.

"Don't scream, okay?" I warned her. Slowly, I released the pressure of my hand on her face.

She clumsily pulled herself up into a sitting position, scrutinizing me the whole time. I backed away and gave her some space.

"Am I dreaming?" she whispered.

"No."

"Are you sleepwalking?"

"Morgan, no! I'm completely awake, and so are you!" I told her in exasperation. "Put your shoes on, we need to go—"

"I'm not going anywhere until you tell me what's going on…" She was acting as if she didn't trust me.

"What? Morgan, it's me…"

"Prove it," she demanded.

"Are you crazy? Just give the eyes a second and they'll stop glowing, okay?"

"Prove that you are Whitnee."

"Morgan, this is ridiculous…" We were wasting time, but she had such a terrified look on her face. "Okay, um, you know all the lyrics to 'Baby Got Back' and rap them shamelessly when nobody is around and…Oh, in ninth grade we toilet-papered Billy Mattock's house because you had a crush on him, and we never told anyone it was us, even though you had all those sus-picious mosquito bites and…uh…You still write letters to Santa Claus, and I only know because I caught you doing it last year—"

"It's a *tradition*!" she hissed in the darkness. "Fine, okay. I believe you. Now what the *beep* are you doing? You look like the creature from the freaking black lagoon with your eyes, and your hair, and the polka dots all over your face…*ugh*." She shivered visibly.

Oh, yeah, I forgot about the toothpaste…

"Sorry, but watch." And I did the shield again—it was becom-ing like second nature very quickly.

She flinched in surprise. "Holy—"

"I know."

"So what do we do?"

"We get our shoes on, and we go down to the river to see what's happening!"

"That is *so* not a good idea, Whitnee."

"Then I'm going alone," I said simply, jumping down quietly to find my flip-flops under my bed. "And if I don't come back, then you probably know where I went."

"*Ughh*, déjà vu…" She groaned but joined me on the floor anyway.

She kept up a running monologue under her breath even as we made it outside, softly clicking the cabin door closed behind us. I couldn't understand everything she was saying (thankfully) but

I did catch the phrases "sneaking out," "horribly mauled by night animals," and "psychotic best friend."

I was in the lead, marching purposefully down the trail but throwing cautious glances all around me. Morgan was close on my heels, even accidentally treading on them a few times. Once we were away from the floodlights of the campgrounds, the trees cloaked us in thick darkness. If it hadn't been for our flashlights, we would not have been able to see a thing. Where was the moon?

I knew the path to the river well, even in such darkness. But Morgan's negative chanting was distracting me, and okay, it was making me more nervous. I stopped dead in the trail and turned my flashlight on her.

"Morgan. Stop panicking."

"Whitnee," she pleaded. "Can we please go back to the cabin?"

"We're almost there!"

"Then let's get Caleb first…"

I snorted. "Oh, sure…if we were caught sneaking into the guys' cabin, we'd be in seriously more trouble than sneaking down to the river. Besides, I can protect us with life forces right now. Look!" And I pushed my free hand out with a force of Wind…only nothing happened. I looked down at my palm. I tried the Earth Shield this time…No green force field came out around us. I tried to use each of the four life forces, and it was the same as before. They felt very close, but I couldn't get the right connection in place.

"Oh, perfect!" Morgan cried in exasperation.

I was dumbfounded, but instead of standing there arguing with her, I spun around and continued as fast as I could to the river. Maybe I just needed to be closer to the portal.

"Wait for me!" I heard her cry.

I didn't slow down until I reached the riverbank, turning my flashlight on the clear water moving ceaselessly over the rock bottom. Across the expanse of water was the rock cliff that we had climbed to reach the other side. And there was nothing extraordinary about it—nothing that would make me think a portal to the White Island resided there.

As soon as Morgan caught up to my side, breathing heavily, I declared, "We have to go over there."

"You gotta be kidding me. It's the middle of the night. We're in our pajamas! What are you going to do, swim? We both know you're not getting in that freezing water with fish in it!"

She had a point. And I was sure Ben would have locked the canoe shed up for the night. But I was desperate, and I didn't want to be logical at the moment. I turned to her in the dim glow of our flashlights. "Morgan, something is happening! I'm telling you…I feel it all inside me. If I ignore it, I'll lose the chance to get my dad!" I could feel my emotions rising to the surface, and I tried to choke them back. Now was not the time to get emotional.

"Whitnee, listen…You're not thinking clearly—"

"Uh, I think I'm pretty clear about what just happened back at the cabin! Don't tell me I'm crazy."

"I didn't say you were crazy, but let's think for a moment…You have toothpaste all over your face. Your hair is a crazy mess. And, granted, your rockstar pajamas may be cute, but they are still, in fact, pajamas…Is *this* how you think people on the Island envision their Pilgrim? And besides that, are you ready to see Gabriel again looking like *that*?"

I paused and thought about what she was saying. I might pretend like Gabriel didn't exist, but the thought of him seeing me like she just described was pretty unappealing.

Before I could respond, she continued a little more gently, "We need to think through this first, okay? We have responsibilities here. We cannot just disappear again. We got lucky last time with nobody finding out…This time we have to be smarter. And there's no way Caleb would forgive us for transporting without him. We have to prepare…and plan."

"How do we do that when we never know when that portal will open?" I cried.

"Whit, has it ever occurred to you that when you're ready to go, the portal will open up for you?"

I met her gaze then. She was the crazy one here. Had she not heard the same stories I had? "Of course that has never occurred to me. Why would it?"

"It's just something I've been thinking about…theorizing," she said carefully. "Remember how Ben said that something about Nathan opened the portal for Will? Well, if your dad really could access all four life forces—like you—maybe there's some kind of connection there with the portal…"

"I don't get it."

"Remember how you were able to activate the portal on the Island by using all four life forces? The portal itself works with the combining of all four…and the first time we met Abrianna, she and Ezekiel were pretty adamant that *you* were the one who transported us there. Whitnee, what if it just takes you going over there and opening it up yourself?"

Her words hung between us like a tiny sliver of hope that I wanted to grab and hold on to. I wasn't sure what to think of her theory. It kind of made sense…except that none of this stuff made that much sense in the real world of science and logic.

"Well, how would I know if that was true without trying it?" I pointed out.

"Duh, we already tried it. Remember three weeks ago when you transported yourself and four other people there? Do you mean to tell me that Abrianna just happened to hit all her switches at the right time when we crossed? I'm telling you, Whit…I really think you are the key here, which is why I think we wait."

"Wait for what?"

"Wait until we're ready," she explained. "Wait until camp is over or something. If you really can do what I think you can, then we plan it out. Listen, I'm dead set on going back with you no matter what, okay? But you said it yourself, this time we do it differently. This time we are the ones in control. We are not Abrianna's puppets this time."

"You know, I never knew you were so convincing in the middle of the night," I teased.

"Sure you did. Don't forget who talked you into toilet papering Billy's house that one night…"

"And y'all blame me for always getting you in trouble…*psh*." I took a deep breath and peered again across the Frio River. "I really hope you're right, Morgie."

"Me too." She sighed heavily. "Please don't hate me if I'm wrong, though."

I just shook my head in response. Then I frowned in the darkness. "Got any theories about why I'm using the life forces on the Main—" But then I stopped. A sound caught my attention—something crashed through the brush off to our right.

Morgan heard it at the same time, because she froze, her eyes widening in fear. Either we were about to be busted or eaten—I wasn't sure yet which I preferred. We both backed away in fright, using our flashlights to scan for danger.

And out ran toothpaste-face Amelia, her eyes wild with fear. "There's an animal chasing me! Run!" she shouted.

That was all we needed to know. The three of us took off in the opposite direction, running clumsily over the rocks along the riverbank. We were scrambling up to the rock ledge overlooking the water when Amelia tripped and cried out in pain. Morgan and I stopped and bent down over her. That was when I fixed my flashlight behind us and saw a terrifying, man-eating, wild…rabbit.

I resisted the urge to cuss.

"Is that what you were running from?" I growled.

Morgan and Amelia squinted carefully into the spotlight of my flashlight. The rabbit paused and sniffed our direction before hopping away through the brush again.

"Stupid rabbit made me give up my cover!" Amelia exclaimed once she realized what had happened. She picked up a small rock and threw it back toward the bushes in anger. Then she pulled up her pajama pants leg and revealed a nice-sized scrape where she had fallen. "Dangit! I'm so mad!"

"Oh, *you're* mad?" I said. "Not only did you scare me to death with the animal thing, but you also snuck out of your cabin! Who should really be mad here?"

"Whatever," she said. "I saw you with your shield in the bedroom! I had to follow you—you're not going to that Island without me!"

"Amelia, we're not going to the Island."

"Then what are you doing out here? And how did you just use a life force here at camp?"

"I don't know," I answered honestly.

"Well, it looks to me like something is happening, so come on! We need to go." She stood abruptly to her feet and began marching her way back down to the riverbank.

"We are not going anywhere except back to the cabin," I told her firmly, but she wasn't listening. "Amelia!" I called.

She had made it to the water's edge and was stepping into the shallow end with her flip-flops still on. How far was she planning to go? I looked back at Morgan, who returned my confusion.

"Get out of the water, Amelia!" I scolded.

She didn't obey me, but she did pause and spin around to look at me. "I want to go back to the Island *now*, Whitnee! I don't want to stay here anymore! Please! Let's just go—"

"I already told you we're not going right now. You need to get out of the river and calm down," I insisted.

"Amelia, come on. No playing around here," Morgan warned.

Amelia had now backed farther into the water, and it was up to her knees. She was getting completely soaked, but in the view of my flashlight, I saw shiny wet tracks on her face too. When had she started crying?

"You two don't understand…I need to go back. Maybe Ezekiel and Sarah would let me live with them! I could be their other granddaughter or something…They liked me. They took me to the Music Center and listened to me sing and play instruments, even when I wasn't very good at it. I just can't stay here, Whitnee! I can't! I'm not wanted…" She was standing there, knee-deep in the river, crying her heart out. This wasn't just one of her drama moments. She was breaking.

"Amelia, please get out of the water, and we'll talk—" I attempted to calm her down, but she was just getting started.

"Oh, you want to talk again? You want to hear the truth about my weekend? What would you say to me if I told you my mom didn't show up again? What if I said she left me with my dad all weekend and wouldn't even answer my calls?"

I stuttered, "Maybe she got tied up with something—" But it sounded hollow in my own ears.

"Again? You're always making up excuses for my parents! If they really loved me like you always say, then they have a crappy way of showing it! If I could just go back to the *Island*"—and she gestured wildly behind her—"then I wouldn't feel so ignored every single freaking day! Maybe it wouldn't hurt all the time... And who knows? Maybe Mom and Dad would even marry each other again, because everybody knows I ruined everything! She left because of *me*! I don't even know what I did...but if she had just been sick of Dad, then she would've at least tried to see me, right? Maybe if I just disappeared...If I could just start over... Please, let's *go*! Take me back, Whitnee. Come on!" She seemed on the verge of a panic attack, like she couldn't catch a breath or calm herself down. And she was backing farther into the water where there was a stronger current.

And I don't know why I did it—I know I didn't give it a logical thought or I probably would have stopped myself—but I rushed into the icy water toward her, ignoring my fear of the river. I could only see Amelia's puffy, despairing face in front of me. I grabbed her by the waist and picked her up...and you know what? She let me. Her face fell against my shoulder, and she became like dead weight. Morgan met me halfway, and we carried her onto the shore where the three of us collapsed and huddled together on the rocks. I took Amelia into my arms while she sobbed into my shoulder.

"I just want to go back..." she repeated hoarsely.

I could understand that part of it all too well. But Morgan, Caleb, and I had already decided that we would never allow Amelia or Kevin to go back with us. It was too dangerous, and they could only become liabilities. Of course, now was not the time to tell Amelia that. But I knew in my heart I could never take her back with me.

"Shh..." I held onto her tightly and rocked a little while Morgan rubbed her back comfortingly. "Just breathe right now, okay, sweetie? Stop talking and focus on breathing." And I held her like that until I was confident we didn't have a full-blown panic attack on our hands. "Amelia, you can't run away from your problems, because no matter where you go, they'll still be there." I spoke softly, but with conviction. "There is no easy way out of our circumstances...Sometimes you stick it out even when you want to give up because you know that on the other side is either a better situation or a better you."

It was probably one of the most profound lessons I had learned in my life, and I believed it with all my heart. I wasn't sure how to make Amelia understand the power of her choices...but if one summer at Camp Fusion five years ago had altered my perspective on life forever, I believed it could do the same for her too.

Amelia's tears were slowing, but she kept whispering, "I'm tired of hurting. I just want to disappear...I just want to go back..."

I smoothed her hair and answered with a sigh, "We all want to go back for different reasons. But we can't forget what's important about us being here too."

The three of us sat there quietly, with the trickle of the water and Amelia's fading sobs as the soundtrack of the moment. And when I glanced at Morgan staring out across the river, I was surprised to see silent tears rolling endlessly down her face.

I WISH I WERE A
HUMAN LIE DETECTOR

Amelia was less edgy and definitely more withdrawn from that point forward. It wasn't like she never talked, but she seemed to lose her spunk. She just did what was expected of her, and I was keenly aware of the signs of depression setting in—especially since I had spent a whole year acting like that after my dad disappeared. No one could reach her—not me, not Morgan, not the girls or her therapist. I did find time to share with the therapist what had happened over Amelia's weekend (leaving out the whole river scene, of course). Sometimes I felt like it was the parents of these kids who should be in therapy more than the kids themselves. I was starting to see why so much of therapy was teaching the campers skills for dealing with difficult people and situations.

Something needed to be done about Amelia. I couldn't shake her words that "just talking" never fixed anything. And I considered myself to be a person of action, so I began to formulate ideas for what could be done to fix the situation. Unfortunately, I didn't come up with much at first.

Meanwhile, the final weeks at Camp Fusion were passing quickly. Day after day I tried "feeling" for a life force, but it never happened again after that night in the cabin. No portal activity was visible on the other side of the river either. Once Caleb got over the fact that we had run down to the river without him, Morgan had shared her theory about the portal with him and Ben, and they felt that it actually made logical sense. After all, Ben had initially designed the portal with Abrianna (even though he never knew it would work until she pushed him through it—*ugh*, still hated her). He seemed to think that we might be on to something.

So we set a plan in motion. The three of us packed "Island survival bags" that included a change of clothes, toiletries, water bottles, flashlights, and snacks. We didn't want to have to depend on anyone to provide what we would need. We decided that the night after the lip sync contest and Camp Fusion Send-Off, when all campers and mentors left camp for good, we would pretend to leave, then double back to Ben's cabin. At that point we would take a canoe across the river and try to transport—Ben agreed to help cover for us on the Mainland end of things. We even formulated a story to feed our parents. We figured the ultimate good of what we were trying to accomplish might outweigh the bad of lying. The story was that we would need to stick around Camp Fusion a few more days to help clean up and debrief from the summer's events. It was a pretty viable story, and none of us thought our parents would have a problem with it.

Once I had a plan formed, I started to feel a little better. I decided that I could actually focus a little more now on my final days at Camp Fusion. Caleb and I had settled into a comfortable, nonverbal agreement about our developing feelings for each other. We kept our flirting mild around other people, but the silly rush I felt when I saw him was something that still surprised me. He started getting creative with his flirting—doing sweet, random things for me that were above and beyond his usual friendly attention. For example, one day he had Kevin deliver a note to me, and all it said was, "Hi. Miss you. –C," with a smiley face. I couldn't wipe the smile off my face for hours.

Another time he offered to escort Morgan and me to the Snack Shack. Oddly, Morgan turned down the offer but encouraged us to go without her. Since it was just the two of us, he bought me an ice-cold Coke and nachos, which we shared. That was when he teased that it was a kind-of date and that he deserved a pay-off at the end—like a kiss—because that's how all good dates end. I pointed out that a kind-of date only earned a kind-of payoff, and he would have to do a lot more than buy me a Coke and nachos to get that kind of reward. We finally settled on the kind-of payoff— I had to seductively wink at him at a time and place of his choosing. He redeemed his reward the next day in the cafeteria in front of all our campers, who promptly informed me that I needed to practice the art of a wink. This resulted in a winking game with the campers that lasted the rest of the day. Pretty sure there's no way to keep a straight face when a middle school boy winks at you…Needless to say, I kept losing the game.

So while things with Caleb were fun and new, other things were not so great. By the time we were in our last week of Camp Fusion, Amelia was still in a slump. I knew I needed to do something, but I didn't have an inspiration until lunch that Tuesday.

"Are your parents coming for the Lip Sync Contest Friday? I mean, it is your big eighties debut!" I asked the girls while we munched on stale corn dogs.

Emily, Madison, and Bailey nodded, but Amelia said curtly, "I didn't invite mine."

"Amelia, you have the biggest part in the song!" Emily cried in shock.

"They might come anyway. Don't they get flyers in the mail with our letters home?" Bailey pointed out.

"I don't know. I don't write home." Amelia shrugged. "I just texted my dad and said I needed to be picked up by six o'clock Friday night after the show, and he said okay."

"What about your mom? Don't you think she'd want to come?" Madison asked her.

"Guess she can't come if she doesn't even know about it," Amelia replied casually.

Her actions were totally making sense to me now. If she didn't tell her parents about the event, then she didn't have to face the disappointment of them not showing up... Incredible how the subconscious mind worked to protect our damaged feelings.

And that was when I got the idea. Okay, I probably should have run it by the therapist first or perhaps not even have given it a second thought. But once I thought of it, I couldn't get it out of my head...I had to act right then.

I looked down the table for Morgan to let her know I would meet them back at the cabin later, but she wasn't sitting with her girls. "Hey, Angie," I called, and the petite dark-haired girl gave me her attention. "Where's Morgan?"

"She left to go back to the cabin," Angie told me with a shrug.

"She always leaves early," Amelia muttered under her breath.

"What?" I turned back toward Amelia.

"You haven't noticed? Morgan always leaves really quick after she eats. Sometimes she comes back before we're all done and sometimes not...I think she has an eating disorder," Amelia stated.

"Amelia, you shouldn't say things like that. Morgan does *not* have an eating disorder." I gave her a stern look.

"I'm just telling you that she acts like it. I've seen girls at my school do it, and I even tried it a couple of times myself—"

"What are you talking about?"

"Bulimia, Whitnee. Do you really not know about that?"

"I know what bulimia is, and it's not funny to joke around about—or do to yourself!" I couldn't believe what I was hearing.

"Well, a lot of girls at my school will eat in front of people in the cafeteria, but then immediately go to the bathroom and make themselves throw it all up. Don't you notice Morgan in the bathroom a lot? Especially right after mealtime? And her stomach never feels good. And, okay, look at her. Her clothes don't even fit her anymore. She's been borrowing one of my belts to hold up her shorts..." She trailed off as she looked up from running her big mouth to see the expression on my face. "I thought you knew. Did you really not notice?"

My stomach dropped. I had noticed it…without noticing it. It wasn't until Amelia started pointing all those things out that I remembered the many occasions she was referring to—but I hadn't strung the evidence together to form that conclusion.

"I have to go. Throw my trash away, will you?" I got up quickly and ran out the cafeteria doors, marching purposefully to our cabin. I tore through the door and paused long enough to see if Morgan was in the bedroom. It was deserted, so I continued to the bathroom. And sure enough, I could see her sitting on the floor in one of the stalls.

"Morgan!" I called out and saw her jump and start moving. "What are you doing?"

"Uh, just a sec…"

I crossed my arms in front of me, praying Amelia was not right about what I was seeing. I just couldn't believe my best friend would get involved in something like an eating disorder.

After the toilet flushed, she came out, revealing watery eyes and pink cheeks.

"Where are the girls?" she asked as she moved to the sink to wash her hands.

"In the cafeteria," I stated, just watching her. "Are you sick?"

"Just a little nauseous…no big deal. Why? Did you come back here for me?" She looked surprised.

"Well, yeah…I did. What is going on with you? You spend a lot of time in the bathroom—"

"Story of my life, Whit. Nothing new…"

"It is something new. I mean, now that I'm thinking about it, it's been worse this summer. You're constantly excusing yourself to the restroom, especially after you eat—and that's on the rare occasion that you actually do eat! Even back at the end of school, getting ready for prom…you kept saying you looked fat in your dress when you so didn't. And every road trip you have to stop multiple times…I've always assumed it was just a weak bladder, but now…"

"What exactly are you trying to say, Whit?" Her eyes were narrowed as she watched me try to string my thoughts together.

"Morgie, why are you getting so skinny this summer?"

"I don't know—I'm not eating enough nasty camp food?" She averted her eyes.

"Why don't you eat enough?"

"Just not hungry—look, where are you going with this?" She crossed her arms too and stared a little coldly at me.

That almost took me off-guard, because Morgan and I didn't fight—we just didn't. We could get slightly annoyed with each other every so often, but we'd never had a full-blown fight. It just wasn't our style.

And yet I knew she was lying to me.

"Morgie…" I sighed and dropped my arms, gesturing with my hands. "You do not need to lose weight. You are not fat in any conceivable way! I promise you don't want to go down this road… an eating disorder is not something to play around with—"

She snorted out loud as if I was being ridiculous. "I do *not* have an eating disorder, Whitnee."

I just stared at her. At this point, it sure would have been nice to use those Geo instincts to help sniff out a liar…

"Then *what* is wrong with you?"

"Nothing is wrong. Just let it go, okay?" And she turned abruptly back to the sink where her toothbrush and toothpaste had been lying. She began brushing her teeth.

I stood there watching her, the silence becoming thick between us. She felt so closed off to me right then, and I couldn't remember a time when it had been that way between us. She was definitely hiding something.

When she finished brushing, I couldn't help myself. In a hurt voice, I finally said, "You're lying to me."

She rolled her eyes and turned to go back to the room. I followed her, listening to her impatient explanation. "Quit being so dramatic. I've had stomach problems my whole life—it's hereditary. And maybe camp food just doesn't agree with me. Where did you get the idea that I have an eating disorder?" She dug around in her bag, acting as if we were having the most casual conversation now.

"The puking, the way you get up quickly after every meal, and, okay…Amelia was the one who brought it up."

Morgan froze in place then. "Amelia doesn't know what she's talking about. She's twelve."

"She seems to have some experience already with it…and she said you've been borrowing her belt."

"Big deal. Can you please drop it?"

"Look, if you won't talk to me about it, maybe you should discuss whatever's going on with a doctor when you go back home tomorrow…"

At that point, Morgan spun around and there was anger in her expression. "Whitnee, this conversation is over. I'm serious. I don't understand where you find the time to have such an imagination. Leave it *alone*." And she actually walked away from me. I watched her move to the front door before she called back, "And do *not* bring this up with Caleb. I don't need him breathing down my back either. Understand?"

I couldn't respond; I was so taken aback. The next thing I knew she had slammed the door behind her.

"What's with you?" Caleb looked concerned as he settled into a wooden rocking chair beside me on the porch.

The campers were at their evening activity with the camp staff, which gave us mentors a break. I had done nothing for the last thirty minutes but sit on the porch, rocking and thinking deeply about the contents of my day. That was where Caleb had found me.

I barely glanced at him before saying, "Nothing."

"Ah, it's the classic girl response when a guy asks what's wrong…which really translates to 'There is something wrong, but

I want you to keep asking me until I'm ready to tell you.' So predictable," he replied lightly.

With a warning lift of my eyebrows, I said, "Or it means 'Back off, jerk, and leave me alone.'"

"Ouch." He put his hand to his heart as if he'd just been shot.

I smiled slightly. "Truthfully, I'm just thinking about things."

Morgan had already left camp. Her mom had scheduled all those appointments for the next day. She had promised to return late Wednesday night, but that was pretty much all the good-bye I had gotten from her. She had been acting so uncharacteristically private about things the last couple of weeks...She had even seemed to lose interest in Drew, Jaxson's best friend and a fellow mentor this summer. Morgan was a flirt and always enjoyed hanging out with different guys without getting into serious relationships. However, she didn't even seem to be that same person anymore.

But she was only part of the reason I couldn't stop thinking.

"Spill it, Terradora."

I took a big breath, because something told me that even though I suspected Morgan had been lying to me earlier today, she had been pretty clear about not discussing it with Caleb. The three of us rarely ever kept secrets from each other...It was just understood that discussing things among the three of us was okay. But for Morgan to actually clarify that she didn't want Caleb in on our conversation was kind of important. And I felt that I should respect her wishes...for now.

So I decided to confess the other thing that was on my mind.

"I think I might have done something stupid this afternoon."

"Who, you? Never..." Caleb said sarcastically.

"Do you want to hear this or not?" I pressed my lips together in a firm line, conveying my annoyance at his jokes.

He immediately straightened up. "Sorry, yes. I'll behave."

"Well, I sort of called Amelia's mom today..."

"Um, does her therapist know—?"

"No, and don't go lecturing me about it either, okay?" I became defensive. "Amelia didn't invite her mom to the Lip Sync Contest and Send-Off because she didn't want to be disappointed if she didn't show up again…but I thought that maybe I could convince her mom to come out for the show as a surprise. I'd never tell Amelia that I called her, but if she showed up…" Caleb was staring at me doubtfully. "Did I do a bad thing?"

"Well…I don't know. Usually the therapists handle stuff with parents."

"Yes, but I couldn't just sit around and do nothing! The poor girl needs some reassurance and time with her mother. Nothing I say can give that to her…but you know how Amelia loves attention. If her mom surprised her, then it would mean the world to Amelia. I don't know, Caleb. Maybe it was the worst thing I could do, but it's done now, so…"

"How did the conversation go, and how did you get her number if you didn't tell Amelia's therapist?"

I had the grace to become a little sheepish then. "I snuck the number off of Amelia's new cell phone…and, well, her mom didn't answer my call. So I left her a long voicemail. I tried to play to her self-serving style of parenting. I told her how many great things I had heard about her from Amelia and how much it would mean to her if she came and surprised her on Friday…how we all wanted to meet her. I begged her not to tell Amelia, that it could be our secret, and I would do whatever to help her get here, blah-blah-blah. I can't remember everything I said, but I gave it my all. And then I left my number for her to call me back if she was interested."

He seemed skeptical, but he did say, "I guess if she doesn't show up, then it's no loss to Amelia because she'll never know. And if she does show, then it sounds like it could be a good thing…"

"Don't tell anyone, please?"

"I won't. I'll add it to my list of Whitnee secrets…the same list that holds the magical Island and all that." He grinned. "You know, you are a lot of things, but boring isn't one of them."

"Yeah?" I grinned back. "Well, I guess I will take that as a compliment. So how about you? Anything new?"

His expression turned contemplative. "Today was a rough day for Kevin."

"Oh, no. What happened?"

"You know, that kid just never seems bothered by his situation—both parents dead, living with his grandparents. He's even got a brother who's only like five or six years old," Caleb explained. "The only time before today that I've ever seen him upset about missing his parents was that one time on the Island when he thought they might be alive there. But one of the boys said something in group session today about a fishing boat or something… and then Kevin just had a meltdown right there on the spot. Apparently, he's coming up on the first anniversary of their death in August. And he suddenly remembered this time last year when they were planning their boating trip…"

I nodded sympathetically for poor Kevin. "The first year is the hardest…because everything about the year before is still a memory with that person in it."

"Exactly. I felt so bad for him. We sent the other boys away early for free time, and he stayed with the therapist a little longer. Kev didn't want me to leave, so I was there for the whole thing. It just ripped my heart out, Whit."

I leaned my head to the side. "Are *you* okay?" I asked, thinking how Kevin's meltdown might have dredged up Caleb's own memories of losing his dad.

"Yeah…" He sighed and ran his hands through his hair. He always did that during an intensely emotional moment. It was my only sign that perhaps Kevin's situation had hit him in a sensitive spot today.

"Caleb," I began, wanting to say something I didn't normally think to tell him, because he was always the strong one. So I paused before passionately expressing my thoughts. "You make such a positive impact on other people because you actually care about them. You are always putting others before yourself…" I reached over and linked my hand with his. "You're patient. You're loving—even with someone like me who doesn't deserve it. From everything you've ever told me about your dad, it seems like you turned out just like him. And I know with all my heart that he would be so proud of the man you've become."

When I finished, he wasn't looking at me directly. But I felt his hand tighten around mine, and then he blinked really quickly several times. "Thanks," he mumbled.

We sat there together for a while after that, quietly watching the day slip away. I wondered how people ever survived without having some kind of support system. Maybe that was really what Camp Fusion was all about in the end...companionship in the darkest moments of life.

NO GOOD-BYES

"Whitnee, I need hairspray!"

"Argh! I got glitter in my eyes!"

"Are you sure I don't look fat in these leggings...?"

"I messed up my nail! Who has the hot pink polish?"

"Moooorgannnn, my hair won't stay like this..."

A tornado of beauty products had blown through our bathroom, leaving a sharp-smelling vapor of hairspray and overheated curling irons. I stood there in the midst of eight girls who were doing their best to achieve the most color-splattered, obnoxious eighties look possible. I only had minutes before I needed to be at the lodge to make sure my sound crew and stage were all set up and ready to go.

"Okay." I took control. "Madison, the hairspray is right in front of you—silver bottle. Sara, try to blink the glitter out without messing up your eye makeup. We don't have time to redo it. Emily, you look awesome in those leggings. Quit worrying. Uh, Angie..." I marched toward the small girl. "Here is the pink nail polish—please don't spill. And, Amelia, if you would just tease your hair a little bit underneath, it will stay... Where's Morgan?"

"In here..." Morgan called out from one of the stalls.

Of course she was going to the bathroom. I gave my attention back to the girls at the mirrors. "Everybody's packed up, right?"

"Yes…" they chorused.

"Remember, you'll have some time to come back and pack the rest of your bathroom stuff before Send-Off, so just leave it here. Don't be late!"

"Just go, Whit," Morgan said, coming out of the stall with a flush. "I've got it under control. We'll meet you over there in ten minutes."

"You sure?" I peered doubtfully at the messy bathroom and the chaotic campers.

"Yes. You don't need to be late either," she reminded me.

"Okay…" I surveyed my own appearance one last time in the mirror. The hot pink hair extensions were bright splashes of color in my usually pale hair. Naturally straight, my hair had been scrunched and teased into a wild mess with the help of too many hair products. Amelia had painted on my thick, dark eye makeup, which made my gray eyes seem much lighter, almost a pale blue. My outfit, a pretty amazing eighties punk rock look, was layered and colorful and tacky all at once. And when I waved at the girls on my way out, my arms jangled with too many bracelets. "I'll see y'all over there…Remember, girls just wanna…"

"Have fun!" they shouted with me and then giggled and cheered. Their excitement made all the stress of putting these little events on worth it.

I made my way quickly to the lodge, hoping my makeup wouldn't melt off in the hot afternoon sun. I was also trying to overcome the nervous feeling in the pit of my stomach that had robbed me of my appetite all day. It had nothing to do with performing; I was pretty used to that. There just happened to be a lot going on today…

First, there was the anxiety of running the Lip Sync Contest. Yes, I was in the show with my girls, but as the music and drama activity camp director, I was in charge. The fact that this event would close out the summer meant that it needed to be good.

All the campers had families coming in for it. Well, except for one…I had never heard back from Amelia's mom. Part of me hoped she might still come—I mean, I had given her all the times and information she would need—but I wasn't holding my breath at this point.

Second, I would have to say a final good-bye to my campers, and I had been dreading that all week. We had already exchanged contact information and made promise after promise to keep in touch. But my heart hurt knowing that this time where my life intersected with theirs was coming to an end. Living and growing together for this long had formed bonds stronger than normal relationships…It was like I had little sisters now.

Third and biggest of all was our impending plan to transport tonight. Everything was set in place. I had called my mom earlier in the day and told her I wouldn't be home for a few days. She had seemed surprised and a little disappointed, but we got through it. Needless to say, I hurried through that conversation before she could tell I was lying—and before Robert's name could come up. Every time I thought about tonight, my heart raced and my palms turned sweaty. What if our plan didn't work? What if the portal was closed and I couldn't open it? What if it *did* work? Who would be on the other side waiting for us? That last question almost had me doubling back to the cabin for fear of vomiting up what little food I had forced myself to eat today.

I had to get a grip. I was stronger, better, more prepared this time. Nothing would deter me from my primary purpose—to find my dad and bring him home. There was no room for anything extra. No drama this time, no complications. Get in and get out. It was simple.

Parents were already beginning to arrive at the lodge, and there was a rush of activity as staff, campers, and families converged.

I was almost to the door when I heard, "Well, hello, Cyndi Lauper." I spun around to find Caleb and his three boys walking my direction.

"Hey, there, Justin Timberlake," I replied, taking in his classic nineties boy band look. The spiked up hair, the layered outfit...I always did have a thing for boy bands. Turning to his campers, I exclaimed, "Oh my gosh! It's *NSYNC! Can I have your autographs?"

"You can be one of our groupies," one of the boys suggested.

I raised my eyebrows at Caleb. "Already teaching them about the life of a rockstar, huh?"

He laughed. "We're bringing the nineties back in style, which means you girls are going to lose the contest! We know exactly how to work that crowd. Right, guys?"

The boys grunted in manly agreement.

"We'll see about that," I responded, having a difficult time taking my eyes off of Caleb. He just looked...different...like a bad rocker boy. I liked it.

"You're working that wild eighties look," he said, appraising my outfit too. "I could get used to the pink hair really fast."

"I was thinking the same thing about you...I mean, the boy band thing and all. It's kind of hot."

"Geez, Whit, if that's all it takes, I should have been serenading you with cheesy boy band ballads all these years."

I just shook my head with a laugh. "I have to go." I backed away. "See you *later*?" I accentuated the word.

"You bet." He nodded, his eyes losing a little of their amusement.

I moved on into the lodge, bumping into people on my way to the stage. I said a brief hello to some of the parents I already knew. Finally, I approached Ben, who was setting up the sound.

"Hey, Ben, are we ready to go?" I asked.

"Think so." He hooked one last cord to the system. "You have your iPod?"

I handed it over, and he quickly plugged it in and started clicking switches on the soundboard.

"Hey, Whitnee, how do you want me to organize the campers?" It was Sharie, one of the other mentors who had helped me with music activity camp.

"Um, have them sit in their groups according to the order they perform. Remember, we're starting with earliest decade to most current," I reminded her.

She nodded and set off just as Steve approached me.

"Whitnee, are you all set? What do you still need?" he asked.

"I think we're good. Just want to make sure everyone gets here on time. You're still going to say something at the beginning, right?" I clarified.

"Yes. I'll welcome everybody and talk briefly about what a great summer it's been…"

"Then we'll start the show—I have a couple of people acting as emcees. While the judges are making their decision at the end, did you want to take that time to explain how the Send-Off will work?"

"Yes, I'll do that." He made a note on the clipboard that never left his side. "Great job, Whitnee."

"Thanks." He walked away to greet parents, and I was about to turn back to Ben when a very beautiful woman pulled her sunglasses off to examine me more closely.

"Did I hear that you're Whitnee?" she asked in a dainty, Southern voice.

When my eyes met hers, there was no doubt who this woman was. She had Amelia's piercing hazel eyes and an older version of her face.

"Um," I was so startled I didn't even know what to say. "Yes, I'm Whitnee. Are you…?"

"Amy, Amelia Robinson's mom. I believe you had called and left me a message?"

I saw Ben's eyebrows rise as he stood there looking busy with the soundboard. Amy was all charming smiles, just like her ex-husband had been when I'd met him. Were these people just really good at faking it?

"Yes, that was me." I finally found my voice. "Wow…I'm, um, so glad you came!"

"Well, of course, if my daughter is performing…I called Jack, her father, and agreed to meet him for the show. Don't tell Amelia, but we are going to take her to dinner afterward together…but that's really all the time I will have this weekend."

Both of her parents were here? I hoped Amelia saw what a positive thing this could be. My heart started pounding when I suddenly considered the multitude of reactions Amelia could have to this.

I stared at her, trying to figure out what to say. "Well, I'm sure Amelia will love to see both of you. It's been a long summer…"

"I know. I've just missed her so much!" she gushed, and I wondered what kind of mother could stay away from her daughter for almost eight months like that…but I wasn't there to judge. I just wanted Amelia to be happy. "How has she been doing here? You know, she has quite a stubborn side…like her father."

And even though Amy continued chattering, I no longer heard her the moment I spotted Amelia entering the room. She led the way for the colorful pack of girls behind her and then her eyes rested on me. It happened so fast, but it felt like slow motion. She saw who I was talking to, her face darkened, and then she wheeled around and shoved her way through the girls and out the door again.

"Um, I'm sorry. Will you please excuse me?" I was running away before I had even finished speaking.

Morgan grabbed me on my way out. "What happened? Why did Amelia just run out?"

"Her mom is here. I'll be back, okay? Just keep the girls calm and ready for the show."

I saw Amelia's sprinting figure leaving the crowd behind and heading in the direction of the old jungle gym. I ran after her, accepting the fact that I would be sweating by the time this was over.

"Amelia!" I shouted. She kept going and I chased her a little longer before finally yelling, "Stop running!"

She slowed down when she reached the playground. I eventually caught up to her. We were both breathing with difficulty. She spun around on me.

"You did this! I know you did. How did you get her here?" she exploded.

"You know what? I did, okay? You wanted time with your mom, and you've got it now!" I replied in exasperation.

"I don't want to ever see her again! I am not going back there—"

"Stop it," I commanded and took a deep breath. "Stop acting so selfish. I'm serious. I just freaking chased you down in hundred-degree weather right before a huge event that *I* am in charge of—I need you to get control of yourself and listen to me."

She actually looked surprised by my words. "I'm not being selfish—"

"Yes, you are," I interrupted. "If you fall back into these immature emotional outbursts of yours, then you're just going back to how you were, Amelia...and this whole summer was pointless!"

"Well, maybe I haven't changed after all."

"Oh, please! Your classic defense mechanisms are getting old!" I erupted with frustration. "You know you've changed. And your parents deserve to see that. They might be the same parents you left when you came here, but you're not the same kid. Don't you want to show them that?"

"But they don't want me."

"If they didn't want you, then why did they both agree to meet here to see you perform and spend time with you afterward? The three of you together?"

She froze, her eyes wide as she looked at me. "They're both here? Together?"

I nodded at her apparent shock.

"I haven't seen them together in a long time," she mumbled.

"And yet they did it tonight...for you." I let my words hang between us for a moment before softening my voice. "Listen, Amelia, just stop running from your problems. Go back in there. Give your mom the biggest hug she's ever gotten from anyone.

125

Tell her you love her and you're glad she's here—and mean it when you say it. Then do the same to your dad, and be thankful that you have the night with them. You can't fix your parents, just like I can't fix you. You can only control your own choices. So *please* do the right thing here. Everything you've learned this summer starts *now*."

She looked torn for a moment before quietly saying, "Okay."

I sighed with relief. *Breakthrough.*

I turned around to head back to the lodge, thinking she would follow me.

"Wait," I heard her say. When I faced her again, she had tears in her eyes that weren't there before.

"Amelia, we need to get back. Please don't start crying now."

"No, it's not that." She looked up at the sky, trying to compose herself. "It's just that…I'm really going to miss you, Whitnee. You're the only person I trust right now. And that's the only reason I'm going back in there."

Tears were now threatening my own eyes. I just moved quickly and encompassed her in a hug.

"I will miss you too. I love you," I said simply.

"I love you too," she told me, and I squeezed my eyes shut for a moment. How amazing it was that I had somehow earned her love over this summer. I vowed to myself that no matter what, I would stay connected to her as long as she needed it.

The Lip Sync Contest was a huge success and an immense amount of fun. Not only was it entertaining to revisit history through music, but it was also hysterical how much the campers and mentors got into their parts. I know I was biased, but from a musical production standpoint, I knew my girls were one of the best acts. Their dance routine was stellar, and Amelia had a personal best performance. She played Cyndi Lauper perfectly and nailed every single line. She got a huge applause and then threw all kinds of air kisses to the crowd—she even waved at her parents before stepping off the stage. I took that as a good sign.

But the highlight of my evening was when Caleb and his boys got up to perform their song...Oh my gosh, I laughed so hard watching him in the middle of those preteen boys lip syncing and acting like teen idols! They had choreography, and they copied every move and crowd-pleasing gesture they could remember from the original boy band. The best part was when they each went and picked a girl from the audience to sing to onstage. Two of the boys picked their moms, Kevin picked Amelia, and Caleb picked...yours truly. I will admit that while I acted embarrassed and surprised, inside I was totally digging the attention. They each got down on one knee as they sang and made hand motions in time to the music. Caleb got the chance to serenade me with a "cheesy nineties boy band ballad," and he made it worth every moment. At the end of the song while the crowd went nuts, Caleb grabbed my hand and kissed it, shooting me a little wink.

I wanted to melt.

As it turned out, the judges made their decision based on overall production, lip syncing ability, and crowd reaction. Our act came in second place. Caleb and his campers got first. I decided I could live with second...especially since first place went to the boy who serenaded me. I was still grinning stupidly about it long after the show was over.

I didn't get a chance to see Caleb again before everyone hopped into action moving the campers out. Everything had been packed up prior to the show—now the families came back to the cabins to pick up luggage and make sure nothing was forgotten. Needless to say, that part of the process was a little chaotic and noisy. Our bathroom needed some serious repacking and cleaning, but with so many moms there to make it happen, it was done in no time.

Before we knew it, it was nearly seven o'clock, and campers, mentors, staff, and families had gathered in front of the lodge for the Send-Off. Steve encouraged everyone about leaving Camp

Fusion and going back out into the world more empowered. It was a beautiful moment, and I actually fought back tears when I realized the moment had come. Camp Fusion would soon be over.

When Steve finished, the parents and campers said one last good-bye to the mentors. I hugged all of my girls at one time and gave them my final encouragement and well wishes. They were crying too.

When Amelia and I hugged, she whispered in my ear, "I know you're planning to go back to the Island. Promise you'll tell me everything that happens. And promise that you'll be super careful. And don't forget me...ever."

I didn't know quite what to say, so I just nodded at her through my tears. She pulled away abruptly and wiped her eyes before rushing off to get in her car. We didn't even say an official good-bye.

And then it was time. The families loaded up their cars with luggage and kids. And the rest of us, as was tradition, lined both sides of the road that led away from the camp. Steve had prepped us about waving and smiling and cheering for the campers as they left—no matter how sad we were about watching them leave.

When I took my place on the road, Jaxson wandered up beside me. We made small talk about the evening's events as we waited for the first cars to start down the road. I couldn't deny Jaxson's charm. But I felt nothing romantic for this college-aged cutie. The poor guy had kind of been pursuing me at the beginning of the summer until...well, until Caleb and then Gabriel took my emotions for a roller coaster ride. After that, Jaxson just had "no game," as Caleb liked to put it. But I still found him pleasant to be around. I saw Caleb and Morgan join the line on the other side of the road. I smiled at them, but Caleb didn't look really excited to see Jax and me talking. He didn't make any territorial moves, like coming over to my side...even though I kind of wished he would. But then it became too late, because the line of cars began their ceremonial parade past us and out of sight.

We all waved and cheered—the campers had the windows down and their heads sticking out as they passed. Parents honked their horns for fun. It was meant to be a happy occasion. But in my own heart, it just wasn't all that happy. I was not very good at saying bye. I hated being separated from people I loved.

I waved to Emily first on her way out.

The next of my campers that went by was Madison, and then came Amelia. She held her phone out and yelled, "Text me if anything happens, okay?"

And I knew what she meant. I gave her a thumbs up. I could feel the ball forming in my throat as I watched her drive away with both of her parents. She would be okay. I had to believe that. Bailey was the last of my girls to pass me, and I waved and called out to her.

But when Kevin drove by in the back seat of his grandparents' car, calling, "Bye, Whitnee! I'll miss you, and I'll never forget!" I completely lost it.

The tears just poured out of my eyes, probably smearing Amelia's stupid mascara. But I couldn't stop.

"Hey, you okay?" Jaxson asked.

"Yeah, of course. It's just sad." I sniffled. "I don't think I can stand here any longer." In fact, I was starting to feel pretty dizzy. Maybe it was the heat combined with not having eaten much today. I felt like I needed to sit or something.

"The line is almost done." He pointed to the last car. "And then it's our turn to go."

I took a deep breath and put on a somewhat happy face for the remaining cars. After that, Steve gathered us on the lawn for one last thank you (which was a short version of what he had already said at our meeting last night) and then freed us to go pack up our cars. I made my way quickly to sign out on his clipboard. Then I turned, hoping to hurry away so I could mourn in private and then emotionally prepare myself for our evening plans.

"Hey, aren't you going to say bye?" Jaxson stopped me.

"Oh, of course…I'm sorry. Guess I was just wanting to check my makeup for smears," I told him quickly.

"You just have one right…here." And he reached out to wipe a smudge near my left eye. It felt really awkward.

"Thanks. I should go. It was really great to meet you this summer, Jax."

"You too. And you have my number, so don't be a stranger, okay?" And then he was hugging me before I had a chance to respond.

So I hugged him back, briefly patting him on the back, and then pulled away with a simple, "Bye." I spun around to head back to the cabin, maneuvering among mentors saying tearful good-byes to each other.

Caleb stepped briefly into my path and muttered, "You know, it's a good thing we're leaving, or I might have to have a talk with him about what physical contact he's allowed to have with you…"

"Don't be like that." I gestured between the two of us and said mockingly, "Just friends, right?"

He rolled his eyes, and it kind of pleased me to know that Jaxson's hug bugged him.

"Look, I feel weird and sick and dizzy. I'm going to go sit and cry in the cabin for a little bit. Just send Morgan for me when y'all are ready."

He frowned at my words, but before he could say anything, Claire interrupted. "Caleb, can I talk to you?"

We both jumped. She did not seem happy. In fact, there was a coldness in her eyes toward me. I could just feel it—in girl vibes.

That was when I decided maybe I felt fine enough to stay around after all.

"Sure," Caleb agreed, and then when I didn't move away from his side, he gave me a mock-puzzled look and whispered naughtily, "Just friends, right, Whit?" The expression on my face must have been too much for him, because he cracked a smile. "I'll catch up with you later, okay?"

He was blowing me off in front of Claire! That was so not okay! Of course, I had just told him I was leaving for the cabin, but whatever…I gave him one dirty look before relenting and moving away slowly so I could listen in as long as possible.

"Can we take a walk?" I heard Claire ask innocently. A walk sounded like more than just a quick see-you-later kind of talk. But they walked away before I could hear anything else.

Dangit. I reminded myself I had no right to get mad—Caleb was not my boyfriend. I didn't even know yet if I wanted him to be. And, truthfully, I was feeling so strange and disconnected that I had to put thoughts of Caleb away and focus on getting to the cabin as fast as possible.

The moment I entered the room, I was so struck with how bare it was without all of the girls' belongings that I collapsed in the middle of the floor and gave in to the tears. I already missed them. I knew if I didn't allow myself these few private moments to mourn, then I would regret it. But, wow, it physically hurt to care so much.

My head pounded with every heaving sob, and I could feel myself start to shake a little. And then I was distantly aware of the toilet flushing in the bathroom. I froze. Someone else was in the cabin. I stood wearily and moved to the bathroom, wiping my eyes self-consciously.

"Morgan?" I was surprised to see her there, assuming she'd be saying her good-bye to Drew.

I immediately became aware of her emotional state too. Her face was flushed, and her eyes were puffy with tears. We were both still in our eighties outfits.

"Are you okay?"

She moved to the sink to wash her hands, and she really did just seem like a wisp of a person—skin and bones. Even her personality had seemed altered the last couple of weeks. She finally mumbled, "Saying good-bye really sucks."

I was about to agree when she suddenly stopped. With the faucet still running, she pressed both frail hands to the sides of the sink, her knuckles turning white. And a horribly mournful sob just ripped out of her.

"Morgie…what is wrong? Is this about the campers?" I moved to her side, grabbing a paper towel and wetting it in the running water. Then I switched the water off and offered the towel to her.

"Oh, Whitnee…" She sobbed and took the paper towel, pressing it to her eyes. "The campers are part of it. I'm thinking about everything right now…losing Carrie, saying good-bye, leaving Camp Fusion, and…" She trailed off and sucked in a breath.

"And what?"

She just shook her head. She inhaled as deeply as she could and tried to slow her breathing. I waited patiently, trying to ignore the way my hands were still shaking and the splitting pain spreading behind my eyes throughout my whole head.

"Morgan, I really want to know what is wrong with you. Is this more than just leaving Camp Fusion? Is it about going back to the Island?"

She checked her reflection in the mirror, and I watched as she completely composed her expression before addressing me.

"I have to go call my parents before we leave tonight…Maybe we can talk when I get back?" she suggested.

I nodded slowly. "Okay."

And then I reached out to hug her, shocked at how much less of her there actually was. She didn't just look skinny, she felt bony. She hugged me back and then sidled past me, calling out, "I'll be back in a bit."

I turned my attention on myself once she was gone. I looked like a mess. I wet another paper towel and fixed my face, even combing my hands through my hair in an effort to tame it.

When Morgan got back, I would find out the truth. I knew her. She always had to process circumstances internally before sharing them outwardly. And she'd been processing for quite a while—so much so that it was damaging her health. Thankfully she sounded ready to share. I hoped her phone conversation didn't take long—I was ready to hear the truth. Whatever it was, we would get through it together…

Suddenly, a paralyzing pain that seemed to split my head in two obliterated every other thought. The bathroom around me disappeared into blackness, and the sharp sensation resonated through my entire body, as if a rubber band inside me had snapped and pitched the whole world out of alignment. The breath was knocked out of me for a brief moment, and I staggered, groping for the sink to keep me upright.

And then my vision returned slowly. I was still in the bathroom. Alone. But when I found my reflection in the mirror, my eyes looked so bizarre that I considered my own sanity for a moment. They weren't just glowing; they literally started flashing colors like an obnoxiously bright billboard—blue, green, gold, silver—and back through them again. I leaned in close to the mirror, with my nose almost pressed against it, watching as if it wasn't me, but some girl with freaky eyes in a really tripped-out movie. I felt each life force course through my body, and just as quickly my head stopped hurting, my hands stopped shaking, and I stood up straight.

I knew then that the tricky connection I had felt to the Island— the one that had an apparent "short" in it—had just wiggled itself into the right position. I sensed everything around me differently. And more importantly, I knew somehow that the portal was in use. I couldn't explain it, but I knew it.

It was time.

I literally ran out of the cabin, hustling to the river. I had to know what was happening, to see if it was true. I half-expected to run into Caleb and Claire on their walk. And surely Morgan would notice something happening from the cliff downriver where she could get cell phone reception.

And yet strangely there was no one around. I halted when I reached the river's edge, staring across the water. There was not even a stupid breeze or weird light or anything. But I knew it was there. I knew it was open. With a cry, I thrust my palms out in front of me and to my delight, the river water receded away from me and climbed upward into a wave about four feet high that waited for my cue to break. I laughed manically and then let it come crashing down, splashing me as it rolled up high on the bank. It was working! Oh my gosh, I needed to find Morgan and Caleb! We needed to go *now*.

I spun around breathlessly to speed back up the trail and instead ran right into the arms of a man much bigger than me. I was going to step back and apologize until I became aware that his hands had deftly grabbed mine and looped them behind my back where another man began binding them together.

"What—?" I was completely startled before registering the fact that something bad was happening. Instinct kicked in and I began fighting to get away. I pulled on my hands. I kicked and was about to scream when the man in front me slammed his hand down over my mouth.

"Shhh. You do not want to fight us."

Oh, yes, I did. They were *tying me up*.

Terror coursed through my body, and my eyes scanned my surroundings for help when the realization hit me that I was not going to overpower either of these men. I had to keep my wits about me. I couldn't give in to the paralyzing fear at the surface of my thoughts. I vaguely recalled hearing that when you were attacked, it was important to remember everything you could about the attacker's physical features and clothing so you could give an accurate description to the police—assuming you got out of a situation like this alive. So my eyes moved to the man in front of me while I chanted in my head, *Think clearly, Whitnee. Remember everything you can.*

Tan skin. Brown eyes. Dark hair. Dirty, white, out-dated clothing. A scar on one side of his face with three slashes. He was soaking wet. And his hand smelled funny and…kind of familiar. Like sulphur. Reminded me of…

I stopped fighting and my eyes went wide and my stomach churned as I stared at the man with recognition.

He grinned wickedly at the expression on my face. "You remember me now?"

The scream ripped from my throat even though it was muffled. This was the same man who had attacked me in the forest of
Geodora...the Pyra who lured me into the woods with an image
of my dad. I recognized his smell. And worse yet, I recognized
that scar on his face where I had clawed him.

"Stop fighting me, pretty girl, and this will be easy," he murmured against my ear, and I wanted to be sick. These men were
Dorians! What did they want?

"You sure we have the right girl? The hair is pink..." The other
man spoke behind me. I tilted my head to try to get a view of him,
but the Pyra in front of me jerked my face back around.

"Oh, this is the right girl...but even if I was not sure, he will
confirm it."

He? Who was *he?* Was it someone I knew?

"Now, as much as I hate to cover those special gray eyes of
yours, you cannot see any more of us..." As soon as he said it, a dark
cloth came over my eyes and nose, and I struggled against them.

Oh, dear God, please don't let them hurt me. They were so bulky
and strong that my thrashing about was nothing to them. And
just when I remembered that I had life force powers here, I felt
something cold, metal, and sharp attach to my wrists. They had
put armbands on me. The bands injected poisonous ocean water
into the arms, cutting off access to the life forces. I felt completely
helpless as the familiar sensation of weakness moved immediately
through my system.

Strangely the two men got quiet, and I heard a third set of
footsteps approach us on the rocks. Was somebody there to help
me? I tried calling out, and then the Pyra removed his hand from
my mouth and stuffed a rag into it. I choked and my eyes started
watering into the blindfold. Who was there? Oh, please, let them
be a friend...

"This is the girl, correct?" the second guy behind me called out,
and they seemed to step away from me.

I felt strangely exposed just standing there not being able to see
what was going on and feeling more and more lethargic.

The third person, whomever he was, must have given an affirmative sign, because he did not speak.

"That was easy. Time to go then," the Pyra stated and jerked me so hard the other way that I fell.

Only his tight grip on my arm kept me from hitting the ground, but I was sure I would have a bruise later where he was gripping me. I heard a grunt from the third person behind us. It was definitely a low man's voice.

The Pyra complained, "Calm down. She is still alive, is she not?"

Still alive? Was that not going to be a permanent thing? The next thing I knew, he had picked me up and thrown me over one shoulder. I could tell he was wading into the water.

I had to fight this. He was going to take me across and transport me to the Island!

When he had moved deep enough into the river that I knew we were somewhere in the middle, I conjured as much strength and energy as I could and threw myself sideways in an effort to escape. I heard him grunt with the force, and then I was underwater in the Frio River. That was scary for a number of reasons—the most pressing being that I hadn't taken a breath first. However, it did release the rag that had been stuffed into my mouth, and when I was yanked back up to the surface I came up screaming as loud as I could.

"Caleb! Morgan! Help! They've got me! They're taking me to—"

But I was slapped brutally in the face, and my words were cut off. I could taste blood in my mouth, and it stunned me into silence. And then the wet rag was back in my mouth again, and I wanted to cry out of frustration.

Please, please let someone have heard me. Please.

"You are not supposed to—oh!" the second guy started, but didn't finish, because then it sounded like somebody else threw a punch at the first guy, the Pyra, who had slapped me. I only knew this because I felt his body reel away and stumble for a moment.

"What was that for?" The Pyra was angry, and his grip on me tightened to a painful pressure.

"You are not supposed to hurt her," the second guy said in a nervous voice.

The mysterious third person, who I realized was the one who punched the Pyra, still wouldn't say anything for me to hear.

"Do you want your identity exposed?" the Pyra exploded at the third person, who must have been somewhere to our left.

Identity *exposed?* Who was this person exactly? It had to be someone who didn't want me to know who he was, but who at the same time seemed to have an interest in my safe delivery to the Island.

"Just let me do my job, and then you can do yours. But if you hit me again, it will be the last thing you do," the Pyra threatened.

"We need to go in case someone heard her," the second guy reminded him.

Oh, please let that be true... The fight in me was fading. I couldn't believe this was happening...kidnapped right there at Camp Fusion by Dorians. And one of them might even be somebody I knew. Somebody I trusted...

I was hauled across the river and then carried up the cliff, with three men to pull me up. I knew once we set foot on the other side it was over. The moment I was on dry ground again, the wind picked up to dramatic strength and began whirling around us. I could feel it happening...just like last time. Only this time I wasn't embracing the magic of the moment. I was crying weakly and screaming inside my head for help.

And then the earth dropped out below us, and I fell into darkness and despair.

REDISCOVERY

A DIFFERENT PERSPECTIVE

I failed to see how things could get any worse, even though I knew it was risky to ever think such a thing. Because, yeah, things could always be worse than they were.

But as I sat there on that cold tile floor, I could not find a silver lining in the situation. The only lining directly in sight was the stain around the rim of the toilet where the water settled inside the bowl. Boy, did I have that stain memorized...I was so sick of this scene. But I could no longer ignore the fact that something was very wrong with me. This was not normal. People shouldn't have to live this way. Constant stomach pain, cramping, vomiting, and other such unlovely means of expelling what the stomach couldn't seem to handle... There had even been blood involved.

But even that hadn't been enough to truly freak me out. No, what scared me was the way the rest of my body was responding to whatever was wrong. The weight loss, the headaches, the shortness of breath at the weirdest of times, the constant rejection of food and liquid...I had even passed out a couple of times this summer—once at home on July Fourth and once in the locker room while on life-guard duty. Fortunately, I had convinced the nurse I had just gotten a little dehydrated. But the complete picture was pointing toward the very thing that family history and genetics had always taught me to fear. I didn't need a doctor to tell me that I was not functioning like a normal seventeen-year-old girl.

The worse I felt physically, the more depressed my thoughts became...and with Camp Fusion finally ending, I could no longer repress the darkness. It wasn't like I had forgotten the reason I came to Camp Fusion five years ago. I still experienced flashes of the afternoon Carrie died. I remembered the hopeless feeling of sitting in the middle of the street with her and the blurry movement of adults all around us. That afternoon had been the last time we would take a casual bike ride together or laugh together or share a private joke. Carrie's life had been taken from her at the age of eleven.

Today was the last afternoon I would have with my campers... the last time I would have to remind Angie to be on time or help Sara find her constantly misplaced belongings. Every good thing came to an end, and I hated it. I had spent the last six years avoiding good-byes—I just couldn't handle the sad stuff.

Combine the events of this summer and my now constant physical state, and it was easy to see why my thoughts had come to such a dark place. As I slumped there against the stall door, all I could wonder was, *Which moment will be my last?*

When the heaving had stopped for a few minutes, I flushed the toilet, even though there was nothing in it but that horrible stain that would never go away. I readjusted myself, wiping my eyes from the tears that always came with dry heaving, and stepped out of the stall.

There was Whitnee.

"Morgan? Are you okay?" she questioned. Her face was surprised to see me, but that suspicion was in her eyes as she took in my whole appearance. She had been crying too, and I knew why.

"Saying good-bye really sucks," was all I could say, thinking that might satisfy her curiosity. But I didn't mean the good-bye we just went through with campers. I meant something far more permanent...like dying.

Geez, I was sick. I felt so suffocated by this preoccupation with death. And just like the state of my body, I knew my own thoughts of death were unhealthy too.

I was *very* sick. And I didn't have the words yet to express that to my best friend.

Admitting that in my mind brought the panic to the surface. I could feel some kind of scream or moan try to escape, and I couldn't stifle it. I gripped the sink tightly in front of me, praying that I wouldn't lose it in front of Whitnee.

"Morgie...what is wrong? Is this about the campers?"

The next thing I knew, she had pressed a wet paper towel into my hands. I covered my eyes so she wouldn't see just how panicked I was.

"Oh, Whitnee..." I couldn't help the tears. If she only knew how deep my fear ran...how completely messed up I was. If I was as sick as I thought I was, could I put her through the same thing I went through with Carrie?

"The campers are part of it," I admitted. "I'm thinking about everything right now...losing Carrie, saying good-bye, leaving Camp Fusion, and..."

I think I'm dying, Whitnee.

"And what?" she prompted me, but I shook my head.

I couldn't say it out loud. This was ridiculous. Just because I felt that way didn't mean it was true. Maybe I had more of a dramatic side than I ever realized. After all, the test results came back today for sure. My parents probably already had them in hand and were just waiting for me to call so they could share the good news. Just because the preliminary tests had been bad...it didn't mean what I thought it meant, right?

I needed to calm the *beep* down before I scared myself—and Whitnee—too much.

"Morgan, I really want to know what is wrong with you," she almost pleaded. I could tell being unable to understand me was killing her. "Is this more than just leaving Camp Fusion? Is it about going back to the Island?"

Ah, the Island. The one ray of hope left in my black world. I had a particularly vested interest in getting back to that Island. In fact, just the thought of it gave me a sense of peace. I felt like I could handle whatever test results came back because we were going back to the Island...tonight.

I gazed at myself in the mirror until I was sure I had pulled it together. I needed to tell Whitnee and Caleb the truth. But I couldn't do that until I knew what exactly I was dealing with.

"I have to go call my parents before we leave tonight. Maybe we can talk when I get back?" I told her, trying to convey in my expression what I knew she was wanting—some reassurance that I would be honest.

"Okay..." Fortunately, she caught on.

I was going to make a quick exit, but then she stopped me with a hug. That simple act of friendship helped me breathe a little bit better. It was good to know that no matter what I had said or done recently, she was still my best friend.

I excused myself and, with renewed strength, I found my way in the early evening light to the little cliff downriver. It was hidden through a thicket of trees, but it was the only place you could get high enough at Camp Fusion to reach a network signal for your phone. My hands shook only slightly as I speed-dialed my mom.

"Hello?" It was my little sister, Maeghan.

"Hey, Mags, is Mom or Dad there?" I asked breathlessly.

"Yeah...they've been in the office all afternoon. Told us to stay out of there, so hold on."

Not good. They holed themselves up in the office when they had important "adult" business to discuss. Maybe it was just financial stuff that had them in there today of all days.

After some scuffling sounds on the phone, I heard some mumbling, and then my mom said into the phone, "Hi, honey."

"How's it going, Mom?"

"Just fine. Are you on your way home yet?" Was it my imagination or did her nonchalance seem forced?

"No, I told you I had to stay a few more days—"

"Morgan, we never agreed to that...not with everything you've had going on. I wouldn't have let you go back to camp this week if I'd known you would ask to stay again." She sounded more sensitive than normal.

"Mom, it's just till next week. Why are you so upset about it? Did you get my results back?"

She paused. I felt my heart sink. She wouldn't have freaking paused if she had gotten good news.

"We decided we would discuss them when you got home, remember, honey? That's not exactly a phone conversation."

I could hear my dad start to mumble in the background.

"So it's bad, isn't it?" I whispered.

She paused again and then gave a shaky sigh. "Morgan..."

"Mom, I'm sorry, but I have things to do before I can come home. Just tell me. I deserve to know," I told her with a very strange lack of emotion. I was starting to feel disconnected from myself and the whole situation. Maybe this was what an out-of-body experience felt like—where you just didn't feel anything at all.

And then she was crying right there on the phone, and I had my confirmation. Our worst fears were justified. I was vaguely aware of my dad taking the phone from Mom and trying to calm her down as well as reassure me. He apologized, saying I was never supposed to find out like this. I don't really remember exactly how the whole conversation went down, just words and phrases like "advanced stages" and "treatment as soon as possible" and "don't worry, honey, we're getting the best doctors" and...I couldn't take it any longer.

I pulled the phone away from my ear while he tried to convince himself that this was all treatable...fixable. Because that was what my dad did. He was a fixer. So of course everything that had a cause had a treatment. But I could hear the fear in his voice, taste the insecurity in his words.

Without any emotion at all, I spoke calmly into the phone, "Dad, if things are going to change as drastically as I think they are, then just give me until next week. I promise after that I'll do whatever needs to be done. But I need to stay here, okay? Just for a few days. Please."

"Don't you feel bad, Morgan? The doctor said that at this point he couldn't understand how you were still functioning normally..."

Well, I wasn't—the doctor was right about one thing. And Dad was probably wondering why in the world I was not ready to come home and get "fixed" by modern medicine. Maybe because I knew with everything in me that this was never going to be an easy fix— no matter how much Dad wanted it that way.

"I feel fine..." I lied. Geez, I had become so good at it. "But I won't always feel this way, will I, Dad? Please just give me a few days before...before all of that starts."

He was quiet, and all I could hear were Mom's muffled sobs on the other end.

"Okay, honey. I understand," he replied very gently, and I heard my mom protest. "But I want you to call us every day, okay? And the second you feel bad, I'll come get you. We love you." When his voice cracked, I knew I needed to hang up.

"I love you both too," I said without promising anything, and then I pressed the button to end the conversation.

Nobody ever really knows how they're going to react to bad news. And until you've experienced what feels like a death sentence, maybe it's just not easy to understand. But I didn't cry. I just stood there, knowing this moment had been a long time coming. After all, this was why I had avoided doctors and complaints to my mom about how I felt for the last year or so. Deep down I had known there was something really wrong with me—and apparently it had been wrong for quite some time. Now the fear that had kept me from getting help was like the first nail in a coffin. I felt numb all over, which was kind of a relief from the constant pain I now carried with me everywhere.

I know I was staring at the river, but I wasn't really seeing it. I saw nothing and felt nothing as if I had already become...nothing.

I wasn't even aware of time passing or even existing at all—until I heard my name. I snapped back into reality and became aware again of sounds and movement around me.

It was Whitnee...screaming for Caleb and me. I felt my numb heart jumpstart. I had never heard her voice sound so distorted and terrified. I paused a moment to figure out where I was hearing her. It was like her voice had echoed all around the river, bouncing off the rocks and cliffs surrounding the water. I stepped as close as I could to peer over the edge of the cliff down into the water.

"Whit?" I called out, but I heard nothing and started wondering if I had hallucinated the whole thing. After all, my mental state was not in its best form. After a brief moment of debate, I leaned out over the water and scanned the riverbanks to my right then upriver to the camp's main swimming hole. There was some kind of movement down there. What was I seeing exactly? It looked like a small group of people carrying...well, it looked like a body. And when I realized the body was wearing bright pink clothing against the others' somewhat neutral-colored clothes, I freaked.

The group had made it to the top of the cliff that bordered the forbidden side of the Frio River—the side that everyone knew never to cross. And then a heavy rush of wind nearly knocked me over as I stood there leaning too far out over the cliff. I was forced to step back or fall into the river. But even though I lost my view of the group, I didn't miss what happened next...a strange burst of light and then...stillness.

"Whitnee!" I screamed. I had a bad feeling...a very bad, horrible feeling that had nothing to do with my own sickness.

I leaned back out over the edge and was not surprised to see the group had vanished. *Oh, please don't tell me the limp body dressed in pink was Whitnee. Please, no...*

Why did things always have to go from bad to worse? Forgetting my own doomed situation, I turned and ran back to camp, fighting back the abnormal pressure in my lungs. I dashed quickly through my cabin, calling for Whitnee, but there was no one there. Caleb. I had to find Caleb...last time I had seen him was at the Send-Off. The camp was looking pretty deserted outside—just a few people still packing up their cars. And then there was Ben.

"Ben!" I practically screamed and ran over to him, clutching his arm to hold myself steady. "I think something bad happened, Ben... We need to...I think..." I wasn't very coherent, especially since I was looking wildly around for Caleb and trying to make sure nobody heard me.

"Whoa. It's okay. Just take a deep breath—"

"I think Whitnee was just taken...to the Island, um, down at the river...It happened so fast. I heard her scream and—" I really wasn't breathing right.

"What?" Ben's eyes went wide. "Morgan, tell me exactly what happened."

"I...I was out on the cliff using my phone and I heard—oh, Caleb!" I cried.

He had just emerged from a path through the trees. And he was with Claire. *Beep.*

As soon as he heard my voice, his head snapped up. I left Ben and ran to Caleb, trying to appear calm in front of Claire. "Caleb, I need you *now*. It's Whitnee...We need to go..." I told him, and I could tell he was trying to understand my desperation while dealing with Claire at the same time.

Claire snorted rather unattractively and crossed her arms in a pout. "Of course it's Whitnee. It's always Whitnee with you, Caleb."

"Claire—" he began.

"No, just go. I'm done with this." And she marched away from us.

I didn't care, but Caleb seemed perturbed as he watched her go.

"This better be good, Morgan, because that girl officially hates my guts now—"

"I think Whitnee was just kidnapped by Dorians!" I exploded, which officially ended any sort of control I had on my emotions. My air supply felt choked off by the huge ball in my throat that had now erupted into tears.

"What in the world are you talking about?" Caleb's face turned deadly serious. "She just told me she was going back to the cabin for a while. Kidnapped? How is that even possible?"

Ben came up behind me and placed an arm at the top of my back and a hand on Caleb's shoulder. "I do sense something strange. Let's go!"

And the three of us moved into action. On our way to the river, I explained through my tears what I had seen and heard. The more I said, the faster Caleb moved and the more distressed he became.

"This can't be happening..." he muttered.

I felt the same way. Ben remained silent as he listened, but his face said it all. He was worried. A small part of me really hoped I was just crazy. I could deal with mental illness...but not with losing another best friend.

All was still at the river, and we halted when we reached the edge of the water.

"Whitnee!" Caleb hollered, his voice echoing all around us. "Whitnee!"

I moved to his side. "Caleb..."

"*Whitnee!*" He called again, and I could feel his fear.

"She's not here."

"She's gotta be around here somewhere if you saw her!" he snapped at me and then called for her again. I watched him help-lessly. "If she's not here, then she's back at the cabin...just where she said she would be. I mean, surely she wouldn't come down here without us..."

We both knew Whitnee. Of course she would come down here without us...if she had a good reason. But whether she came on her own or not, it was clear something had gone wrong. I had never heard her so afraid. And I shuddered at the echoes of her screams in my head.

"Caleb, she's not here. I'm telling you...they took her over there!"
I insisted, throwing my hands out toward the other side of the water.

"No! No, that's just not possible. Come on." He shook his head.
"We need to go find her back up at camp. Right, Ben?" Caleb was
already backing away.

But Ben had not moved. In fact, he was standing very still, facing the water as if he was trying to hear something. "I don't know,
Caleb," Ben said quietly, his face a mask of concentration.

"You're both crazy! I'm going back up there—" But when he
turned around, something stopped his progress. *Someone*, I guess
I should say.

I gasped, and Ben turned around at the shock on my face.

Standing there in our pathway stood a soaking wet Dorian we
knew pretty well...

Gabriel had come to the Mainland.

THE TABLES TURN

There was a moment when stunned silence was about the only thing we all had in common. Gabriel was here...at Camp Fusion. Before I could think through the implications of his appearance, things turned ugly.

Caleb launched himself full-force at Gabriel, grabbing handfuls of Gabriel's wet tunic. Gabriel appeared shocked as Caleb yelled an inch away from his face, "Where is she? What did you do to her? Tell me *now!*"

"*Caleb!*" I cried out and ran to them.

He was out of control and looked about to tackle Gabriel and start throwing punches. Ben was faster than me and grabbed Caleb by the waist, ripping him away from Gabriel with difficulty.

"You better start talking, man! I'm serious!" Caleb shouted as Ben pulled on him. "Ben, let me go!" Caleb's face was enraged, and I stepped in front of him, placing my hands on his tense arms.

"Caleb, stop. Gabriel wouldn't hurt Whitnee," I protested, throwing a glance back at the confused Dorian.

"Oh, yeah? Then tell me how it is that he shows up here right after you're telling me some Dorians kidnapped her! Pretty convenient timing! I totally believe you now...and *he* knows something!" Caleb spat and shot furious looks at Gabriel.

"I do not know what you are talking about, Caleb!" Gabriel replied, his face just as angry. But he was keeping a safe distance away from us.

"*This* is Gabriel?" Ben broke in, staring hard at him. "Abrianna's *son?*"

Gabriel cocked his head to the side at Ben's words. "Do I know you?" he asked taking a closer look at Ben.

"Oh, for the love...we have so much to explain here—" I sighed, but Caleb interrupted me.

"Start with why your people took Whitnee!" He pulled away from me and moved toward Gabriel again. I quickly put myself in between the two of them. Caleb was frustrated when he growled, "Morgan—"

"I'm sure there is a good explanation for why Gabriel is here. Maybe we should all just *stay calm*," I suggested, taking a deep breath myself. I needed Caleb to think clearly—he was not typically given to such outbursts. I knew only Whitnee had the power to bring out that crazy protectiveness in him. But Gabriel was here for a reason, and we needed to hear what it was.

I gave Caleb a pleading look.

"I won't touch him, okay?" Caleb pacified me.

"No, you most certainly will not," Gabriel agreed ominously, the fire of anger in his dark eyes.

Ben had approached us again. "Let the boy speak," he told Caleb, but then directed his next statement at Gabriel. "And it had better be good, or you will have more to deal with than just Caleb's wrath."

I peered up at Ben with wide eyes as he surveyed Gabriel—there was mistrust all over the older man's face.

Was violence really the best way to deal with all these intense emotions? Men. Why couldn't they just cry like us girls and get rid of it that way?

Gabriel looked directly at me and asked, "Please tell me first. What has happened to Whitnee?"

"You tell us," Caleb retorted before I could answer.

"I do not know." Gabriel gestured with his hands as he spoke, clearly frustrated. "I just transported here...I came across the river and started walking and then heard you screaming for Whitnee. I came back this direction as fast as I could."

I squinted at him through my puffy eyes. "That's impossible. I saw three men take Whitnee through the portal about fifteen minutes ago..."

"Gabriel was one of the three!" Caleb accused.

"No, I was not!" Gabriel protested. "I told you I just got here, and I came alone. I have seen no one until you...Why would I take Whitnee like that?"

"That is why you're here, isn't it? To take her back to the Island!" Caleb pointed out.

Gabriel narrowed his eyes at Caleb and then said arrogantly, "We both know I would not have to resort to kidnapping to get her to go with me."

Even I could understand guy talk—and that was a direct blow to Caleb's ego. Caleb's fist sprang into action before I could stop him. But Gabriel was ready for the reaction this time. He grabbed Caleb's arm, the muscles in his own arm flexing with the tension. I sucked in a breath, afraid that the two of them would not be happy until someone was bleeding.

Gabriel hissed at him, "Maybe you should stop fighting me and instead help me understand what has happened here. I am not your enemy."

"Gabriel's right," I spoke up, earning a dirty look from Caleb. "We need to focus on finding Whitnee! Gabriel, if you're telling the truth, then we all have the same problem here. Somebody has taken Whitnee against her will."

The two guys dropped their fists again, and I pulled on Caleb to back away a little bit. Gabriel might not be Caleb's enemy, but he was certainly his competition. I had never seen Caleb behave this way. I mean, Gabriel was supposed to be the emotional Pyra, not logically minded Caleb. Caleb was clearly not going to back out gracefully this time around when it came to Whitnee and Gabriel. And if I hadn't been off about reading Whitnee's behavior lately, Gabriel had more competition than he knew.

"We need to go through that portal *now*," Caleb decided, and then glared at Gabriel. "And you're taking us."

"I will not go back through that portal without Whitnee," Gabriel protested.

"That's impossible, because she's *not here*," I insisted. "I'm telling you the truth! Three Dorians kidnapped her—do you know how they could have done that without your knowledge?" Wouldn't Gabriel have seen them along the way during the weird time warp thing that happened every time we transported?

"I wonder..." he paused. "Someone would have had to send people in ahead of me and—"

"And what?" Caleb said.

Gabriel shook his head. "I do not know." But he looked as if he was thinking heavily about something. He glanced back at the river, his brow furrowed. "Perhaps we should hurry and cross over again..."

"Whoa, now. You two are not going anywhere with him until we make sure what Morgan saw was not just another one of Abrianna's illusions. What if Whitnee really is still around? While we look, Gabriel can kindly explain more of his purpose here," Ben suggested with wary glances at his fellow Dorian. "Morgan, it would be wise to check the cabin again, don't you think?"

I nodded, even though I didn't doubt my own eyes.

Caleb replied, "Fine. Then we all go back up there together. Morgan doesn't go anywhere alone. And neither does Gabriel." He was still casting suspicious looks at Gabriel.

Gabriel grunted but gave a brief nod of acceptance. He was outnumbered, so I don't think he saw any other choice. I was struck with the way the tables had turned. On the Island, Gabriel was the one with authority—the one who told us what to do. Here on the Mainland, Caleb had the upper hand. It was totally unfair that

Whitnee couldn't be here to watch this switch take place. How would she have handled that? But the coldness of terror seeped in again at the fact that she really was gone, and I didn't know what was happening to her.

"We must hurry then…the portal will not stay open much longer." Gabriel commented, glancing back across the river in doubt.

The sun was beginning to set as we hurried back along the path with Caleb taking the lead. The tension among us was high. I felt like I needed to break down some of that by getting these stubborn men to talk.

"Why exactly did you come here, Gabriel? Is something happening on the Island?" I asked, trying to sound neutral.

"I received confirmation from Abrianna that Whitnee's father is still on the Island," he replied unemotionally.

We all stopped short, turning to peer at him. Didn't see that one coming.

"Start talking," Caleb barked.

"Apparently he has been there for six years—since he disappeared from here—helping Abrianna, though I do not know with what or why," Gabriel informed us, and I couldn't really read his expression. He was staying so emotionless.

"Does Ezekiel know of this?" Ben spoke up.

Gabriel turned to give Ben his attention, pausing as he surveyed him curiously again. "He does now," he answered cautiously. "Whitnee's father appears to be some kind of prisoner, extremely well hidden and protected. Abrianna acts as if he willingly lives like that. I came to share this information with Whitnee."

"We already knew Nathan was on the Island. Abrianna told Whitnee that herself. That's why Whit was going to stay instead of transporting back with us," I told him.

I saw a muscle in Gabriel's jaw tighten. "I should never have forced her through the portal like that. She belongs on the Island—"

Caleb snorted. "So now you regret trying to protect her from your psychopath mother? And who are you to decide that she belongs on the Island?"

"There is no question where she belongs. She is our Pilgrim!"

I think it was the first time I had ever heard Gabriel confirm such a thing. I exchanged meaningful glances with Ben.

"If that's what you believe, then it's pretty obvious that you don't know everything about Whitnee's dad," Caleb said.

"What do you mean?"

"I mean that you only have part of the story—the part that Abrianna wants you to hear, Gabriel. She just gave you a good enough reason to come back here and get Whitnee! Truth is, your dear, old mom wants Whitnee's abilities. She promised to help Whitnee find her dad if Whit would give all her life force powers over to Abrianna."

"That would be impossible...Besides, a person will eventually cease to exist on the Island if they lose their connection with the life forces. Surely you are mistaken," Gabriel said doubtfully.

Caleb and I looked to Ben for confirmation of this belief. He nodded slightly, still training his eyes on Gabriel with suspicion.

"How could Abrianna ever accomplish such a thing?" Gabriel asked, almost more to himself than to us.

Caleb gave me a frightened look and threw his hands up. "Who knows? But I'm afraid Whitnee might be close to finding out now that they took her. And, for the record, I still don't trust you. You could just be one of Abrianna's minions sent to do her dirty work—"

"Enough!" Gabriel's emotion broke through as he replied fiercely, "If you think I am that stupid about the Guardian's real motives, then you underestimate me. You are right. She is after Whitnee for reasons I do not completely understand. And she will apparently go to extremes for it...as evidenced by this situation. I admit that I did come all this way on her orders to retrieve Whitnee, only to find out that Whitnee is already gone. Do you think I do not see what is happening here?"

I hadn't considered that part of it yet. If Abrianna was going to kidnap Whitnee anyway, then why send Gabriel here?

But Ben had already followed that line of thinking through to its ugly end. "Don't be so sure that portal will stay open for you," he said darkly, the heavy weight of experience in his words.

Could Abrianna really be sick enough to trick her own son into coming here just to do the exact same thing to him that she did to Ben? On that ominous thought, we picked up our pace again and finally arrived back at the camp. I ran inside the deserted girls' cabin, once again calling for Whitnee but knowing I wouldn't find her. All of our packed bags were lined up against the wall, including our Island survival bags.

Whit! How do you get into these situations? I thought despairingly, my fingers grazing her bag.

What had possessed her to leave the cabin? Alone in the room, I could feel the fear creeping back into my mind. I could not let it overtake me again. I had to think clearly. I had to be strong—for Whitnee's sake.

I heard the door open and Caleb's voice. "Morgan? Can we come in?"

"Yeah, she's not here," I replied flatly, my hand still resting wearily on Whit's bag.

Caleb found me there in the empty room and said quietly, "Let's stick to the plan, okay?"

I turned my gaze up to meet his eyes. He was afraid, just like I was, but he was back in control of himself.

"Let's load up your car. I'll go move it to Ben's. With Gabriel here, we might still be able to transport."

"And what if Abrianna doesn't keep the portal open? I really believe Whitnee was the key."

Gabriel's voice sounded from behind Caleb. "Even if she closes it, I think we will still be able to get back." We peered skeptically at the tall Dorian whose large stature filled the doorway. His expression was determined and had a glint of confidence in it. "I did make my own preparations in the event that someone in my *loyal* family betrayed me."

Caleb narrowed his eyes. "How can we trust you? You came because Abrianna ordered you to."

"I came because I wanted to help Whitnee reunite with her father. Yes, my instructions were to bring Whitnee back...but *only* her, not you. However, I never expected Whitnee to leave the two of you behind. And I am not doing this for Abrianna, no matter what she might believe." Then he gave Caleb a pointed look. "Thanks to you, I do happen to have some friends on the other side now."

My mind moved to the group that had traveled with us for protection last time—Eden, Levi, Tamir, and...Thomas. I perked up a little bit, thinking of the exotic blue-eyed Water boy who had occupied a lot of my attention on the White Island.

Caleb and I exchanged glances as if we were translating a silent agreement of trust. I felt a tiny spark of hope flicker to life.

With a nod at me, Caleb said, "Change your clothes. We need to go."

That was all the prodding I needed.

When I came out of the cabin, changed and ready to go with both survival bags flung over my shoulder, there was only Gabriel standing on the porch, surveying the surroundings with curiosity. Guess that meant that Caleb and Ben had already left to hide the car...

"So I take it Caleb trusts you now or you wouldn't have been left alone," I said lightly.

"I suppose. He really is a Geo. Always suspicious, always questioning." He sighed, looking out over the campgrounds that must seem so different to him than the sugary white beaches of the Island. "So this is Camp Fusion? Where you work?"

I settled into a rocking chair and nodded. "Yep. This is it." I pulled the last piece of gum from my pocket and offered Gabriel half of it.

He dismissed my offer with a slight shake of his head. Gum was the only thing I could chew that didn't make me sick...kind of wished now I had picked up another pack before tonight.

"It is peaceful here. And it smells different," Gabriel remarked quietly, looking up at the sky. "Amelia and Kevin...where are they?"

"Gone. Camp ended today, and they went home with their families," I replied sadly. "They're going to be mad when they find out they barely missed seeing you!"

Camp Fusion was actually over. It was weird to think that when I came to camp eight weeks ago my life had been somewhat normal. Now everything had spun wildly out of my control in a single evening.

Gabriel turned to examine me closely as he lowered himself into another rocking chair. I had forgotten how intense his eyes could be. "How long has it been here since you left the Island?" he wanted to know, probably noting my weight loss that had become increasingly harder to hide.

"Six weeks."

He shook his head. "It has only been about five weeks in my time. How is that possible?"

I just shrugged. "We were on the Island five days, but only missed one day here. No one but Ben even knew we were gone." The time issue with the portal was something I just couldn't wrap my brain around.

Gabriel grew quiet and directed his gaze across the camp again. I took my turn to study him carefully. He looked the same—except his usually long hair was cut short. It was still curly, and he had that rich tan skin that was so characteristic of a Dorian. But Gabriel was not just any Dorian—he was a gorgeous one. Even I couldn't ignore how sexy those finely toned muscles were. It was obvious why Whitnee went all weak-in-the-knees around him. But outside of his physical appearance, Gabriel was just not my type. He was too serious, too moody for me. Whitnee, on the other hand, had been able to break through that and bring out the lighthearted side of him. There was something beyond just physical attraction between the two of them. Even I had noticed that. Caleb might not trust Gabriel, but I couldn't help trusting him...because Whitnee did. And my best friend was usually a pretty good judge of character.

"Have things changed much...in six weeks?" Gabriel finally questioned.

"Um, some things," I answered truthfully, wondering if he was fishing for certain kinds of information about my best friend.

"Whitnee? How has she been?"

His casual act didn't fool me. Poor guy was desperate for details.

"She's been doing pretty well. Things got really ugly at first after we went through the portal." His eyebrows went up, so I continued, "She was pretty mad at all of us. She thought she was going to finally find her dad, and we all ruined it for her."

Gabriel's face turned dark at my words, and I quickly added, "But after about a week, she just snapped out of it and starting plotting and planning a way to get back. Whitnee's like that, you know. Once she makes up her mind about something, she's going to make it happen."

He smiled slightly.

I didn't tell him that a good majority of Whitnee's initial depression had been over missing him, even though she had never admitted it. I couldn't explain that she had forbidden us to talk about him the last six weeks so she could get over what happened on the Island between them. And I wasn't about to clue Gabriel in on the changes between Whitnee and Caleb, although I thought some of it had already become kind of obvious to him. No, that would be up to Whitnee to explain if she chose. I just hoped she would get the chance to make that choice for herself.

I couldn't help asking, "Gabriel, do you think they will hurt her?"

"No," he stated firmly. "She is too valuable to them." His face was a mask of concern, and I couldn't tell how much he believed what he said.

"But if they try to take her life forces...Could it kill her, even though she's not a full Dorian?"

"That is a troubling thought. I did not even know it was possible to *take* someone's life force. We need to hurry back to the portal."

I was about to ask him more, but a car pulled up to the cabin. We grew quiet as we watched Claire bounce out of the driver's seat with the car still running.

"Morgan, I thought you guys had left—" Claire started when she spotted me on the porch, but trailed off when her eyes rested on Gabriel. "Oh, hi."

I grew apprehensive. "Um, we were just about to leave. What are you doing back?"

"I left something in my room. Who is this?" And she had that look in her eye that I was starting to think most girls got when they discovered Gabriel.

He stood up and bowed to her. "I am Gabriel," he introduced himself.

I stood up too, panicking at how foreign he was acting. Nobody in America bowed unless they were onstage.

Claire loved it. "Oooh, your accent is so cool! I'm Claire. Are you a friend of Morgan's?"

"He's...Ben's grandson." I lied quickly, causing Gabriel to give me a funny look.

"I didn't know Ben had a grandson!" She moved closer to us, never taking her eyes off of Gabriel's face. "But I do see a family resemblance now that you mention it. Are you just visiting, or do you live around here?"

For a moment I was thankful Whitnee wasn't here. If she had seen the way Claire was eyeing Gabriel...Claire had an uncanny knack for treading on Whit's territory—even without knowing it.

"He's just visiting...from far away," I jumped in again. "In fact, we're just waiting for Caleb and Ben to get over here so we can leave." I was trying to hint that she needed to leave too.

"Oh. Well, is everything okay? Where's Whitnee?"

Gabriel and I both kind of tensed up at her question. *Why did I just say I was waiting on Ben and Caleb?! Stupid!*

"She is...fine," I mumbled.

"I didn't mean to act like such a jerk earlier. It's just that Caleb's fascination with Whitnee gets old...I don't know. Don't you feel weird about your two best friends acting like that? It's sick how she just leads him on...She either needs to commit or set him free."

I shifted uncomfortably. This was awkward, especially with Gabriel listening so intently. I didn't like conflict, and I wasn't all that great at speaking up and taking sides. But she was talking about my two best friends, and I had a problem with that.

About ten different snarky comments came to my mind, but I went with the nicest option. "They've been through a lot together. Nobody knows what goes on in a relationship but the two people involved in it. So we probably shouldn't judge them..."

Oh, for the love...please leave. Her car was still running.

"Whatever." She sighed. "Just seems like nobody can compete with her. Is she *always* the center of attention? I don't know how you put up with it as her best friend."

Her words frustrated me, but for reasons I wasn't sure how to explain—reasons I didn't understand myself.

Maybe she noticed my hesitance, because she quickly said, "I'm talking too much. They're probably perfect for each other, and I'm just insanely jealous."

Probably so, I thought, my teeth grinding my gum into pieces.

She gave me a weak smile, and I tried to smile back.

"You said you left something in the cabin?" I reminded her.

"Oh! Yeah..." And she ran inside.

Once she was gone, I made a face at Gabriel. "Sorry about that."

"Am I understanding she is more of Caleb's friend than Whitnee's?"

"Apparently neither of them now."

"It appears that more has happened in these six weeks than I understood," he said softly with a grimace.

At that point Caleb and Ben rounded the corner of the cabin. Caleb took one look at Claire's running car and directed his attention back to me as if confirming the fact that she was nearby. I nodded and rolled my eyes. That was when Claire came running back out.

"Okay, I'm leaving now! Gabriel, if you're going to be in town for a while, give me a call." And she handed him a piece of paper with her name and number on it. "I don't live too far from here and would love to show you around south Texas..." She gave him a charming smile as he took the paper.

Holy beep, the girl was shameless. For all she knew, Gabriel could've been *my* boyfriend, right?

"Bye, Morgan!" she called and bounced down the stairs before she caught sight of Caleb standing there.

She paused ever so briefly, and he just stared at her.

"Bye, Caleb," she told him less enthusiastically, and then climbed into her car and drove away. I slowly stepped down from the cabin, trying to read Caleb's face.

"What do all the numbers and dashes mean?" Gabriel looked confused as he tried to decipher Claire's piece of paper.

Caleb snatched it from him, balled it up, and shot it with perfect aim into the garbage can several feet away.

"Let's get out of here," he grumbled and started toward the river.

I sighed as the male rivalry continued.

CALEB AND FABIO

Crossing the river was pretty anti-climactic. Nothing happened when we got to the other side...and I mean *nothing*. Not even a greeting by a bird or a lightning bug or anything. It was dead still. The portal had been closed. I tried to withhold the panic that I could feel rising in my chest. The longer we were stuck over here, the more time passed on the other side...and the more danger my best friend was in.

Gabriel had assured us it would open back up soon. How he knew this he didn't explain exactly. He just kept saying he had friends on the other side with a plan and that we needed to trust that they would come through for us. So we had no other choice but to camp out there and wait.

After we had calmed down from the big disappointment of nothing happening, I had slouched down on the ground and glanced across the river at Ben, who was sitting there perfectly still, watching and waiting. Poor Ben...my mind kept replaying that last conversation before we had canoed over.

Ben had pulled Caleb and me aside with an anxious look on his face. "Listen, you two," he started. "I have a bad feeling about you going back to the Island with him. I can't shake the fact that he's Abrianna's son and came here on her orders..."

"Ben, he's different from her," I tried to explain. "I mean, he was very protective over all of us last time—"

"Maybe so, but was it for your sakes or his own? I don't like the idea of you transporting now, but somebody has to get Whitnee." He spoke quickly and quietly, as if he couldn't get his thoughts out fast enough. "What Gabriel said about Nathan being there to help Abrianna...I guarantee you it has to do with the portal or this new thing she's onto about taking someone's abilities. But there is *no way* he is staying willingly. I know Nathan. She threatened or guilted him somehow...And I just can't believe Abrianna would take Whitnee like this—it seems like such a desperate move and not even Abrianna's style. She's more of a manipulator than a person of force."

"Ben, are you sure you don't want to come with us? We could really use your help—" Caleb said.

"No," Ben responded firmly, and threw a hesitant glance at the silent Gabriel who stood upriver from us. "I'm sorry, but no...I just can't do it. Besides, I need to stay here on this side and keep an eye on things. I'm only giving you four days. After that I will have to contact your parents and tell them something." Beads of sweat had popped out on his forehead as he spoke. I had never seen Ben that serious or upset. He always seemed so cool and collected. What happened to Whitnee had clearly shaken him.

Suddenly, I thought of something and reached into Whit's survival bag. "Ben, take this." It was her dad's wedding ring that she had carefully wrapped up. "You can use this as proof, if you need it. Please don't lose it. Whit would never forgive us."

He took the ring, a look of sorrow crossing his face. Carefully, he tucked it into his work bag and then pulled out two small containers. "Take these for extra protection...at least until you are gifted with life force."

In his hand were two small pepper sprays. I didn't tell him that I already had one in my bag. I took one and placed it in Whit's bag, which was now hanging over Caleb's shoulder.

"Thanks, Ben," we chorused.

"Keep your eyes and ears open, and don't trust anybody. I know that sounds harsh, but I'm serious. I would bet my own life force ability that Abrianna has her spies everywhere..." And he shot another meaningful glance in Gabriel's direction.

I had to admit that Ben's words made me more nervous. I was already afraid of what was going to happen on the other side, but I guess with Gabriel and Caleb taking control I hadn't really started piecing together what we would do once we got there. Now as I sat there staring absently across the river and trying to ignore the waves of cramping in my stomach, I did wonder how we would ever be successful. It had seemed a much easier task just to retrieve Whitnee's father. Now our focus was on rescuing Whitnee too.

"I know who Ben is from my history lessons as a child," Gabriel spoke up, his sharp gaze following my line of vision. He sat down next to me but still kept his distance. "It took me a while to place his name and image. He was the Guardian before Abrianna. What I do not understand is what he is doing here."

"That man right there," Caleb pointed across the river, "could have been your grandfather. He was like a father to Abrianna."

"Until she tricked him through the portal and never let him come back through. I think she was only about our age then." I let those words sink in and watched for his reaction. It couldn't be fun to have such a rotten, evil skank for a mom.

"I knew she became Guardian when she was eighteen, but why would she do that to him?" Gabriel's eyes had grown intense in the fading rays of daylight.

Caleb lowered himself down on my other side. "Because he supported the Council's decision for Nathan to lead the Island instead of her. Did Abrianna tell you that Nathan was born on the Island two years after her? To Ezekiel and Sarah?"

Gabriel was genuinely shocked. "No."

"Born with no tribal birthmark, a pale complexion, and white-blond hair. Now does that remind you of a certain prophecy?" Caleb's undertone was still snarky.

"I suppose he can use all four life forces too, like Whitnee?" Gabriel clarified.

"That we still don't know," I responded. "Ben suspects it, but apparently Nathan never admitted it. Either way, he was taken into Palladium care at a young age so they could protect him and ultimately decide what to do with him. It seemed most people believed he was the Pilgrim at that point."

"That must be whom the old rumors are about..." Gabriel mused, "though no one ever talks about it. It is against Palladium orders to speak any more of the Pilgrim. Of course, since Whitnee came and went, people are talking in every village. What else do you know about her father?"

Caleb said, "Your mom and Whitnee's dad were raised together and were apparently close..."

I gave Caleb a look, warning him not to say anything about Ben's speculations over a romance. That might be as uncomfortable for Gabriel as it was for Whitnee.

"There was a huge fight between Abrianna, Nathan, and Ben the night that the Council made their decision... Ben was never seen again."

Gabriel remarked distantly, "History says that Benjamin the Guardian grew ill in his mind after years spent obsessively and unsuccessfully trying to understand the connection between the Mainland and the Island. They say he either drowned himself or sailed away before his Guardianship was over..."

"That is so unfair!" I cried. No wonder Ben had no desire to go back there. He was known as a crazy. I watched him sadly across the water. He hadn't moved an inch from his post.

"I assume you know then that Benjamin the Guardian was Ezekiel's younger brother?" Gabriel pointed out.

I nodded slowly. "Yes, which makes Ezekiel Whitnee's grandfather."

Gabriel let out a heavy sigh. "So she is a Dorian after all. And Ezekiel must have known...Did you really not know any of this before you came to the White Island?"

"We found out when we got back. Ben told us everything he knew," Caleb said. "It was a lot for Whitnee to take in at one time."

"I can understand that," Gabriel mumbled. "So if Nathan was born and raised on the Island, at what point did he come here?"

"A few years after the night of the big fight, he came in search of Ben. But then he met Serena here at camp—"

"That's Whitnee's mom. And it was love at first sight for him," I jumped in, because I found this part of the story extremely romantic. "And he stayed here for her, leaving the Island behind forever..."

Gabriel looked away from me then, a strange emotion on his face, and Caleb elbowed me in annoyance. I was confused. That was how the story went, right?

"*But*," Caleb said. "not long after he got here, Abrianna opened the portal up again..." He proceeded to fill Gabriel in on the story of Will Kinder's disappearance and Nathan's retrieval of him that ended in memory loss.

I frowned at how unromantic Caleb made Nathan's choice sound, as if Nathan might not have stayed for Serena if he hadn't forgotten the Island. It was like he wanted to downplay the whole sacrificial love aspect that was such an important part of...*Ohhhh*. So that was his problem. He didn't want Gabriel to get any bright ideas.

I shifted my gaze to Gabriel as he stood to his feet and mumbled, "I just need to walk around for a moment."

I felt bad as I watched him stalk away from us, one arm reaching back to grip his neck as if he was thinking really hard. I had a feeling we had just overwhelmed him with all that information. But he didn't look like he doubted us. Many times I had gotten the impression that Gabriel was aware of Abrianna's dishonesty—even if he didn't know the full truth.

"I can't believe we know more about his mother and the real history of the Island than he does...How is he ever going to do a good job as the next Guardian?" Caleb muttered quietly to me.

"Caleb, can't you show a little more sensitivity? You're being so abrasive," I griped at him. "We're all worried about Whit, not just you—"

"Um, *worried* doesn't even describe it! It's more like I haven't breathed normally or had one freaking normal heartbeat since you told me what happened." The fear that he had been keeping under control was now plainly visible in his eyes.

"I know. I feel the same way. When I think about what they might do to her—"

"Stop. Don't even bring that up. We have to believe they're going to protect her because they want something from her. Morgan, please be honest with me." He leaned in close and whispered, "Are you sure Gabriel wasn't one of the men with Whitnee? Did you recognize any of them?"

I thought hard and pictured what I had seen. "I couldn't see them very well. But I'm pretty sure there were three of them, and they were all dressed in similar clothes, and it was far upriver...I honestly couldn't tell you if one of them was Gabriel or not. But I believe him when he says it wasn't him."

"So what? We're supposed to just believe that Whit was transported out of here at the same time Gabriel transported in? How would that have worked?" I shook my head in confusion. "I don't understand why you and Whit have always automatically trusted him when he has lied over and over about stuff. Is it because of his looks? Because that would really tick me off—"

"No...maybe some of us are just better at seeing the good in others."

He gave a sigh and then gazed out across the river. "I think I'm going to lose her. If Gabriel isn't the lying, conniving jerk that I want him to be, then he has a right to be with Whitnee. And we know she wants to be with him."

"We don't *know* that, Caleb," I began and had to pause just to think through what I should say.

I had been very careful with both Caleb and Whitnee when it came to my personal opinions about their relationships. Did I know from the start that Claire was just Caleb's attempt at getting over his crush on Whitnee? Yes. Did I have my ideas about who Whitnee truly loved and should be with? Yes. Was I ever going to share that with her? No. She had to figure that out for herself. I just happened to be the best friend who sometimes knew her better than she knew herself.

So I said carefully, "You are one of the most important people in Whit's life. And something has definitely changed between the two of you. Maybe you're not giving yourself enough credit."

"Maybe, but sometimes it sucks to be lumped into the best friend category when I want more... *You* know I've always wanted more." He gave me a pointed look.

"Yeah. I know."

About a year ago I had confronted Caleb about his attraction to Whitnee. At the time he couldn't even admit to himself that he liked her as more than a friend. But it had become obnoxious when the three of us were together. Whitnee would make a comment about a cute guy or tease Caleb innocently about other girls, and he would become sullen and annoyed way too easily over it. I finally figured out his real problem. *He* was in love with *her.* But Whitnee had been clueless, and even Caleb hadn't thought through all of his feelings about it. I didn't want Caleb to get hurt, so I had warned him to slow it down. She just wasn't ready. Whit never found out about that conversation, but I had known for a while now that what Caleb felt for Whitnee was quite different from what he felt for me as his friend.

I gave him a sympathetic look. "I know it was hard to tell her the truth. And even though the timing seems bad—"

"The timing was the worst! Before I even got a real chance, Fabio showed up." He rolled his eyes in Gabriel's direction.

I couldn't help but crack a smile. "Fabio?"

"Yeah, you know—the guy on the cover of all my mom's old romance novels."

"I know who Fabio is." I laughed. "My mom used to gush over him too." I briefly pictured Gabriel posing on the front of a smut novel, and I chuckled a little harder before finally saying, "Look, you can blame *Fabio* all you want, but the truth is that you kissed Claire—"

"And I know Whitnee kissed Gabriel!" he hissed and then dropped his face into his hands, as if he could block the idea out of his head. "Ugh. Everything sucks."

I decided to back off. "Whitnee cares about you too, Caleb. I can't tell you how many times this summer she's admitted that you gave her butterflies in her stomach...You know what a big deal that is to her."

"Really? She said that?"

I nodded with a sly smile. I hoped Whitnee wouldn't mind that I told him.

"Huh..." He half-smiled too. But then he shook his head, and his face grew solemn. "But what should I do, Morgan? Don't you think she'll forget all of that once she's around Gabriel again?"

I bit my lower lip and thought for a moment. I honestly didn't know how to handle that question. Because as sure as I was that Whitnee felt something new for Caleb, I was just as sure she felt something powerful for Gabriel too. "I don't know how things will be...I'm just hoping we can get her back safely right now. But once we do, my best advice is to not be the clingy, insecure guy friend. Let her choose what she wants, even if it means giving her some space."

He sighed heavily and rubbed his forehead with one hand. "I just wish...I mean, when she was taken I was trying to smooth things over with Claire so she wouldn't leave on a bad note. And all I can see in my head now is Whitnee acting all hurt when I walked away with Claire instead of with her. Kills me."

I shut my eyes for a moment. "Yeah. I blew her off in the bathroom and left. She was crying, and she wanted to know why I was crying, and I just couldn't..." I stopped then, suddenly reliving the contents of my evening. That's right...it was a confirmed fact that I had an incurable sickness, and I still hadn't told my friends. I had planned to come back from my phone conversation and tell Whitnee the truth no matter what the news had been…but I'd never gotten the chance.

"You saw her in the bathroom before it happened? Where did you go?"

"I…I went and called my parents." My voice grew shaky and Caleb noticed.

"Wait, why were you crying in the bathroom? Is there something else going on?" He was peering at me as closely as possible in the fading light.

"No," I lied. "I just feel like you do—I wish I would have stayed with her instead of leaving, you know?"

"Morgan, why do I have the feeling there's something you're not telling me? You haven't exactly been acting like yourself lately."

I hesitated. So Whitnee wasn't the only one who had noticed… but was now really a good time to tell Caleb the truth? I knew I could trust him, and I knew that his logical explanations and encouragement might bring me great comfort. Maybe I wanted to hear him tell me that everything would be okay—even if they were just empty words.

But I just couldn't give him any more bad news. My problem could wait until after we found Whitnee. Besides, once I got to the Island my situation might change. I mean, I was a Hydro on the Island…and Hydros had extraordinary healing abilities there.

I shrugged.

"Morgan, you'd tell me if something was wrong, right?" His voice was full of concern, and I felt him press the palm of his hand to my back. His intuition was like a knife cutting through my resolve. I could feel the pressure behind my eyes again as the tears threatened to form.

I took a deep, shaky breath. As I opened my mouth to respond, I felt the ground beneath us start to vibrate slightly, and a powerful gust of wind blew my hair into my face. I couldn't see Caleb's expression, but I heard him suck in a breath.

"It's opening!" Gabriel exclaimed from several feet away.

We scrambled to our feet.

"Hold onto me," Gabriel commanded, holding out an arm.

I grabbed on to him with one hand and felt Caleb grasp my other hand tightly.

"Bye, Ben!" I shouted.

If he called back, I didn't hear him, because the wind had begun its circular rotation around us. An orange mist stole quickly toward us from the tree line, lighting up the ground.

"Here we go," Caleb breathed. "Don't lose me, okay?" He was pressed in closely to my side.

I was suddenly afraid of the pain of falling again. And I leaned into Caleb for reassurance, squeezing my eyes shut. When it felt like an earthquake shook the earth below, we dropped into nothingness.

And though I tried desperately to stay awake, everything went blank as the darkness overcame me.

MOONLIGHT SPRING

The first thing I became aware of at the surface of my consciousness was the perky, laughing sound water makes when it moves quickly over and around natural barriers. I stirred slightly, and everything else came into focus. The pains in my stomach were still there, but other than that I wasn't aware of any new injuries. Maybe I had landed better this time.

I pulled myself weakly into a sitting position only to realize that the lower half of my body was submerged in water. My bag had landed a couple of feet away. As I backed up onto dry ground, I stared in amazement at the beautiful brook that originated from the waterfall to my left.

Incredible...

I had arrived in the exact same place as last time. The water cascading majestically down its rocky path and bubbling right past me spilled into a small spring that might have been deep enough to swim in. Tonight the spring was pristine and sparkly in the silver moonbeams that broke through the trees hovering over this private spot.

The first time I had landed here, I had been unable to enjoy this sight. Now, in the calm of night, I allowed myself a moment to reflect on that first experience. I remembered having no idea where I was and finding one of my arms tucked underneath me, bending my wrist at a painful angle. One confusing minute had gone by before I had heard Amelia's screams nearby. Caleb and I had converged simultaneously at the place where Amelia had been freaking out. He had pointed us in a direction and instructed us to go find Whitnee on the beach; he was still looking for Kevin. That had been chaotic. Frightening. Surreal. But this time was different.

I was here. Again. Back on the White Island—where anything in my imagination seemed possible.

I stood, not really surprised that I had once again become separated from my friends. I leaned down and splashed some of that cool water on my cheeks, just to keep me refreshed. I missed the days when I didn't feel weak or tired all the time...the days when I could actually eat and burn off the energy that food gave me. Now even eating was a chore, because the effects were so horrible. Nobody knew—not even my parents—how badly I had deteriorated over this summer. Whitnee thought I had an eating disorder, and I guess it was kind of true.

I *was* beginning to starve myself, but not for the reasons she believed. Food in my digestive system brought pain. Sometimes I had nightmares that I was chained to a hospital bed by a feeding tube.

I shuddered at that thought, staring absently at the water trickling through my fingers and over the palm of my hand. Everything was going to change now that I was here. And if it didn't...well, there was nothing left to do.

I knew I needed to figure out which direction the Southern Beach was, because Caleb would probably go there first. While I contemplated this, I allowed myself to admire my pretty little oasis in the middle of the jungle. The night was beautiful, warm without being suffocating. I only wished it wasn't marred by the desperate situation we had found ourselves in. I was about to straighten back up when

I heard movement in the foliage around me. I remained hunched down, my senses suddenly alert as I listened.

There was someone moving in the darkness behind me and another person directly across the brook. The crunch of human footsteps was unmistakable.

"Caleb?" I called out. "Gabriel?" The footsteps paused, and all I could hear again was the waterfall.

Not good.

If it had been one of them, they would have called back to me. A rush of adrenaline seized me, and I crept quickly over to my bag. I couldn't use a life force until someone had gifted me...but I had pepper spray.

At the same time I moved, the person in the jungle directly behind me started crashing through the foliage in my direction. I fumbled desperately with the zipper but couldn't get it open. My fingers were practically numb with fear. I kept looking back, but the stranger hadn't appeared yet. So I grabbed the bag and began running, following the edge of the little brook to the pool of water ahead. Maybe I could find a place to hide beyond its perimeter. I knew my lungs would not hold out if I tried running far. Darn my sickness! Darn everything about this situation!

I darted around the spring, trying not to slip over the rocks and uneven ground. Just as I crossed an open patch where the moon was a spotlight on my path, I tossed a quick glance behind me at the dark figure emerging from the trees.

"*Morgan?*" My chaser blurted loudly.

I stopped short from my wild dash. I knew that voice.

"Thomas!" I cried, spinning around.

He made a strange gesture with his hand and then ran effortlessly over to me. I was startled all over again at how blue those eyes of his were even in the moonlight.

"Oh my gosh, I'm so glad it's you..." I took a deep breath, and before I could think, I launched myself at him for what I had intended to be just a friendly greeting hug.

I felt his arms slide completely around me as he hugged me back without hesitation. It felt unexpectedly amazing to have someone hold me for a moment.

"You made it back," he breathed, pulling away but keeping his hands on my shoulders. His eyes danced with genuine excitement as they moved all over my face. "We were looking for you."

"Did you find Caleb? And Gabriel?" I asked quickly.

"Yes, yes. We separated to find you, but I will contact them." As he spoke, he reached into his leather satchel and pulled a metal cube out. I knew that was a zephyra—an Island communication device that used live images of the person you were contacting.

"And Whitnee? What about her?" I searched his face and felt the sinking feeling return at his expression.

He shook his head slowly but didn't speak as he gave his attention to the zephyra. I threw another cautious look back where I had landed, remembering I had heard someone else over there.

"Gabriel," he spoke clearly into the device.

The little paddles inside the cube began spinning and an image of Gabriel finally appeared. He looked stressed.

"I found Morgan," Thomas told him simply. "We are at the spring not far off from the cove."

Gabriel nodded quickly. "We are searching the ruins again. Keep her safe there until we contact you."

And then the zephyra shut down. Thomas redirected his attention on me, this time studying me more seriously.

"Are you okay?" he questioned.

"I...I think so. Um, who else is with you?" I was peering into the darkness again.

Thomas looked around almost forcibly and then glanced back at me. "There is no one else here. Levi was my only companion, and he is with Gabriel and Caleb now."

"Are you sure?"

His eyes moved to the exact spot I had been looking at, and he was quiet for a moment. "I am sure."

I wasn't convinced he was right, but I also never seemed too convinced lately that I was right myself.

"Thomas, please tell me what has been happening here," I begged him. "I'm so confused. Three men showed up and kidnapped Whitnee—"

"Three? I only saw two," Thomas interrupted.

"You saw them?"

He nodded. I was sure there had been three. I grew a little nervous at this inconsistency. Surely Gabriel hadn't been the third kidnapper after all...It would just not make sense.

"Levi and I have been camping out down here waiting for Gabriel to return with Whitnee. He was gone for several hours. While patrolling the area, I heard someone scream for help. Levi and I split up to track the voice. Then I discovered two men who I did not recognize carrying Whitnee through the forest. I followed them as closely as I could without being discovered. But then I lost them somewhere around the Watch Tower ruins. They just...disappeared. It was bizarre, Morgan. We have scoured the area and found no one. That was about three hours ago."

"Wait...three hours ago?"

That puzzled me. So the passage of time stayed the same between the Island and the Mainland this time? Because it had been about three hours since I saw Whitnee on the other side of the river. Maybe time only jumped unpredictably when you transported to the Camp Fusion side...but stayed the same when you transported to the Island?

"So Gabriel used the portal earlier today..." I clarified.

"Yes. But he just informed us when he arrived that she had already been taken by the time he got to the Mainland. He is in quite an emotional upheaval." Then he paused. "How are you? This must have been extremely difficult for you too."

I nodded. "Yeah. I don't understand what's going on. I'm scared."

He placed a hand on my shoulder again, and the sensation of his touch gave me another little adrenaline rush—even in the middle of such horrible circumstances.

Looking fiercely into my eyes he assured me, "We will find her. We have more help than you know." It was a cryptic thing to say, and I was going to ask him to explain, but he continued, "Would you like to sit down for a moment? You look as if you might fall over."

Had I been swaying? Maybe I had...I certainly felt faint. We sat on the ground, and I curled myself up into a ball, tucking my knees up to my chest and wrapping my arms all the way around. Sometimes this position helped with the pain. I desperately wanted to sleep. Fighting off the fatigue had become almost impossible.

"Here." Thomas held out a bottle of Pure Water. In the blue glass bottle the clear liquid sparkled even in the night. I took it from him and drank a little bit, feeling it trace its path through my empty digestive system. It almost burned, which caused my eyes to water immediately.

"Morgan..." Thomas was frowning. "I do not wish to pry into your life if you do not want me to, but you seem very different since I last saw you."

"Some things have changed since I was last here," I answered quietly.

"Please tell me what is wrong. Do you need a HydroHealer? Do not misunderstand me—you are beautiful as ever—but you do not seem well."

"I'm sick," I confessed, staring out at the water. Why was it so hard to tell my two best friends, but now that I sat here on a foreign Island with a guy I barely knew, I suddenly wanted to spill it all? "It's not contagious or anything...but it's something that can't be healed on the Mainland. It makes me hurt—so much that I can't eat or breathe right. I'm tired all the time...And I haven't even told Whitnee or Caleb that...that...things are this bad." I squeezed my eyes shut and dropped my face into my arms, which were resting on my knees. My eyes no longer watered from the pain in my stomach—I was actually crying now. It was ridiculous for me to behave this way in front of Thomas. He probably regretted ever asking. As I hid my face, I willed myself to stop the tears.

But then I felt one of his arms slide across my back and pull me closer to him. His other arm wrapped around me from the other direction, and then I was completely immersed in his comfort. He didn't even say anything at first, but the tender firmness of his embrace freed me to cry openly.

"Should I take you straight to the Healing Center? There are people there, trained people who can—"

"No." I was adamant. "Not until Whitnee is found. I can't—" And my words got lost in another sob.

"What should I do? You know I cannot heal very well." He held me tighter.

"You can't do anything, Thomas." I wanted to say that I was so ready to be done with it that I thought too much about death. But no, I couldn't let him that far into my private darkness. "I'm just s-so tired of the pain...I don't feel anything anymore except the constant pain..."

I felt him pull away from me, and his hands slid down my arms, forcing me out of my balled-up position. He sat up on his knees as his hands found mine. I watched through misty eyes as he pressed our palms together, lacing his tan fingers through my own thin ones.

"Can you feel this?"

A bright blue light began to glow between our hands, and his eyes lit up like blue diamonds as he stared intensely at me. I knew exactly what he was doing. With every last bit of strength in me, I accepted the life force gift.

A cold river of thriving energy surged through me...like a dam had broken. The precious, pure Water flooded every empty space until I felt completely filled up with the cool and relaxed ebb and flow of life force.

When the transfer was complete, I knew my eyes were glowing blue too. Instead of dropping my hands, he held onto them, and we stared at each other. Every time Thomas gifted me, it felt like a transfer of his very soul. The permanent connection to a life force was such an inherent part of a person on this Island. It was the one thing Whitnee experienced that Caleb and I never could quite understand. Gifting, on the other hand, was an intimate experience between two people, almost unexplainable in some ways. But it wasn't permanent—just like the gas tank of my car, it eventually ran low, and I would need a refill. But for now...for now it was like a recharge to my very existence.

"Thank you," I whispered, my face still wet with tears.

"Maybe you could heal yourself now," he suggested.

I hesitated. Whitnee had been the natural Healer of our group. Last time we had been here, I had secretly practiced on myself whenever I felt the stomach cramping coming on. It had worked temporarily, but the symptoms always came back. However, now that I knew what was actually wrong with me, maybe I could use my biology knowledge to completely fix it...Didn't Whitnee say that knowing the functions of the human body had helped her heal others?

Thomas noticed my hesitation and said, "It is much easier to heal yourself than heal another person. Just try it. Come here." He stood up, hauled me to my feet, and placed the Water bottle back in my hands. "Drink all of it and then concentrate on healing your infirmity. Maybe you should get in the spring water too..."

I glanced at him skeptically and then at the spring in front of us.

"At the HydroHealing Center they often completely submerge a patient in a body of Water in order to heal more serious illnesses. The Water works from all angles that way and is easier to control," he explained. "This spring is fresh water."

Well, the lower half of my body was already wet from earlier... and I always loved an excuse to enjoy the water. But getting in with my clothes on was not ideal. I thought of the swimsuit in my bag, but I couldn't exactly change into it here without things getting awkward. Not to mention the fact that I had become extremely insecure about how bony and sickly I looked without clothes on.

I shrugged mentally and kicked off my socks and shoes, even though they were already wet. I guzzled down the entire bottle's contents before stepping into the spring fully clothed. It was surprisingly cool despite the warm evening. Once I reached the middle where the water came up to my ribs, I turned around and saw Thomas wading in behind me. And, *holy beep*, he had taken his tunic off. With his back turned, I could see his Hydrodorian birthmark etched into his right shoulder. The tropical fish with the four zig-zagging waves looked more like a tattoo...And tasteful tattoos on a guy were *sexy*. Now was not the time for Thomas to distract me with his exotic good looks.

When he turned around, I was still staring unapologetically, and he just grinned lightly at my attention. With a dismissive shake of my head, I stood before him and lifted my shirt enough in the water so that my stomach was exposed. Closing my eyes, I rested my hands there and concentrated on pushing the Water's healing properties to my abdomen. I could feel the trickle of the Water life force moving within, and it was so cold that it felt hot as it matched up against the disease growing inside me. At some point in my concentration, I became aware of Thomas's hands pressing down against my bare stomach—transferring his own attempt at healing. After a few minutes, the pain started to loosen and release me, receding like a tide washing away from the shore. Once I could feel nothing but sweet relief, I relaxed and opened my eyes.

Thomas was only a few inches taller than me, and he had moved in close...*really* close. I was more than a little aware that his hands were still on my bare stomach.

"Did it work?"

I paused and thought for a moment, trying to sense the responses of my own body. Something had undoubtedly changed...the tightness and the muscle cramping was gone. My stomach felt more relaxed than it had in a long time. Could it really have been that simple? Was this Island and its life forces powerful enough to heal me just like that?

"I feel...much better," I whispered. A slow, tentative smile broke out on my face.

He smiled back. I liked his white teeth and the way his smile reached his illuminated eyes in the dark. And maybe it was his hands on me or the way the drops of water glistened on his bare chest, or maybe I was just crazy out of my mind over what had just happened...But one minute his eyes were swimming in front of me, and the next his lips were locked onto mine.

I don't even know who initiated it or if we both went in for it at the same time. I just knew that the pressure of his mouth and his kisses were all I wanted in that moment. I loved the feel of his cool skin, and I became really fuzzy when I felt his hands inch from my stomach to grip my waist and pull me in closer. It had been too long since I had felt anything other than my sickness. Now I couldn't get enough of Thomas, becoming way too wrapped up in the sensation of full body contact with him. I was practically clinging to him, not wanting the moment to end. But it had to—before I crossed lines I wasn't willing to cross. I knew myself, knew my weaknesses.

And a blue-eyed boy with a tattoo-like birthmark was one of them.

I broke off the kiss rather abruptly, realizing I had just become one of *those* girls...the kind who was so emotionally unstable that she threw herself at a guy just because he was there to comfort her! I could already hear Whitnee lecturing me...

"I'm sorry. I'm so sorry," I apologized.

"I am not sorry. Why are you?" he said, that boyish grin on his face. His eyes were a little glazed, and I knew that look on a guy's face—had seen it many times.

He was feeling the same thing I was, which was yet another reason we needed to stop. The Water around us seemed to dance in the moonlight, shimmering and rippling in unnatural artistic patterns, and I didn't know which one of us was causing it.

"I just...I shouldn't have done that. I'm just kind of an emotional wreck lately and...I'm sorry."

I had not kissed a guy since my ex-boyfriend at school, and truthfully, he hadn't been that great of a kisser. A little sloppy. Thomas, on the other hand, did not have that problem. And I was starting to wish he did, because with the moonlit setting...the two of us in the Water...it was a little too perfect for a make-out session. I turned like I was going to get out of the spring, but he stopped me.

"Where are you going?"

"Out." I gestured behind me. "We need to dry off in case they call for us."

"Do you regret what just happened?" he asked, looking slightly hurt.

I paused, trying to decide.

In my silence he jumped in. "Do you remember that one night in Hydrodora after the Water games? You were having so much fun and laughing as if you had belonged there in my village your whole life..."

Oh, I remembered that night...very clearly.

He hesitated and then took a step closer to me. "I wanted to kiss you that night...in the Water. And I have been unable to get the thought out of my head since then."

I thought I was surprised at his words until I heard myself say, "Me too."

What? Did I just admit that out loud?

He smiled and reached for me. "We have more time. Do not leave."

I shook my head but couldn't help the smile from spreading across my face. "You know, if you don't behave yourself, a scary water creature might attack you." And I pinched his side in the water.

He jerked away with a laugh.

"Oh! That's right...I forgot how ticklish you were." I laughed at his reaction.

"I would risk battle with a scary water creature for one more kiss from my blue-eyed Traveler," he said, and I felt a little shiver of excitement at his words.

I put a hand to his chest to push him away from me, and with the other hand I sent a ripple across the Water with my life force. Tilting my hand and fingers just right, I manipulated the Water into taking the formation of a huge shark fin swimming in a circle around us. Thomas watched with amusement.

"Even this water creature?" I started singing the tune from *Jaws*. "Dun-dun...Dun-dun..." And I moved the watery version of the fin around quicker as I chanted faster. At the climactic part of the song, I crashed it into Thomas's back, engulfing both of us in a powerful splash. We laughed as the Water dripped down our faces. I don't remember the last time I truly laughed. Probably that night in Hydrodora.

"What the beep was *that*?" He chuckled. At my surprised reaction, he added, "Did I use the *beep* word correctly?"

"Um, that was *perfect*." I nodded, laughing even harder. He remembered our joke! "And that was from *Jaws*! You've never heard of *Jaws*?" I exclaimed. "Well, of course you haven't. It was this really great cheesy movie back in the seventies about a shark who ate people—wait, you know what a shark is, right? Big ugly fish with a mouthful of pointy teeth?"

"Yes, I know what a shark is. What were you chanting?"

"The theme song!" I told him, and he just laughed like I was the biggest dork. "Oh, come on. It scared you, didn't it? Just admit it! Everyone gets scared when that music starts. Especially Whitnee." And saying her name sobered me up.

"Uh..." He rolled his eyes and laughed again. "I will tell you what is scarier than a shark. There are legends about a water beast that stalks the ocean surrounding the Island...like a shark, but much bigger, much faster...and very unfriendly."

He used the Water life force to mimic his words. A ripple on the Water moved near us as if there really was something larger than life beneath the surface.

"They say the beast is as ancient as our Island, but nobody I know has ever actually seen it. According to legend, it attacks the boat of any Dorian who tries to sail away from the Island and capsizes any ship that tries to find the Island."

I watched wide-eyed as he manipulated the Water to look like a huge spiky tail that hit the surface and then went back into the deep. I shivered at his words and at my memories of Will Kinder's drawings...Hadn't he warned us about the water beast that guarded "the tank?"

"Do not look so scared, Morgan." Thomas caught the frightened look on my face. "It is a silly legend, designed to scare people away from ever leaving the Island. It does not really exist."

"What if it did?" I breathed. "What if it was guarding something more than just the Island? What if it protected a tank?"

He looked at me like I was crazy. "I do not understand—"

"Have you ever heard of a tank anywhere on the Island? Like maybe a fish tank or something?" I know I didn't make any sense to him—especially from the look on his face. Truthfully, it didn't make that much sense to me.

"What would be in this tank? Where is it?"

"I don't know," I told him.

"Nor do I." He shrugged. "Never heard of anything like that before."

I was considering what to say about this when I thought I saw somebody move in the jungle behind Thomas. I sucked in a breath.

"What?" He turned to follow my gaze.

"There is somebody there," I whispered, grabbing onto him in fear.

We were silent for a minute as he scanned our surroundings. Finally he turned back around.

"I do not see or hear anyone." And he grinned at me, teasing, "I think *somebody* was a little afraid of the water beast legend."

"I'm not playing around, Thomas. There is somebody out there."

"Well, if there was, maybe they realized they almost interrupted a private moment and they left. Trust me. You have nothing to fear out here," he assured me, and I couldn't understand why he didn't take me seriously.

I was sure I had seen a shadow of a person or something. But I couldn't think about it much longer, because Thomas had that look in his eyes again. And he was leaning down closer.

"And speaking of privacy...We might not have much longer with just the two of us before Gabriel contacts me again..."

Tempting...oh, so tempting. But now I was a little more on edge and remembered that dangerous things were going on around this Island. I was starting to think someone had been watching us. And that creeped me out.

"I would love to stay here with you...but we really should get out."

He sighed heavily. "You are determined to make me behave..."

I took him by the hand and started backing up toward shallower water, pulling him with me. "Thank you for helping me tonight. And for getting my mind off of...everything." I paused and shook my head, still a little shocked that I might have actually just healed myself. "Just so you know...I don't regret kissing you. But that's as far as it goes, Thomas."

His face grew mischievous. "Of course." But then his grip on my hand tightened, and I was pulled back toward him.

As his arms moved to envelop me, he charmed the spring into swirling magically around us, creating a column of Water that stretched high above our heads. And then it was just him and me inside this beautiful private water tunnel with moonlight pouring in from above. I gasped with delight. His eyes were bright as he openly searched my face.

"You're such a show-off." I tried joking, but I sounded breathless.

"I do not know when I will get another chance...so just one more kiss. That is all I ask."

And I didn't argue with him. His lips moved slowly toward mine, and he kissed me very differently from before. It was incredibly romantic and unforgettable to see the tenderness there...to know that right then spending time with me was his priority. I had never begrudged the attention that Whitnee drew everywhere we went on this Island. But something in me took pride in knowing that Thomas wanted this moment with me and only me. And it had nothing to do with being the supposed Pilgrim's best friend.

He did behave by ending the kiss this time, but his arms were still around me. I looked at him seriously and said, "Can I ask you something?"

"Anything."

"Will you keep what happened here tonight a secret? I haven't told my friends about the sickness. If I really am healed, then there is no need for them to ever know. Can you promise not to tell anyone?"

He nodded. "If that is what you want, then yes. I will never say a word. Will you be honest with me if you start feeling pain again?"

"Yes," I agreed.

Then he grazed his fingers softly over my cheek. "You have lovely eyes, Morgan. They seem as deep as the Blue River itself. I have missed you very much."

I actually blushed a little bit, something I didn't normally do. I was about to respond, but my words got lost in a massive gust of Wind that knocked over the Water tunnel, drenching both of us completely. All I could see at the edge of the spring behind me was a bright light that made me feel very exposed there in Thomas's arms.

"Thomas!" A voice barked at us.

"Gabriel?" Thomas sounded annoyed at the interruption.

My heart jumped into my throat when I saw Caleb and Levi flanked on either side of Gabriel. Levi lowered his hands, his eyes silver in the darkness. The bright light was issuing from Gabriel's palms, and he was flushed with annoyance.

Holy. Beep. This looked so bad. Thomas was shirtless, we were in the middle of a spring holding each other, and...Caleb's face said it all.

I had screwed up.

PALLADIUM SPIES

"What were you thinking?" Caleb hissed at me as we trudged through the jungle, the Dorians leading the way. "We've been trying to reach you on the zephyra since Eden contacted us. I just knew something bad had happened to you, Morgan! I had no idea you were just ignoring us so you could make out with Thomas!"

"I'm sorry," I whimpered, trying to keep up with him. "It wasn't like that, though—"

He gave me a seriously annoyed look over his shoulder. "You mean it wasn't how it looked? You weren't really just kissing him inside your little Water world thing?"

I paused. "Okay, it was kind of like that but not the whole time. How long were y'all standing there?" I remembered the strange shadow I had seen in the trees. If it had been one of them, I was going to be pretty angry.

"Not even thirty seconds before Levi blew the Water away to see what was going on." He ran his hands through his hair in a frustrated way. "Morgan, you know I don't butt into your business— I've always tried to like the guys you date. And this isn't even about Thomas—he's a nice guy. But come on!"

"Caleb, please don't be mad at me." I linked my arm with his so that he would at least walk by my side. I felt that fluttery feeling of panic in my chest when someone was upset with me, and it caused me to cast apologetic eyes at my friend. "I said I was sorry."

"Sorry does not take back the last thirty minutes when I thought I'd lost you too! I swear, I feel like I've had at least ten years taken off my life in just one day," he muttered.

I remained quiet while he calmed down. At least he wasn't pulling away from me. I was extremely embarrassed about what had happened—I had no idea what to say or how to defend myself. I couldn't tell Caleb the exact truth...but I wished he knew that making out with Thomas wasn't the only reason we had been in the water and hadn't seen the zephyra going off on the shore.

Finally Caleb said in a softer voice, "I just don't understand how you could do something like that right in the middle of Whitnee's situation. Nothing about you lately makes sense to me, Morgan."

Ouch. That hurt.

My eyes prickled a little at his words. I let go of him, feeling defeated and keeping my gaze on the ground as we hurried along. "Can we please drop it?"

He just sighed in response, but I noticed that he willingly kept pace with me after that. I glanced ahead at Thomas, who I knew was trying to listen in on our conversation. Gabriel had been really upset with him too, but Thomas had remained true to his word and kept my secret. Even though I felt a huge amount of guilt, I couldn't help thinking somewhat defensively that Gabriel was forgetting how his attraction to Whitnee had derailed him in his own duties not too long ago. Yes, Thomas was supposed to be awaiting Gabriel's call and, yes, he had been instructed to remain on guard in the area. But he had also been specifically ordered to protect me. What Thomas had done was not unforgivable nor was it that difficult to understand.

"So tell me again where we're going?" I asked Caleb, trying to change the subject.

"All I know is that Eden contacted Gabriel with the news that a group of suspicious people had been spotted moving north of here...They were most definitely transporting something important, and Eden suspects they have Whitnee. She's staying at the Palladium, where she believes they're heading."

"Why was Eden at the Palladium?"

"She's the one who opened the portal for Gabriel."

I considered that. How would she have been able to get in the Palladium undetected? And she would have needed help opening the portal. Eden could only control the Earth life force. The portal required someone in each tribe to open it—or someone who could control all four life forces. Like Whitnee.

"Well." I sighed. "At least you and Gabriel are working together now."

His face was grim. "Only until I have Whitnee back."

And for the first time I grew a little apprehensive for the moment Whitnee would have to deal with these two guys.

We came to a clearing, and I was not that surprised to see a gigantic bug resting there, waiting for us. Yes, I said a *bug*. It was like a dragonfly; only it was so huge that it could fly with six people in a carrier on its back.

"We're going by thunderfly?" I asked Caleb, observing the peaceful creature.

"Only to a certain point. It will get us there faster." He surveyed the bug and then mumbled, "I wonder if this is Boomer."

The bug shifted on its legs and seemed to look directly at Caleb and me with its big, buggy eyes.

"Yes, it is Boomer," Levi confirmed. "He says hello again, and you can identify him by the circular design on his tail." Levi paused as if listening to a voice in his head.

Caleb and I peered curiously at the thunderfly's tail. Sure enough, there was a strange circular mark—almost like a tie-dye design.

Levi continued, "He is very sorry to hear the news about the *Whitnee Pilgrim*. He offers his loyalty and aid."

Caleb appeared a little skeptical about speaking to the bug, so I said, "Thank you, Boomer. That is nice of you."

Needless to say, I didn't hear a response. But I thought I detected a slight nod from Boomer.

We piled quickly into the carrier, and Thomas made sure he was seated beside me. He seemed to have already recovered from our embarrassing interruption. Maybe guys just got over that stuff faster...or maybe they were proud of it. I don't know. But once I sat down, I became very aware of hunger pains that I hadn't felt in several weeks. This was a good sign. I actually wanted to eat! Once Boomer had started his wings, we were up in the air with the wind blowing through the carrier, and I could feel the cool night air drying my wet clothes—and giving me chills.

Gabriel directed his attention to Thomas. "Tell me again everything that has happened here since you saw Whitnee."

"Well, when the kidnappers arrived and you did not, we"—Thomas gestured to himself and Levi— "decided that something had gone wrong. In that case, we did exactly what you asked. I immediately contacted Eden, and she moved into place for our contingency plan."

"So Eden had no problems getting into the Palladium?"

"Apparently not. Michael saw to it that she and the others made it safely to the portal. Whatever they did must have worked, because you are here now."

Gabriel nodded approvingly. "If Levi was with you, which Aerodorian did Eden take with her?"

"Hannah," Levi answered.

"Hannah?" Gabriel, Caleb, and I all repeated.

"The Hannah who took us to the Nightingale?" I clarified.

"Can she be trusted?" Gabriel asked, and he looked uncomfortable.

"Yes," Levi said.

Gabriel seemed doubtful, and all I could remember was the somewhat nervous housegirl who had been like a personal servant during our stay in Aerodora. Granted, Hannah had been very knowledgeable, but she didn't strike me as the type who could handle espionage activity very well. And it sounded like Eden had to be very sneaky to get into the Palladium unnoticed.

"Eden trusts her," Thomas commented, as if that settled it. "And Eden was adamant that it be girls only in the Palladium. Some kind of plan she had..."

"So who else went with Eden?" Caleb questioned curiously.

"Michael was the Hydro—"

"Is Michael a girl too?" Caleb interrupted Thomas, who looked to Gabriel to explain.

"No. Michael is a servant of mine—he lives at the Palladium," Gabriel said shortly.

"Can he be trusted?" Caleb mimicked Gabriel's question with an equal amount of mistrust.

Gabriel gave Caleb a sharp look. "Yes. He is loyal to me above my own parents."

I could tell it wasn't something he really wanted to talk about, so I jumped in, "And who was the Pyra to go with her?"

That was when Gabriel had a weird reaction. The muscle in his jaw flexed, and his eyes narrowed slightly. He hesitated a moment and then said, "Jezebel."

"And let me tell you, my friend...Eden was not happy about that choice." Thomas shook his head in amusement.

"Eden needs to stop being so judgmental. Jezebel was the only Pyra available that we were sure could be trusted." Gabriel sounded annoyed.

"I think that is Eden's problem. She does not trust her because—" Thomas began.

"I do not care what Eden thinks of Jezebel," Gabriel retorted sharply.

"And Jezebel is...?" Caleb prompted.

"I think I remember you talking about her last time..." I interjected. Gabriel's eyes shifted nervously to me. "Wasn't she the one we were supposed to meet in Pyradora the day we left? I think you told Thomas and the others to find her and stay with her until the storm passed. Am I right?"

"Good memory, Morgan." Thomas smiled, and I felt him give my hand a squeeze. He didn't let go of me after that.

"And what's so special about her again?" Caleb prodded, and I was more than a little curious myself.

Thomas and Levi again remained silent so Gabriel could explain.

"She is just a family friend. But she is a little...well, I do not know the word for it." Gabriel paused.

"Self-absorbed?" Levi supplied at the same time Thomas said, "Crazy?"

I raised my eyebrows at this and felt Thomas snicker beside me.

Gabriel just shook his head. "She is useful for different reasons, and I believe she can be trusted. Again, she is somebody that I feel is more loyal to me than to my parents. And those people are hard to find these days." He grew quiet, and his expression grew sour.

"So do we have a plan in place for when we arrive at the Palladium?" Caleb finally questioned.

"I think that once we confirm these people have Whitnee, we attack the Palladium. If I know my parents, force might be the only way to retrieve her..."

I did not miss the knowing looks that Thomas and Levi exchanged, but Gabriel and Caleb did not seem to notice. I gave my attention to Thomas, trying to question him with my eyes, but he just squeezed my hand again and gave an almost imperceptible shake of his head, as if warning me to stay quiet. What was going on here?

Gabriel continued, "Eden will need to gift Caleb as soon as we arrive. I am assuming Morgan has already been gifted?"

Thomas and I nodded.

We grew quiet then inside the carrier as we each became lost in our own thoughts and anxieties about what would go down in the next few hours. I was scared. Something weird was going on, and the only reason I wasn't questioning it was because everyone seemed to be working for the same goal—rescuing Whitnee from the hands of whoever had her. But the inconsistencies in the story bothered me.

I knew I had seen three men take Whit. Thomas said there were only two.

I was pretty sure I had seen and heard another person in the jungle—twice—when we were at the spring. Thomas was confident I was wrong.

Whitnee and her kidnappers had disappeared around the ruins...but how had they randomly appeared way north of there without anybody seeing them prior to that?

The whole thing reeked of inconsistencies. My thoughts instinctively led me to lean against Thomas, and I felt him shift his weight toward me too. He kept a protective hand looped around mine, and even though I was feeling all kinds of uncertainty inside, he didn't seem worried at all. What had he said earlier...? *We have more help than you know.* What exactly did that mean? I cast a suspicious glance at Gabriel—his handsome face was completely expressionless as we flew through the night sky above the Island.

It wasn't long before Boomer started descending into a dark part of the Island, clearly nowhere near villages. I could see the Palladium lights not too far away. It was hard to miss the huge silver dome that glinted even at night. The Palladium was the formidable residence of the Guardian, Abrianna. And the location of the portal to Camp Fusion was buried deep in the ground below.

We alighted quickly from the carrier, and Boomer quieted his wings. In the cloaking darkness we began our hike across the hills, approaching the Palladium from the southwestern side. I prayed my energy would hold out. Even though I felt ten times better than before, I still remembered how long it had been since I'd eaten. Once we got closer, Gabriel halted our progress and made us get down on the ground.

"I think I see something," he whispered.

Caleb was directly next to him, and I watched the two of them hunker down together and stare out into the night. I lay flat on the ground and felt Thomas's protective hand on my back. When I glanced at him, his eyes were shifting suspiciously in every direction. My heart pounded heavily against the ground.

"There is a wagon—" Caleb reported.

"Coming from the south," Gabriel added. "I only count about four guards—but I cannot see who they are. We could probably overpower them easily."

"We should move closer to the Palladium—we have to stop them before they take her inside!" Caleb agreed.

Without any further conversation, we crept across the field that stretched before us, staying low to the ground.

Gabriel led us to a darker section of the Palladium gates on the west side. "Right here is the only blind spot for Palladium guards," he explained softly, pointing up to the ledge where the guards patrolled. "They have to physically send a guard out here every hour to survey the area. Should anything happen, come back to this spot until you find an escape route." Then he gave the other Dorians his attention. "While we have the opportunity, we should take out the wagon. Keep the guards alive—we need to question them. Caleb will secure Whitnee, since he has no life force and cannot fight."

"I can fight without a life force," Caleb reminded him grimly.

"Even so..." Gabriel told him. "Your job is to get Whitnee away from there no matter what. We will do our best to protect both of you and to keep them distracted." Caleb nodded—he was not going to argue with that assignment.

"What about me?" I asked, wondering where I fit into the plan. I did have access to life force, and I wasn't that bad at using it.

Gabriel instructed, "You stay here with the zephyra and be ready to contact someone for help if we need it."

"But I can help," I protested.

"That is helping, Morgan," Caleb told me and squeezed my shoulder in reassurance.

I wasn't crazy about having to stay behind, but they were right. We did need a lookout, and I knew Caleb would never approve of me engaging in a physical fight. To be honest, I didn't really enjoy that idea either.

"Let's go!" Caleb prompted, and I felt Thomas push his zephyra into my hand.

I watched as the four guys peered back out into the darkness before launching into action.

"Wait..." Gabriel murmured and held out his hand to halt the others.

"What the—?" Caleb sounded confused. "They aren't stopping. Where are they going?"

I tried to see what he was seeing, but he and Gabriel were in the way. Gabriel was silent as he watched.

"Why aren't they coming this way? I thought you said they were going to the Palladium!" Caleb huffed.

"That is what I was told..."

"They're moving straight north. What's north of here?"

"Nothing but mountainside and ocean," Gabriel answered, clearly puzzled by this.

Levi looked back at Thomas, and a look passed between them.

"Gabriel, my friend," Thomas began. "We should contact Eden immediately and tell her of this change. She will know what to do. She has people—"

"No, I refuse to play this game anymore. I am confronting the Guardian directly for answers!" Gabriel announced, opening up his zephyra. Levi grunted, and Thomas vehemently shook his head.

"That is not a good idea, Gabriel," Levi protested, shutting Gabriel's zephyra with one hand. "The Guardian does not know that you have returned. Perhaps it should stay that way for now."

"She was planning to leave me on the Mainland!" Gabriel growled. "The fact that I have caught her in the midst of her deception might prompt her into telling me the truth. I can threaten her—"

"I actually agree. I want answers too, and we know Abrianna has them."

My mouth dropped open slightly. Did Caleb really just agree with Gabriel on something important?

"You should contact Eden first," Thomas insisted.

"Since when was Eden the one in charge around here?" Gabriel muttered angrily, glaring at Thomas and Levi as if they had betrayed him somehow.

Levi frowned. "Since you went through that portal and needed her help."

As if perfectly on cue, Levi's zephyra lit up. The argument paused as everyone stared at it for a second. Levi opened it, and Eden's face appeared. She looked gorgeous—almost like she was going to a dinner party and not doing secret spy stuff in the dark of night. Her long black hair fell in loose curls that framed her face, and she had a white star-shaped flower tucked into one side. I didn't remember Eden wearing makeup the last time we were here because she had that naturally pretty thing going on. But tonight she was all glammed-out.

"Where are you?" She spoke quietly into the zephyra, her eyes moving around the whole time as if she were walking while she talked.

"We are here on the west side of the Palladium," Levi answered her. "We saw a wagon of people moving north just now, passing the Palladium. Four guards that we can see."

"What do you mean they are passing the Palladium? I assumed—"

"Let me speak with her," Gabriel barked and grabbed the zephyra. "Eden, what is happening? Where is the Guardian?"

"I do not know. When we arrived, she was very distracted. Michael moved us to the portal once she excused herself to the Dome. But at some point while we were in that dreadful portal room, she left the Palladium, and we lost her...Ugh—Jezebel, I told you to stay by my side! We need to get out of here."

I heard another female voice complain, "I cannot move that quickly in this dress! It might get damaged!"

"Curse these dresses," Eden muttered, adjusting her own.

And then Hannah's recognizable voice said, "Just hold the skirt like this. Oh! Eden—someone is coming down the hall!"

Eden paused in place and grew quiet. We listened breathlessly to what was happening inside the Palladium. For a moment all we could see was the bodice of Eden's dress in the zephyra—and, yes, that meant a focused shot of her cleavage. I was more impressed by the cut and design of the dress and how well she wore it, but Thomas turned his face away and stifled a laugh. Caleb and Levi stole amused glances at each other while Gabriel rolled his eyes in annoyance.

Men.

I elbowed Thomas to stop laughing and gave the other three a stern look. At least they had all done the gentlemanly thing and looked away...

Finally Eden's face became the focus again. "Sorry. Nobody is there after all. We are about to exit on the east side. Can you meet us?"

"Eden, we are losing that wagon!" Gabriel exclaimed.

"Not for long! We will just need to catch up."

"Which will be impossible in this dress!" Jezebel screeched behind Eden.

Eden's face was so completely annoyed that it was almost comical. She looked Gabriel right in the eyes through the zephyra. "You and I need to have a talk later about your choice in allies...and about that portal! You failed to inform us that it would interrupt our connection with the life forces."

"What? What do you mean?"

"I mean that none of us who powered that device could use a life force until just a few minutes ago. There is something very unnatural about that portal."

We all exchanged confused glances at this news, and my mind returned to those few moments after we had left the Island the first time. Hadn't Whitnee turned on the portal and then had trouble reconnecting with her powers? We had just assumed it was because we were on the Camp Fusion side...What if it was something else about the portal?

"I did not know that would happen..." Gabriel was puzzled, but Eden was too rushed to care.

"Talk later! Get moving!"

"Wait, how did you—" Gabriel called, but Eden's face had already disappeared. He slammed the zephyra shut in frustration.

I knew from experience that Gabriel and Eden butted heads about as much as Whitnee and Caleb did. I am sure it vexed Gabriel to no end to be in Eden's debt and to have to consult her for the next move.

Impatiently, Caleb barked, "Let's go!"

FIREWORKS

Caleb surveyed the guard ledge and then moved forward without waiting for Gabriel. We were close on his heels and attempted to be as covert as possible. After we edged our way around the gates to the other side of the vast Palladium grounds, we found Eden, Hannah, and the girl I assumed was Jezebel in a huddle at the edge of the hill.

"There you are!" Eden called as Gabriel approached her first.

If she had been pretty through the zephyra, she was stunning up close. Even Gabriel seemed to soften a little when he saw her.

But she seemed oblivious to this fact as she briskly greeted us. "I am so glad you made it here." She briefly hugged Caleb and me.

We greeted Hannah, the kind-hearted, fashion-conscious Aerodorian. But then I turned my attention to this Jezebel girl, and I'm sure my eyes widened of their own accord. The girl was *beeping beautiful*—she had the exotic Island features like the rest of them, but she looked more like she belonged on the cover of a magazine back at home. Her skin even seemed paler than the other Dorians. She was tall and thin like a model and had almond-shaped eyes. Even her full lips were well defined in the dark of night. I could only assume she knew her own physical beauty because her dress was kind of...Let's just say my parents would have killed me if I tried to wear a dress like that.

"I wish I had known formal attire was the requirement for chasing kidnappers," Caleb quipped, giving Eden's arm a friendly squeeze. "You girls look nice."

Jezebel sniffed as she peered at Caleb and me. Clearly she was not impressed.

Eden graced Caleb with a sardonic smile. "I have missed your humor, friend. Come here..."

I watched in fascination as they joined hands, and the Earth life force passed from her to him. As soon as she had broken off contact, Caleb's eyes were lit up green.

"Remember how to use that shield? You will need it tonight. They will not give Whitnee up without a fight," Eden warned.

"We must go," Gabriel reminded us impatiently. "The girls will stay here, and we will go retrieve Whitnee."

"I am not staying *here*," Eden replied indignantly.

"Eden, you have a cover to maintain with the Guardian now. We do not need to ruin that. Besides, look at you. That dress...is not practical for fighting."

She crossed her arms. "Dress or no dress, I can still fight. You know that."

They glared at each other until she gave in—almost too easily.

"Very well. We will stay a short distance away from you. But—" She held up a finger to him. "If it looks like you are losing control of the situation, I am intervening."

Gabriel gave a short nod of agreement, and then it hit me that these people I cared about might get hurt through this. I cast a fearful glance at Caleb, wishing he would just stay here with me.

"Be careful, please," I whispered, throwing my arms around him.

"Of course." He hugged me back tightly. "Stay here. Regardless of what happens, promise me you'll avoid danger, please?"

"I think we're already in danger. But I promise. Just get Whitnee back," I pleaded, not wanting to let go of him. That familiar panic was starting to make my heart race again.

He released me too soon, and we both directed our attention to the others.

Eden was speaking heatedly to Gabriel. "Jezebel should go home now. You know it is not wise to let her stay here. Besides, we might need to use her house as a hideout later since we are so far north."

"Gabriel..." Jezebel put on a pouty face at Eden's words, and there was something slightly annoying about the way she said his name.

A bad feeling started nagging at me. She came up to him and looped her arm through his. "I do not wish to go home and miss all the fun."

"Jez." Gabriel sighed and tried extricating himself from her embrace. "Trust me, this will be fun for no one. I would prefer you were not in harm's way. And Eden is right...We might need to hide at your house tonight."

"*Ugh*, very well." She withdrew her hands sharply.

There was a strange closeness there that I had not seen between Gabriel and anyone else but Whitnee. Surely it was not what I was thinking...Gabriel had assured Whitnee he was not romantically involved with anyone on the Island.

Jezebel laid one hand intimately on Gabriel's arm as she passed him. "I will see you tonight."

He was guarded as he gave her one short nod. I watched Jezebel curiously as she departed. She held up one part of her dress daintily in one hand and then snapped her fingers on the other hand so that tiny sparks flashed in the dark.

That was when the guys started to move away. My eyes connected with Thomas's, and he gave me a sort of half-smile and a wave as he backed away. I waved back at him nervously, wondering why it was that boys seemed to relish the idea of a good fight—especially playing the part of a hero.

And so I was left there, a frazzled mess of nerves on the inside and aware of how underdressed and plain I probably looked next to these exotic Island girls. I was still damp from the spring water, and my hair turned wavy when it dried naturally.

"We need to stay close enough to see what is happening," Eden said to Hannah and me as she motioned for us to follow her.

I knew the two of them were constantly surveying our surroundings, but I could only keep my eyes trained on the guys as they moved stealthily in the dark. It was obvious they were trying to take a shortcut that would place them in the direct path of the wagon. But since nobody seemed to know where the wagon was heading, it was risky business. The White Mountain, which was really a dormant volcano, rose up like a black tower stretching toward the sky on my right. The wagon was following a twisting, chalky path in the moonlight. The trail appeared to wind through steeper hills and rocky territory the closer it moved to the mountain. But then my vision was limited beyond that. Somewhere in the distance was the ocean. So where exactly was the wagon going? To the ocean or to an unknown location on this side of the mountain?

As we crept, I finally asked, "Why are y'all so dressed up?"

Hannah smiled. "These dresses are lovely, are they not? I designed them!"

Eden gave me a wry look. "I am sure it was obvious last time you were here that the Guardian appreciates finer things. That was our key into the Palladium tonight. We made a special delivery."

"Custom-designed dress for the Guardian and a new perfume Eden has been working on," Hannah explained. "It was the perfect reason to show up for a visit."

"Oh...well, that was smart," I agreed, as we traipsed along in the dark. "And what was Jezebel's excuse for being there?"

Eden groaned. "We needed a Pyra for the portal, and the Guardian adores Jezebel. Her role was simply to charm Abrianna into thinking our visit was innocent."

"And she did a good job!" Hannah remarked.

"Too good of a job...which is why I do not trust her." Eden's voice sounded annoyed again in the darkness.

"Yes, but she took a personal risk by helping us tonight. If the Guardian found out what we did, I am positive Jezebel would no longer be her little pet," Hannah pointed out.

"What exactly is Jezebel's relationship to Gabriel?" I worried maybe I was being too nosy, but if there was something going on there, I had to look out for my best friend.

"Nobody really knows. Gabriel's family has always been close to Jezebel's family." Eden shrugged. "Gabriel and Jezebel grew up together too."

"Gabriel is so complicated..." Hannah sighed, and I remembered the suspicions Whitnee and I had formulated that Hannah had a mad crush on Gabriel.

"He is *not* complicated." Eden dismissed Hannah's remark with a flip of her hand. "I have no trouble reading those emotions of his. I just find them exhausting."

"That is because you have known each other so long...and I do wish I had those Geo instincts about people," Hannah said wistfully.

"Hannah, how exactly did you get involved with all of this?" I wanted to know. I still had a hard time picturing Hannah, who had drawn our bath water and picked out our clothes, capable of hurting a fly.

"Because Hannah is in Ezekiel's circle of trust," Eden answered. "And she is extremely gifted and highly trained with the Wind life force. You do not want to be on the receiving end of her attacks. Trust me." And Eden turned around to grin knowingly at Hannah.

"Really?" I was shocked, almost forgetting to keep walking.

"Well, of course." Hannah laughed at my reaction. "You did not believe Ezekiel would allow just anyone to care for Whitnee in

Aerodora, did you? He would never have allowed you to venture to the Nightingale that night without highly trained protectors. Believe me, I am more than just a housegirl."

"I guess we just didn't think about that," I said, considering the validity of her statement. I suppose it made sense—we had thought Ezekiel just considered Whitnee the Pilgrim last time we were here, which would have been a significant enough reason for him to take extreme measures in protecting her. But we had since learned that he knew all along Whitnee was his granddaughter and had been unable to speak the truth about it. I am sure that just reinforced his protective nature. Of course he would have offered her the best of everything while she was here.

"Look!" Eden warned, and we froze. "They are in position."

The three of us were at the top of one of the hills overlooking the mysterious wagon as it shifted directions into yet another small valley that lay between us and the mountainous volcano. I could barely make out three figures who by pure luck were now in the perfect place to attack. Where was the fourth guy? And which one was he? I held my breath. It was now or never. But then one of the men in the back of the wagon shouted to another and seemed to point right in the direction of the guys. The guards in the wagon were all peering that direction now.

"Do they see them...?" I fretted, and Eden groaned.

"I guess he needs my help after all. Hope they are ready," she muttered. She knelt down in her dress, pressed both hands to the ground, and whispered something. When she stood up, her eyes were vivid green in the dark. With a stretched voice, she said, "That wagon is pulled by hipposoles. They are peaceful Earth creatures and sensitive to the life force. I sent them a *danger* message—"

She stopped explaining because chaos broke loose below, starting with the hipposoles, who bucked and reared and snarled, pitching the wagon sharply. I looked on with wonder and dread at the scene unfolding.

A line of Fire snaked viciously around the wagon, snapping and hissing at those inside its boundaries. By the light of the Fire I could actually see what was happening. There was a lifeless, blanketed bundle about the size of a person lying on the floor of the wagon. Two guys immediately ducked down to protect the bundle—which my racing mind assumed was an unconscious Whitnee. A green Earth shield went up over her. One man stood up, and his hands became like blowtorches shooting flames back into the darkness. Another guy jumped off the wagon and began extinguishing the boundary of Fire with Water sprays that sent up steam.

Suddenly, a piece of wood shot out of the dark and hit the Pyra in the back, reminding me of a skill Levi had taught Whitnee. The Pyra stumbled at the impact, and then Levi tackled him and knocked him off the wagon. They were now out of my line of vision, but I was distracted from their scuffle when a whip corded of pure Fire wrapped around the Hydro on the other side. Out of the blackness of night came Gabriel. However, the Hydro used a technique I recognized as the Mist. His body became like a Water sprinkler, and the Fire cord disintegrated around him. That was when Gabriel turned to his own fists for attack.

I was scanning desperately for Thomas and Caleb when a thick fog began to spread over the entire area, creating more confusion for everyone down there. It was difficult to see with the unnatural cloud hanging over the site. This couldn't be good.

"Should we go help?" I asked in a high-pitched voice.

"Not yet..." Eden answered slowly. "Thomas is producing a Fog. Very smart, especially if Levi has the Pyra under control. He cannot burn through it. Now if one of them is Aerodorian, we might have a prob—"

She was interrupted by a small whirlwind that sucked up Thomas's fog and cleared the air. Unfortunately, that revealed a startled Caleb who was poised to launch himself into the back of the wagon. Instead he came face to face with the angry Aerodorian.

"Oh no!" I screeched, clapping my hand to my mouth.

Without a word or sound from beside me, Hannah flung something long and silvery-violet at the Aero about to attack Caleb. It almost looked like a sword that glinted in the moonlight on its way down. With perfect aim, it hit the Aero straight in the chest with a bright flash like a camera…and he fell backward and over the side of the wagon.

I turned wide eyes on Hannah.

"I could not help myself." She shrugged innocently when she caught my gaze. Her eyes were a silver color. "Lightning arrows are my favorite."

Lightning?! I think I visibly shivered and made a mental note to never get on Hannah's bad side.

Caleb instinctively used his Earth shield, but he did not remain under it for long once he realized there was just one guy left in the wagon—the one who still guarded himself and Whitnee underneath an identical shield.

"How can he get her out?" I wondered aloud, my hands pressed to my face as I watched.

But Eden was searching for something—she kept darting glances all around us. That was when a few dark shadows came running past us, shooting at the wagon with the palms of their hands.

"Caleb!" I screamed without thinking.

Magical weapons bathed in blue, red, green, and purple light ricocheted everywhere with the presence of these new fighters. I jumped up.

Eden grabbed my arm. "They are on our side!"

The hipposoles were going nuts with all the activity and jerked forward unexpectedly, tipping the wagon sideways. I watched with horror as Caleb, the guard, and Whitnee toppled to the ground. The guard's Earth shield went down with it, and the blanket slipped off, revealing that it really was Whit beneath. But it was a disturbing sight to watch her fall like dead weight.

Caleb recovered quickly and did something I'd never seen him do—he held out his hands in a strange pose with one in front of the other and then released a green force that boomed like a shotgun. It smacked the man in the stomach, and he doubled over. Before the guard could recover, another light—blue this time—pierced his side. That was when Thomas launched himself at a high speed directly at the man, tackling him to the ground.

Caleb took advantage of the distraction and scooped Whitnee off the ground. When he began running, Eden could hold me back no longer. I took off sprinting down the hill.

Distantly, I heard my name but ignored it. I could only see my two best friends—and the possibility that they might not escape the rebounding life force attacks behind them. Caleb had Whitnee cradled in both arms as he ran as fast as he could. I reached his side and ran along with him.

"Watch behind us!" he panted, and I repeatedly threw frightened looks back at the wagon.

But then there was a massive explosion that sent Caleb, Whitnee, and me flying forward and landing hard on the ground. The green light of Caleb's shield flashed over Whitnee's motionless body, protecting her fall. My breath was completely knocked out of me when I hit the earth, and in that space of time when my body was reeling from the shock I rolled over and blinked up at the star-lit sky above me. The strangest things came into focus at that point...I really believed in that moment that I was staring at the Big Dipper constellation above me...the only constellation I actually could recognize on my own. And it felt very odd to see something so familiar when I knew I was on an untraceable landmass somewhere in the world.

The stench of something burning hit me, and my eyes watered. My view of the sky became obstructed by thick, black smoke. I sat up, coughing, and looked back in surprise.

For a scary moment all I could see were bright orange flames and billows of smoke. There was no human movement visible. The wagon had been completely obliterated, and wooden pieces like mulch rained down in what seemed like slow motion. I was vaguely aware of the hipposoles trotting away from the scene. What had just happened?

"*Jezebel!*" Eden screamed in anger on her way down the hill.

Hannah was close behind, blowing away the smoke. With relief I saw Thomas stand slowly, coughing. He immediately started dousing the flames with Water. I scanned all around me. People were starting to move out from the debris and smoke. I could hear different orders shouted.

"Secure him with armbands—"

"Do not let him move!"

"We have an injury over here..."

Levi eventually came into my sight, aiding the others in putting out the Fire. But Gabriel...Where was Gabriel? I felt trapped inside this surreal moment where nothing that happened even seemed real. I was like an outside observer in the middle of the chaos. Nobody even seemed to notice me as I stumbled closer to the destruction. Still lying on the ground behind me was Caleb, who was brushing Whitnee's hair from her face with shaky hands, his eyes and mind focused only on her, his mouth whispering things to her I could not understand. She was still unconscious. The people who had emerged to help at the end of the fight were subduing the prisoners.

"Jezebel, you could have killed all of them! That was completely foolish of you!" Eden was screaming at the beautiful girl standing victoriously at the top of the hill with golden eyes and golden hands in the dark.

When had Jezebel come back? Had *she* been the one to blow up the wagon?

"Caleb, you have Whitnee? Good. Gabriel!" Eden called out in frustration, and when there was no response, everyone looked around expectantly. "Where is Gabriel?"

Nobody knew.

Eden moved closer to the damage, growing more desperate. I found myself following her, even though she seemed blind to my presence. She had the strange look of a tragic damsel searching blindly for her lost love. Finally, she came to a heap on the ground several feet away.

She dropped to the ground and cradled his face with her hands. "Gabriel? Can you hear me?" Her voice had this instantaneous tenderness to it that I had never heard before.

Gabriel did not stir.

"I need help over here!" She turned, and that was the first time she spotted me standing there. "Morgan, come quickly!"

I moved to her side, wondering what in the world I could do to help. "What's wrong with him?"

"I do not know..."

It was clear that Gabriel was breathing, but he certainly was not moving.

"He seems to have been rendered unconscious. Can you help him?" Her green eyes connected with mine, and I tried to read the emotion there. "Maybe you could wake him up with a splash?"

"Can I do that without a bottle of Water?"

"Yes, as long as you have Water in your system. We need to leave here immediately, and I need him to be okay...Everything depends on...I swear, I am going to strangle that reckless Pyra girl..." She stopped blabbering and focused her attention back on his face.

I concentrated on the movement of Water within my body and built up the pressure in my hands lightly, like a garden hose that was being pinched. Then I released it and splashed the cold Water on Gabriel's face and chest.

He stirred, and his eyes flickered open. Eden stretched a gentle hand toward his face and gave a sigh of relief, but the next thing I knew Jezebel was at our side throwing her scantily clad body practically on top of Gabriel. She was crying, but in a very dainty way where tears just pooled in her eyes without dropping and marring her perfect face.

"Gabriel!" she cried. "I am so sorry! I was only trying to help you!"

He sat up in confusion. And once it was obvious that Jezebel was taking over the role of emotional wreck, Eden rose to a standing position.

Gabriel ignored Jezebel and gazed up at Eden. "Where is Whitnee?" were his first words.

Jezebel's sobbing immediately paused as if turned off by a switch.

I watched Eden become completely expressionless as she replied robotically, "She is in our possession now. Prisoners are secured. We need to leave immediately."

"We will go to my house!" Jezebel declared, then she ran her hands over Gabriel's chest as she informed him, "I already have my servants preparing food and beds."

Eden just gave a brief nod and walked away, the swish of her dress leaving behind the faint scent of sweet flowers.

"Eden, wait!" Gabriel called, trying to maneuver himself out of Jezebel's arms. "Jez, give me a moment, please."

I began backing away, trying to ignore all the weird intuitions I was having. I wanted to find Caleb and Whitnee again anyway. Surely Whit had woken up by now.

Out of the corner of my eye, I saw Gabriel grab Eden by the arm and spin her around to face him. "You have a lot of explaining to do here."

"So do you," she replied coldly.

"Who are all of these people working with you? How did you know when the wagon was spotted? You need to start being honest with me...now."

She did not seem moved by his forcefulness. "I will explain when we are in a safe place. For now we need to focus on getting away from here before your parents find out that we have Whitnee."

I didn't find out what his response would have been, because Caleb called out to us from across the destruction. He sounded so uncertain and scared at the same time that I bolted his direction without another thought. He was still in the same spot hunched over Whitnee, who lay still in his arms.

But the horrified way he was staring at her sent chills down my spine.

"She won't wake up," he choked. "They did something to her! Look!"

When I fell down beside him, I knew exactly what he meant. She wasn't breathing. Her skin had taken on a greenish hue that seemed magnified against her bright pink outfit. Flashes of Carrie's lifeless body whirled through my mind. My stomach clenched as the cold grip of experience confirmed what I was seeing.

Caleb was holding a dead body.

REBIRTHING

There are moments in time where it seems the whole world stops spinning just for you—as if it is your destiny to be lost in that one beautiful stroke of the clock forever. Like a first kiss...when your mind floats in an abyss of happiness, basking in the warmth of a new memory.

This was *not* one of those times.

I now knew that there were other moments—dark and disturbing moments—when time itself was lost. And waking up from nothingness was worse than waking up from a totally realistic nightmare. It was like being born for the first time. Before that moment of awareness, there was simply...nothing.

"Oh, Whitnee...please, please wake up!" a girl sobbed, her voice echoing through a tunnel. There was a mournful tone to her voice, as if she didn't really believe her pleas were going anywhere.

There was another voice—a male. "How long is it supposed to take?" This voice was filled with a desperate and persistent hope, and it stirred something within me as it drifted through the tunnel.

At his words, a slew of voices echoed in the empty space—none of which I recognized or understood.

One minute I had no thought, no mass, no awareness, and the next minute I was slammed into a strange reality. My body was stiff, and my limbs were stretched tight like invisible strings were attached and pulling on them. My head was thrown backward, and in that moment where my eyes saw nothing but bright light, I came to life. My heart took its first beat, and I sucked in one immense breath. It came through my dry throat like a choking wheeze. The rest of my body followed suit.

It was an agonizing experience. The blood pumping through my veins carried the lick of torturous pain with every pulse, and my heart hammered my chest so hard that it felt bruised. My lungs wanted to burst with every short intake of air. I know I screamed once breath became possible. There was a person with a familiar scent—with strong arms holding me still—and I instinctively turned my face into his torso and muffled my screams there. I gripped his shirt tightly until my fingers were numb.

"Baby, it's okay…You're okay. Just breathe," he coached.

There were other people, other sounds around us, but I just focused on the tender and vaguely familiar lilt of his voice as he soothed me.

"What's happening to her?" He directed the question away from me.

"She is waking up. Once her body finishes the reset, the pain will fade. Give it another minute." This voice I did not recognize, but I was glad to know that whatever was happening to me would be over soon.

I panted and sweated, enduring the throbbing as it coursed through my entire body—even down to my toes. And then it began to fade, and I felt my muscles relax. The last thing I did was unclench my fists from his shirt.

Then the blinding light took shape, and I was in a room with several different people watching me closely—none of whom I recognized immediately. In fact, I could not remember a thing… not one thing before this moment. And that terrified me more than the strange, curious faces peering back at me. Why was I here? *Where* was here? And with an eerie detachment, I wondered…

Who am I?

"How do you feel?"

I peered up at the green-eyed boy who spoke to me, whose arms were still around me. I knew then that I *must* have had some kind of existence before now, because even though no details or images came to my mind, I became very aware of emotions.

For example, the boy—the one with the familiar scent and comforting voice—I knew I trusted him. I studied his signs of relief, noted the attractive way his hair framed his face, the slash of a scar across his right eyebrow. He stared back at me with such intimacy I had to assume we had known each other longer than just these few minutes of torture.

"Whit?" A soft and broken girl beside me placed her hand on my arm.

She had vividly blue eyes that seemed unable to believe what she was seeing. Her cheeks seemed sunken in and held the wet tracks of many tears. She looked pale, sickly, and incredibly sad. I felt a bond of trust with her too. In fact, a chord of protectiveness unexpectedly ran through me. I felt like there was something I needed to remember about her…something that made me feel anxious.

She lowered her face to my arm and clung to me tightly, whispering, "Thank you, God." Her thin shoulders jerked as her sobs slowed.

And then my eyes scanned the rest of the room for familiarity. There were many faces I just did not recognize…all had browner complexions with rich, dark hair. A few girls dressed very fancy… a few men who looked unshaven and rough. And then there was one standing a few feet away that caused another pang of emotion. He studied me from a distance with piercing eyes. I felt a dramatic assault on my stomach, as if I couldn't breathe again.

He was tall with powerful arms crossed over his chest. And he was fiercely beautiful. My heart began racing again just as it had

finally settled. But there was something dangerous about him…
Perhaps there was something I wasn't sure I wanted to remember.
He made no moves to come closer, so I finally tore my eyes away
to gaze back at the handsome green-eyed boy by my side.

I tried to sit up, so he gently lifted me into a sitting position.
Someone else—one of the unshaved, rough-looking men with
vibrant green eyes—pressed a bottle into my hand and instructed
me to drink. I didn't question him, as I was very aware of my
parched throat.

"Do you remember anything that has happened to you?" the
gruff man questioned.

I stared at him wide-eyed and shook my head. "Wh-where
am I?"

A stunning girl in a sparkling green dress spoke up from behind
him. "You are at a house in Pyradora where it is safe. What *do* you
remember before now?"

I noticed the contrast between the two of them, wondering
curiously when the last time the man had showered. He looked
like he'd been sleeping in the grass.

"Nothing…" I whispered, my eyes flicking warily around the
room again.

"What do you mean, nothing? What about what happened at
Camp Fusion?" the boy asked with a frown, still keeping a protective arm around me.

I stared back at him in confusion.

"Another temporary side effect. The memory is usually the last
thing to return," the man explained, and then he turned back to
me. "I am Seth, an Herbal Technician for the Geodorians. You
were drugged with a rare concoction designed to put your body
into a temporary state of death. Just as you had to restart physically, your mind is still restarting. Your memories will come back
in pieces within the next twenty-four hours."

I didn't respond as I took this in. What a bizarre explanation.
And what were Geodorians? They sounded like aliens.

217

"Are you sure that's all they did? She's acting weird..." the blue-eyed girl asked him softly.

"She has no memory." Seth shrugged as if that explained everything.

"No memory of what happened or no memory at all?" The girl's voice wavered as she looked into my face like she expected me to say something.

I slowly shook my head at her. "I...I don't know what's going on. I do know you, right?"

Her face fell at my words, and the boy next to me said angrily, "Did they already take them from her? What if they permanently messed her up?"

Took them from me? What did he mean?

"Please..." I begged fearfully. "I don't even remember who I am. Somebody explain to me what's happening. Who are you?"

And I couldn't help glancing at the mysterious guy across the room who took my breath away. He had a scowl on his face and appeared impatient about something.

"You're Whitnee...and I'm Caleb. And this is Morgan..." Caleb said slowly, watching my face for signs of recognition.

And, yes...I did recognize my name. *Whitnee*. I knew my name! "And...we're friends, aren't we?" I said to Caleb and Morgan.

Though I had no specific memories, I felt a connection with both of them. And they clearly felt a closeness to me as evidenced by the lack of personal space at the moment.

Morgan nodded and smiled through her tears. "Yes, the best of friends," she said, and Caleb nodded with less enthusiasm.

At that moment one of the dressy girls, the one in purple, interrupted. "Whitnee, I am Hannah. Will you come with Morgan and me back to a bedroom where we can wash up and change your clothes? We will answer all of your questions there."

I looked down at myself and realized I was dirty, and my clothes were torn. There were suspicious bruises around my wrists where the skin was raw. This frightened me even more. What had happened to me?

"Yes, that is a good idea," the girl in green agreed. She seemed distracted, but I also decided she was the one in charge when she started giving commands. "Jezebel, perhaps you can have some food brought out for everyone?"

A girl in a red dress that left little to the imagination nodded lazily and gave me one last curious look before disappearing.

"The rest of you should refresh yourselves as well. It might be a long night. Seth, is there anything you can give her to stimulate the memory? We need to know *tonight* what she remembers."

Seth gave her a grim look. "Doubtful. But let me see what I can create." He grabbed the leather trunk full of small bottles and tubes and moved to the table to work.

I took a brief moment to look around the room—it seemed to be someone's expansive living room, filled with lots of abstract paintings and oddly-shaped statues. Combine that with the vaulted ceilings, and it almost felt like a foreign museum. The light in the room was bright but cast itself in shimmery patterns, highlighting perfectly the red, gold, and white decoration. I was sitting on an overstuffed, tall-backed white couch, which I hoped I hadn't tarnished in my filthy state.

Caleb's arm reached around and pulled me close. "Everything will be okay," he whispered in my ear.

I decided I really did like him—even if I didn't remember all the reasons why. And there was something about his scent when he leaned in that close that sparked something in my stomach.

The girl in the green dress then turned her attention on the silent, brooding guy a short distance away who still had not moved or taken his eyes off me. "Gabriel," she called. "We need to handle the prisoners out back."

Gabriel...Yes, there was something about that name too...but what did I remember about it? I glanced sideways at him, trying to decipher my feelings.

"Caleb, perhaps you would like to go with us? There is nothing more you can do for Whitnee right now," the girl said gently.

Caleb gave a sigh and looked straight into my face. "I don't want to leave you…not when I just got you back."

I stared back at him, not sure what to say. I actually felt a little jolt of panic about him leaving me too. "Are you going far?" I questioned in a pathetically weak voice.

"No…I will still be here on the property. Morgan will take care of you though, while I'm out back." And he turned to the sad blue-eyed girl and helped her to her feet. I watched him embrace her quickly and ask, "You okay?"

She nodded and patted his back. Watching the apparent closeness between the two of them filled me with warmth, despite my circumstances. These two were allies…friends.

Both Caleb and the silent Gabriel appeared reluctant to leave but finally moved to the door with the girl. I watched helplessly as they disappeared from sight. And then all I felt was disappointment, but I wasn't sure for whom or where it came from…the cute boy I trusted? Or the mysterious guy who did not speak one word to me?

"Whitnee?" Morgan's voice broke through my thoughts. She followed where my gaze had been and then gave me a half-smile. There was something very familiar about that smile. "Come on. I'll explain what I can…" She held out her hand and helped me to my feet. "And we need to take a look at that busted lip of yours."

I pressed my fingers to my lip and was surprised to find it swollen and painful. What exactly did I look like? I couldn't even remember my own reflection. This body didn't even seem like my own. Nothing felt right…except my name.

FIRST IMPRESSIONS...ALL OVER AGAIN

I soaked awkwardly in a tub of hot water that smelled like lavender. Hannah had insisted it was my favorite scent "last time I was here." I was too overwhelmed to care. The bubbles in the water covered up my body, but it was still strange to have others in the room with me in such a vulnerable state. Morgan had immediately dived into my hair, pulling out tangles. At one point I thought I saw pink clumps in the mess, but she said they were extensions, not my real hair. I listened as the two girls filled my blank mind up with all that had been happening while I was apparently knocked out by a powerful drug. Most of what they said did not make sense to me, but I listened attentively, hoping for it to spark some memories.

"I was kidnapped?" I think my voice sounded unnaturally high-pitched and fearful when I heard that piece of news.

Morgan nodded. "Yes, I saw them take you through the portal."

"Well, what did they do to me besides drugging me? I mean... I can't remember anything." I started shaking all over at the unknown. I hadn't missed the random bruises that had started popping up on my body, not to mention the achiness I felt in my muscles. What *if* they had done something horrible to me that I could not remember? I saw Morgan and Hannah exchange worried glances.

"Relax, Whit." Morgan hid her expression as she spoke calmly. "You're safe now...I don't think there was nearly enough time for anything to happen to you. They seemed to be rushing you to a particular destination instead."

"Like where?" I asked.

"We don't know yet. But I'm sure we'll figure it out soon," Morgan assured me.

"Well, why did they drug me with that stuff?"

Morgan looked to Hannah with a raise of her eyebrows.

Hannah said, "From what Eden and Seth said, that kind of drug is a dangerous concoction that is illegal to use here on the Island. We are fortunate to have Seth on our side—he is very learned in such dark experiments. He used to work exclusively for the Guardian, but he left her ranks a few years ago. That was the only way we knew you were not...Well, he was the one who recognized the effects of the drug, instead of mistaking you for..."

"Dead," Morgan finished with a shudder. "That's interesting that he worked for the Guardian before..."

I didn't know why that was so interesting to her. I didn't even know who the Guardian was.

"Yes, that is why Gabriel was a little surprised when Seth appeared." She paused as if considering something and then directed her attention back to me. "As for *why* they drugged you... It was probably the best way to subdue your powers, since the armbands affect you so negatively."

"M-my *powers*?" I was confused. "What powers?"

Morgan sighed. "You can manipulate certain life forces. You know, Wind, Fire, Earth, Water...You name it, you've got the power to use it. You're kind of the most powerful person on this Island, assuming they didn't take them from you..."

I stared at her incredulously, wondering if she was joking. But both girls looked serious. "I'm so confused." I shut my eyes for a moment.

"I think I will go borrow some of Jezebel's clothes for her." Hannah gave Morgan a knowing look. "Maybe you two need to be alone for a moment."

Morgan nodded, and Hannah left the room.

When it was just Morgan and me, I decided I was ready to get out of the water. I stepped out into a huge blanket-like towel and wrapped it completely around myself before settling weakly onto a nearby sofa chair.

"I'm sorry...I just don't remember anything. This is so weird," I mumbled to Morgan, who cleaned up around us, tossing me curious glances every so often.

"You really don't remember a thing? Not even the last time you saw me...at Camp Fusion?"

I shook my head in frustration. "No...Why? Is there something specific I should remember?"

She grunted. "There's a lot you should remember. But don't try too hard right now. Seth is working on making something to help you."

"Who exactly is Seth? Who are all these people? They're obviously very different from you and me," I commented.

"Yes, they are," she agreed before plopping down on the sofa chair next to me.

"Tell me more about Gabriel...He seems familiar," I prompted her.

She immediately cast intuitive eyes on me. "What seems familiar about him?"

"I don't know...I have very mixed feelings around him. Do I know him very well?"

I was surprised when she smirked and shook her head, as if pitying me. "Yeah, you know him...probably better than the rest of us."

"Yet he didn't speak to me back there..." I trailed off, remembering that disappointing feeling.

"Well, there was a lot going on, and he's in the middle of being in charge."

"Really? I thought that girl Eden was in charge," I told her honestly.

"Is that how it seemed...?" Morgan mumbled as if thinking this idea over. Then she gave me another cryptic smile. "Don't worry about Gabriel. I'm sure there will be time soon when you will have a chance to talk with him. But I wouldn't rush that conversation until you remember *everything*."

I felt myself frowning. "That sounds ominous. At least I trust you and...Caleb. He seems very, um, concerned about me. Is he always like that?"

She nodded again, almost as if she was enjoying my commentary. "Yeah, Caleb is pretty protective. And you have way more memories with him than with Gabriel."

"Is he..." I paused, not sure if I should ask this or just wait till I remembered. "There was something about the way he held me and talked to me and about the way I felt...Is Caleb my boyfriend or something?"

She gave kind of a strange sputter, almost like a laugh she was trying to stifle. "Umm...that's a complicated question. Technically, no."

"Huh." I felt a slight disappointment at her words. "Sure would love to get all those memories back soon..." I sighed, cuddling into my towel.

Before Morgan could respond, there was a knock at the door. She jumped up to answer, and I shrank back. I could hear her at the door talking to a male voice I did not recognize.

"Are you girls okay?" he asked from the other side where I couldn't see him.

"Of course. How about you? Your leg?" she questioned back softly.

"It is fine now." There was a pause before I heard him whisper, "Does Whitnee remember anything yet?"

She glanced back at me before shaking her head.

"We cannot get any information out of those guards that were with her. We really need to know what happened...if they already took her life forces or not..."

"We can't rush her. She's been through a trauma and doesn't even really remember me or Caleb. Surely Gabriel has ways of making those guards talk..." she murmured.

"You would not want to know," he responded with a sigh. "He is still out there with them. I just wanted to check on you. Is your...I mean, are you still feeling better? You promise you are okay?"

"Yes, I promise. Thank you for asking."

There was a pause and a shuffling...like maybe he had hugged her or something?

"Come out as quickly as you can. Jezebel's servants prepared a meal. You need to eat."

"Okay, we will. Tell Caleb and the others that Whitnee is fine—nothing appears to be seriously wrong with her besides the memory loss."

He must have nodded or given a sign of affirmation before she shut the door. When she turned around, there was a flush to her face that hadn't been there before.

"Who was that?" I asked, surveying her change in expression.

"Thomas. He's a Hydrodorian," she answered casually.

"Whatever that is...Is he your boyfriend?"

Morgan stared at me for a second before smiling with slight exasperation. "You're killing me with the questions. I need your memory back, because I need my best friend back!" And when there was nothing left to do or say about this ridiculous situation, she just started laughing and sighed. "I'm so glad you're okay."

She hugged me, and I couldn't help grinning back at the sincerity in her eyes.

I stared back at the girl. Pale hair hung loose and straight down past her shoulders. Pink streaks peeked through the blonde layers. Her grayish eyes had dark circles beneath them as they moved restlessly. Her cheeks had a bit of a flush to them, and her lower lip was still cracked and bruised on one side. She looked familiar, but more like in a déjà-vu kind of way.

Strange to look at yourself in the mirror and not know it's you.

"Whitnee, you ready for some food?" Morgan's reflection appeared behind mine.

She had cleaned up and changed into a soft blue dress. I tore my gaze away from myself after a moment and nodded slightly. I was wearing a pink tunic-style dress that was loose in the arms and tight across the top. In fact, it was a little too low-cut for me in the bodice. Or at least it felt uncomfortably low for me... Maybe I dressed like this all the time and just didn't remember. Hannah had said it belonged to Jezebel, but she thought it would look good on me. The dress came to right above my knees. I could only imagine how short it was on the tall, slender Jezebel. But I wouldn't complain when someone else was offering me their own clothing and hospitality.

"Love the dress!" Morgan exclaimed. "I brought us clothes from home, but Eden thinks we will stand out less if we dress like locals."

"Are you sure the pink hair is necessary?" I was doubtful as I fingered the little flashes of hot pink—remembering in awe how Hannah had dried my hair *with her hands*. "Surely that will stand out..."

"You're going to stand out anyway. And with the pink dress and the pink highlights, you have this whole anime look going on— it's rockin'. You look great—except for the lip. I guess I could fix it for you, but I'd rather wait for the HydroHealer to do it right."

I had no clue what she was talking about. "I suppose anything looks better than how I was."

"True. But still…You might make a few heads turn in there. Or at least two heads turn."

I turned around to face her straight on. "Will you please explain yourself and all these hints you keep giving?"

"No, I think I'd rather let you live in ignorance for now. Trust me." She rolled her eyes. "I'm doing you a favor. Once that memory returns, you'll have plenty to deal with. Let's not rush it."

"Well, it's weird to go out there and see these people who I'm supposed to know…"

"You don't have much of a choice. Besides, there are a lot of decisions that will need to be made, and you need to be there for them—since they mostly have to do with you. Now come on. I'm actually pretty hungry myself."

She grabbed my hand and dragged me out of the bathing room. We passed through a fascinating, high-ceilinged bedroom. There were about four beds in the room, but they were built into the walls. It was like each bed had its own little cavern. The walls themselves were carved with patterns and designs. But the most impressive feature I kept noticing everywhere in this house was the bewitching way the light played off the color and architecture. It was as if an artist had not only designed the strange sculptures and the carvings in every room, but also the lighting to give the art a sort of surreal appeal. The bedroom was decorated in rich golden tones, and the soft lighting almost made the walls sparkle as if splashed with liquid gold.

When we re-entered the main living area—the one with white furniture and red and gold art—I was greeted by the smells of fresh food. Conversation quieted at our entrance, and I tried to ignore the faces staring curiously at me.

Hannah smiled cordially as we veered over to the glass table where she and Jezebel stood talking. An array of exotic foods was artfully displayed, but I was more distracted by how openly Jezebel was appraising me.

"Why did you not heal your lip?" she asked, her eyes narrowed.

"What do you mean?" I asked, pressing my fingers to my mouth.

"I was told you have Hydro abilities, including the power to heal yourself. Why did you not use them?"

"Jezebel—" Hannah started.

"From what Gabriel told me, she supposedly healed herself once without even knowing it. Perhaps they really did take her abilities, if she cannot even heal a simple cut." Jezebel sighed, but there was a satisfied tone to her words.

I gave Morgan a confused look.

"We didn't want her to try anything until she remembered how to use them," Morgan spoke tersely. "You weren't around before, but her abilities are extremely powerful. We wouldn't want them to get out of control…in your *house*."

I watched Morgan stare Jezebel down and was thankful for her defense. I was picking up on some kind of animosity between Jezebel and me. Had I offended her sometime in the past? Or was she just like that to everybody?

"I suppose we shall see what she remembers then…" Jezebel trailed off, eyeing me again, and I did remember I was wearing *her* dress.

"Thank you for the use of your clothes." I smiled weakly at her.

She waved her hand dismissively. "Pink is *not* my favorite color. You can just keep the dress." And she gave me a disdainful look.

"Thanks." I tried to smooth things over. As I picked up a plate to help myself to some food, I continued, "Your house is beautiful. Where did all of the art come from?"

"I created them. Every piece of art is mine," Jezebel said proudly.

I think my mouth dropped open. "Really?"

"Yes. I am a Sculptor." She nodded, her thickly lashed hazel eyes skimming the room as if making sure everything was still in its rightful place.

I guess that explained why the house was so strategically lit—and colorful. I started scrutinizing the room too, and I'm not going to lie—most of her art was very pretty. But some of it was very odd—like the painting across the room that looked like an incriminating blood splatter from a murder committed in this room.

She must have noticed my wandering eyes, because she said, "My house is my gallery. The art pieces you see here are my favorites. I cannot bear to part with them. Everything else I sell and ship to the other villages."

"Wow." I was genuinely impressed. "Even this?" I gestured to the stunning centerpiece on the table.

She nodded with a soft smile as her eyes followed my gaze. The centerpiece featured four red glass-like tubes that spiraled upward, weaving among each other and growing thinner toward their tips like flames in a bonfire. But the design wasn't the most interesting part…It was the twinkle of lights that seemed to move within the glass, as if tiny fireflies floated carelessly inside the sculpture.

"That's incredible," I breathed appreciatively. "How do you get it to light up like that?"

"This particular piece is very special because it is the most difficult to accomplish. The sculpture is infused with Firelight," Jezebel explained.

"It is Jezebel's signature touch," Hannah added.

"Yes, well, Gabriel actually taught me how to do it. Firelight is his specialty."

"It is?" I repeated blankly. Anything about Gabriel seemed to spark my curiosity. Mesmerized by the little flickering lights inside, I stretched my hand out and barely grazed the glass with my fingertips.

"Youch!" I exclaimed when the burning sensation started spreading through my fingers. "It's hot!"

"It is Firelight. What did you expect?" Jezebel rolled her eyes at my apparent stupidity.

But how was I supposed to know that?

"Well, you are a very gifted artist, Jezebel," Morgan commended her.

She seemed pleased by our compliments enough that her cool facade seemed to soften toward us a little bit. "My art is my life," she said simply, but I thought it sounded kind of sad.

I tried to catch a glimpse of her expression, but she turned away from me and moved into the living area.

"Jezebel is one of the most talented Sculptors on the Island," Hannah whispered, tossing a cautious look back at the gorgeous girl who had settled herself on a couch.

Even though she was just sitting there, she had the look of someone who was posing for a camera.

"And does she live here by herself or what?" Morgan whispered back, and I noted the obscene amount of food she was piling up on her plate. For someone so skinny, she certainly had a healthy appetite.

"Her father owns some of the best land in Pyradora. He built her a house up here with all the scenery and inspiration she would need to paint and sculpt. Just wait until you go outside and see the view. But she has not lived with her family since she was about sixteen years old. Her father is a busy man and..." She paused and her voice dropped even lower. "He just leaves her to her own entertainment. That is why this is a perfect hideout for now. Not only are we secluded on the mountainside of Pyradora, but nobody checks in on Jezebel."

"Wow. Doesn't she get lonely?" Morgan asked, and the three of us had to try not to stare at Jezebel lounging across the room.

"If so, she does not show it. She is extremely social and is rumored to be a little...wild. You never know what she is going to do or say next."

"Yeah...like blowing up a wagon," Morgan muttered, which elicited a laugh from Hannah.

"She seems sad to me," I murmured.

Hannah gave me a thoughtful look before adding, "Jezebel is like an art piece herself. Her father displays her proudly, but that is all she is to him...a prized possession, a trophy. She is right when she says art is her life...It really is all she has."

Our conversation was interrupted when the door swung open, and Eden and Caleb came marching in. Caleb was perspiring slightly, and he seemed perturbed as he scanned the room. When his eyes found me, his face relaxed, and he moved quickly to my side.

"You okay? How's the memory?"

"Still nothing, but I feel fine," I told him, watching his mannerisms curiously. He was genuinely concerned for me...and I kind of liked it.

"Well, you look..." He stepped back and his eyes swept over me. "Dang, Morgan," he sputtered. "Couldn't you have found something a little more modest for her to wear? I mean...geez..." And he ran his hands through his thick, brown hair as if appalled by how I looked.

"It's Jezebel's," Morgan replied nonchalantly and moved past us into the living room, using her elbow to motion me forward. "And it's not immodest. It's just—"

"Totally hot," he finished as he followed her into the living room.

"Wow," I responded with wide eyes, feeling myself blush. "This might not be so awkward if I remembered my relationship with you, but really...Do you always talk about me this way?"

Caleb's head snapped back to look at my face, his eyes a little guilty. Morgan laughed out loud as she sat on the floor with her plate of food.

"No, sorry...I just..." He didn't seem to know what to say. "Normally you like it when I compliment you. Well, actually, you act all annoyed by my flirting...But deep down I know you like it."

"Really?" I blinked at him. "Am I that complicated?"

"Not to me."

"You act as if you know me pretty well."

"I do."

He was so confident that I found myself slightly flustered. I so desperately wanted to *remember*. It bothered me how everyone knew me better than I knew myself.

"Well, maybe you're not always right," I remarked lightly.

"Amazing how you still find ways to argue with me even when you don't remember me. Are you sure you're not faking it?" Caleb joked, shaking his head in amusement.

I decided I didn't need to remember him to find his smile and the twinkle in his eyes attractive.

"Okay, give it a rest," Morgan jumped in. She turned to Caleb with a pointed look and muttered, "*Loverboy* needs to go easy on her until she remembers *everything*. Come sit, Whitnee."

I settled on the chair closest to her, not quite comfortable with floor seating in this dress. Caleb took the spot next to me, and I tried not to cast too many curious glances in his direction. Before I could take my first bite, Eden called everyone to attention. I glanced around the room as conversations halted and some people moved in closer. I scanned for Gabriel, pretending that I hadn't already involuntarily looked for him when I first walked in the room earlier. He was still not there. The Geodorian Seth was still working at the table in the corner, his eyes focused on mixing and pouring and flipping pages in an old book. I certainly hoped he could come up with something quickly.

Eden cleared her throat, and though she seemed completely in control of herself, her eyes looked tired. "We will be staying the night here. It is just not safe to transport Whitnee anywhere else on the Island right now, as I am sure the Guardian has discovered that she is no longer a captive."

"And do we know for sure the Guardian is the one behind the kidnapping? Those men were not Palladium guards," a man leaning against the wall asked.

I was trying to draw connections between the things they were saying, but it still did not make complete sense to me.

"Even still…Gabriel seems to think so. And we have many other reasons to believe it." She nodded as if that settled the matter. "It is important for each of you to remember that, as far as we know, the Guardian still does not know of Gabriel's return. We need to protect his presence here as much as Whitnee's."

"So what exactly is the plan?" Caleb jumped in. "Are we just going to sit around here and wait? We need to work on finding Whitnee's father."

"My father?" I repeated in shock.

Caleb barely glanced at me. "Whitnee and Gabriel both believe he is on the Island, Eden…"

"We are working on that—" Eden sighed, but was interrupted by a deep voice from behind her.

"I guarantee that the Guardian has him well hidden." Gabriel was standing in the doorway, his face flushed and his eyes dark. I couldn't stop the pounding of my heart at the sight of him. What was my problem? "We are still debating about how to handle retrieving him. I believe now that we have Whitnee we should try negotiating with the Guardian to release him to us."

"And I believe we should wait and see if Whitnee remembers something that would be helpful. I would rather not negotiate with the Guardian," Eden pointed out, frowning at Gabriel.

"The longer we wait, the more time they have to plan against us. We should act on the element of surprise," Gabriel argued.

"This is not a time for emotional impulses, Gabriel," Eden flung back harshly.

"It is not emotion—" Gabriel growled at her, anger clearly on his face.

The room began to erupt into arguments. I didn't understand half of what they were saying. So I sat there and listened to the opinions of the twelve or so people in the room, feeling quite overwhelmed and small.

"Enough!" Gabriel finally shouted over the voices. "We will stay here for now. But I want guards on duty rotating throughout the night—"

"I think I have it!" Seth blurted from his workspace in the corner, completely oblivious to the fact that he interrupted something important.

All eyes turned on him as he held up a bottle of brown liquid triumphantly.

Racing over to me, he placed the bottle in my hands. "Drink it."

"Whoa." Caleb pressed his hand to my arm and gave Seth a skeptical look. "Are you sure it's safe?"

Seth shrugged. "It should be. Of course, I have never created something like it before, so there is no real way of knowing."

Oh, perfect.

Caleb stared at him like he was crazy. "I don't like this idea. Maybe we should just let her memory return normally."

"Seth is the best Herbal Technician on the Island, Caleb," Eden reminded him, and I thought I heard a suspicious grunt from Gabriel.

I stared at the tar-like substance in the bottle. It was dark and thick and smelled like a putrid mixture of citrus and rotting vegetables.

"*Ugh.*" I turned my nose away.

"You don't have to do this, Whitnee," Caleb asserted.

I looked around at the expectant faces in the room. Gabriel moved several steps closer, his face expressionless once again as he watched me. I wondered what he was thinking.

"No, I'll do it. I want my memories back," I said quietly, trying not to gag at the smell.

"Drink it down really fast," Morgan suggested.

I brought the bottle to my lips and followed her advice, chugging until I gagged and had to take a breath.

"Oh, that is awful," I whispered, my eyes watering at the nastiness of it. It was surprisingly cold, and I could feel it snaking its way to my stomach. I wanted to throw it back up.

"Just a little bit left, Whit. You can do it," Morgan coached.

"I will get her some Water…" I heard Gabriel mumble, and he moved out of my cloudy line of vision.

I was miserable, but I made a mental note that he still had not addressed me directly. And the desperate curiosity about what had happened between us was enough motivation for me to finish off the remainder of the concoction.

I groaned and got to my feet quickly, wanting that Water and hoping I wouldn't throw up on Caleb and Morgan, who had once again invaded my personal space. I handed the stained bottle off to Seth. Caleb made a move like he was going to follow me, but Morgan cleared her throat and shook her head at him. If she was trying to be subtle, it didn't work. But Caleb did halt his movement and, instead, kept a watchful eye on me from a distance.

Just as I made it to the table, Gabriel spun around with a Water bottle in hand and appeared startled to find me right behind him.

"Thanks." I grabbed the bottle and our fingers brushed. I felt a little tickle in my stomach that had nothing to do with the unpleasant substance I just swallowed. I tried to mask my reaction by drinking as much Water down as I could handle, washing the taste out of my mouth. He took a step back from me and stood there awkwardly, as if he wasn't sure what to do with himself. I heard the group in the living area return to their arguments and opinions.

Finally I set the bottle down on the table and gripped my stomach for a second, feeling everything slosh around uncomfortably.

"How do you feel?" he asked quietly with a gentle undertone to his voice that I hadn't heard all evening.

"Um…" I thought for a moment, trying to ignore the amazing depth of his eyes as he stared at me.

Up close he was even more gorgeous…and a lot bigger than me. The top of my head only came to his chest. And just as I was pondering these things, I started to feel very fuzzy and almost fatigued. I turned away from him to press my hands on the table, leaning on them while I squeezed my eyes shut for a moment. A prickly sensation started along my neck and traveled down my spine, causing me to shiver.

"Whitnee?" Gabriel's voice was very close, and I opened my eyes in time to see his hand move to touch the bruise on my wrist. His skin was hot, and I could feel his body warmth very near me…

But I was no longer just standing there at the table. There was a man with feverishly hot skin forcing my hands behind my back, his scarred face laughing cruelly at my terror. Another man was behind me, tying me up, and the two were much taller and stronger than me. Right before one of them put the blindfold over my eyes, I screamed furiously. An unnatural vortex of wind surrounded me, and the scene vanished as quickly as it had come… but the Wind did not.

MISTY, WATER-COLORED MEMORIES

I wasn't really sure what was happening, except that it felt like I was floating. My mind cleared only when a sickeningly loud shatter of glass pierced the air and a flame exploded right in front of me. Gabriel shoved me aside, while his hands moved out protectively, almost seeming to swallow the Fire that threatened the entire room. But now the food and dishes and tiny red glass pieces were flying everywhere.

"Whitnee! Release the Wind!" Gabriel shouted, finally taking my hands into his and covering my palms.

A white-hot sensation pulsed through my arms.

I felt suffocated and feverish, and the light, airy feeling left me. That was also when the Wind in the house died. I turned my eyes up to Gabriel's as he held my hands in his. He was breathing quickly as he searched my face. The whole house felt very quiet—and all eyes were on me.

"You still have your abilities," he whispered, and I thought I heard relief in his voice.

"What *was* that?" I choked. I was so confused, especially when Jezebel's screams pierced the air.

"How could you?! You just blew up my favorite sculpture!" I glanced at her, thinking she was yelling at Gabriel. But, no. Her eyes were on me, and she was enraged. Everybody else was already on their feet, their faces tense and uncertain.

Gabriel released my hands and gave her his attention. "Jez, it was an accident—"

"But, Gabriel! My Firelight sculpture!" she screamed and cried at the same time.

"If I did that, I didn't m-mean to…" I stuttered as I looked about at the damage. There was food flung everywhere, sharp pieces of glass littering the floor, and a burn mark on the wall and ceiling above the table. But no pretty sculpture.

"What did you do to her?" Caleb asked accusingly as he stared Gabriel down from across the room.

"Caleb—" Morgan had a warning in her voice.

"Do not blame him for what *she* did!" Jezebel marched up to Gabriel's side, tears streaming down her face. She pointed a finger at me. "You are clearly dangerous and out of control!"

"I-I'm sorry…" I looked again to Gabriel. Had I really broken the sculpture without knowing it?

"You acted as if you were seeing something that I was not seeing," Gabriel told me softly. "Did you remember something?"

"Uh, I saw something," I mumbled. "Like a flash of…Only I thought it was really happening…I thought you were…"

"What did you see?" Caleb asked.

I cast frightened eyes on him and looked at the eager faces around the room, finally settling back on Gabriel's face. I could not explain why, but something about Gabriel made me very nervous and suspicious then.

"I don't know how to explain it," I lied.

"Well, it had to be something! You nearly destroyed my house!" Jezebel yelled again.

Eden interrupted her tantrum from the living room. "Hannah, maybe you should take Jezebel back to her room so she can calm down."

"I am calm!" Jezebel snapped at her.

"I think that is a good idea, Jez." Gabriel spoke somewhat sooth- ingly. "I am sorry about your house. We will get all of this cleaned up. But you are very upset, and it is not helping the situation."

She made a sour face at him, her mouth moving as if she wanted to argue. Finally, she let out a frustrated snarl and stormed from the room, muttering curses. I watched her go, feeling incred- ibly guilty and sick.

"Seth, what exactly did that potion do?" Eden questioned.

Seth shook his head. "Exactly what you wanted. Increased her mind's functionality so she can remember. The flash she had must mean it is working."

I was listening to their conversation, but I was getting a weird feeling.

"Are there any other side effects we should know about?" Caleb asked sharply, picking up the bottle and sniffing it. I wondered the same thing...especially since the room was now spinning.

"Well, there is a powerful sleeping draught in it. Her mind will reset faster once she is asleep. But it does not seem to be affect- ing her—"

And that was the last thing I heard before I fell into a deep, dark sleep. I know a pair of strong, heated arms caught me because they were the last thing I felt instead of the floor rushing up to meet me. And there was something strangely familiar about those arms...as if I had done this before.

Seth was right.

Sleep brought dreams that seemed to organize themselves into the empty files within my mind. Some of the dreams were extremely vivid and detailed...like making heart-shaped pancakes with my mom on a lazy Saturday morning or riding with my dad in the car, the wind blowing our hair and both of us singing loudly to old rock music. But other dreams were blurry, interrupted shreds of memory. I hadn't realized how very little I remembered the year after my dad disappeared. Memories of Camp Fusion came in bright colors and sparks of emotion. I saw Morgan and Caleb as children and how much they had changed over the years. I remembered too well how much I had wanted Caleb to kiss me in the pantry...how sick Morgan had been and our last conversation about it. I remembered that Mom and I had not left each other on the best of terms and that I was on a mission.

And then the memories I had wanted to forget played mercilessly before me in painstaking detail...an Island, a boy, a greedy ruler, and a lost father.

My eyes fluttered open as real-time consciousness flooded in. I was startled to find myself in a cave, shrouded in semidarkness. I sat up immediately to look around and realized I was actually in that bedroom in Pyradora...where the beds were set into the walls. I breathed a sigh of relief and willed my heart to slow. Soft, faintly flickering light fluttered over the walls and ceiling in the room, reminding me of the nightlight I had as a kid that changed colors. There was a thin blanket, and Morgan was curled up in a fetal position beside me. She was breathing deeply and evenly and seemed so comfortable and peaceful—not at all like she had been at camp. I stared at her for a moment, trying to imagine fully all that she must have gone through since I was kidnapped.

Kidnapped.

I shuddered again at the clear recollection I now had and then gazed around the rest of the room. I immediately recognized the figure sleeping in the bed across from me. Softly I pushed the blanket off and stood to my feet, noting I was still in Jezebel's pink dress. A pair of sandals was waiting beside my bed, and I slid my feet inside. Tiptoeing across the room, I gazed down at Caleb's almost comatose state. He was lying on his side, holding a pillow to his chest. His mouth was slightly open, and I was filled with a deep longing to curl up beside him and take the place of that pillow. Poor Caleb must have lived a nightmare from the moment I disappeared at camp.

But I turned away, because he wasn't even the reason I was out of my bed right now. No, there was someone else I needed to find first. Someone who owed me some explanations…immediately. And so I shoved away the guilty feelings I had about leaving my sweet, sleeping Caleb to go find *him* first.

I surveyed the occupied beds in the room. One held Eden, who did not appear to be wearing her fancy dress anymore. Another bed might have held Levi—I couldn't tell exactly, but I thought I recognized the close cut of his hair. It must have been the dead of night, because everyone seemed completely out of it. But I didn't see the one person I was looking for in the room, which kind of surprised and disappointed me at the same time. He had always insisted on staying by my side last time.

I found my way quickly and quietly to the door, hoping to come across him somewhere else in the house, ignoring the creeping shadows that the strange moving lights cast everywhere. The living room was darker, and someone appeared to be asleep on the couch. I moved closer, but one sniff told me it was Seth. That man needed a bath. I certainly hoped he wasn't soiling the pretty white couch.

I moved around in the darkness, trying to see my way carefully across the room. But a movement in the kitchen caught my eye, and I froze like one of Jezebel's statues.

A figure emerged from the shadows and whispered, "Who is there?"

I immediately recognized Thomas.

"It's Whitnee," I replied and padded quickly to him.

"Whitnee? What are you doing awake?" he asked, surveying me closely in the dark.

"Got my memory back, and I was just looking for…Wait, why are you up?" I asked, noting that he was carrying two Water bottles.

"On guard duty with Gabriel," he said.

I sucked in a breath, and he cocked his head a little.

"What did you say you were looking for?"

"Um, actually, I need to talk to Gabriel…Where is he?"

"Out front. I was just about to take him this bottle."

"Oh." I stared at the bottle. "Listen, do you mind if I take it to him? And maybe you could just keep yourself busy a little longer? I just need a minute alone with him..." I gave him an innocent look.

He smiled like he understood my real motivations—which I'm sure he didn't. "Sure, okay. I will do some rounds out back first." He handed me one of the ice-cold bottles.

"Thanks." I sighed and made my way in the dark to the front door.

But I stopped short and ran my fingers through my hair to pull out any lingering tangles. I took a few deep breaths and noticed someone had mercifully healed my lip and bruises while I slept. Good. Now I just had to face Gabriel...*Be strong, Whitnee.* I had a purpose in mind, and I would not be distracted by my attraction to him. No way, not this time. My reactions earlier were natural, given the fact that I didn't remember anything. But now that I did remember, I could control myself better. Mind over matter. I straightened my dress, softly pulled the door open, and clicked it shut behind me.

The night air was cool, and I almost lost my focus when I saw the view before me. There was a wide, stretching lawn and then nothing but night sky glittering with the most brilliant display of stars I'd ever seen. Against that backdrop stood a tall, perfectly carved figure of total masculinity that made my stomach flip. His back was to me as he surveyed the surroundings in front of him. Either he had not heard me or he was just assuming I was Thomas.

I walked up to his right side and held the Water bottle out, purposefully staying a little behind him. He didn't even look as he reached for the bottle and took a drink. I crossed my arms in front of me and took a moment to study him. His profile was sharply defined, and I could see, even in the starshine, when he clenched his jaw muscles after swallowing. His hair was cut shorter than I remembered, and I found myself missing the softness of those curls...

Dangit, Whitnee. Focus. After a silent moment standing there, I began wondering how long it would take him to realize it was *me* beside him.

"You know, we need to do something with those guards," he began, corking the bottle again and glancing my direction. That was when he froze, and his eyes widened as if he was seeing a ghost. "Whitnee." He said my name low, like a statement…like a breathless realization.

And normally I would have laughed, maybe even teased him for not knowing I was there so long.

But I had no smiles for him. I kept my face expressionless and my body language closed off when I declared, "We need to talk."

THE RIDDLER

"You have your memory back," Gabriel remarked and, again, it wasn't a question. He turned his gaze away from me and back to the night sky, giving a barely perceptible sigh. "What do you remember?"

"Everything," I answered, frowning slightly. "Except for what happened after I transported. I'm assuming that will come back soon. But, Gabriel…" Just saying his name again, right here to his face, made me feel all nervous inside. I had spent weeks avoiding thoughts of how I would react when I saw him again—a good thing too, since I never could have planned the way events had unfolded. But he still had this completely intimidating effect on me.

As if he knew I was struggling, he looked down at me sideways. Could he sense my determination to ignore any romantic feelings I might have?

"Yes?"

"Morgan said you came to the Mainland…I need to know why."

"I came for you."

I tried to ignore how romantic that sounded.

"Why?"

"Abrianna told me your father is alive on the Island, and I believe her...even though she withheld the full truth from me."

I felt a twinge of anticipation at the mention of Dad, but we would have to come back to that issue later. There was something else I needed to deal with right now.

"So you came all the way to the Mainland just to tell me that? Morgan said the Guardian sent you to bring me back."

"True. Abrianna arranged for me to find you."

"And did she tell you to *kidnap* me?" I inquired tartly.

This time his whole body turned my direction. "What are you implying?"

Now that I had his full attention and the force of his eyes on me, I grew a little apprehensive. "Did you..." I started, a little tremor trying to fight its way into my voice. But I had to know the truth. I had to ask. "Did you help them kidnap me? Were you there?"

His expression grew angry. "Are you really asking me if I had something to do with you being taken and mistreated by those fools?" His voice was dangerously low as he watched and waited for my answer.

I stumbled at the horror on his face. "Morgan said you were on the Mainland...that they found you minutes after I was taken! And there was a third person there that I never saw..." My voice trailed off as I observed him becoming more agitated. "I just need to know. I just need to hear you say that it wasn't you. Make me believe that it wasn't you, because..."

"Because why? You already suspect it was me." He glowered at me.

"I have a really strong feeling that it was somebody I know well...somebody I trust."

"It was not *me*! I would *never* do that to you, Whitnee. I would never allow someone..." And then he let out a low growl and kind of spun away from me. While he paced in irritation, I felt increasingly horrible for accusing him of such a thing. I mean, this was *Gabriel*. The same guy who held me in his arms and confessed his feelings for me…the one who kissed me as if I was the only person in the world who mattered…the one I had tried unsuccessfully to forget…

Now that I was standing there with him, how could I believe he would do that to me? Even so, I still couldn't wrap my brain around the fact that he had arrived so close to the time the kidnappers had.

Finally, he faced me from a few feet away and with a biting undertone said, "Must I work all over again to gain your trust, Whitnee?"

I sighed and pressed my hand to my forehead. "Do you think I'm just looking for reasons to not trust you? It's not exactly fun to wake up and realize *you* look the most guilty."

"Why am I always the one who looks guilty to you? After what happened last time you were here and everything that has happened since…" His voice trailed off.

"Maybe you should start being completely honest with me," I retorted. It wasn't as if my suspicions had been completely unfounded. He had lied before. "I'm not just a mysterious Traveler this time. I'm part Dorian, Gabriel. This Island is as much a part of me now as it is you. I want you to treat me like an equal, like a partner this time around and not some little girl you always feel like you have to protect. Open up to me—quit hiding things."

He glared at me a moment longer. I matched his expression, thinking that even with an angry scowl on his face he was still way too attractive.

"I will be honest if you will assure me you do not really believe I had anything to do with your kidnapping." He was deadly serious.

"I believe you, okay?" I softened my voice just a little. "Now explain to me how you got to the Mainland."

He began pacing slowly. "I have been trying to understand all night what really happened. When Abrianna brought me to the portal, it was already open. The kidnappers must have gone through ahead of me. If I had just arrived there sooner, I might have stopped them." He was talking more to himself than to me at this point. "I might have learned of her plan to take you…and to leave me there." He stopped and looked back at me. "Did Morgan tell you that part? That Abrianna closed the portal behind me?"

I gave one nod of affirmation. "I'm sorry about that." I meant it. I couldn't even imagine where I would be right now if he hadn't planned ahead. And something about Gabriel being on the Mainland without me seemed wrong.

"Fortunately, her plan did not work. But I keep wondering… how many more times can I outsmart her? The more I keep trying, the more I become just like her. Lying, asking others to put their lives and reputations in danger for my sake…" He shook his head in disgust.

"You are *not* like your parents, Gabriel," I insisted. "They are twisted by their own selfish motives…You're different."

He snorted derisively. "I wish that were true…" I stared hard at him, waiting for him to explain. But he changed the subject. "Tell me exactly what happened to you before I came to the Mainland."

So I recounted my experiences from the time I felt the portal click on in the cabin bathroom to the last thing I remembered, which was falling through the portal.

"So you really believe this third person was somebody who knew you? Somebody whose identity they were trying to protect?" he clarified.

I nodded with a frown. "And it's not just that. I never got to tell you this, but your mother kind of led me to believe that night at the Palladium that someone who traveled around the Island with us was really manipulating things to help Abrianna get what she wanted from me. When Kevin and Amelia were kidnapped in Geodora…I don't know. She made me think she just staged all of that to get me to send the kids to the Palladium…She wanted me to think that everything I did on this Island was my own choice. But she was behind the scenes manipulating every move."

Gabriel barely moved as he took in my words. Finally he said, "I knew something was suspicious about that night in Geodora. Are you saying you believe the same person she was referring to could be the same person who helped kidnap you on the Mainland?"

I directed my gaze at the stars as I tried to piece things together. "Maybe," I responded, a chill running down my spine.

Our eyes met, and I was sure we were thinking the same thing. *Who?*

"It couldn't be Eden, Hannah, or Jezebel. They were on this side opening the portal for me," he muttered.

"No, I'm pretty sure it was a male. And the only others who traveled with us before were Thomas, Levi, and Tamir...and speaking of, I have not seen Tamir yet tonight. Have you?" I remembered the tall Aeroguard who worked for my grandfather, Ezekiel.

"I believe Levi contacted him earlier and asked him to come."

"That's probably a good idea. Does Ezekiel know I'm here yet?"

"No. We cannot risk communicating that information on a zephyra right now. But someone has been dispatched to tell him."

With a sigh, I said, "Realistically, I cannot think of one person we know who would betray our trust like this."

"Except for me," he remarked bitterly.

I pressed my lips together and gave him a look. "Surely you understand why I would think that at first—"

"I wish I did not," he replied sharply.

I opened my mouth to apologize, but he continued in a business-like tone, "And you do not remember anything once you were on the Island?"

I thought for a moment, and there was a hazy flash of something on the beach, but I couldn't bring it into focus. "Actually, something did happen, but I can't remember that part yet. Listen," I said forcefully, "all that matters to me now is finding my dad. And I need your help. That's, uh," I swallowed with difficulty. "That's really my only purpose here. I don't want to talk about prophecies. I don't want any *distractions*...I just need my dad back."

Gabriel stared at me, and I got the impression he was trying to decide what exactly to say. I wondered if he'd caught my double meaning. "We will find your father," he assured me gruffly.

"I want to talk to the men you captured," I told him.

"Absolutely not."

"You don't have the right to tell me no—"

"I am only protecting you—"

"Um, I believe the last time you tried to *protect me*, I got pushed through a portal. Now look where we are," I remarked bitterly, and he bristled visibly at my words. Okay, so it was a low blow, and I knew it, but *seriously*. "We're partners this time, remember?"

I turned on my heel and started marching around the side of the house. Hadn't Caleb said they were out back somewhere on the property?

"Whitnee!" Gabriel grabbed my arm and yanked me to a stop. "You cannot reason with men like that—"

We were interrupted by Thomas, who was coming around the house from the direction I was heading.

"Everything okay?" Thomas called.

Gabriel released me, but before he could respond, I asked, "Thomas, where are the guards you captured?" I moved quickly out of Gabriel's reach.

Thomas looked surprised. "They are back in Jezebel's storage building—"

"Thomas!" Gabriel snapped, to which Thomas looked even more bewildered.

"Thanks!" I called and took off jogging the direction he pointed.

I heard Gabriel instruct Thomas to take the front guard and that he would be back soon. He called after me, but I did not stop. The terrain grew rocky behind the massive house Jezebel lived in. The ground off to my left seemed to lead directly into the mountain through the gaping mouth of a cave. I turned my eyes away, wondering vaguely what was in there, and finally reached the nondescript storage building.

There were blocks of that sparkly white rock piled outside—the same material that some of Jezebel's sculptures had been designed from. Tools and random equipment were visible through the open door of the spacious room. The light in the storage building was dim, and immediately I caught sight of a pair of legs sticking out. Someone was sitting on the floor in there.

That was as far as I got. Gabriel pulled me away and placed the bulk of his body between me and the storage building.

"Why are you so stubborn?" he blurted.

My chest was moving up and down as I caught my breath. "Is one of them a Pyra? With a scar on his face?"

Gabriel stared at me as if he was unsure he should answer. Then he nodded.

"He was there at Camp Fusion—he was the one trying to protect the identity of the other guy. And Gabriel, he was the same one in the forest the night that I got lost in Geodora! That scar on his face? I did that!" I told him breathlessly.

The implication of my words hit him slowly, so I finished his thoughts for him. "He has seen my dad! He used an image of him to lure me into the woods, so...so he knows where Dad is!" I finished, feeling impatient. I tried to move around him, but he blocked my path.

"Gabriel!" I huffed.

"Whitnee, he is a bad man...a dangerous man."

"No kidding, Sherlock," I retorted sarcastically, but Gabriel's eyes burned with intensity. "Do you know him or something?"

"His name is Saul. I have been searching for him for a very long time now. He has caused more trouble on the Island than I care to recount. Remember that Fire in the jungle when we were on our way to Geodora? I am fairly certain he was behind it. And the night I was held in captivity by the rebels...You remember my injuries?"

My eyes widened, and I felt sick. I remembered what they had done to Gabriel that night...and remembered those final tender moments I had spent with him in Hydrodora as I healed his wounds.

"Then...he is not really a rebel. He works for the Guardian!" I exclaimed.

Gabriel said grimly, "That is what I am afraid of. Or that there really were no rebels after all...just a pointless assignment she has given to keep me busy."

Before I could respond to this, a sick, distorted laugh that sent chills down my spine sounded from the interior of the storage building. It was slow at first and then picked up to a maniacal fervor before turning into a hacking cough. Gabriel and I exchanged meaningful glances.

"Please let me talk to him," I whispered.

"No—" he protested.

"He can't hurt me with you there."

"It is not your physical safety I am concerned with at the moment. I fear more about what he might say to you."

I stared pleadingly into those gorgeous hazel eyes of his until he relented.

"Very well." He shook his head as if he thought he was making a mistake. "But do not get close to him."

"Oh, don't worry about that."

Carefully we entered the storage building, Gabriel in the lead. And there he was...the man who had attempted on two occasions to abduct me. He smiled crookedly like he'd been expecting me.

"There is my pretty girl. Come back for more?" He spoke in a gravelly voice, and I masked my shudder.

For more *what*? His comments scared me—especially about the parts of my journey that I still couldn't recall. My eyes flicked around the room nervously, even though he appeared to be tied up pretty well.

"I knew you would miss me."

"Shut up, Saul," Gabriel growled.

"Well, I tried that earlier, and you did not seem to care for my silence. But now…give me a few minutes alone with her, and I will tell you anything you want—"

He was silenced when Gabriel gave him a hard kick to the torso. I tried not to react to the violence. Even though the guy deserved it, the whole thing sickened me. Maybe this wasn't my best idea.

I spoke up, successfully keeping my voice steady. "Tell me where my father is."

He laughed through his groans of pain. "He used to be on the Island."

"What do you mean, *used to be*?" I clarified sharply.

Gabriel stood close by, his body so tense I could almost feel him vibrate.

"You could say he is technically not *on* the Island at this moment." He grinned at me with a sinister gleam to his eyes. "I will tell you where to find him, if you will only lean down and let me smell your hair again, maybe even give me—"

"Enough!" Gabriel yelled and kicked him again.

"Gabriel, stop!" I ordered him.

Saul's eyes were watering, and his face was scrunched up, but he kept laughing, acting as if the pain gave him some kind of satisfaction.

"What do you mean he's not on the Island? Tell me what you know!" I demanded.

Saul spat. "That is all I can say. You decide for yourself."

I stared hard at him, my anger rising. What would it take for a man like this to just tell the truth? I decided to try another question. "Who sent you to kidnap me? Was it the Guardian?"

Saul wheezed, and then stared at me as if trying to figure something out. Finally, he said, "I do not work for the Palladium, if that is what you are asking, pretty girl."

"He is lying. There is no other way to access the portal but through the Palladium." Gabriel muttered.

"And yet, somehow you came back through that portal without your mother knowing," Saul pointed out, a gleam in his eye.

Gabriel and I grew silent as we contemplated his words. Was he trying to make us believe Abrianna was innocent? *Psh.*

Then Gabriel moved in closer to me, reaching out as if he was going to direct me back outside, and said, "We have already questioned him, and he only talks in riddles. This is doing no good."

"Wait." I held up my hand. "Saul, who was the third person who came with you to the Mainland? The one you wouldn't let me see?"

"It could be anyone, could it not? Hmmm...who do you trust the most on this Island?" He grinned lazily at me. "It will be fun to watch you pick apart your little group...living with doubt and uncertainty...questioning each person's loyalty. You think they all want to see a Pilgrim come and take their life forces away? You think everyone wants to see you rule over us?"

"I did not come to take anyone's life force. I came to find my father...Now, just answer my questions!"

"I tell you what," he whispered, and I couldn't stop from bending down a little farther to hear him. "Just lean in a little closer... that's right. I will tell you..."

I must have leaned too far, because Gabriel yanked me back. "No. Stay away from him." He kept his hand on my arm, which prompted Saul to another laughing-slash-coughing fit.

"Oh, now I understand." Saul half-wept, half-laughed. "You just want her all to yourself! Do you think you are in love with her, Gabriel? I thought there were rules about that...If she is the Pilgrim, you are not allowed to love her like that, are you? Or do you just want her like I do? Nothing but a pretty face and a warm body to—"

I had heard enough of this guy's dirty mouth. Before Gabriel could react, I had already moved into action. The sharp, iron-looking tool that I had noticed across the room flew through the air and levitated at Saul's neck...stopping a mere hair's breadth away from cutting his throat. He appeared shocked as he stiffened and glanced down warily at the instrument.

"You are really starting to piss me off!" I spoke heatedly, knowing my eyes were now ablaze with the silver hue of an Aerodorian. I had one hand stretched out in front of me, controlling the weapon.

"Whitnee—" Gabriel warned, but I ignored him.

"Tell me where my dad is or, I swear, I will slit your throat and not look back. If you won't help me, then I'm sure once you're dead your other friends will be happy to talk." It was like I was only seeing Saul and the whole godforsaken storage room through the haze of rage. Was this what a crime of passion felt like?

Slowly and with more solemnity, Saul spoke. "Let me ask you something first."

I let the sharp side of the instrument nick the tender skin at his neck. "I'm not playing around here," I threatened.

"I realize that." He gave a weak grin before his eyes turned serious. "Let me be honest with you now. Have you ever considered the idea that your father does not want to be found? He has been gone for, what, six years now? And yet you have come and gone from this Island twice in a few months. Surely, if he had wanted to see you—wanted his life on the Mainland back—he would have already left by now."

My hand wavered, and the instrument slipped an inch from his neck. I glanced to my side at Gabriel and tried to decipher his expression. Why was he just standing there, looking as if he might actually believe these lies?

"He is a prisoner here!" I protested, turning my attention back on Saul.

"Is he?" Saul questioned darkly, and I just stared at him, debating if I really had the strength to just kill him.

"Whitnee." Gabriel spoke my name gently, and I felt his warm hand move over mine and close the palm of my hand.

And just like that I snapped out of the feverish need to hurt and destroy. The iron instrument fell with a clang to the ground, and Gabriel kicked it far away. I could feel the tremors start in my chest and move to my hands and legs. I couldn't breathe. I needed to get out of there.

Shakily, I told the man lying there on the floor. "You better hope that we don't meet again."

I began to back away, pulling my trembling hand out of Gabriel's. I was almost to the door when Saul called out to me. It was so strange to hear him say my name that I froze without turning around, afraid that he would see how much his words had shaken me.

"I will tell you this," he began. "I will not be stuck here for long. And *when* we meet again, because we *will*—"

At this, I did turn my head back to look at him. His eyes were alight with a sick pleasure.

"You better hope there is somebody else there to protect you."

That was all the prompting Gabriel needed. I turned my face away from the beating he inflicted, desperate to drown out the violence in my head and my ears. I didn't know where the other prisoners were being held, but I had to get as far away from this scene as I could. So I ran.

I thought I heard Gabriel call my name, but I couldn't even see straight. Somehow I ended up climbing into the mouth of the cave I had observed earlier. I felt along the walls, moving farther into the dark until I was completely removed from the outside world. I didn't even consider what else could be lurking in there. I just shrank as far into the blackness as I could and slid down the cave wall until I was just a pathetic heap on the hard ground.

DOWN THE RABBIT HOLE

It wasn't long before the deep resonances of Gabriel's voice echoed my direction, accompanied by approaching soft light. I didn't respond immediately. He would find me if he kept walking this direction. I wasn't crying; in fact, I felt like I wasn't even blinking. The darkness was thick around me as I tried to shut out the savage emotions that had so readily coursed through my body.

Truthfully, as I sat there on the cave floor, I really wanted Morgan and Caleb. I wanted their nearness, their goodness… because I did not feel like a good person right then. But then I never wanted them to know about the murderous monster that apparently lurked inside me. And so my friends suddenly felt far more removed from me than just asleep in the house.

Gabriel finally found me, and I blinked vacantly at the light shining from the palm of his hand. We gazed at each other in silence until I tore my eyes away to notice the random sparkles that were now winking at me inside the cavern. I reached my fingers out and rubbed the rough rock of the cave wall…no glitter on my hand. But it was definitely sparkling in Gabriel's light, and I was mesmerized.

"I wanted to kill him," I whispered, not meeting his eyes.

"You would not have done it," he told me confidently. "Wanting to kill somebody and actually doing it are two different things."

"Have you ever killed someone, Gabriel?" The question was out of my mouth before I decided if I really wanted his answer.

"No…but I have wanted to." His voice was low and soft, but it still echoed. "You should go back in the house. Try to get some sleep before the dawn."

I considered that for a moment. The cave was warm, and I couldn't explain it, but I felt safe in its shadows. Tilting my head up to look at him again, I spoke in a small voice. "Will you sit with me for a second? I just want to talk."

He was hesitant but eventually lowered himself to the floor and leaned against the wall across from me. His choice of physical distance between us did not go unnoticed.

He extended his lit hand out in front of him, and a golden bubble, like the head of a round light bulb, popped out and hovered above us, enshrouding us in a soft cocoon of light.

"Jezebel said your specialty was Firelight," I commented flatly.

"I suppose so," he answered.

"I didn't know that." There was so much I didn't know about Gabriel. When I fixed my gaze back on him, I asked, "What is it that you do every time you touch my hands? You did it when I broke Jezebel's statue…and then again in the storage building. It's like you suffocate my life force or something. Makes me all calm and rational again." I held up my palms and examined them.

"It is a Pyradorian ability, but it is not affecting your life force…just your emotions. You are the one who decides to release the life force."

"What do you mean?"

"Pyras have access to a tranquility force that helps us balance out our emotions—otherwise, we could never contain the Fire within us. It is similar to an alarm that kicks in when we need it… but we can choose to ignore it. I can transfer it to others through my hands." He flashed a yellow light at me from his hands. When he used his life force, his blazing golden eyes were breathtaking.

With a slight smile begging at the corners of his mouth, he added, "I have had to use it many times with you. Makes me wonder if you are not really a true Pyra behind those gray eyes."

"I am *not* a Pyra," I insisted, slightly indignant. Not that it was a bad thing to be a Pyra. From where I was sitting, Pyras—or at least one in particular—were pretty special. "So, wait. When, besides tonight, have you done that to me?"

He shrugged lightly. "I believe the first time was when we were on our way to Aerodora after I found you on the beach... Remember how you almost knocked Caleb and Morgan over with your anger in the jungle?"

"Uh..." Yeah, I did remember. And it seemed like so long ago.

"There were other times...in Geodora mostly..." His voice trailed off, and I was no longer remembering the times he calmed me...more like all the times he excited me. And our explosive kiss outside the cabin. It was ridiculous how well I could conjure the feel of Gabriel's warm, full lips on mine...the way his hand cradled my head...

"Ah, Geodora." I sighed, but it came out more as a moan, and my face immediately grew hot. I cleared my throat and looked up at the high ceiling. *No distractions*, I told myself. So I changed the subject. "You want to tell me why you almost looked as if you believed him back there...about my dad not wanting to be found? What exactly do you know about my dad?"

"The word *know* seems so relative lately." He drummed his fingers on the floor as he spoke. "After putting together the real story of your father's birth and considering the way Abrianna talked about him...I feel as if I know nothing, Whitnee." And when he let out a quiet sigh, I noticed how tired he really was. There were bags under his eyes that seemed exaggerated when he leaned his head back to rest on the wall.

"Do you think there was...or is...anything romantic between the two of them?" My insides grew cold, despite the warmth of the cave.

I saw him frown.

"Do you think he is really here to be with her? I mean, I know she's married to Eli, and well, he's technically still married to my mom…" I broke off because the thought of my dad having an affair with Abrianna, the devil's spawn, was just too far-fetched. That would mean I never really knew my dad's true character. The man I remembered, the man I loved and called Daddy, was a hero in my eyes—a champion of all that was good and right in the world. Not a backstabbing, cheating jerk.

"I think they are very close…closer than I have ever known my mother to be with someone else, and yes, that includes Eli," Gabriel admitted and then turned to see my reaction.

"But how would you know that? Have you seen him?"

"No, I have not seen him. But they communicate…in their minds. I have watched it happen more than once, and I cannot ignore the change in her face when she is talking to him." He shook his head, as if imagining it again. "I could not hear either of them, but she goes blank for a moment. She finally explained to me what was happening. And, though it was subtle, she was different while she was talking to him. She became like…I do not know how to explain it. Almost weaker…maybe softer?"

"Mind communication. That is a rare Aerodorian ability, right? I just didn't know it worked like that." I thought about how I had been able to hear Boomer's voice in my head, but I hadn't been able to communicate back unless I spoke out loud. Then I considered Abrianna's apparent personality change around my dad. "Ben said they grew up like brother and sister. Maybe that's all it is."

"Maybe," he agreed, but his face was doubtful.

I think we both tried to ignore the awkward idea of our parents having some kind of romantic history together.

I started thinking aloud. "She told me that night at the Palladium that my dad was predictable…that if she gave him the chance, she knew he would contact me. She made it sound like she had manipulated him into action to achieve what she wanted, which was to get me to the Island and later to the Palladium."

"When did he contact you on the Island? What are you talking about?" Gabriel looked confused.

I stood to my feet and started pacing. "I never told you. I had a dream the night I was in Hydrodora. I talked to my dad…It was really him, I know it was." My words came out more quickly as I paced, thinking through it all. "All I could see in the dream was a room that appeared to be made of concrete. It was completely empty, and it shifted and groaned…But no, I was standing on the water bed while I dreamt, so that must have been…" I paused to think.

"What happened in the dream?"

I threw my hands up in frustration. "He told me to leave. He said he had been trying to protect Mom and me and that if I didn't leave the Island, all of it would have been for nothing. He said to go straight to the Palladium, told me where to find the portal…and I did what he said…" I halted and stared off into the unlit cavern. What if Dad had lied to me just to make me go to the Palladium? What if he was in on things with Abrianna?

But, no.

No.

My dad was *not* a liar.

What was it about this place that made me lose all loyalty and trust with people I cared about? My mind pictured that stupid scar-face Pyra I should have killed…

"Whitnee, listen," Gabriel started, probably noticing the multitude of conflicting emotions flitting across my face. He rose to his feet and faced me. "You were right about your father being a prisoner here. I am just unsure about what *kind* of prisoner he is. A willing one? I do not know. But after you went through that portal, she told me I would not be able to find him. I have searched all over this Island for weeks, hoping to recover him and bring him back to you instead of bringing you here again—"

"You did?" I stared wide-eyed at him, not really sure why that surprised me. "You've been looking for him all this time?"

"Of course. Secretly."

I blinked at him.

"But Abrianna was right—he is somewhere I do not know. And when Saul said he was not on the Island—"

"Saul is a liar," I stated flatly. "He's here somewhere."

"Yes, but I feel like he gave us some kind of clue. I do not believe for a moment that Abrianna would have let him leave the Island. What if he was on a boat or someplace we could not reach him on land?"

My eyes widened as I realized what he meant. We needed to start thinking the way the enemy would think. And who better to help with that than Gabriel, one of their own?

I was staring at the sparkling wall that towered high above Gabriel's tall and broad frame when I realized there was a gigantic marking on it. I grabbed him by the arms and pulled him away from the wall. He seemed confused by the sudden physical contact, but he definitely didn't try to stop me. A huge swirl was carved—or maybe burned—onto the rock wall.

"Will Kinder has been here!" I cried.

"Who?"

I reached my hand out and touched the swirling symbol before venturing farther into the darkness, remembering the schizophrenic man's words...*I went inside the mountain where it sparkled everywhere like stars.* And there had been a sketch of this marking on his wall—a sketch of this cave!

I was too excited to explain. "What is this place? Where does it lead?"

"You mean the cave? Jezebel's father owns this property, and she uses the stone for her sculptures. Where are you going?"

I ran my hands along the walls curiously, not even realizing how naturally I had lit up my hands with Firelight. Gabriel's little bubble of light floated behind me. There had to be something remarkable about this place. What had Will said again about a cave? I hadn't really thought much of what he said was real... until now.

The cave. It is where they fought. I liked it there, though. It was warm, and it sparkled like the stars…Have you seen the Big Dipper?

The stars outside…and the glittering walls…and the symbol. Holy cow, what did it all mean? And who fought here? Over what?

"Do you know what the Big Dipper is?" I questioned loudly, thinking Gabriel was still back at the symbol. When I spun around to find him right in my shadow, I actually jumped.

"I have no idea what a big dipper is. Tell me what has gotten you so excited all of a sudden."

"Um, we met a man named Will…" I breathed, wishing I could take a step away from him, but I was kind of blocked in by a cave wall. I explained briefly who Will was and our experiences visiting him earlier in the summer. While I spoke, I carefully slid to my right in order to put some space between us.

"Something important happened here." I continued my exploration deeper into the cave. "Does the cave lead anywhere else?"

"No, it does not. Jez digs her material from it. Whitnee, you are just moving in a huge circle."

My hands paused their sweeping gestures over the wall, but I didn't look at him when I said, "You sure know a lot about Jezebel and her property."

"I have known her my whole life."

"Yeah, you guys seem so *close*. I mean, you even have a nickname for her…which is sweet, I guess. I mean, everyone who knows *me* really well calls me Whit. Except you. You never call me anything but Whitnee or—"

"Little One?"

Hearing him say it made my heart skip a beat, but instead I said, "Which could be demeaning if you think about it." I was thankful that I didn't have to look at him.

"But for someone so little, you have quite a bit of…power. Does it bother you that I shorten Jezebel's name?" he called after me.

"Not at all! I said it was *sweet*."

Oh, just shut up, Whitnee. I was trying to sound casual, but I don't think that's how my voice was coming out. I didn't *even* want to know what he was thinking right then.

I finally came to a spot in the wall that jutted out sharply. I examined it with the Firelight from my hand. Was it my imagination or did it sparkle more over here? I was about to reach out and touch it when I felt Gabriel move in close behind me. He wasn't touching me, but I could feel the heat of his Pyradorian body and smell his sultry, Island-y scent.

"I suppose you could say I am close to Jezebel." He was speaking quietly.

Slowly I turned around to face him, not shying away from his nearness. What was he trying to do? Earlier he wouldn't come near me and now…

"How close?" I asked, my heart pounding in a jealous rage. What was that in his eyes? Hesitation? Fear?

Gabriel had a secret…about Jezebel. It was all over his face.

"Why are you so interested?" he asked, skirting around my question.

"Why do you think?" I snapped in frustration. "You're keeping something from me again. How are we supposed to be partners if you keep lying?"

"You insist on total honesty, Whitnee, but some things said aloud have the power to hurt people. Are you sure you want complete honesty between us?"

"Yes, I do. It's the only way we're going to figure all of this out," I insisted. But deep down, I was becoming afraid of the truth about him and Jezebel. "I've told *you* everything…"

"Ah, really? *Have* you told me everything? Because I have the distinct impression that you and Caleb are more than just friends this time around. Yet you have not said a word about it."

My mouth dropped open.

"I am not discussing Caleb with you."

"Then you understand my point. Some things do not need to be said between us. I can read the signs anyway," he finished sharply, leaving me to wonder how much had been revealed of the developing feelings between Caleb and me. "Now we should probably return to the house before the others wake up. And Thomas is alone on guard duty. I told him I would only be gone for a moment." He backed away to leave, but I just stood there.

"I am not leaving until I have fully explored this place. I have a feeling there's a secret here." I put my hands on my hips stubbornly.

"The only thing we can reasonably conclude is that your friend Will was once here. It does not mean there is something special about this cave."

"He was with my dad...on Jezebel's father's property...in this cave! Of course, that had to be before you and Jezebel were even born, but still...How can you pretend that's not important somehow? I'm not going back to the house yet. Just go handle your business, and I'll stay here."

"You know that I cannot leave you by yourself." He was becoming aggravated, but I didn't care. "We can come back in the daylight."

I shook my head, feeling annoyed with him for keeping secrets...and for bringing up Caleb like that. It was none of his business. He moved toward me again, like he was considering just dragging me out of there himself. I took a step back, realizing I was only pinning myself in the crevice between the wall and the jutting rocky piece of the cave.

But instead of shrinking against a hard surface, I fell *through* the cave wall.

TRUTH OR DARE

I gave a startled cry as I felt myself falling backward into empty space. Gabriel's alarmed face disappeared for a moment. I thrust my arms out, trying to catch myself, and ended up being caught by his powerful hands. I was slammed back into him, wrapping my shaking arms around his back while the world righted itself again. The floating bubble of light had extinguished, leaving us completely in the dark. We held each other for a moment, and I hated that I fit so perfectly into his arms…that my head rested at the perfect spot on his chest and that his heartbeat was so familiar.

"That was scary," I whimpered, but decided I wouldn't mind staying there like that for a while longer.

"There must be a gap there that we did not see," he said. "Are you okay?"

If I said no, would I get to stay longer in his arms?

"Yeah. I'm glad you caught me."

We pulled away from each other, but his lingering hand around my waist made me think he was just as reluctant as I was to let go. I turned around to face the wall again while Gabriel cast Firelight over my shoulder. It looked like just a normal crevice of rock. But when I reached out, my hand went through the wall and disappeared! It was as if it was just a holographic image…

"It is a screen. How bizarre to find one here," Gabriel murmured.

"A screen?"

"Remember how Pyras can create illusions…images that appear real but are not? A screen is a stationary image meant to block out something visually. They are made to resemble their surroundings." He plunged his hand through to the other side.

"Sooo…it sounds like I was right about finding a secret in here." I couldn't keep the sly grin off my face.

"You would like that…"

"Let's go check out what's on the other side." I started forward, but he took the opportunity to wrap his large hands around my stomach and pull me back. *Dang.* The physical contact was starting to affect me—in the ways I was hoping to avoid.

"Wait. It could be dangerous."

"Well, good thing you trained me so well to defend myself. Come on." I pried his hands off of me and pulled him forward.

"We really should check back at the house first…" he mumbled half-heartedly, but I was moving through the screen, desperate curiosity pushing me ahead.

I probably should have listened to him…should have turned back and marched straight to that house. But I had my mind set—I was going to follow the clues until I found my dad.

With my hands illuminated, I pushed through the thin screen and found myself in a small chamber maybe ten feet in diameter. Directly across from our point of entry was the swirly symbol again…only smaller.

"Look!" I cried as I moved quickly across the space. There were thin, almost imperceptible cracks that ran from the floor in a square around the symbol. "It's a doorway," I realized, glancing back at Gabriel squeezing himself through the small screen entry behind me.

His eyes roamed everywhere in the chamber before finally resting on me. "Watch out for traps," he warned.

I turned back around and used my entire body to push against the door—but with no luck. It would not budge.

"Gabriel, come open it." I moved out of his way and watched him pit all of his strength against the door.

Nothing happened. Finally, he stepped back and, with one glowing hand, he leaned against the door and shook his head.

"I really think we should come back later to explore—" he said, but stopped when my eyes widened.

One of the four swirls in the symbol had begun to glow red, starting from its outermost tip and moving inward to the center of the spiral. He pulled his hand away, and the light faded.

"Maybe you have to use—"

"All four life forces to open it?" he finished, examining the symbol closely.

"Wait, step away. Let me—"

"No. Bad idea." He shook his head before I even had a chance to complete my thought. "You know what happens every time you combine life forces."

"That was because I hadn't built up enough life force stamina before. I got better by the time I was leaving. Come on…just let me try it," I begged.

"You have never used more than two at once. What if you…"

"Explode?" I joked. "I don't think that will happen."

"That was not exactly my thought."

"We don't even know if I can use all four together. At least let me try. Just once." And I reached out both of my hands and rested them on the surface of the wall.

"Please, Whitnee…"

I inhaled deeply and focused. My breathing, my emotions, my thoughts, and my very existence all molded into one concentrated beam of energy. In that moment I felt a complete connection with the Island…as if the Island itself were gifting me…as if my body were merely an extension of the ground beneath me. The different sensations of Wind, Fire, Earth, and Water coursed through me like an electric current contained deep within the mountain.

In fascination, I watched as the swirls on the wall began to light up—one each in blue, green, red, and purple. Just like before, they began at the outer tips of the symbol and spread inward. At the point that they reached the center, the symbol flashed bright white, and the door in the wall pushed backward, leaving a darkened walkway into a tunnel.

I was about to drop my hands to my side and release the life forces when I discovered that I was glowing…and I don't mean my eyes. I mean my skin, my clothes…Everything on me was illuminated, as if a radioactive film had settled over my body. The power and energy that surged through me was inhuman. I felt strong enough to break through the rock wall by myself. And yet, I had the sense that I was light enough to fly…It was the strangest thing I'd ever experienced. Everything around me looked and felt different, like it had a shimmery, unreal quality to it. Even the air in the chamber seemed like a thick, moldable substance that I could manipulate if I wanted.

I was holding my hands out, gaping at what I was seeing, when I spun around and faced Gabriel. The expression on his face was a mix of terror and fascination. Slowly, he reached his hand out, as if afraid to touch me. My fingers met his in the air, and it was like a shock the moment we touched. We both jumped and pulled away.

"What is happening to me?" I immediately tried to break off the connection with the life forces.

"Your eyes are rotating through the colors…" he whispered incredulously, but his face was grave. "Whitnee, make it stop."

"I'm trying!" I cried. I shook my hands out as if trying to fling the glow from them. Instead, two white lights—I don't even know exactly what they were—shot out of my hands and exploded the part of the cave where they landed. Chunks of rock blew up into the little chamber. I conjured a shield instinctively and practically threw myself on top of Gabriel. I didn't even care if we were both electrocuted by this weirdness—I only thought of protecting him from the collapsing room. There was a shock between our two bodies, but it was only for the first moment we came into contact. He fell backwards, gripping me tightly and taking the brunt of the fall. I maintained the shield, which was pummeled mercilessly with boulders and rock pieces. I shut my eyes, wondering if we would be buried alive together inside this mountain.

But then the rocks finally came to rest, and all was still again inside the chamber. I opened my eyes and discovered I was no longer glowing...except for the green hue of the shield around us. We were both breathing heavily, and I was too afraid to move. Gabriel's arms remained around me.

"You know," he said with a groan. "If we are going to be *partners*, it would help if you listened to me just once."

"Fine, you were right. Did I hurt you?"

"Other than a shock to my heart a couple of times, I think I am going to live. What about you? Are you going to be sick?"

"I feel fine...I think. But I don't know how long I can hold this shield up. It's probably a matter of time before I have to release it and we're crushed to death."

Oh my gosh, I had sentenced us to our deaths.

"What are you talking about? Just let it go," he said.

I looked up through the transparent arc over us. Okay, maybe there wasn't a mountain of boulders on top of it.

"Unless you just want to stay here with me longer...I probably would not argue with you." His voice had an inviting undertone.

I released the shield and then buried my face in his chest, allowing him to tighten his arms around me. I think we were both a little overwhelmed with what had just happened. And lying there together while our breathing slowed seemed completely comfortable...and needed. I felt the last bit of Earth life force drain from me. Once it vanished, I was fatigued and shaky.

"Thank you for the shield." Gabriel finally spoke into the darkness.

"Please. As if I actually did something *right*," I replied sarcastically, wanting to close my eyes and sleep. His body heat was intoxicating.

"I suppose we should get up and survey the damage," he suggested.

I tried to hide my drowsiness by willingly maneuvering myself away from him. The last thing I wanted was for him to believe I couldn't handle using all four life forces—even though it was pretty obvious I couldn't.

I found enough strength to pull myself up into a sitting position and lean against the wall. Once Gabriel took a look around, I thought I heard him curse—in Dorian.

"What?"

He ran one hand along his face and stared at the screen...or what used to be the screen. "We are blocked in. The rocks..." He sighed heavily.

"Oops," I mumbled.

"It could take a long time to move them out of the way."

"I'll help," I pushed myself up and stood...but not for long. The wave of dizziness had me grappling for the wall to steady myself. My legs nearly gave out.

Gabriel immediately steadied my other side and remarked, "Now who is the one not being honest?"

"I'm fine. I just need a second to—"

"Stop lying, Whitnee. It weakened you like it always does... Just sit down and try not to cause any problems." His voice was a little harsh.

I gave him one stubborn I'm-not-happy-about-this look before sliding to the floor again. There was no point in arguing with him when I was clearly incapable of helping. He set to work, shuffling huge rocks around the chamber. Instead of making myself ignore the way his tunic stretched tightly over those rippling arm muscles, I decided to just enjoy the view. I was a captive audience, after all.

"Do you have your zephyra? Maybe we could contact Thomas," I suggested.

He grunted. "I left my satchel at the entry of the cave when I came to find you." He shifted a few more boulders around before pausing to scrutinize the remaining destruction. "There is no way I can move that...It is too heavy."

In the dim light, I could faintly see what he was talking about. One chunk of the ceiling had collapsed, and it was huge. "Could you use one of your Fireballs to smash it into smaller pieces?"

"You mean a Firedart? No, I would not chance using one here. This room is too unstable and might cave in completely if we add any more pressure."

He gave a short sigh and set back to work without another word. I was thinking I wanted to learn how to make a Firedart when I got out of there. I grew silent then and let my eyes wander over to the doorway I had opened.

"Gabriel, look!" I called out.

"What now?" He dropped a heavy rock before turning around.

I pointed to the tunnel where another little bubble light was floating in midair. He crept closer, and I made myself get up and stumble that direction with what little energy I had remaining.

We peered together into the new tunnel.

"Maybe we should see if this leads us outside somewhere," I whispered, not sure why I was talking so quietly.

Gabriel just stared suspiciously at the floating light.

I took a shaky step forward, and he stopped me. *Of course.* I was about to launch again into my arguments about why we should continue our exploration when he spoke.

"I will go first and take a look around. You stay here and rest."

I gave him a look that clearly said, *Yeah, right.*

"Very well. Then stay behind me this time. And do not touch anything."

I agreed with a nod and followed after him. We had to duck down to get through the doorway. There was nothing on the other side but a hollowed-out tunnel featuring one little glowing light in the middle of the pathway. The floor of the tunnel sloped down into darkness until I thought I glimpsed another tiny pinpoint of light.

Curiously I reached out to touch the bubble and Gabriel slapped my hand away as if I were an obnoxious child. "I said... Do. Not. Touch. *Anything.*"

"O-*kay*." I gave him a dirty look.

He edged past the light without coming near it, and I copied him. We padded quietly down to the next light, and I struggled to walk straight. Looking ahead, it was clear that the tunnel kept going. If this was going to take a while, then he was probably right. We should go back. I desperately needed some pure Water to replenish myself. I knew from experience that Water was the only thing that "fixed me" when I was like this. And, truthfully, I had a sudden attack of conscience about Caleb and Morgan. They would kill me if they missed out on exploring this place. Not only that, but they kind of still thought I had no memory of them.

"Wait," I said as he sidled past the second suspended light in front of me.

I was so weak, I had to pause and lean against the wall.

He turned around and tilted his head, regarding me suspiciously through the light between us. "I think we should go back...I mean, we should get Morgan and Caleb. They deserve to know what we're doing."

"Finally you agree with me." He rolled his eyes. "I will pretend that your real reason is not because you know you are sick and need Water..."

"I'm thinking of my friends too!" I retorted, giving myself away.

"Can you make it back up the tunnel to the door?"

"Of course!" I raised my chin defiantly and pushed away from the wall. But the slope seemed steeper than I remembered coming down, and I felt myself waver and start to stumble backward... right into the floating light. Gabriel caught me from behind, but I had already tripped into it—and apparently tripped something else I shouldn't have.

We felt something vibrate on the tunnel floor and heard the unmistakable scrape of rock against rock.

"The door!" Gabriel exclaimed. I moved out of his way, holding onto the wall for support, while he ran back up the slope. I heard him yell and then curse again before the vibrations stopped and all was quiet.

"Gabriel?" I called out in fear.

"Yes...I am here. The door is closed." His irritation echoed back through the tunnel.

I slumped down to the floor again, exhausted and defeated. Boy, was I screwing up a lot.

Eventually, after he scuffled about and grumbled to himself for a few minutes, he came back down to where I was.

I couldn't look at him. "If you give me a second to rest," I stated quietly, "I'll go back up and open it."

"Absolutely not. You are not using all four life forces like that as long as I am around. Besides, there is no symbol on this side. It will not open the same way." He knelt down across from me on my right, and his legs brushed mine.

I suddenly wanted to cry. "I'm so sorry." I leaned my head back against the wall and swallowed the lump in my throat. My eyes closed easily, and my breathing felt so unnaturally slow that I could just fall right into sleep.

"Whitnee, stay awake!" Gabriel said, and I felt his hand on my knee, shaking me.

"I am..." I mumbled, but my eyes stayed closed.

"Open your eyes." I think he leaned forward, because his voice was closer.

"Maybe if I sleep, my strength will come back," I suggested softly.

"Try to stay awake! Talk to me."

My eyes fluttered open and tried to focus on his concerned face. "About what?"

"Whatever you want to talk about."

"Really? Anything at all?"

He grinned. "Maybe that would be a bad idea. How about a game? Is there a game that would keep you awake?"

"A game?" I gave him a doubtful look. Was he serious?

"We are trapped here with nowhere to go but forward. We might as well entertain ourselves...at least until I am satisfied you are well enough to keep going. Teach me a game you play on the Mainland."

"Um, okay." A game. What game could I teach him? Then the words were out of my mouth before I thought long enough about them. "Truth or Dare."

"Truth or Dare…How do you play?"

"Well, you ask someone if they want to take a truth question or a dare that you make up for them."

"A dare?"

"Yeah…it's a challenge to the person to do something kind of crazy. Something they might not normally do. Like, 'I dare you to go moon the neighbors' or something."

He frowned in confusion. "How do you *moon* somebody?"

His question startled me enough to laugh out loud. No *way* was I explaining that to Gabriel. "Um, never mind about that one…" I choked, feeling a little adrenaline from the laugh that helped me focus better. "We should probably avoid dares anyway if we play. It's not like we can dare each other to do something when we're stuck in here."

"I might be able to think of something," he responded suggestively, and my eyes widened at him.

Did he mean what I thought he meant? "Uhhh…" I stumbled awkwardly, trying to ignore the amusement on his face. "I'm usually more of a truth kind of girl…unless I'm playing with people who I absolutely trust not to dare me to do something morally stupid."

What?! Why did I just say that? I was really supposed to be avoiding distractions with Gabriel…and a game of Truth or Dare definitely sounded distracting. But at this point, I was having a difficult time remembering why I wanted to forget him and why it wasn't okay to flirt with him and why I was supposed to ignore our past together and…

"Very well. Let me make sure I understand correctly," he said. "We take turns either daring each other to do something or asking each other questions that must be answered truthfully?"

"Yes."

"And what if someone lies?"

I shrugged. "Most people don't. They just won't answer."

"What happens if they do not answer?"

I looked him straight in the eye. "Then they're out. And in our case, if one of us gets out, the other is the winner."

He raised his eyebrows. "I do not like to lose."

"Me neither," I told him.

"You go first then."

I sighed. "Okay, truth or dare?"

"I choose truth."

I thought for a moment. What did I want to know about Gabriel? Oh, so many things. But I decided to start out easy on him while he learned the game. "What's your favorite color?"

"Pink," he said without hesitation.

That made me sit up a little more and stare at him skeptically. "Pink?" I repeated. That couldn't possibly be true. But a smile spread across his face as if I wasn't in on a joke. That was when I glanced down at my dress…and remembered the pink highlights in my hair. "You're supposed to tell the truth!" I accused him.

"I am."

"There is no way that pink is your favorite color—"

"Okay, then I will change it to…what is it that Mainlanders call it? Blonde?" His smile had turned wicked now.

"Gabriel…"

"Gray?"

"Stop it!" I had to smile at his attention. "I get your point. But if you're not going to play by the rules—"

"I am being perfectly truthful, Whitnee. My favorite color is whatever you are wearing." And his face did lose some of its amusement.

Was he really being honest or just trying to goad me so that the fatigue would wear off? I will admit that this game was starting to chase away some of that drowsiness. He had my attention now.

"So it is my turn?" He looked at me through narrowed eyes. "Truth or dare?"

"Truth...always," I answered, ignoring the anticipation in my stomach at what he might ask me.

"When you were missing your memory, you kept giving me strange looks. What were you thinking?"

So much for *him* going easy on *me* the first round.

"Truthfully? I was suspicious of you, but I didn't know why. And I felt something for you...but I didn't know what." Was that too much information?

"You felt something for me? Now that your memory is back, what was it?"

"Sorry, you only get one question per round," I reminded him.

He leaned against the wall and studied my expression. I tried not to show anything on my face, which was difficult.

"My turn. Truth or dare?" I prompted.

"Truth."

I decided to go for the thing that bothered me most. "What in the world were you thinking when you handed me off to Caleb in the portal?"

He took a deep breath and waited a moment before answering. "I was thinking that you were in danger, and I wanted you to see that I was not completely selfish and...perhaps I wanted to rebel against my parents just once. Either way, I felt that you were too good to be real...Like you did not belong in my world." He stopped talking and got this really intense look on his face.

I took advantage of his pause. "Well, you should have trusted me when I said I needed to stay. That was one of the worst moments of my life, Gabriel...I was so mad that I practically beat the crap out of Caleb on the other side for pulling me through."

"You hit Caleb?" His eyes widened at me.

"Well, sort of...I mean, I'm pretty sure I at least gave him a bruise. But, *ugh*, you have no idea what that did to me. And then Ben told me all this *stuff*. It completely rocked my world. And all I could think was, 'What if I never get back?' It was horrible."

I didn't know why I was telling him all of that. I guess it had been building up in me for six weeks. He needed to know how I really felt.

His expression grew pained. "Whitnee, I am telling you the truth when I say that I have regretted that decision since the moment you disappeared. And not just because of the trouble it caused both of us or even because I interfered with your plans to find your father, but because..." He stopped again, appearing torn.

"Because why?" I sounded breathless.

He gave a sigh and closed his eyes for a second. "Never mind."

"What? What were you gonna say?"

"I believe you only get one question per round," he finally said, and stared hard at the ground.

You've got to be kidding me, I thought in frustration. "Your stupid turn," I grumbled.

"I am assuming you choose truth again?" he clarified.

"I guess." I rolled my eyes, thinking maybe we should stop playing and just talk for real.

"I want a truthful answer to this one." He finally raised his eyes to mine. "Have you missed me at all?"

Every freaking day, I immediately thought. But I remained silent, contemplating the best way to handle this question. To be truthful would be to admit something that I'd been trying to ignore for six weeks. And what good would it do either of us to admit the truth? I was dead set on not growing attached to him again. I knew that once I found my dad, I was leaving this place—and Gabriel—forever.

"Since you are not answering me, I assume you are forfeiting—"

"Yes," I blurted.

"Yes, you are forfeiting a win to me?"

"No. I mean, yes, I missed you."

Why? Why do I torture myself this way? Bad Whitnee.

"I missed you too," he admitted, and then without warning he leaned forward and cupped my face gently with one of his massive hands.

I should have stopped him, should have cut off the whole vibe between us right then.

But I didn't. Because I really had missed him.

His eyes roamed freely over my face, and his voice was so tender. "I have missed everything about you. The expressions on your face, the way you smile at me, the look in your eyes right before I kiss you..."

I was trembling now because his face was so close. And I so badly wanted him to kiss me again that every rational thought escaped my mind. I was fully awake now and ready for whatever happened next...

But he backed away and removed his hand from my face. Something in his expression told me that he was the one who had some kind of attack of conscience this time. There was no way I gave off a vibe that I didn't want it.

My head was spinning with confusion when he said, "I believe it is your turn to ask a question."

I took a second to compose myself. Something had made him think twice about kissing me. Last time, Gabriel had not been afraid to steal a kiss from me when the moment presented itself. So what exactly was his hesitation this time?

That was when my heart picked up to dramatic speed, and I felt a chill go down my back. "Tell me the truth, Gabriel. What exactly is your relationship with Jezebel?"

His face changed immediately. I got the impression he had been waiting for this question to come up again and was now resigned to finally answering it. He became expressionless, and it felt like some kind of uncrossable barrier slid into place between him and me.

"If everything follows according to plan," Gabriel said robotically, "Jezebel will be my wife when I become Guardian next year."

DISTRACTION

I think I stopped breathing for a full minute before I exploded.

"You're *engaged*?! To be *married*?" I shrieked. "Since *when*?" I knew I was talking in italics, but I couldn't help it.

He was completely unmoved by my reaction, as if he had prepared for it. "Since Jezebel was born about six months after I was," he replied calmly. My mouth was opening and closing like I was going to speak, but my thoughts were totally jumbled in a million directions. I mean, what was I *supposed* to say? *Congratulations*? And was it just me, or did the walls in this tunnel suddenly feel like they were shrinking?

I was no longer lethargic. My girl senses were on Code Red Lockdown. In my shock, I pulled myself to my feet. I didn't want to be physically close to him anymore.

"So…so you lied? In Aerodora…when you said you weren't romantically involved with anyone!" I pointed at him. "Why? Why didn't you just tell me then? We could have saved ourselves a whole lot of confusion!"

Had he been playing with me and my emotions this whole time? I stepped over his legs, carefully avoiding the little suspended light, and moved farther down the tunnel before spinning around unsteadily again.

"I was not lying…Jezebel and I have never made it official." He stood up and looked down at me from several feet away.

"Official? Are you kidding me? You're planning to marry the girl! Sounds pretty official to *me*," I practically yelled. The tunnel was definitely closing in on me at this point. I was suffocating to death as I tried to make sense of what I was hearing.

"Whitnee, if you would just calm down, I will explain it to you—"

"You know what? I actually don't want to know—" I held out my hands as if I could block him out of my view. "I really need out of here. I mean, it's hot, I can't breathe…We need to go. We need to get away…Game over."

I started marching down the tunnel without waiting for him. I had to mask my wobbly walking by tracing one hand along the wall as I went. I wasn't quite as well as I thought I was, but I couldn't stay there. I felt like such a fool! All this time I had thought we had something special…something he didn't have with anyone else! And dang him if he hadn't encouraged me to admit I missed him just in time for him to drop his happy little news on me!

"Wait, Whitnee," I heard him call, but I was not waiting.

I was going to find my way out of there if it killed me. And it might. The path kept descending farther into the mountain, and it was uncomfortably warm. I could actually feel the Fire life force very close to the surface of my emotions.

He caught up to me and said, "I do not wish to marry Jezebel, if you want to know."

"Right. Like I'm going to believe you have no desire to marry supermodel Jezebel with her long legs and gorgeous face and perfect body! Oh my gosh, I've been such an idiot," I started muttering. "It makes perfect sense now…your little nickname for her and the way you know her house and her art and every little thing about her…not to mention how *she* acts around you! No wonder she hated me." He was trekking closely behind as I darted around the floating lights, but I refused to look back at him.

"Jezebel and I have never been given a choice! Our betrothal was constructed by our *parents*. So yes, we have formed a friendship over the years." He punctuated the word "parents" like it was a curse word. "Her father owns all this property, and I am, of course, the next Guardian. Our families saw it as an advantageous marriage that would ultimately give us more power…"

"Good. Great. She will look perfect on your arm once you're the all-powerful Guardian!" I replied. "And I'm *so* glad that I could just be some girl you used as a pathetic distraction before you're a *married man*!" My voice caught with emotion. Wow. It actually hurt to say that out loud. I felt so used. With horror, I realized I was the *other woman*.

I'm gonna be sick. I slowed a little and grabbed my stomach with one hand, trying not to throw up. My body felt feverish now as I subdued the Fire within. Why was there not one breeze in this godforsaken passageway?

He took my pause as an opportunity to spin me around. I was too weak to fight it. "Is that what you think you are to me? A distraction?" His eyes were burning into mine.

"You never should have kissed me…or said all those things to me. Not when you had such a huge commitment to another girl. I mean, I'm not like that. I didn't come to this Island to find someone who…I would never have let you…*ugh*."

My eyes were stinging. I could not let myself cry over this. No way.

"Whitnee, please understand. My life has been planned out for me since before I was born. I have no freedoms, no choices." His grip on my arm grew tighter. "But when you came here, everything changed. You were the most unplanned, unexpected thing to happen to me. And the connection I had with you was something nobody could control, not even my parents. Why can you not see that I care about *you*?"

"Because you're going to marry Jezebel!" I cried.

"I said that was the plan…but Jez and I have always resented the plan. Neither of us is happy about how our lives have been dictated to us. If we could find a way out of it, we would."

I blinked up at him, wanting to believe what he was saying. But I must've been a sucker for heartache, because I asked, "Have you ever kissed her?"

He was silent…and *guilty*.

"Dangit, Gabriel! How can you tell me that you don't care about her like that?" I yanked my arms out of his grip.

"It was before I met you…and it did not mean anything to me! If anything, I realized I could not make myself feel that way toward her."

I think I snorted at that and turned my back on him to keep following the tunnel. "I can't believe I trusted you with so much… I shared my feelings with you and my secrets and…my kisses. You know, it's not like I just give those out to anyone."

That did it. My eyes filled up with the dreaded tears, and I felt one escape down my cheek. Gabriel either heard it in my voice or was especially sensitive to emotional climates, because he darted in front of me and stood directly in my path where he could see my face. I stopped short and took a step back away from him, trying to hide the fact that I was crying.

"Oh, Whitnee." He sighed. "I expected you to be mad that I withheld this from you…I expected it to hurt your trust in me. But I did not expect this…" And he reached his fingers out and wiped the tear from my face.

I pushed his hand away. "These"—I choked, pointing at my teary eyes—"are not for you, Gabriel. I just don't feel well, and I'm tired and confused and…" I knew he wasn't buying my excuses, so I stopped. "Does Jezebel know that you and I…that we kissed and all that?"

He shook his head. "She might suspect my feelings for you, but I did not share those details with her. I know she keeps company with other men when I am not around. We just agreed not to discuss those things with each other until the marriage plans were announced publicly."

"That's so...weird," I said. What kind of a relationship was that? Then I wiped my eyes self-consciously.

"You said that you do not kiss other people..." Gabriel began. "But what about Caleb?"

"What *about* Caleb?" My face turned angry. *Caleb.* My heart pounded harder. How dare he bring him up again!

"I just assumed...perhaps wrongly, but...have you ever kissed Caleb?"

"Not that you deserve to know any more personal information about me," I said bitterly, "but no. I have never kissed Caleb." I hardly felt it necessary to tell him that I had certainly wanted to kiss Caleb before...about as strongly as I had wanted to kiss Gabriel only a few minutes earlier. I also tried to push away the thought in the back of my mind that Caleb would never lie to me or mislead me the way Gabriel had.

"If not Caleb, then were there others...?" His voice trailed off, and I gave him such a disgusted look that he added, "Consider it my last truth question."

I took a deep breath, wishing for some fresh air in there. "I don't know why you care so much, but yes. There was one other guy in ninth grade who tried to kiss me, but he doesn't really count. I was so naïve that I didn't know what I was doing and ended up laughing in the middle of it...which embarrassed him and, well, we never tried it again. End of story. Now can we keep moving? I want out of here!"

Was that a smile trying to break on his face? "So...I was the first one to 'count'?"

I averted my eyes and tried to maneuver past him. I wanted the conversation to be over. But he blocked me again.

"Gabriel," I pleaded. "Let's not do this. I don't even know what to think right now. I'm so mad at you...and at myself. I didn't want any distractions this time around."

"Do you consider me a distraction?" He was intentionally taking up my personal space again.

"Um, *yeah*." I rolled my eyes and tried to go around the other side of him. No luck. Darn his big, muscular bulk of a being! "Please let me go…It's gotta be dawn by now, and we need to find a way out of here."

"I will, but I want to tell you one more secret…for the sake of complete honesty between us."

I stared up at him, my hands on my hips. I didn't think I could handle any more of Gabriel's secrets at the moment.

"When I came to the Mainland…" He was speaking slowly and softly. "A huge part of me expected—and hoped—that Abrianna would close that portal behind me and never open it again."

I started shaking my head. "I don't understand."

"I am trying to say that it would not have been the worst thing in the world for me to be stranded on the Mainland for the rest of my life, to find a home away from here…away from all the responsibilities and the lies and the manipulations. The idea of leaving this place…It was almost exciting to me." I couldn't take my eyes from him as he spoke. "But then I arrived there and you were gone. And all I could think about was returning to the Island… because I realized it was never about being on the Mainland. For me, it is about being wherever you are."

Air. I needed air.

"Gabriel…"

"I promise that I am going to help you find your dad. I am defying my parents and all that is sacred to my Island because I believe we need to right what was wronged a long time ago. I will be your 'partner' and listen to you and fight for you, but I want to know…Is there—" He paused and tilted my chin up so that I had no choice but to continue making eye contact with him. "Is there a reason for me not to marry Jezebel?"

His eyes were so brilliant and so vulnerable, even in the semi-darkness. I could feel my anger cooling and, with it, my body

284

temperature. I gazed back at him as I contemplated what to say. Whatever he was asking me to confirm sounded huge.

"I refuse to be the reason you do not marry Jezebel," I told him, my eyes glistening again with fresh tears. "You have to make that decision on your own...by doing what is right for both of you." I reached out and laid a gentle hand on his chest.

He immediately covered it with his own hand, and I was pretty sure he was trembling. "I no longer know what is right," he whispered.

"Yes, you do. Gabriel, at some point you need to take control of your own future. You have a huge amount of power and influence right at your fingertips. What are you going to do with that? Are you going to run away from that responsibility? Are you just going to be your parents' puppet...or will you do something that changes the world? There is always a choice."

"I want to be a better person...and I feel like I can do that as long as you are by my side, Whitnee." He sounded like he was pleading.

I smiled regretfully at him. "You don't need me to make the right choices, Gabriel."

He closed his eyes and brought my hand to his face where it rested on his cheek. His face was hot against my cool hand. He seemed younger than nineteen years old as he stood there in front of me. The amount of compassion I felt for him was overwhelming. Had he ever been truly loved by another person? Who was looking out for Gabriel? Who had his best interests at heart? Everybody close to him just seemed to be using him. I was instinctively thankful for my friends and family who unconditionally loved and accepted me. But who did that for Gabriel?

"I *dare* you to change your world, Gabriel," I challenged him, thinking it was my turn in the game anyway.

He opened his eyes and the emotion there had changed. "Whitnee..." he whispered, and before I had time to object, he had leaned down and pressed his lips to mine...gently at first.

His lips were full and so, so warm. The sensation of kissing him again was everything I had remembered and yet so different. There was desperation this time. As his kiss grew deeper, I felt his arms move to encompass me. And then I was kissing him back with fervor. I had denied myself the memories of this for too long, and now that I was here...now that we were together...

But I had never envisioned I'd be kissing an engaged man. And I didn't care if his parents had been the ones to orchestrate the engagement; he had still willingly conformed to their wishes. He had still planned even up until now to follow through with marrying Jezebel. And what we were doing felt wrong.

"No!" I cried and shoved him away—with some unnecessary force. I drew a shaky breath and leaned against the opposite wall. "I'm not going to do this. We can't be like this anymore, Gabriel."

"Why? Am I mistaken here? Do you not feel the same thing that I do?"

"Not everything is just about feelings!" I told him, slightly exasperated that he just wasn't getting it. "There's something to be said about integrity too! You have a commitment to Jezebel. And unless that changes, you and I are just partners...*nothing more.*"

He narrowed his eyes at me, the hurt he felt plainly visible there. But it only lasted a moment, because he must have seen some kind of unyielding resistance as I firmly held his gaze. I would not be the "other woman." I would not be played with when there was no real possible future there. I watched as cold resolution came over him, and all vulnerability in his eyes completely disappeared. That invisible barrier between us went back up.

I was almost jealous at how well he could turn off the emotions. Just like that.

DRAGONS HAVE FEELINGS TOO

After that, Gabriel took the lead through the winding tunnel, and I followed behind him silently, trying to come to terms with my multitude of emotions. I felt angry, betrayed, irritated, and, yes, guilty. I worried about Jezebel and how I would feel if I had been promised to a guy my whole life and then some random girl showed up and took him away from me...And then there was Caleb. Now that I was thinking clearly and not so wrapped up in discovering everything I had missed about Gabriel, I couldn't get my best friend out of my head.

How would Caleb feel if he knew Gabriel and I had just kissed again...after everything that had happened between us this summer? If it was true that Caleb and I were technically just friends, then why did I feel like I had just cheated on him? Why, when I was out of the haze of Gabriel's spell, did I suddenly hate myself? A very clear picture of the uncertainty in Caleb's face every time we talked about going back to the Island flashed through my memory...and my heart hurt. I truly cared about Caleb and never wanted to hurt him. But once again, it was clear that Caleb had known me better than I knew myself. He had suspected all along—and rightfully so—that I was not as "over" Gabriel as I had wanted to be. And the very thing he had feared happening...

had now happened. I was right back in a twisted web of feelings for a guy I still barely knew.

But this time the Caleb feelings were still there too. Not even kissing Gabriel had erased those stirring emotions I had for my best friend...like the way Caleb knew me so well—too well—and the comfort I felt when he was around, the ability he had to make me laugh, and the way my stomach actually jumped when he flirted with me in his confident, boyish way. Even the burning annoyance we could bring out in each other was just another powerful emotion we shared. And right now, loyal and protective Caleb was looking a whole lot better than the guy who had just announced his lifelong betrothal and then proceeded to steal a kiss from me anyway.

But how I could hide from Caleb what had happened here in this mountain with Gabriel? I couldn't remember a time Caleb didn't see right through me. I already expected him to be furious when I showed up, having spent all this time alone with Gabriel... while he was probably worrying about what happened to me. We needed to get out of there.

"It feels like we are somewhere in the bowels of the stupid mountain by now. Seriously, it must be a hundred degrees in here! Where are we?" I complained to Gabriel, who had not glanced back once to check on me.

"Obviously, I do not know," Gabriel snapped. His elevated body heat just added to the sweltering temperature in the passage.

I could sense his growing anger and injured pride, and it only frustrated me. Wasn't I the one with the right to be upset here? Geez...he was such a Pyra.

The walls themselves had grown warm to the touch, and the little glowing lights had become brighter and more frequent the farther into the mountain we traveled. I now understood why the Pyras chose to live near the volcano. The Fire life force was definitely more powerful here...I could barely contain it myself.

I darted around another light before asking, "Do you think Jezebel knows about this tunnel?"

"I doubt it," he grumbled in response.

"How could she not? It's on her prop—"

"Could we not discuss her right now?"

"But if she does know, then she'll figure out where we are once they find your satchel…" I pointed out.

"She does not know," he insisted.

"Well, then aren't you a little worried about what everyone will think when we're gone?"

"Of course I am worried!" he replied harshly. "I am worried that we are losing valuable time. I am worried about what Eden will do when you and I are both missing. And I am worried that our traitor—whoever he may be—might already have revealed our plans to the Guardian. Yes, there is much to worry about right now!"

The traitor. Oh my gosh. I had forgotten that somebody—maybe someone back at the house—helped kidnap me. What if he hurt Morgan and Caleb?

"Oh, geez…my friends could be in danger." My chest tightened just considering it, and when he didn't answer me back, I grew more afraid that he was having the same thoughts. "Hey," I stopped following him, feeling panicked and slightly hysterical. "What if this is just a dead end? What if we're just going so far into the mountain that we'll end up in—I don't know—a lava pit or something? Maybe we should just go back and work on opening that door and removing those rocks—"

He stopped and turned around to look at me. "Are you being serious?"

I just stared back at him in anxiety.

"We cannot go back. We are over halfway across this mountain!"

"But we just keep going down…"

"Yes, but we are still headed in a linear direction. If my sense of direction and distance are correct—and they usually are—then we are closer to coming out on the other side than we are to going back." He pointed ahead, but I started shaking my head.

"I can't do this! I need to get out of here." I wasn't typically claustrophobic, but I did need fresh air, and my emotions were starting to reflect how I felt physically.

"Then we need to keep moving! This was *your* idea. Do not give up on me now!"

"Stop yelling at me!"

He sighed and shook his head, trying to soften his demeanor. "We need to continue this direction. I need to see what is hidden here—What?"

I must have made a terrified face, because at the sound of our raised voices a huge reptilian creature had emerged from behind Gabriel...a version of a creature I had only seen in movies. *And it was staring at me.*

"Oh. My. Gosh," I whispered, and he turned to look.

Very slowly, he reached a hand out toward me.

"Whitnee." His voice was completely calm now. "Take my hand."

"What!" I hissed. "We should run! That looks like...like a dragon!" I was panicking for real now and backing away.

The dragon just squatted there, not even a foot away from Gabriel, looking back and forth between us with its red eyes, slit nostrils, and sharp teeth as if it was trying to understand what we were saying. It was about six feet tall with red scales and spikes down its back. The skin was leathery looking but seemed flecked with a shimmering gold that glinted in the flickering light. I saw no wings on this dragon.

"Stay calm. If a drakon reads the wrong emotion in either of us, he will attack."

"Well, what the heck is the *wrong* emotion?" I screeched.

"Probably the one you are showing right now." He spoke softly, but I could detect his sarcasm. "Trust me, take my hand."

I hesitated to move closer, but then the dragon—er, drakon—locked its eyes on me and snarled, tiny wisps of smoke escaping from its mouth. I jumped in fear and rushed to Gabriel, placing my hand in his and taking shelter in the shadow of his tall frame. He placed himself between the reptile and me.

Instantly I felt a soothing, peaceful sensation spread through me, and I realized Gabriel was using his little magical tranquilizer between our hands. Part of me resented him for it; the other part of me was grateful.

"Time to turn around..." I said between gritted teeth, resting my forehead on his back and reluctantly loving the way he smelled. There was no description for the perfect combination of "tropical" and "male."

"If we turn around, we will never know what he is guarding," Gabriel pointed out, and that made my head snap up.

It was guarding something?

"Just keep your emotions indifferent, and he will let us pass. As long as we do not feel whatever he is trained to attack, then we are fine."

"I don't like this idea..." I whimpered, but he was already pulling me toward the drakon. I chanced a glance at the creature who was regarding us too closely for an animal. He made me feel like he could see right through me...and I didn't like it. Gabriel kept his eyes trained on the drakon as we maneuvered past him. True to Gabriel's words, the drakon let us pass by and did not attack. But the creature's intrusive eyes followed our every movement.

Gabriel whispered, "Whatever happens, whatever we find, we need to keep moving through here." After we escaped the drakon's reach, I stepped up to Gabriel's side so I could see.

The tunnel opened up into a vast circular chamber with sparkling lights around its circumference and I wasn't sure which sight to take in first. The ring of colorful drakons clearly posted as guards around the cavern? Or the tips of towering stone posts that rose up from a pit in the center of the circle?

Gabriel and I stopped and stared, our hands still locked together. The birthmarks of each tribe were sketched onto the stone towers. We had entered the room closest to the Hydrodorian tower. My gaze trailed from the symbol down to what lay below. There were stairs that bottomed out to a flat arena with a glittering floor. And in the center of the circle were two flat tables that looked as if they were carved from the cave floor itself. Aside from those tables, there was something familiar about the layout of this place...

Gabriel and I exchanged confused glances. I was desperately curious to take those stairs down to the bottom and find out. But no sooner had the thought entered my mind than the drakon snarled again from behind me.

"Keep moving," Gabriel said, his voice sounding small in the wide open space.

We started edging around the circular pit toward an opening in the wall on the opposite side. We would have to pass a blue drakon, who was already standing rigid, only his eyes moving as he stared at us.

"We can't leave..." I mumbled, shuffling along beside him. "Gabriel, this looks like..."

"A portal? I know," he muttered grimly. "I think I can see now why my parents have been so invested in gaining access to Jezebel's property."

"And why they want to keep it in the *family*..." I added pointedly. Was this really the reason for aligning Gabriel's future with Jezebel's? It sure seemed like a shady and calculated move—just like Gabriel's parents. The real question, though, was did Jezebel or her father know of it?

"What do you think those tables are for? Are you sure we cannot just go down there and look closer?"

He seemed to pause and think about it, mirroring my own curiosity. He released my hand. "Only one way to find out. Stay here until I say."

His eyes conveyed a command I was not to defy, so I nodded in agreement. He knew the drakons better than I did. With caution, he slowly stepped away from me in the direction of the stairs. My eyes moved back and forth between Gabriel's progress and the blue drakon ahead of us. He was watching Gabriel but made no moves to attack. Gabriel placed one foot on the first step down into the pit…and still nothing from the drakon except a suspicious stare.

"Okay, Whitnee…just remember we are only looking. Apparently that motivation is acceptable to them." He reached his hand out to me, and I grabbed onto it. Carefully and slowly, we made our way downstairs.

The moment I set foot on the flat surface of the pit we both knew we had made a terrible mistake. The cave floor began to vibrate, and I immediately felt all four life forces ripple through my body and activate the towers around me. It wasn't even something I could control…I glanced at my hands, expecting to see my whole body glowing again. I still looked a normal color. At the very instant that the vibrations began, the drakons moved into offensive stances on the ringed platform above us. Their roars were deafening and strangely high-pitched. If Gabriel hadn't reacted so quickly by casting a protective Wall of Fire around the entire arena, we might have been burned to death by the Fire-breathing creatures.

"What did you do?" he yelled, turning in circles with his hands projected in front of him.

"Nothing! It just reacted to me!" I shouted. "We need to get out of here before something bad happens, Gabriel!"

I could feel the life forces mixing together—both inside me and around me. Four beams of light shot out of the now-glowing birthmarks on each tower above us, and I felt like I couldn't breathe. The Fire around us, the snapping and snarling of the drakons, and the vibrating ground had my senses in overload. I had one random thought: *Morgan was right. I trigger a portal without even trying.*

"Run!" Gabriel commanded, shoving me ahead of him while he maintained his Wall of Fire.

I darted across the expansive floor beneath the towers, passing through the stone tables. Up close, I saw what appeared to be a pair of handprints deeply impressed into the top of each table and draped in leather straps, but I didn't have time to study them further. A dense fog was percolating above us, and if we really were standing in the middle of a portal, we were about to be transported somewhere.

I rushed up the stairs, and Gabriel's long strides caught up to me. But when we neared the top, the Fire was so hot I had to cover my eyes with my hands.

"The drakons will be on the other side waiting for us! Are you ready?" Gabriel bellowed.

"Yes! Let's go!"

The Wall disintegrated, and we hurtled up the last step, simultaneously scanning for the escape tunnel while assessing where all the drakons were positioned. Unfortunately for us, we found ourselves between two drakons—a green one to my left and the blue one on Gabriel's right—spitting Fire and looking ticked. I barely ducked to the ground in time before the green drakon screamed and shot a flame from his mouth. His emerald scales even seemed to flash with the effort. I scrambled away from him, bumping right into Gabriel, who was about to launch an offensive attack at the blue drakon on his other side. Unfortunately, our collision knocked his shot off-target and hit the wall above the blue drakon. Rocks exploded around us. Instinctively, I tried to conjure an Earth shield, but it didn't work. Instead I shielded my head with my arms while Gabriel and I were pummeled.

"Go!" Gabriel cried, yanking me away from the green drakon, whose teeth snapped way too close to my head.

I spun to launch a force of Wind at the reptile to buy us some space to move, but again, nothing happened. I thrust my hands out with more force...and the drakon only growled back at me, his viridescent eyes glaring.

"I can't use a life force! Something's wrong!"

"Get to the tunnel immediately! I am right behind you!" Gabriel gave me a shove in that direction, which put me within cooking distance of the blue drakon blocking our way.

I was more than a little freaked out that I couldn't seem to conjure a life force, and now I was in a face-to-face standoff with a huge reptile whose very teeth were blazing with blue flames to match his eyes.

But from behind me came a whip of Fire that looped itself several times around the blue drakon's mouth and body. He flailed about, trying to rid himself of the binding force, and his massive tail slashed into the wall and shattered more glittering rock. I glanced back at Gabriel, who was exerting all of his strength in controlling the creature. With a shout, Gabriel yanked fiercely on the powerful whip, and the drakon went tumbling down the stairs.

Our way to the passage was cleared. I forced my feet to sprint that direction, taking note that another drakon—this one a majestic purple color—was trotting toward us. The green drakon was close on our heels, but Gabriel's attention was trained on dealing with him. The tunnel entrance was *right there*…only a few more yards…but the purple drakon was also closing the distance between us too quickly. I pushed myself harder, feeling like my head and my lungs might explode with all the heat and energy in the room.

Just a few more strides. I threw a curious look to my right just to see what was happening in the pit. An illusive curtain had unfolded inside the portal, revealing a picture of a beautiful, white sandy beach.

Was it a portal to another part of the Island? I wondered. I tore my eyes away just in time to see the purple drakon rear back its reptilian head, preparing to fry me with its breath.

But Gabriel took that moment to throw me into the tunnel— yes, *throw me*. I landed hard on the ground as the burning heat of flames seemed to engulf the space above me. When it cooled, I pulled myself up on my hands and knees, noting that Gabriel was not with me. I screamed his name and turned back. He was still in the cavern, grappling with the purple drakon. I watched in fascination as he expertly dodged every snap and flame the drakon threw at him. Finally, he shot a few massive Firedarts at the drakon's chest. The creature reared up to at least twelve feet tall on his back legs before falling awkwardly to his side. Not realizing I had wandered back toward the danger, I stared in shock at Gabriel from the tunnel entrance.

The guy had some *serious* power and skill...I mean, not that I didn't already guess that. It was just incredible to see it in action. Behind him, the green drakon was struggling with ropes made of Fire tied around his mouth and legs.

Gabriel took a deep breath before noticing me standing there with my mouth hanging open. "You were supposed to keep running!" he yelled in irritation. He marched in my direction, and I was going to say something, but my words got lost when the blue drakon suddenly rose up from the pit and struck Gabriel on the back with his front claws.

I screamed as the pain and shock on Gabriel's face registered before he fell face forward at my feet.

OCEANFRONT PROPERTY

I tried with everything in me to use a life force to fight back, but I could not access even one of the four. The drakon pulled itself up and stared down at the fallen Gabriel.

I immediately threw myself over Gabriel's body and shouted at the drakon, "No! Please...we are trying to leave!"

I didn't think the drakon could understand me, especially since he pulled his neck back and cocked his head to the side much like a dog would do. But if drakons could read emotions, maybe he could read the right one in me. I stared up at him, meeting his calculating blue eyes. I wasn't there to hurt him or even to use that portal. I just wanted out of there.

The red drakon had skulked around to our side of the circle, and the two of them seemed to look at each other and make strange sneezing sounds that resembled staccato horn blasts. Finally, they gazed at us and sat back on their haunches in a non-threatening stance. But their defensive positions were clear. They might be letting us go, but we would not be allowed back in that cavern.

I think I might have said thank you, I don't know, because I was suddenly aware of the rapidly spreading blood that was spilling from Gabriel's back. His tunic was ripped open, and the claw marks were deep...so deep that I was sure muscle had been slashed.

"Gabriel, can you get up?" I asked, my voice unnaturally high-pitched.

Was he even conscious? There was so much blood. He groaned and attempted to push himself up with his arms.

"I'll help you. Come on." I reached under his chest and tried to haul him up, which, believe me, was no easy task. All the while, I kept a watchful eye on the drakons who just peered at us in their suspicious manner as we struggled.

"Gabriel, get up!" I told him a little more forcefully.

We managed to get him to his knees and then finally on his feet. I held onto him, rushing us as fast as I could away from the cavern and the shimmering drakons.

He was unsteady on his feet, but adrenaline propelled both of us forward. The tunnel was now carved out at an upward slant, making our efforts even more difficult. Once we seemed far enough away from the cavern, I tried to stop him so I could take a closer look at his back.

But he just gasped, "Keep going!" and I obeyed, because I didn't know what else to do.

I know I was babbling encouraging statements and trying to sound positive as we followed the tunnel, but I wasn't sure if it was more for Gabriel's sake or my own. I tried to ignore how badly he was wounded, tried to pretend like he might not bleed to death before we ever got out of there. And I was still extremely disturbed that I had no life force abilities anymore. Something in my connection with the Island had slipped out of place again.

We managed to carry on, and I was not even aware of how much time was passing…only that we needed to get help. Gabriel was quietly enduring the pain, though I heard a little moan escape under his breath every so often. His motor skills were off, as evidenced by the fact that he wasn't walking straight even with me holding onto his side. His feet would catch every once in a while, like he was trying not to pitch forward.

"We're almost there…" I told him, even though I had no way of knowing that for sure. The only change I noticed was that the air was cooling, and I thought I detected a slight breeze in the passageway. The occasional floating lights were growing dimmer and more spaced out.

But then we hit a dead end. The tunnel just…stopped. And we were staring at nothing but a wall.

"No…" I murmured. "No, no, this can't be right! There has to be another secret passageway here…"

I left Gabriel to lean on his side against the wall, while I ran my hands all along the tunnel. There was no screen—only a deeply grooved wall in front of me. This couldn't be a dead end. We could not go back across the mountain. Gabriel wouldn't make it. I wasn't even sure I would make it.

"Gabriel, tell me what to do. Is there a trick or secret lock here or something?"

He didn't answer me.

"Gabriel—" I turned back around just as his eyes rolled back in his head and he started to fall forward.

I caught him, but he was dead weight, and I crumpled underneath him. Fortunately for him (not so much for me), I was able to soften his fall to the ground. He was completely passed out… on top of me. And my hands were now covered in his sticky blood.

I freaked out.

"Gabriel…" I half-choked, half-sobbed. *Please wake up.* Once I wriggled out from underneath him, I lay flat on my back, trying in vain to slow my breathing. My gasping made lonely echoes in the dark space.

I had no life forces, no way of communicating with anyone, and no way of helping Gabriel. I tried to ignore the blood on my hands, but it only added to my fear. What if he never woke up again? Gabriel couldn't *die.* I stared up at the tunnel ceiling and started to pray for help.

And then I saw it…a trapdoor. In the ceiling. Don't ask me how I knew what it was in such darkness. I could just *see* it. Suddenly I had a flashback to the first time we crossed the Frio River. We had used the rope ladder to reach the top of the cliff, but I remembered Caleb saying that the cliff had such deep grooves that it was practically "made for climbing." And I knew what I had to do.

I rolled over on my side and grazed the back of my hand over Gabriel's forehead. "I'm going to get you out of here," I whispered, the metallic, sickening smell of blood filling my nostrils. I swallowed back the bile that threatened to come up in my mouth and wiped my hands on the ground as I stood.

The grooves in the wall were set in such a way that one could easily climb it—but I was still nervous. I was not known for my agility or athleticism. After taking it slowly, I made my way to the top and reached up to the door. It was heavy—clearly made out of rock. I wasn't sure I could lift it with my own fading strength. I shoved as hard as I could, holding my breath with the exertion, but it didn't budge even a tiny bit. I ran my fingers along the surface and was surprised to find a hollowed-out section in the shape of a rectangle. I felt along the inside until I thought I sensed a lever of some sort. It took me a few tries, but I finally yanked it in the right direction, and the rock door just slid open of its own accord.

A faint, grayish light filtered down through what looked like a blanket or rug covering the door. Cautiously, I pushed it aside and wound the material around my hand to remove it. Then I pulled myself up with tremulous hands, slightly thankful that Gabriel was passed out and unable to see the view of me in a dress clumsily climbing through a trapdoor.

The light was bright, and I had to squint after the darkness of the tunnels. I was shocked to find myself in a very normal-looking bedroom. There was a fluffy bed, like the ones in Aerodora, a wooden desk with papers strewn across it, a spacious armoire on one wall, and windows on all three of the others. I was in someone's house! But I resisted the urge to call out without knowing who lived there. After all, the house contained a trap door that led to a portal that I was pretty sure only a few people (the Guardian included) knew about.

As I scanned the room, I was immediately distracted by the view from the windows. This little house had an uninterrupted panorama of the beautiful ocean flanked by the rocky backside of the mountain and the lush vegetation that grew down there. We had to be on the ocean side of the mountain between Pyradora and the Palladium. And one quick assessment of the view, combined with the dusty state of the room, told me that there was nobody even remotely near this place. It looked like it had been abandoned for at least several weeks.

I wanted to cry.

How was I going to get Gabriel up here? I rushed out to the front balcony where two chairs sat facing the ocean.

"Hello?" I yelled, but the only answer I received was the call of a distant bird and the patient rolling of ocean waves. I took a few deep breaths, thankful for fresh air…even if it was filled with the saltiness of the ocean.

And then it came back. My life force ability. I could *feel* it. To test it out I extended my hands and exhaled with concentration. A silvery draft of air emitted from my palms, causing the dangling wind chime hanging from the porch to clang loudly.

Yes!

I ran back inside and started rifling around, looking for anything I could use to help Gabriel. There was nothing on or in the desk except books and papers that I would have to explore later. A shelf above the desk contained oddly shaped knickknacks and different colored rocks. I came to the armoire and yanked open the doors where a scattered selection of clothes hung. On one shelf inside there sat a bright blue bottle of Water, half full, its contents winking at me through a layer of dust in the morning sun.

I grabbed it and then peered through the trapdoor to Gabriel's still figure lying there in a growing pool of dark blood. How would I get him up here? I held my hands out and conjured a silvery draft of Wind that swept around him. I tried the levitating technique Levi had taught me, hoping I could raise him oh-so-carefully through the trapdoor. I had only ever levitated small objects—certainly not a person and never anything that weighed as much as Gabriel.

I got him an inch off the ground and no further. He was too heavy, and I got lightheaded the harder I tried. With frustrated tears in my eyes, I was forced to lower him to the ground. I shakily climbed back down into the tunnel, the Water bottle clutched in my trembling hand.

I tried to wake him up by shaking him gently and calling his name. But there was no response, and he looked so oddly pale. Somehow I managed to pull off his tunic, which had started to stick inside his wound. Then I pressed the tunic on his back and tried to mop up the blood and apply the right amount of pressure to get it to stop.

Healing with the Island's magical properties of pure Water had always come naturally to me, usually because I relied on my modern knowledge of the human body and its functions to conduct the Water. But I was not always great at healing open wounds… especially something this deep.

Quickly, I swallowed some of the ice-cold Water for myself then poured some onto Gabriel's feverish back. He didn't even flinch. Finally, I pooled some in my own hands, careful to save enough for him to drink when he woke up. I had to close my eyes for a moment, because the wound looked so nasty that I couldn't stomach looking at it for too long. Pretty sure I did not have a future career in medicine ahead of me.

I lowered my frigid hands to his lacerated flesh and focused on the sensation of healing Water flooding through a wellspring deep within me and outward to the stinging open tear of Gabriel's back. I ran my fingers gently across the four ripping claw marks, using the life force to push the Water deeper and repair the muscle and skin. Water and blood mixed together, and after I had worked for what felt like enough time, I was surprised to still see open wounds. They seemed shallower, but I wasn't sure I would have the strength to go much longer.

Not only that, but I was getting a frustrating achy feeling in my own back the longer I crouched over him in that tunnel. When he started to stir, I pulled away.

"Hey, try not to move yet," I told him softly and used part of his tunic to dab around the wound.

"How long has it been?"

"Since you passed out? I don't even know…fifteen, twenty minutes?" I guessed. "I found Water in the house up there and was finally able to access a life force again. That was so weird."

"It was the portal," he said, trying to pull himself up. "Eden said when she and the others turned it on, it temporarily interrupted their connection with their life force…"

"Huh." I was too exhausted to theorize on that at the moment. I was starting to feel the Water life force trickle inward like it does right before vanishing. "Gabriel, your wound is not healed well enough and the only way to get up there is by climbing."

He took a moment to assess our surroundings, and with a grunt of pain he pulled himself to his feet. But then he seemed to grow dizzy and had to take hold of the wall. And now that he was standing shirtless in front of me I had to ignore the sight of those rock-hard abs again. Did he just work out all the time or what?

"I think I can make it," he said. "Just give me a moment."

"Um, no. You need to sit down before you pass out again."

He wasn't listening to me. The thought of him losing consciousness again terrified me. After all, he had lost a lot of blood and the wound was still oozing. "Gabriel, I'm serious. Don't be stubborn. You have no idea how heavy you are. If you leave me again…" My voice sounded a little pinched with fear.

He finally focused his gaze on me in that way that made me feel like he was memorizing everything about me. And it always made me self-conscious. I must have been quite a sight…My dress was dirty and stained with his blood. My hands were sticky, and I don't even have a clue how my face and hair had fared through this whole underground mountain ordeal.

"I am sorry," he told me, and then sank to the ground again. If he did it because I asked or because he knew he was going to faint again, I don't know.

"It's not your fault...You totally protected me from four dragons. That was pretty amazing."

"You call them *dragons*...Are your dragons on the Mainland the same as our drakons here?"

"No, actually...dragons are fictional creatures in my world. I never actually knew they existed." I smiled faintly and got to my feet. I had to think of an easier way to get him up to the room. "Oh, and they can fly in our fairy tales."

"That is impossible," he scoffed lightly.

"Don't even get me started on *impossible*," I replied, surveying the height of the trapdoor. "If only we had stairs then you wouldn't have to use your back to climb..." I sighed, and my gaze rested on the Water bottle. That was when I got a crazy idea.

I snatched the Water bottle up and took a big gulp. Then I handed it to Gabriel.

"Here, drink this and do not move. I am going to try something."

"I do not like the sound of that..."

But I ignored him. I positioned myself a few feet away from the trapdoor opening. With the cold Water seeping through my body again, I activated the life force. But this time I used the Wind to control the temperature of the Water.

With a sharp flick of my finger, a bright blue droplet fell from the surface of my skin and shattered into teeny-tiny crystal shards...which then melted into wet spots on the cave floor.

"Was that...?" Gabriel's voice was disbelieving.

"Yeah," I smiled with excitement. "I just made *ice*. Now watch this, Fire Boy."

With concentrated effort, I combined the two life forces again, but with more power behind it. From the palms of my hands a blue waterfall cascaded and turned to ice upon contact with the ground, emitting a blue fog around me. I stacked the ice as thickly as possible until a roughly designed set of glimmering stairs stood in front of us.

When I turned to Gabriel, his eyes were wide in fascination. "Quit staring and get up there before it starts melting," I commanded. It was slightly amusing to watch him test his weight on the ice, but I did breathe a sigh of relief when he made it up all the way. I ascended my own slippery, uneven creation and let go of the life forces.

I admired my work through the trapdoor. "That is *cool*," I mumbled, and then smiled. If Caleb had been there, he would have appreciated my pun.

"Where are we?" Gabriel mumbled, taking in the room with one sweep of his eyes.

"As if I would know...It seems abandoned. Why don't you go lie down for a minute while I clean myself up?" I suggested, his gray pallor even more noticeable in the daylight.

He didn't even argue. As he collapsed on his stomach upon the bed, I opened the windows and let the fresh ocean breeze filter into the stale house. The pleasant sounds of the rumbling ocean waves and chirping sea birds filled the atmosphere of the little room. I was suddenly exhausted...and freezing. My little ice sculpting experiment had given me chills that rocked my whole body.

I left him in the bedroom to find a small bathing room where a few half-empty bottles of bathing liquids and one ragged towel were left. My eyes looked wild in the mirror, and I could barely control my trembling as I washed my hands and face. I placed Gabriel's bloody, torn tunic in the small basin to soak. When I reentered the little room, he peered at me sideways from the bed.

"You are sick again from the life forces," he noted.

"No, I'm just cold...and I kind of wished I would have let myself sleep longer at the house." My body felt like it had been through a horrible workout regimen; every muscle felt ready to give out. And my back was actually throbbing.

"You need to drink the rest of the Water."

"I drank plenty…I really should keep working on your back. The wounds are still open."

"You did a fine job starting the healing process. But I believe I will need a HydroHealer for the rest of it," he assured me with a grimace. And then he instructed softly, "Come lie down."

I stared back at him uncertainly. "Do we really have time for rest?"

"We do not have a choice…I feel like I might slip out of consciousness again, and you are about to fall over with exhaustion."

"I feel fine," I lied.

"Whitnee, I am too tired to argue with you. I can tell when the life forces have drained you because your eyes grow foggy, you start shaking, and you have no color left in your face," he pointed out, but I was still hesitant to climb into the same bed as Gabriel. *Hello.*

He watched my reluctance through glazed eyes. "I promise not to touch you. But there is only one bed and two of us. We will rest for a few minutes and then determine where we are and how to communicate with the others."

Slowly, I made my way to the other side of the bed, frustrated at my mixed feelings over his promise "not to touch" me. The moment I slid onto the softness of the bed, pulled a separate blanket up to my chin, and rested my head on the pillow, I could actually hear my muscles crying for joy. My eyes took the warmth and softness as a cue to start shutting down.

"We don't even know whose bed this is," I murmured with a yawn.

"Try not to think about it," he suggested, his voice becoming sleepy too.

"We really should find our way back…Don't you think Eden will have everyone out looking for us?"

He was silent, and I thought he had fallen asleep until he said, "Do you find it strange that Eden has so many random people helping us?"

I turned over to face him. "No. Should I?"

"I told Eden nothing about your father or what had really happened in the portal room until it was almost time for Abrianna to send me to the Mainland. The next thing I knew, you were kidnapped, and I came back to find that Eden had people from every different tribe helping us—and she *knew* things. Like what was happening the moment it was happening. And then you tell me that someone we trust is actually a traitor working for my parents...I am more uncertain than ever about whom to trust beyond you and your friends."

"Well, I feel like we can trust Eden. But if you didn't order all of those people to help us, then why are they here? What's in it for them?"

We stared at each other, puzzled.

"We have tried to keep the truth about you very quiet on the Island. We told the people you had gone back to your homeland and would not be returning. Most people accepted that and moved on, though there is still chatter and rumors of your abilities in every village."

"What about Ezekiel?" I thought of my silver-haired Aerodorian grandfather and remembered the letter my grandmother, Sarah, had slipped into my pocket before I left. She had given indication in the letter that she wanted to tell me the truth about my dad and my real heritage here on the Island, but it sounded as if she had been threatened not to speak of it. "How did he react when he found out I was gone?"

"I went to see him...as soon as I could get out from under the prying eyes of the Palladium," he said, his warm eyes wandering all over my curious face.

"You did? What did you tell him?"

"The truth. I told him everything about how you left the Island, what I had learned about your father, and that I believed him to be on the Island but did not know where. I asked for his help."

I don't know why hearing that surprised me so much...I suppose I hadn't realized how much Gabriel had grown to trust Ezekiel over his own parents.

"So then he told you who my dad really was and that I was his granddaughter?"

Gabriel's thick eyebrows furrowed. "No, he did not. I was honest with him, but I now know he did not return the sentiment. He said he would start looking further into my theories and appreciated the confidential information. In retrospect, I do not believe Ezekiel trusts anyone very easily these days. He probably had no reason to trust me with his side of the story." His eyes turned dark. "But that is nothing new. It seems I do not appear as a trustworthy person to most people."

I felt a twinge of guilt at his words, having fallen into the category of "most people."

"I really believe he is under some kind of threat from Abrianna not to speak of my dad or the Pilgrim, Gabriel. And, yeah, maybe he wanted to test you out first and see if anything he said got back to the Guardian," I answered, my eyes heavy with the need for sleep. "You are being too hard on yourself. Ezekiel trusts you more than you realize…Don't forget he allowed *you* to accompany his own granddaughter around the Island."

Gabriel just watched me thoughtfully, his eyelashes so long and thick that every time he blinked I wondered how they didn't tickle his cheek.

"And remember how he deferred to you in that meeting with the Tetrarch Council over whether I should travel to the other villages or transport back immediately? He practically handed the decision over to you…In retrospect, it's more clear to *me* how much Ezekiel trusts you."

I watched Gabriel shrug ever so slightly and close his eyes.

"Hey," I whispered, and he opened them again. "Thank you for getting us through that mountain…and for everything you've done to help me find my dad."

He graced me with a half smile, and then we could fight the drowsiness no longer. The bewitching rhythm of the surf rolling up and down the shore outside lulled us both to sleep, where we entered separate worlds filled with our own personal nightmares.

THE LUCKY SHIRT

When I landed on the beach, not even the softness of the sugary sand could save me from the jarring blow of falling from another world. I didn't take the time to figure out my exact location—or even to take in the amazing fact that I was back on the White Island. I had an uncanny knowledge that I was on the Southern Beach again—perhaps in the same place I had woken up before. Everything around me was like déjà vu…with the slight differences of being tied up and blindfolded this time.

"She is over there!" the Pyra shouted in his surly voice from down the beach. My blindfold was starting to slip down past one eye, affording me a partial view of the jungle that I remembered avoiding the first time I came here. I struggled to my feet and ran in the opposite direction of my captors—toward the Watch Tower ruins that I knew were hiding just behind that green. Perhaps I could lose them in there somewhere. I shook my head furiously in an effort to free my vision completely of the blindfold. No matter how fiercely I yanked my wrists, I still couldn't get rid of the armbands.

I was almost to the cloak of the jungle when an invisible force from behind struck and knocked my feet out from under me. I tripped and fell face first into the ground, my fettered arms powerless to cushion my fall.

I cried out, not just in pain, but in righteous anger. The men were quickly upon me, and I kicked and screamed for help the moment the scar-faced Pyra aggressively picked me up off the ground.

"We need to get her in the tank immediately!" the second man panted, his voice still sounding slightly more panicked than the Pyra's. He was the one who had tied my hands up and who now, in full view, was clearly a Geo. A really *big* Geo. I searched wildly for the third man…the one they wouldn't allow me to see. The man I was sure I knew.

But there was no one else in sight.

"The tank?" I screeched, the Geo's words finally resonating with me. Will Kinder had mentioned a tank. In fact, he had referred to the Watch Tower ruins as the tank! "What's the tank? Where are you taking me? Help!" I screamed loudly again, hoping someone in the jungle would be close enough to hear me. But no one came to the Southern Beach because local legend said it was haunted.

"If you do not shut your mouth"—the Pyra warned, pinching hard on my side as he threw me over his shoulder— "I will do it for you. And you will not like it." He spun around and addressed the Geo. "Fix her now!"

The last thing I saw was what should have been a peaceful view of the ocean slipping into dusk before the blindfold was tightened and some kind of rag stuffed back into my mouth. Where was the third man? The one who kept the Pyra from hurting me? I had a feeling of dread that he was no longer around. I tried to keep my sense of direction as I was dragged away from the beach. We were definitely heading to the Watch Tower ruins, and my theory was confirmed when I heard their heavy footsteps hit the stone. But we wound around the ruins in places unfamiliar to me, since I had only spent one night there.

And then a heavy, grating door swung open and slammed shut behind us. Was this the tank?

A voice I did not recognize laughed mirthlessly. "Someone is going to be very happy with you boys. We are ready for her in room two. Where is your other partner?"

"Reporting back," the Pyra answered. "He has another job, you know."

"And since I do not see the collateral here for our little girlfriend, I am assuming that is his next job. I would not wish to be in his position."

"There was not enough time to retrieve the 'collateral,' as you put it. Not with that ignorant, lovesick fool transporting in behind us. We had to get out. And this one has a bigger mouth than I expected." He jolted me to make his point.

I grunted lightly to show my displeasure at his words, but he only laughed. I was intentionally keeping quiet and still—cooperating for the time being in the hopes that they would keep talking. I was also trying to rely on my hearing to pick up on details that might help me later. The way their voices echoed made me think we were surrounded by metal, not the traditional stone of the Island. And it smelled musty...and wet. I tried counting the steps he took to room two, but I lost track at thirty-two. The farther we moved, the more creaky and vast the place sounded.

Finally he paused, hardly winded after carrying me so far. Another door opened, and we entered, only for me to be dumped onto a cold, flat surface.

"Does the Guardian know anything?" the Geo piped up.

"No," the new guy said, a reserved edge to his voice. "And you better see to it that she and everyone else stay in the dark. Those are the orders." I heard people shifting around and the clinking of glass. "Once we are finished here, you know where to take her?"

There was an affirmative grunt from the Pyra, which was when I felt his hot breath on my face. The overwhelming smell of sulphur made me feel like gagging. "You can scream all you want in here, and nobody will hear you." He took the material out of my mouth.

"What are you going to do to me?" I choked, trying in vain to keep the fear out of my voice, wishing I could see the room and what they were doing.

"For now, we are just going to ensure that you stay within our control. But later…I have some ideas for you." His meaning was made pretty clear when he ran his dirty finger across my cheek and over my lips.

I snapped my teeth down, wanting to inflict pain on him for talking to me like that.

I heard him laugh again, and the new guy said, "Now, Saul…you know you have to behave with this one."

"Yes, well, once they acquire what they want from her, I have been promised I will get my turn." And his hand tangled in my hair and pulled threateningly.

"You should not speak of such things…" the Geo said nervously.

"Yeah," I agreed. "Like I would *ever* let you get away with touching me."

"I believe I am getting away with it now, pretty girl." He snickered, and I felt his hand trace a line down my face to my neck and then farther…

Somebody slapped it away. "Stay calm, Pyra. Leave the room while I work, if you must." There was silence and grunting, and then the new guy addressed me. "This might hurt just a little."

He lied.

Whatever he did felt like a dagger slicing its way into and up my arm until the pain had surged viciously through every part of my body. And the horrible shrieking and crying that echoed off the walls was the sound of me dying.

"Whitnee!"

The shrieking hadn't stopped, but I had full use of my arms and hands again. I made fists that punched and slapped my attacker, who took a firm grip on my flailing arms.

"Wake up, Little One! Whatever you are seeing is not real!"

I stopped fighting back and realized it was my own hoarse screams that were faltering as reality filtered back in. My eyes fluttered open, blurry with fresh tears, and I found Gabriel leaning over me. It was his hands on me, but in a firm and gentle way. Not like my kidnappers.

I shut my eyes again and swallowed against the pain in my throat. I might have just shredded my vocal cords through my screaming fit. He released me, and I curled into a ball and buried my face in the pillow, trying to erase the sounds in my head. My shoulders heaved with terrified sobs. It wasn't just a dream. It was a memory, and it felt like I had just lived it for the first time. It was the final memory I needed...and wished I didn't have.

"I'm sorry...I'm sorry," I repeated in shame, my voice muffled in the pillow. What did they do to me? Where were they taking me? And that Pyra...Saul...scared the crap out of me. My crying became more hysterical just remembering the things he said and the way he had treated me.

Gabriel pulled me into the shelter of his powerful arms. I knew it couldn't have been comfortable for him with his back still ripped open. He didn't even say anything at first; he just held me and stroked my hair as my cheek rested against his bare chest. Eventually the sound of his steady heartbeat, combined with the tiny tugs on my hair, left me calm enough to speak.

"It was Saul...and it wasn't a dream," I finally whispered into the stillness. I immediately felt his body stiffen as his hand paused on my head.

With a dangerous undertone to his deep voice, he said, "Depending on what you tell me next, Saul just might be the first man I willingly kill."

I pulled away from him to peer at his face, which was set like stone. His eyes glittered with the fever of fury.

"Gabriel," I started, my mind still making sense of my memory. "I don't think the Guardian was the one who ordered my kidnapping."

After sharing with Gabriel everything I had seen and heard, a renewed purpose was born in both of us. We rummaged around the little house, hunting for a zephyra and other things we might be able to use on our journey.

"I knew there was something strange about the Watch Tower ruins. When Thomas said you disappeared around there, we searched the area...but then they reappeared with you farther north," Gabriel thought aloud.

"I think it's all underground. There were tunnels that went on for a while," I reasoned as I opened up the armoire again to search through the shelves, drawers, and clothes hanging in there. Gabriel was shuffling through the desk. "Tunnels kind of like the ones we just went through in the mountain...only they sounded different inside. Like they were made of metal or concrete—something smooth and hard."

"It could be argent—the silver substance that the Palladium Dome is made of," Gabriel suggested, inspecting papers as he spoke.

"The Dome where you can't use your life force powers?"

"Yes. That is the work of the argent—when you apply freezing temperatures to the mountain rock it forms argent and works as a life force control. The armbands we use on prisoners are made of argent, as well as certain buildings where we would want to limit visitors' usage of a life force—like the Dome."

"Interesting," I mumbled as I rifled through the clothes, hoping for something a little more practical and modest to wear. I needed out of this bloodstained dress. *Good thing Jezebel hates pink*, I thought. I had definitely ruined her pretty pink dress. Surely it would be okay if I borrowed an outfit from here, even if they looked like men's clothes?

"Likewise, if you apply extreme heat to the mountain rock it forms the clear material we make our bottles and windows from."

"Glass," I answered back, my head buried in the armoire. "That's what we call it on the Mainland." My hands groped in the far recesses of the back of the armoire, and I felt something foreign and familiar at the same time…a type of rougher material that I knew I hadn't seen on the Island.

I pulled it out into the light and unfolded it.

Gabriel had his back to me and was studying the papers in his hand. "Whoever lives here apparently works closely with the Palladium. These are letters, requests for aid in the villages, building plans, diagrams of something I cannot understand with notes detailing each life force, laws of life force usage…And then these drawings of the human body? I do not even know what all of these labels mean…" He finally turned to face me as I gaped at what I had laid out on the bed. "What is that?"

In a daze, I ran my fingers along the pair of faded men's jeans, the scattered holes ripped fashionably along the front. Then I held up the old, thin t-shirt that I knew so well. I pushed my finger through the familiar hole under one sleeve.

Speaking slowly, I said, "I think my dad lives here."

Gabriel was silent as he watched me bring the shirt to my face, breathing deeply the scent of the cotton. I couldn't remember what my dad smelled like, but I *knew* this was his shirt. And suddenly he felt more alive to me than any other moment in the last six years.

"Years ago, my mom and dad went on a date to a U2 concert," I explained softly. "I've heard the story a million times. Mom accidentally spilled her drink on Dad's shirt at dinner, so she bought him this U2 t-shirt at the concert to make up for it. He's always called it his lucky shirt, because he said that was the night they found 'their song'…"

I paused because there was a lump forming in my throat as I thought of my mom and dad being separated from each other for so long. It was just wrong. No matter what my mom was trying to make herself feel for Robert or what kind of relationship my dad may or may not have with Abrianna, I was one hundred percent sure my parents loved each other. And I vowed never to question it again.

"Dad took this shirt with him on every research trip, even though it's old and faded, and we used to tease him about the holes in it. It was what he wore the last time anyone saw him."

At that point I brought my eyes to meet Gabriel's across the room. His face was curiously tender when he asked me, "What was their song about?"

I smiled ironically. "It's about not being able to live with or without somebody you love."

There was a reverent pause between the two of us. Finally, Gabriel asked the one question we both wondered. "Why would your father live here—so close to a portal—and not use it?"

"Maybe it's not really a portal…Maybe it's something else. I don't know, but I intend to ask him myself when we find him." I shoved Dad's clothes into an old empty satchel Gabriel had found in our search. "We need to get to those ruins as soon as possible. I have a strong feeling they're holding him there." I gave him a pleading look, wondering what objections he would come up with, what excuses he might have in the name of my protection.

He nodded slowly. "I agree."

"Good. So…what's next?"

As he organized the papers in his hands, he turned his back to me.

I gasped, and my stomach turned queasy. "Gabriel." I breathed and dropped the satchel on the bed. "Your back is infected or something…" My eyes watered as I moved to take a closer look. Spidery little lines branched out from the open wound, like a web of raised veins ready to pop.

He heaved a sigh, and I pulled on his arm to make him turn around and face me. I studied him closely and was surprised to see him sweating. The guy walked around with an abnormally high body temperature, but I had never seen him sweat. And the normal golden hue of his skin tone was still gray.

"Tell me what's happening to you."

He tried to avoid meeting my eyes, but I could clearly seen pain there. "Drakons carry a venom in their claws…There is nothing you could have done…"

"Venom? You mean you were poisoned? Geez, Gabriel, we need a Healer for this!"

"Yes, we do. But I still have a few more hours before it becomes too much of a problem."

"Why didn't you tell me? I could have gone for help…We could have done something!" My heartbeat echoed in my ears with the heavy thud of fear. He had to pry my fingers off his arm.

"You needed rest first. And I thought maybe the drakon hadn't released the venom…I was wrong," he concluded. He moved away from me to shove the papers in the satchel on the bed.

I stared after him in exasperation. "Well, what are we going to do? You need help!"

His response was to toss me a tunic and drawstring pants. "Go change. Let me think."

"Gabriel—"

He held up a weak hand. "Please. Just give me a moment."

I shook my head and stomped off to the little bathing room. Not good. This was not good at all. I ripped the dress over my head and pulled on a tunic that was too big. As I tied it in a knot behind my back, my mind whirled through everything that had happened, trying to draw conclusions and put pieces together that shouldn't fit. I felt like I was stuck in a puzzle where the pieces connected, but the picture was ugly and distorted.

I pulled on the drawstring pants and tied them as tightly as they would go, which still caused them to inch down my waist a bit. While smoothing my hair in the mirror, I couldn't help wondering if the only person who could help Gabriel right now was the Guardian. We couldn't be far from the Palladium—which had to be closer than our friends in Pyradora. What if we went there for help? Yes, it was jeopardizing my mission, but Gabriel…

His own stubborn side would kill him someday.

I opened the bathroom door and started, "Hey, Gabriel, what if we went to the Palladium and found—"

I stopped. Gabriel's expression and posture were tense. And he was not alone.

"Nobody is going to the Palladium." Someone familiar spoke to my left. I turned in surprise.

"Tamir?" Confusion colored my voice. The tall Aeroguard who had been one of our trusted companions last time was looming near the bathroom door and watching me closely. I would have felt relief at the sight of him, except that something was off in Gabriel's attitude. I could sense it all the way across the room.

"Hello, Whitnee. It is good to see you alive and well."

"Of course I am alive…What exactly is going on here?" I looked back and forth between Tamir and Gabriel.

Tamir's voice was calm and nonthreatening. "I was about to ask the same thing. Do you know how many people are looking for the two of you? Jeremiah and I"—Tamir gestured to the other man who was positioned in front of the door, as if to block our exit— "had a suspicion we might find you out here."

Gabriel took a step closer to him. "And how exactly would you know that, Tamir? I did not even know of this place." I moved closer too, but Gabriel threw an arm out in warning. "Stay back, Whitnee. I do not trust this situation at all."

Tamir raised his eyebrows. "I am just following orders. You took Whitnee without warning, and you have the audacity to question *my* motives?"

"Gabriel didn't *take* me anywhere against my will. And what exactly are your orders?" I asked.

"To find you and make sure that you two do not disappear again," Tamir answered in a matter-of-fact tone. "I am sorry,

Gabriel, but if you do not cooperate and come with us immediately, we are going to have to put you in armbands."

Gabriel stared at him as if trying to read something in his expression.

"You can't do that!" I was appalled and took a few steps closer to Gabriel, preparing my hands for defense if it became necessary.

Jeremiah and Gabriel also took defensive stances. Surely Tamir was not the traitor…not after everything he had done to help us?

"Who is giving your orders, Tamir?" Gabriel growled.

Tamir seemed slightly amused by our alarm. "You *know* the answer to that. Jeremiah, get on the zephyra and let her know we have them." He smiled cryptically at me. "We are what you might refer to as the *real* rebels."

To be continued…

BOOK 4 of the PHANTOM ISLAND series

COMING SOON!
www.KrissiDallas.com

ACKNOWLEDGMENTS

The *Water* books took me two years to write—and another two years to publish. The fact that the first half of this volume is finally in the hands of readers right now is a surreal and terrifying thought!

Melody Duckworth, your life story is beautiful, and I love how it has aligned with mine for so long. Thank you for letting me pick apart your thoughts and experiences so that Morgan's voice could make a debut in this volume. I know it's not always easy to recall the past. Your strength and your heart inspire me every day.

Thank you to my inner circle of trust—Bonnie Inman (my mom), Sam Dallas (my husband), and Katrina Elsea (my friend and original editor). Thank you for following my vision blindly and supplying me with plenty of encouragement and patience through every obstacle this book presented.

Sonia Pennington, you have *God-given* talent. Thank you for sharing your artistry with me so that the White Island could have a map. I miss having you in class every day.

Thank you to Letty Camacho for helping me with my Spanish! (And for letting me name Aunt Letty after her.)

To Jessie Sanders, my conceptual editor, thanks for sticking out this project with me. Your gifts in grammar and vision have made a huge difference in this series. Thank you to Kristen Verser, my cover artist, for always giving *Phantom Island* books the right "face" so that people will pick them up.

Special thanks to Renea McKenzie, Loni Fancher, Amy Meade, and Ali Evans for previewing *Watercrossing* and *Watermark*—four amazing gals whom I am always glad to have on my Phantom Island team!

Thank you, Secret Squirrels, for stressing me out by flip-flopping in the Caleb/Gabriel debate, supplying me with Junior Mints through late night writing stints, and sending me real-time reactions to the story by text and e-mail. You make the writing process so fun!

And to those fans who have been with me since the first edition of *Wind*—I kept you tucked in my heart with every word I wrote on every page. The continuation of this story is a testimony of your love and support for *Phantom Island*. Thank you.